Tell Me Everything

Tell Me Everything

MARIE BRENNER

E.P. DUTTON & CO., INC.   NEW YORK

Library of Congress Cataloging in Publication Data

Brenner, Marie.
  Tell me everything.

  I. Title.
PZ4.B8392Te [PS3552.R384]   813'.5'4   76-17571

ISBN: 0-525-21470-4

Published simultaneously in Canada
by Clarke, Irwin & Company
Limited, Toronto and Vancouver

For my mother and father

Tell Me Everything

"What do you mean, *'he's locked up behind closed doors in meetings all day'*? Did you tell him Florida Burns was on the line?? B-U-R-N-S? Tower Syndicate columnist? That Tell Me Everything's on deadline and it's *crucial* that I confirm an item with him? Did you tell him *all* that? . . . Oh. And what did *he* say? To *'take a number'?"* I was devastated, but hoped this underling was too unconscious to perceive my dismay. I drew in a breath but tried to stay calm. I didn't want a secretary to be the first name on my so-far-unblemished Tell Me Everything enemies list. (Gossip was no easy business when what one craves is *love.* But one also craved an item, so I plunged right along.) *"Look.* I don't know if you understand the importance of what I'm about to print. . . . No! I can't tell *you* what it is, I'm going to have to talk with Mr. Smolins himself. That's right . . . *himself.* So, if-you-could-be-so-kind as to just take a note into Zev Smolins right-this-minute which says, 'Florida Burns, Tell Me Everything correspondent, Tower Syndicate, will be at the following number for the next fifty minutes—that's 988-7654—and he's to get back to me. . . . do you have all that? Should I repeat it? Not necessary? *Terrific. I'll wait here for his call."*

1

For emphasis, I slammed the receiver down. The book-case lurched in response. The Lomitas High *Lomitian* and a paperbound copy of *Cellulite! Get Rid of It!* crashed to the floor. I ignored them, then picked up the other phone.

"Hello? Is this the Century Apartments? Marvelous! Are you the cooperative leasing agent? Marvelous! This is Marie Hélène de Rothsch . . .—" I slurred the last syllable, just one of my telephone tricks. "I am *desperate* to find twelve rooms to buy, perhaps you can help me? I have something *specific* in mind. The other night . . . a penthouse . . . I believe it was *oh, I'm not sure*. But it belongs to that Frenchman . . . *Monsieur . . . Monsieur . . . mais quoi?"* A pause to enhance the dramatic effect. "*Oh, dear me.* What was his name? *Ah, oui!* André Michelin? The director? *Ah, oui!* That was it, Penthouse Three! Marvelous place! Is it perchance for sale? *Divine! Mais, quoi?* You believe it's been sold? Oh no, could you double-check?" Sniffing victory, I tried not to let my smile show through the phone. "It has? *Absolument?* Rotten luck. I'm so disappointed. . . . *No,* I'm not interested in anything else. . . . Oh, excuse me, just *one more thing.* Could you tell me if the flat sold with all its furniture? Yes? And—pardon my questionable taste—but, could you tell me by any chance . . . Yes! I'd adore to know the price. . . . *I see!* A bientôt! You've been *so very kind.*"

Bingo. I dragged the Olivetti across the oak dining table that doubled as my desk. This was a break. On canary proof, I began to type. Then the phone rang. Quickly, I soft-pedaled the score of *Gigi* blaring from my stereo on the floor. What would my sources think if they knew the truth: that Florida Burns was a tough-skinned-but-mushy-insided push-over, a media *crème brûlée.* I mean, what would it do to my reputation if word leaked out that Florida Burns still gets misty when she hears "Gigi" being crooned by someone as silly and old-hat as Louis Jourdan. "What miracle has made you the way you are . . ." was shoved into low gear. I allowed my arteries to harden, my lucite exterior to slip on. *Please God,* let it be Zev Smolins, president of Homerica Pictures.

"Florida?"

"Yes?"

"You might be interested in this. Sophia Loren starts a world-wide promo tour on her latest . . . probably sometime at the end of this month and she'll be accompanied by both Ponti and . . ."

"*Harvey. I'm on deadline. Please.*"

"I know, *stupid.* That's why I'm doing you a favor." I heard Harvey Kaplan talking to his secretary. "Will you tell him to hold, hold on please? I'll be done with *this* in . . . two minutes! . . . So, Florida? Are you going to use it or not?"

"*Hey.* Give me something hot! What about Jason Jaffe, your star client, huh? Give me something about him! I don't want these leftovers."

"Look, Florida. I can't feed you the things that go to Earl Wilson, *you know that.* Give-me-a-break because now, I must-must run. Last chance on the Sophia Loren?"

I sighed, then I caved in. "*All right.* What do I care? The only people who are going to see it are suburban housewives stuck under dryers. It's not like any of this is *real.* You would get me on a day when I'm against the . . . Are you going to dictate? Is it all already written? I don't want to waste any more time than . . ." As Harvey read, I felt my stomach rumbling, then I started to peck. "Wait! Harvey? Do you think I can say something like 'The usual rumors of a split between Loren and Ponti are . . .'"

"I don't care what you say. All I care is . . ."

I knew Harvey's next line by heart. "Just spell the name right?"

"*Right.*"

I checked out the clock: twenty-five more minutes. This was the part I hated: the actual writing; but more: the feeling that maybe I was doing someone in. Could I take care of Michelin and my phone call to Andy Marks all within the next 1430 seconds?

3

FOR: IMMEDIATE RELEASE—TOWER SYNDICATE
FROM: FLORIDA BURNS
RE: ANDRE MICHELIN (note to Brian: you think of a title, ok? fb)

Is émigré French director André Michelin about to make his peace with his less-than-beloved France? "Pale Dreams"— Michelin's homage to Jean-Paul Sartre which never made it across the Mason-Dixon line (merci à Dieu)—proved a real "No Exit" for its tiny, captive audiences. As Tell Me Everything correspondent Florida Burns discovered this week, the failure of the privately financed film may signal Michelin's return to the lucrative world of French TV commercials. Michelin has already quietly unloaded his super-posh twelve-room co-op on New York's Central Park West—avec furniture! But New York wags suggest that anyone who turned in a film as confused as "Pale Dreams" might board the wrong plane and wind up in Hollywood, where a failed film means a bigger budget next time out. Bonne chance, Monsieur Michelin!

(Brian: Can you patch it up, if you think it needs it?? XXOO, fb)

Quickly, I reread it. Yes, it was a Perfect Item. Luck was with me. I still had nine hundred seconds. Which meant there was just enough time to scrawl in the date (April 3rd), grab my leotards (were the purple ones clean?), stuff the Odorono and Lubriderm into my bag, then fly out the door. But before I did that, once again I picked up the phone.

Great! Andy Marks *was* home. "Honey-I-gotta-talk-fast-because-I'm-rushing-but-I-just-wanted-to-let-you-know-that-piece-you-wrote-in-the-*Somerset-Reporter*-about - the - endangered-Vermont-mountain-wolves-was . . . a positive work of art!" I took a breath. All the twenty-four-year-old Tower Syndicate copyboy needed to get ahead was a little encouragement from an up-and-coming star. I planned to give it to him. "So! While wildlife preservation may not be *my* thing . . . I can't tell you! I was just knocked out by it! A final stroke. "And-. . . don't you let Brian Milman make you think you don't know your ass from your elbow. He'd die to be able to have Andy Marks' writing talent and . . . *complex overview!*"

4

I was out the door by the time Andy Marks had the chance to say thanks. Today was *indeed* my day! By magic the Dakota elevator had found its way up to the ninth floor. At the press of a button, the steel doors wheezed . . . open! This was no minor miracle. Usually I'd have to wait for what seemed like an absolute year.

I collapsed on the elevator's black leather bench. *Christ!* It was one thing to be able to say you were the only single girl and *subleasette* in the chicest, oldest, and best-known apartment building in New York, but it was quite another actually to endure life in one of the reconverted maid's rooms. The twelve-minute ride down that landmark building's hydraulic lift was no picnic either. Still, Florida Burns wasn't about to trade in her views of iron gargoyles and an Italianate courtyard, her glimpses of famous neighbors (Rex Reed! Lauren Bacall! Roberta Flack! John Lennon! Yoko! Leonard Bernstein!).

Let Eloise have her Plaza Hotel, I have my Dakota. Sure, it would be nice to swap a hotplate and sink for a real kitchen, but I had something that pleased me much, much more. An Address. You'd have to be crazy not to like seeing limousines and tourists form constellations outside your door. The fact that they weren't for me was only (I hoped) temporary.

Don't get me wrong. There was much more than a desire for status involved in my residential love affair. There were acres of antique woods and polished brass, miles of marble stairways and hand-carved mahogany doors. The spirit of Henry James and Old New York fairly oozed from every floor. Now I ask you, would an exile from a Texas suburb choose three rooms in a modern high-rise over this cultural and aesthetic feast? Would the only child—and heiress to the Burns supermarket chain—pick even the trendiest air-conditioned East Side address when real class was available? *Mais non!* Not this exile, anyway. I might not yet trade bon mots with Rex Reed, but at least I was a vicarious keyhole focused on a world that I aspired to be in. If nothing else, I had found temporary (if humble) asylum in a much-fantasized promised land.

If only I wasn't always rushing out. And this day I was

really in a hurry. I spilled into the northeast lobby (one of four), excused myself for plowing into the Raleigh carriage (and the nanny) of the heir apparent to America's number-one rotisserie manufacturer, sprinted through the first-floor hallway, and landed at the front desk just in time. The *Arnold* (Maryland) *Bugle* tear sheet of my column had arrived. Outside in the doorway, a moving van was pulling up. Ever romantic, I hoped it was *a sign.*

"Somebody moving out?" I asked the concierge.

"A new man is moving in," she replied.

"A new man?" I asked, trying not to seem as if I cared. "What kind of man? A family man? A married man?"

"No, Miss Burns. I think his name is . . . *Markman.*" She turned away to pick up a phone.

I stuffed my column into my tote, then I spotted the clock. Panic! Three minutes to bolt five blocks. I raced out the beckoning door. A new man in the Dakota, huh? That meant (with my luck) that there were two possibilities: Mr. X.— *Markman*, she'd called him—was bound to be married or a fag. Because for sure no unmarried up-and-comer could afford those maintenance payments. You didn't have to live in New York City to be aware that the Dakota was "high-rent." Certainly we were no luxurious singles complex.

Pamela ("Peaches") Rosen was waiting patiently in the foyer. Her canvas sacks were getting heavy, she had pressed "Bradshaw, A." twice already. "Who is it?" Finally, a garbled voice had squawked from behind the door's steel grille. "Pamela Rosen? From A New Leaf? You called for a plant?"

Only then had a loud buzz ushered her in. This might only be her second house call of the day, but Peaches Rosen hoped it would be her last. She dragged her canvas tote bags up the stairs, then stopped to tidy up her load. Dirty gardening gloves and shovels covered with peat moss had fallen on the floor. She leaned down, then reinserted her supplies in their proper pockets. Damn! Why were they falling out? Peaches Rosen had

6

designed her carry-alls to do just that, so each one had half a dozen special compartments. They were a walking advertisement; "A New Leaf" was stenciled on all sides. At least once a week, somebody would stop her on the street and ask her where she'd bought them. Half-smiling, Peaches Rosen would admit she'd made them, but she'd try not to seem too proud.

Peaches Rosen had always been terrific with her hands. Take the apron she wore. When they'd started the business, door-to-door green-thumbing, Peaches had wanted to look . . . *different.* Her partner (now married, living in Georgetown) had said, *coveralls,* Levi-Strauss coveralls, you know with the pockets? That's what they should wear. *Something practical.* But Peaches had opted for the unique, the special, the individualized design. For weeks, she'd made dozens of drawings, then discarded them. She'd haunted the boutiques, searched every store for a perfect style. Finally, she's scored. Navy linen! Peaches Rosen had found the most sublime wrinkleproof blend. Her concentration had paid off; this fabric was tailor-made for her apron's needs. She had stitched sixteen pockets of assorted sizes all over the front. Pencils, tools, papers, pencils, soil samples, pesticide foil packets . . . everything had its place. Her obsession had been rewarded. Saks Fifth Avenue had wanted her apron for their Christmas catalogue. Peaches had turned them down. The last thing in the world she wanted was to see Rosen knockoffs everywhere she went.

Now she was an original. A Jewish girl from Atlanta with blond hair and green thumb? That you didn't find every day, not in New York City, anyway. She had raised her specialness to an art form and for $25 a house call, she planned to keep it that way.

Perfect. This job would be easy. Pamela Rosen's eyes had darted through the apartment the very second she'd breezed in the door. This woman was a new customer, she'd spotted one of A New Leaf's *Village Voice* classified ads. Peaches smiled, then started making mental notes on her customer's botanical profile. A few hanging plants (she could tell from a distance all they needed was fresh soil). The bamboos? Maybe more sun. With any luck—and no interruptions—she might be able to make the gym for her twelve o'clock class.

Not that she'd rush through the job. Pamela Rosen loved working on greens; adored the pruning and the trimming and the futzing with sprays. She always sprayed. Peaches Rosen believed in giving her clients their money's worth. Plant paranoids were what kept her alive. Midnight calls! One brown leaf and they'd be on the phone, hysterical. Coleus treated like pet poodles. People singing to ferns. Chatting with holly. She had a hundred stories. On Tuesdays and Thursdays when the shop was open, she kept a journal. Someday she'd write a book. Her best friend, Florida Burns, had suggested a title: *Confessions of a Whore-to-Culturist,* but it hadn't been one of her better puns. Only the two women had laughed at the joke.

Today wouldn't be book-writing day, not with these sagging vines. Peaches had stuck one finger in, two inches deep. "Really, all I think you need on all of these—they are just *lush,* I swear—are new pots. That's all." She paused, then fingered one leaf. "Maybe a few nitrates. . . . But, that's just an option. Basically, they're . . . *okay.*"

"Just okay?" Her customer looked anxious. "I really try to take as good care of them as . . ."

"Better than okay! They look *fine.*" She sought to reassure her. "These are some of the healthiest spider ferns I can remember."

"Thank God," the woman said.

Peaches Rosen had been left alone to stalk the mealy bugs, and she was glad. Alone, she was at her best; she was focused, yet removed. She was lost in the vagaries of her own time and rarefied pace. Fantasies! She spun entire scenarios with Peaches Rosen cast as the star. Some of her best interior dramas had been acted out while she stood silently stripping dead leaves. She had much to reflect on. Like Roger Rausch. They had been living together for (could it be?) almost six months. Still, Peaches wasn't sure she was really in love. She might be comfortable enough to wear her Clearasil to bed, but this rampant domesticity had done nothing to quell her rich inner life. Every woman's magazine she picked up only made her feel worse. She wasn't sure that a twenty-nine-year-old stockbroker (on his way up) was what *Cosmopolitan* would prescribe for a mind-throbbing sexual life. She longed to be taken over, swept away. She thought that maybe there was something wrong with her. Why couldn't she achieve these research-documented "waves of multiple orgasms"? Relationships! Hers might be "meaningful," but she was lucky if she came once every three weeks. Well, she would work on it. "Think about how he gives you such emotional support," Florida had told her when she'd started to complain. *"That you don't find every day."*

Of course Florida had been right. Roger was there—understanding, sympathetic—whenever her clients and her responsibilities started getting her down. He was level and solid, an absolute brick. But had she picked herself up from the suburbs of Atlanta to find happiness with a pale chunk of buffed stone? Peaches Rosen was still young enough (twenty-seven in February) to think that romantic love involved glass slippers and being upended from her feet. She still had her illusions and was unsure that a "safe harbor" could be enough.

She wasn't about to walk out, though, not till she found someone else. Roger Rausch wasn't perfect, but he was a lot better than being left to go it alone. At least, with Roger she could allow herself to experience inner peace. She was left alone to withdraw, have her moods. The one thing Roger Rausch did offer was a responsiveness to *her* needs.

Misting! This was the fun part: how she loved soaking, really soaking, each city-parched plant. Peaches Rosen had refused to turn in her hand-held sprayer for an automatic. Sometimes she squeezed the red plastic handle till her palm went raw. She might have sore tendons, but she was sure the exertion was her safety valve preventing an all-out Rosen-Rausch emotional debacle. She had accepted her velvet-hammock existence, but she didn't feel trapped. Not by a long shot. Whenever she felt like walking out, she thought about

9

her two closest friends. The stark reality of Florida Burns' and Marcie Laster's lives instantly sobered her up. Whatever her vague feelings of discontent, she was surely better off than they were. Both Florida and Marcie had fabulous jobs, both were super overachievers. But they were both alone. Both of them skipped from man to man; their pattern was spotty, and between affairs was a lot of white space, sometimes over a year.

Peaches didn't know how they could take it. *Well,* they'd explain, *we have our jobs.* And they had their telephones. Peaches had become accustomed to Florida or Marcie occasionally calling (for job-counseling advice!) after two o'clock. In the morning! What were they doing with that kind of work-related insomnia at this stage in their careers? Sublimation, Roger had called it; he meant: "What they need is to get laid."

But that wasn't true. What they needed, Peaches felt sure, was to be *understood* by a red-blooded member of the opposite sex. She wished that Roger had more friends so she could, at least, fix Florida up. Peaches Rosen knew it was old-fashioned—an anachronism, even—but she was a man's woman. She had always had boyfriends; what's more, she liked it that way. She was Southern and petite ("soft, pink, and fluffy," Florida called her), but was that the only reason she hated being alone? Peaches Rosen might look fragile, but her backbone was pure flint. Cohabitation didn't mean she'd lost her identity or "submerged it": was that what the feminists said? Crap! Most of the women she knew would give up their expense accounts for just that chance. Peaches Rosen knew. How? Easy! That was all any of them ever talked about, except for their jobs.

One minute more and Marcie Lester thought she would scream. There was no way to open this skyscraper's window. She was thirty-three stories over the Hudson, hermetically sealed. She couldn't even commit suicide with one meticulous jump.

But she had thought about it the very minute she'd

10

unlocked her office door. One manuscript, three sets of galleys, and four books were piled up on her desk at Metropolitan Pictures. She should complain to the readers' union, if only there were an East Coast branch. The note from Troy Younger, Metropolitan's East Coast story editor (and her boss), had been short, but far from sweet: "Marcie, all you need to do is an index card, fifty pages of each one, okay? By noon, *please.*"

It was now twenty-five till. She had done only half. One more bank heist or last picture show, they'd have to carry her out on a stretcher. She was exhausted. She was locked in a cell with a hangover and hundreds of pages of blizzard-cold type. Why couldn't she learn to pop two Excedrin before she drifted into bed? She carried a diaphragm with her everywhere, but . . . aspirin? No way. Being a walking drugstore wasn't her idea of neat. She was paying the piper now, all right. She had to escape for an hour, to steam out in dry heat. She knew Troy would have a cat if he came back from lunch and discovered she'd left for the Ponce DeLeon. Fags! They never understood that sometimes a woman needs her gym.

Well, fuck Troy Younger and the entire homosexual cabal of Metropolitan Pictures, Inc. Marcie Laster had her own life to lead and it did not involve playing God about a bunch of fourth-rate "literary properties for filmic consideration." Fuck that, too. It wasn't like anything she and Troy ever recommended would be bought by the Coast. About the best they could hope for was lunch with Mike Nichols' gopher; maybe Gene Hackman's reader would also come along, if they got really lucky.

A glamour job! She'd beaten out a score of other applicants all eager for her mingy pay. Now she stared out an airtight glass wall. A warm April day and she was stuck, staring at the river, charting the progress of a barge slogging past the New Jersey piers. She sighed. *Just one more, maybe she could wade through one more virgin-born tome.* A pink and orange pseudo-patent-leather floral cover caught her eye. Just from the flyleaf she knew this stinker didn't have a Chinaman's chance. Chemical warfare . . . a spoof, a joke? Who did they think they were

11

kidding, she read the *Times*. Marcie Laster dashed off a well-practiced bouquet of acid lines: "What do you say about a 'comedy' that has a village of Indians done in by rotten chemical cheese? You say it stinks and even a little bit more. *Earth Cloud* is a pretentious mish-mash of sadism and trivia. This is A. L. Potter's third novel. When will somebody tape his fingers together (for good)? I say *Pass-adena*. Or, as they say in Texas, 'El Pass-o!' "

Eat your heart out, A. L. Potter, wherever you are. With a flourish she initialed her index comment card "ML." How she loved composing a truly sour one-liner! How she dreaded getting something "hot," something she might even take a shine to, might hope the studio would buy. Then she'd have to work all day, getting her syntax just right. After all, her report (sometimes fifteen or twenty pages) would be sent all the way to California. You never could tell who might actually read it. George Cukor! Dino DeLaurentiis! The mind boggled. They would all see her initials, or even Marcie Laster's full *name,* proudly riding the top. That was power, but it took special care. More care than Marcie Laster could bestow upon her morning's chores. She was still thinking about last night's blind date, still hoping that each time the phone on the outside desk chimed twice it would be *him* who would call. A media buyer at Benton & Bowles? Whoever thought that for him (after three hours), she'd fall . . . blindly into bed. But Marcie knew Bruce Firestone would be different, she knew from the way he'd looked at her that he would call for sure. She frowned for the briefest instant; a wave of self-doubt washed over her. Nonsense! She was just (as they said in group) "doing a number on herself," and her shrink had implored her to act from the gut, to always do what she felt like doing.

Well, she had felt like fucking. Was that such a crime? If she and Bruce Firestone hadn't gone to bed on the first night, it would just be a question of time. So why not? Get the most obvious part out of the way first. Then they could really get to know each other. "Without all the bullshit," Bruce had said. Female Assertiveness Training, Marcie! Take heart. She shoved herself into her estian space, she drew breath and

concentrated on her mantra . . . or was it her "barrier"? *Fuck.*
She could never remember. Well, Werner Erhard (her latest
guru) taught that "whatever is, is," so that meant . . . she could
relax, enjoy. Bruce Firestone would either call or he wouldn't
call. Whatever happened, *it was his problem.* She felt a rush of
blood come up from the base of her spine and she began to
feel . . . better. Maybe the fifty dollars an hour and the
weekend retreats were helping. Now she could concentrate on
what was really important.

Her work. But she had no time for good words today.
Today any "property" that crossed Marcie Laster's desk would
land in a mined and treacherous internal war zone. All these
turkeys were destined for the much-feared steel file box.
Siberia! (Via one three-by-five index card.) At first she'd been
conscience-stricken. How would she react if her own words
were someday treated the way she decimated others'? Was this
why her hands froze into paralysis the moment she sat down to
her college Royal she kept at home? Because she was afraid
someday another Marcie Laster would write "pretentious
mish-mash" all over her? Quickly she scribbled a note. She
must take this up with the analyst, perhaps it would appear in a
subsequent dream. Writers! You couldn't very well make it in
New York these days unless you were somehow "in print." Yet
here she was, a short-haired double for Ali MacGraw, and she
was stuck in this gig, reading others while she knew in her heart
of hearts she deserved others to be reading her. Well, you had
to be philosophical. Marcie Laster thought herself to be some
tough judge, but anything decent wouldn't land with her anyway. It would be shuttled (by air express) right out to Metropolitan's men at the top. And they were all in Los Angeles,
where Real Movie Power lay. She and Troy Younger were just
jerking off—in Hollywood terms, that is.

Enough of this maudlin introspection, she'd be late for the
gym. She glanced at her calendar while she stood up to go.
"Lunch—April 4th—FRANCIS COPPOLA'S Executive Assistant."
In agate type she had scrawled in his name. She hoped that
someone would stroll into her office and read her date book
upside down, let them freak out at what *her* week held in store.

13

"Be back at two," she screamed at Arnold Schill, Troy's Associate Story Editor (in training) and all-around secretary/office boy. Another gay. Yes, she was surrounded, but at least Marcie Laster didn't have to play office sexual politics. She took comfort in that. With Troy Younger and Arnold Schill, Marcie Laster knew where she stood. It was Hollywood quicksand, but so far she hadn't sunk.

The three of them were a mini-team, a troika of creativity lost in a corporate sea. Metropolitan was a small company, not a studio by any stretch. Certainly no competition to Paramount or Warner Brothers. Three movies a year they produced, and distributed a few pickups. Something they had distributed last year in the U.S. and Canada was shown out-of-competition at Cannes. Troy was hoping that Metropolitan would reissue it now. He could screen it and invite his hundred closest friends. Maybe for this one they might actually come.

No doubt about it, Troy Younger was devoted to his job. "Listen, honey. These jobs are a revolving door with movie companies, *a fuckin' revolving door.* So don't think that you— that any of us—will be able to last here for more than a year." Troy had told that to Marcie three years before, when he'd first hired her. She'd started as his secretary, then had been promoted. Junior Story Editor. That meant three days a week she read and wrote synopses. The other two were taken up with appointments: agents, publishers, junior editors, people from the book clubs.

"Listen, honey. It's all about levels. The head of Simon & Schuster is *not* going to have lunch with you. The head of subsidiary rights for Simon & Schuster is not going to have lunch with you—maybe she'll give you twenty minutes in her office, but *that's it.*"

Marcie asked Troy who would have lunch with her, now that she had an expense account of $125 a month.

"I would try the assistant to S & S's subsidiary-rights girl. Maybe she would do it. Even though *you're* not a studio, you never can tell."

Troy only allowed her out to have lunches twice a week. Marcie had cut her Tuesdays and Thursdays back to just one fancy voucher a week. On $125 a month, you couldn't go far, but Marcie Laster had it all figured out. Simple! It was better to be seen once a week at Le Madrigal (where company presidents, executive editors, and Jackie O. go) than to be seen twice as often somewhere else lower-brow. You had to know how to play the game, and Marcie Laster did. If only she could figure out how to get the West Coast to agree that her cab fares would be put on the tab.

Still, a big part of the game was looking good, no matter what the let-it-all-hang-out crowd might think. That's why MWF (noon till two) Marcie Laster checked herself into the Ponce DeLeon Health Club. She wanted to be ready when opportunity struck.

Besides, in a women's gym, you never could tell what you might learn. In the sauna (last fall?) Marcie Laster had overheard two women talking, she had thought (at first) about her. "She's the kind of girl . . . I don't know, a perfectionist! The kind of girl who would have her legs waxed every few weeks, even in the winter." A throwaway line, but for Marcie Laster, a twenty-four carat one. She's made the appointment at Elizabeth Arden's the very next day. Over the winter, she'd wondered if the women had noticed that Marcie Laster (on the next bench in the dry heat) had incorporated and digested their casually mentioned sterling character trait.

Mike Markman, the "fast-food boy wonder" and self-styled media savant, lay blanketed under a mountain of newsprint. His boyhood Indian quilt blanket was tattered, but pulled up to the tip of his chin. A single Tensor beamed an amber shaft over his bed, leaving the rest of the room shrouded in deep inky blue. Midnight blue! Walls, shades, and bookcases were freshly covered with navy paint. This was no bus-and-truck, common garden blue. It was like . . . lapis lazuli, yet more intense. He had even conferred on this custom mix a Markman, Incorporated copyrighted name. "One A.M." now clung to his walls, creating the perfect private quarters to house a young mogul.

15

In short, Mike Markman had designed the ideal nocturnal space. The twenty-nine-year-old taco prince did his best (and only) work all through the late hours, each and every night. Bio-rhythm! His was that of an all-night diner; Mike Markman could only achieve deep alpha sleep when the dark first began to be edged with gray. He would stay curled up till he heard the thud of his morning media-drop, then he would stumble out (sometime around nine) to pick up the logpile of twenty-two morning newspapers stacked like kindling outside his door. Half-dazed, he would stagger back in, then he would plow through hundreds of pages, searching for trends, bits of whimsey, maybe a few grains of hard news.

Luxury! Mike Markman had convinced himself this indulgence was the key to what others might call his "meteoric" success. He might own a chain of high-class taco stands called La Taquita, but that didn't mean Mike Markman could afford to let his outer-directedness slip. His twenty-two newspapers (suburban, local, trade, international) could be hard to coordinate, but they were necessary (he thought) tools of his trade. Anyway, it was all in who you knew. Mike Markman knew the guy who owned the Hudson County News Company. They were friends, which meant he'd arranged for one of his New Jersey truckers to bring Markman's morning madness in. So along with the biggies—the *Journal,* the *Times,* the *News, Women's Wear Daily, Variety,* the *Hollywood Reporter,* the *Boston Globe,* the *Paris Trib,* the *London Times,* the *Express,* the *Telegraph,* the *Philadelphia Inquirer,* the *Washington Post* (and the *Star*), *Newsday,* the *Atlanta Constitution,* the *Los Angeles Times,* the *Dallas Times Herald,* the *San Francisco Examiner*—Hudson County News also supplied his suburban barometers: the *South Orange Outlook! The Charlotte Northside Sentinel! The Arnold* (Maryland) *Bugle!* If La Taquita was to keep its profit picture in the dozen small towns where he had opened shop, Mike Markman had to be right there, tuned in to each market's specialized news.

Just about now—a few minutes on the downside of noon —was when Markman, Incorporated went into action.

Excited, he reached for the phone, but in the half-light he

16

fumbled—the *Arnold* (Maryland) *Bugle* was clenched in his other hand. The receiver slipped from his grip, tortoise-shell frames fell down his nose. *"Shit . . ."* His fingers stretched for the bed lamp; a soft light crept over the room.

Now he was purposeful. Dialing his number, he jammed his glasses back into place. *"Is he there?"* Mike Markman barked into the phone; then, not missing a beat, he continued to talk. *"What do you* MEAN *what do I mean?* SCREW THAT! I'm telling you I want to unload it! DUMP IT! I'm not throwing good money after . . ."* Mike Markman smiled. It never failed. Always his broker asked for his source, never did he ever give it away. He smoothed down the edges of the *Arnold* (Maryland) *Bugle,* then his voice dropped. "Never mind who told me. The *same* person who always tells me. He was right about Paramount, wasn't he? Didn't he put us in Universal months before *Jaws?* So? Just get rid of it! My friend warned me about Homerica. . . . No product, their stuff in development stinks. . . ." Mike Markman listened for a moment, his eyes on the clock. The fingers of his free hand pulled at his hair. He was squirming; his Indian quilt was a heap on the floor. He wanted to get going, he had so much to do, not the least of which was winding up this phone call, the first of the day.

His broker was conspiring to keep him on.

"Look, Barney. I know you want me to hang onto it, but everybody knows about summer pictures! Sock 'em in and out of the drive-in circuit and in two weeks if they don't hit . . . La Taquita takes a fuckin' bath." Mike Markman reached for his date book, the receiver clamped to his neck. He was standing up now, completely nude. His foot tapped on the rug. He was imposing, but just not quite tall enough for his vanity to be gratified.

In the next room somebody was dusting, *psst* went an aerosol spray. Damn! When was Juanita going to understand he didn't want her buying any more of those? Twice he'd told her about the ozone level; twice he'd failed to make the point. "Okay-okay-okay . . . I've got the whole thing figured. Sixty-five thousand shares of Homerica, right? Unload forty at eight and a half. . . . Wait! Punch up the machine and tell me where

17

it's at. . . . Okay! That ain't so hot. Maybe we'll get lucky on the stuff we have left. I'll hang onto a few. Who knows? No source is perfect, even mine! Anyway, *le show biz* makes me nervous. . . ." He laughed easily and often, after business was done. "What was it those turkeys at Goldman Sachs wrote up about La Taquita? 'Get Mike Markman out of food and he's a downside risk'? You know what? *They're probably right.*"

He was still smiling when he threw on his clothes. Every day he wore the same thing: tennis shorts, tennis shirt, white leather Adidas. Even in winter, he never got cold. He yelled to the maid, "*Qué haces allá afuera? Juanita!*"

"*Muy fresco, Señor Markman. . . . Muy fresco y . . . poquito frío.*"

Where was an envelope, any envelope? He was grabbing papers, scooping up rackets, running late. He'd have to sprint twenty blocks to get to the bubble on time. He hated to make any partner wait.

The second hour of Mike Markman's day was always the same. One set, maybe two, but certainly a gut-clenching, jet-powered session of tennis, seven days a week, at one o'clock. He never missed a day. He felt it gave him a good start on life. Just look at Max Whitehead, age seventy-one, who always played on the next court. Never missed a shot, the old coot! And he was all-city seeded, in the age-sixty-and-over's. Hell, he hoped he would be as active when he got to be Whitehead's age.

Who was he kidding? He hoped he would be as active when he got to be half Max Whitehead's age! The way business looked headed, he couldn't be sure. He was sure of one thing: his next birthday was August 4th and he had only one aim: to get La Taquita on the big board by day one of his thirtieth year. He was ready. He had twenty-seven locations and sales of five million a year. Now the bankers were coming to *him* with ideas, even though he was still considered a *pisher* at this franchising game.

It had been a long uphill fight—three years. At first, the money men wouldn't even take his calls. "Mexican food?" they had howled. "No way, not in these backwater states." They had encouraged him to try chicken, maybe hot dogs boiled in beer. "Look at Lum's! Just take a look at those figures!" But Mike Markman had known he was right. He had been convinced that Maryland, the Carolinas, Kentucky, and the Virginias were long overdue for the pleasures of Tex-Mex.

Which, to his Southern-California and Mexican-bred mind, meant this: a disgustingly packed greasy beef-and-cheese taco iced with heaps of shredded green and red. Bursting burritos! Flour tortillas overstuffed with beans, chiles, and meat . . . exploding in your mouth, all over you! And that was just the first bite. Mike Markman's Mexican food would be served well—no tissue-paper wraps for him—but, more important, it would be served *fast.* And it would be delicious. His aim was to be called the Rimbaud of Fast Food. He would bring in the poetry, surfeit his La Taquitas with hanging plants, tile floors, ceramics, even piped-in music (Vivaldi? The Tijuana Brass?) to finish off the ambiance. Why, he was doing a public service, both for himself and his hungry customers. Nobody else could offer that Markman quality, certainly not five years ago, when he was first starting out. Seventy-nine cents a taco! He had blown them off their heels, but he'd started small. A deserted Whataburger in Bowling Green, Kentucky, was Latinized within weeks; that lease, his first, he got for just eight hundred dollars down. Eight hundred dollars! From there he fanned out, next stop Arnold, Maryland; he'd found a run-down Arby's in the classifieds. They were only too glad to sell everything but the Arby's name.

That he didn't want. He had his own name. "La Taquita" was soon riding on six storefronts with a newly decorated "Mexican potting shed" look. Who said venture capital was dead? Who said a new business couldn't make a go? Within the first three years his sales had risen to over one million a year. And he was smart; he would keep La Taquita within his control. He kept fourteen fingers in everything; he wouldn't let go. The tiles in the new Durham restaurant were imported from southern Spain. He'd found them himself on his last

19

vacation, three years ago. "Those are the ones . . . I must have those!" In perfect Spanish he'd pointed to a sample square on display.

"Impossible, señor. I paint each one myself, with a tiny paintbrush. It would take days." The old woman was all alone, and unswerving. These tiles were souvenir tiles, $5 a piece. For the briefest instant Mike Markman let his enthusiasm flag. Then he got The Idea. It would only cost him $10,000 to put the old woman (and her daughter) on retainer for a year. And he got seventy-five thousand tiles, a bargain besides.

He was a perfectionist, an adventurer, a loner, and prematurely gray. But he was still too caught up with the immediacy of his success (his new co-op) to let a myth make him complacent. So! Why had he started a chain of fancy-shmancy sit-down taco parlors in the hinterlands? Could you answer me that, Mr. Success? In his mind, his bankers took on voices, sometimes Moses, but mostly Shelley Winters. He was only too glad to lay the Michael David Markman theory of corporate success on their heads: give the public what they don't have, go where the market is crying to be tapped.

He knew. Mike Markman had been two years out of Stanford but was already bursting with ideas. The year was 1971, for him a watershed. When the flower children wilted, Mike Markman had never been happier, he'd experienced an absolute energy release. He felt he was part of the new wave, the King of Now. Why? The pop-top world of Palo Alto hipness had bored him from his freshman year. For Mike Markman, all the San Francisco weirdos were absolutely déjà vu. How could he be impressed by David Harris when his very own mother had taken off "to find herself" before his thirteenth year? She'd turned up in Cuernavaca a few miles from Ivan Illich's door. And there she'd stayed all through his high school years, leaving Mike Markman to groove with her during the summers and during the school year to function back in the Palisades, very much on his own. But Toby Markman was no deadbeat, no gigolette. Within a year of her divorce, she was running a thriving cooking school. By the time Mike Markman

20

graduated from high school, she'd published not just one *"comida típica"* cookbook, but two.

Manny Markman always said, "The apple doesn't fall far from the tree," and his only child had proved *that* old chestnut to be doubly true. From both his parents Mike Markman had gotten his incredible drive; he had run Stanford Student Marketing, demanded personal tutorials for himself when the campus was closed down. He was a cynic, a nihilist, an apolitical savant. Had his draft number not been 321, he might be somewhere selling tacos (or spicy broiled chicken) somewhere in Vietnam.

But he wasn't in Vietnam. He was unpacking the last packing crate in his new five rooms over Central Park. And now the money men came to him—to his office—his reconverted bedroom in an obscure shade of blue. The parade of suppliers, wholesalers, union leaders, subfranchisers (*never!* he'd tell them), brokers, and money men. The heat was on: "Take La Taquita public." En masse, or one-to-one, they were banging down his door. But Mike Markman was careful, he made mental notes. And he was watching, always watching, the way each supplicant leaned in, oozing sincerity, but still . . . tense. His last apartment's leftover Castro Convertible practically buckled under the strain of all those Peel Brothers brogues and Paul Stuart three-piece suits that were applying the pressure in his office-at-home every single weekday afternoon. Flattered! He was gratified (but not humbly) that these bankers wanted to take La Taquita, as they said, "over the top." But he was cautious and more than a little bit anxious when he saw projections that would turn his baby into a "growth capital" machine. Okay, he might be self-involved, but he wasn't a Bernie Cornfeld. Not for him was the idea of future castles and hordes of women and publicity schemes. He was worried about exposure, his possible downfall. The Heisenberg Uncertainty Principle! Would La Taquita change under an imminent microscopic probe?

Money! That was the key, as good as sex, as good as love. And certainly, revenge. His first salvo would be aimed at

Goldman Sachs. Hypocrites! They hated him, but for the last two years were falling to new lows kissing his ass. But they were his bankers . . . and apolitical Mike Markman hated their dichotomies, couldn't wait to give them the ultimate run-around. A Jewish firm doing business with Arabs? "Sell a million of Xerox. . . . Buy a half of AT&T warrants at XYZ!" the dark-haired block traders would scream into consoles, with lunches served to them at desks. While upstairs in the anemia-haven of Corporate Finance, strings of palomino-faced men would lie in wait to poison young entrepreneurs like Mike Markman over a drunken $40 expense-account lunch.

Fuck . . . Money was money, but he had to sprint eastward toward his game. He had scribbled in his book, then let his eyes rest for a moment on his library shelf. The middle row! An offender! Where his prized collection of forty-seven Hardy Boys was lined up, someone had knocked an antique photo askew. "Bathers at Coney Island, 1935" was teetering on edge. He had righted it, lodging it back into its proper place. Perfect! It balanced over Hardy Boys Number 39; he loved that one! Thirty-nine was the one in which Mike Markman had first learned the word *spelunking*.

But he had been staring at the women in the photograph, staring at the books he had treasured since he was nine. He hoped someday to pass them along to his sons. He knew he would have several, although girls (if he could train them) would be okay. Maybe some of both, yes! That would be ideal. Odd, it was easier for Mike Markman to visualize his sons—they would, of course, look just like him—than it was for him to bring their mother into view. What would she look like, Mrs. Mike Markman, mother of his children, wife of the insomniac taco king? But worse, how would he ever meet his ideal when work was his mistress and La Taquita occupied his every day?

He zoomed out his double oak doors, taking the marble steps two at a time, ignoring his phone ringing off the wall. If he stopped—even to say hello-goodbye—his timetable would shoot up in flames. He glanced at his watch, cursed the world's slowest elevators when he was already halfway down. His tennis shoes sailed over the cobblestone courtyard. The Dakota!

He had just settled into his five massive rooms. He had just gotten used to the fact that he was approaching the liquid half-million-dollar league which, among other things, had enabled Mike Markman to move into this German-Renaissance apartment building which had always represented his urban house on the hill. He was a shareholder in the Dakota, which meant that he was "involved" in its regulations and its communal problems. *If only he had someone to share his life with . . . but enough!* Mike Markman was never given to complaining, although he must write himself a memo to get the co-op board to do something about that elevator.

He frowned, then felt his calves scream as he burst into Yorkville Tennis City just in time. All through the first set, the question plagued him: was the next Dakota board meeting a week from Tuesday, or had he missed it last night?

REPRO: ARNOLD (Maryland) BUGLE
Tell Me Everything/ F. Burns

Two years ago, 27-year-old Boy Wonder Quentin Wallace burst upon the Hollywood scene with his independently financed production of "Cloud 8"—which was memorable less for its soggy love story than its spectacular $30 million gross. Last year, the golden boy racked up more reams of praise when he and Molly Madden had that blistering—and *very* public—affair. Their final breakup (Hollywood still hasn't stopped talking about their screaming "disagreement" at Mr. Chow's in Beverly Hills) only fueled Wallace's already high profile, and early this year, at 29, Quentin Wallace became Homerica Picture's youngest chief executive.

Now, Tell Me Everything's West Coast Early Warning System insists, Quentin Wallace may be on the way out of Homerica's revolving-door presidency. Already, gossipmongers have dubbed him the company's "Guest President," but this week, in a sensational (and very hush-hush) development, Homerica's Board of Directors huddled after a screening of Wallace's first Homerica production, the $10-million "Evening Up." Early viewers had suggested the Homerica brass would rename this picture "Disaster Area,"

23

and apparently the honchos couldn't have agreed more. Wallace, my spies report, will soon be named head of Homerica's cable-TV division—if he'll accept that "transfer."

Quentin Wallace, as might be expected, is taking no phone calls, but your ever-curious correspondent has located him at California's ultra-posh Golden Door Resort, where, I'm told, Wallace checked in over a week ago for rest and massage. A week ago? Doesn't that explain why Wallace wasn't at the Homerica meeting? Whatever the conclusion of *this* thriller, expect the other shoe—or bomb—to drop before the week is out.

*

Confident superstar Ronnie Crawford—you know him as the hit-maker who recently confessed on the Carson show he had been a sexual switch-hitter—has decided to give up the title of Numero Uno Hollywood Heartbreaker. Constant companion Sharilee Acuff will be the first-ever Mrs. Crawford and the date's even been—sort of—set for the nuptials: this weekend somewhere in Las Vegas. Reached at home by Tell Me Everything's Florida Burns, Crawford would only say that he's opening in Vegas this weekend, but while we were chatting, the operator *did* break in with an emergency call from a Mr. Larsen at Tiffany's—so I think we might as well draw the obvious conclusion. While this bride won't be wearing white (Sharilee was once hitched to Les Nelson, leader of the country-western band that first gave Ronnie C. his start), everything else will definitely come up spotless for Sharilee. She'll become mistress of Ronnie's half-million-dollar white stucco hacienda in Bel-Air, and she'll have her pick of Ronnie's white Cadillac, white Mercedes, and white Silver Cloud convertible. The pool is blue and the tennis courts are green, but that's life—and love—in Hollywood: nothing's ever quite perfect enough.

XXX

That was a mistake. I watched this week's Tell Me Everything drift out of Marcie Laster's hands. When was I going to learn? I never should have given Miss Metropolitan Pictures a look at real dish. Silent, I retrieved my *Arnold* (Maryland) *Bugle* tear sheet from the Ponce DeLeon's floor. Maybe she

24

had learned something new, something hot. I searched Marcie's face for her reaction.

She looked at me. "Does your mother know what you do for a living?"

That hurt. "Tell me you can't wait to run back to Metropolitan and start spreading the Quentin-Wallace-in-trouble-at-Homerica story."

"Everybody knows about *that*. I'm surprised that *Variety* hasn't run it already." Marcie's legs had stretched into a perfect straddle. Underneath carnation tights, her inner thighs tight-- ened, then relaxed. "*Anyway*. I heard this morning that it's not happening. The latest word is that Wallace's father—since he's still on the board—is forcing Homerica to keep the asshole on. At least for a while."

"Was it Gertrude Stein who once said, 'Interesting, if true'?"

Marcie folded herself into an inverted scissors. "I wasn't there at the time. I knew Gertrude's cousin Selma though; she was the *real* bitch." She looked around the gym, her lips a narrow line, then she smiled. "What's new?"

I said "not much" and let my eyes follow hers. At that moment I saw what Marcie Laster saw. Women in leotards (black, red, pink, purple), pantyhose with runs in them, or men's shirts pulled over tights were clustered everywhere. Hardly a spot remained. Those unlucky ones who had not laid claim to foam rubber pillows hovered near the machines: whirl-a-bikes, knee presses, walking joggers, slantboards, pulleys, weights, sprockets, and widgets. About the last place I wanted to be was next to Marcie Laster when she was on the attack, but we were too close friends for me to allow myself to do anything so obviously hostile as changing places. Anyway, I wasn't sure if Marcie Laster was on the offensive; sometimes it was tough to tell.

Instead I looked to see if Ozelle, *la profesora,* or my best-friend-in-the-whole-world, Peaches Rosen, was on the horizon. Ozelle! Never take Advanced Body Jazz and Respiratory Aerobics from an ex-belly dancer (Turkish). Not if you wanted to keep your life on any kind of timetable. Ridiculous! Already she was four minutes late. Worse! Never once had she apologized for holding us up. Didn't she realize that we were working women trying to keep our lives under control? Insulting! Her very behind waddling through the door would exude contempt, her buns would shake like dancer's bells. Ozelle hadn't worn the veil in seven years, but she still knew how to give a workout. For a $150 Ponce membership, did one have a right to demand anything more?

I would be forced to talk to Marcie.

"Got any items?"

"Maybe."

"I'm dying. Just dying. I don't have a thing this week."

Marcie kept half an eye on the door. "You know about *Ruby Slippers,* the remake of—"

"*Marcie!* That was in the *Hollywood Reporter* last week!"

" So what? *That's* never stopped you before." She began to laugh.

I rolled on my back and watched my legs climb through the air. Upside down, they didn't look so bad. "Come on. I'm serious."

"Whoa-kay. Items-items-items. Question: all the stuff I feed you . . . why don't you ever quote *me?* Not famous enough?" She seemed genuinely concerned.

"You'd want me to? Couldn't you get in trouble? Like get fired or something?"

"I don't see why—"

"What am I going to call you? 'Marcie Laster—Production Exec'?" This was getting ridiculous. I was getting pressured by a close friend. And I was feeling guiltier than . . .

"That's exactly what I want you to call me. 'Marcie Laster, Production Executive'!"

I started to answer—to say something "smart"—but Marcie was way past me; her head spun like a *dredl.* I thought she was taking in the clock (now at 12:07) or the twenty-odd pair of leotards in various stages of limbering up. I was wrong.

Marcie Laster was taking in *me.* "Your hair! What did you do to it?"

26

Everywhere there was glass, a mirror covered all four walls. I looked to see what she was talking about. "Oh, this? Just a perm. You know, the Bette Midler look? What's the matter, you hate it?" I fluffed out my new $25 Afro, hoping that would help.

She waited. "Well . . . 'Hate' isn't exactly the right word. I mean, I like the style. I'm just not sure if it's right for everyone. . . ." Marcie stared at my face, then she smiled. "Maybe I'll get used to it."

"What about the color? I used henna, can you tell?"

"So-I-see! Are they still doing that?" She paused and held two fingers above her eye like she was using a viewfinder. "I guess it's . . . not bad. Although, I don't know. Well, don't ask me. I haven't seen a copy of *Vogue* in ages. . . ."

Ozelle saved me. She crawled on her platform and reached for the mike. The screech rang in my ears like her voice, but she turned away from us and bounced a needle onto a disk. Neil Diamond! Wouldn't you know it! We had heard "Holly Holy" at least ninety-seven times. Musical lead-ins were not one of Ozelle's flashier assets. Not like the clothes, anyway. Today she was in her one-piece lilac stretch lace, zipped up crotch to boobs. Scuffed mauve ballet shoes completed The Look. *Tacky.* I gave myself the once-over in the nearest mirror. Ivy League! I liked what I saw: regulation scoop-neck dancers' black; tights (also black) chopped off above the ankle bone. Pulled over them were argyles (green and red). Just because Marcie Laster had a Presbyterian button nose and her Presbyterian hair cut in a wedge three years before anyone had ever heard of Dorothy Hamil didn't mean she was *always* right. I liked my new auburn sausage curls. They brought out the color of my eyes (blue)—kinky hair made me look real.

Anyway, some friends are competitive, what are you going to do? I always have believed: you gotta like people for what they are and (as my father always says), *don't expect anything more.* I had been taught that I wouldn't get it.

What I was getting was pain, all from Ozelle. *Please! Not the jumping jacks, not the running in place. That kind of pain nobody needs.* Ozelle! Do you have any idea what it feels like to have two grapefruits bouncing in time to an R & B beat? Do you have any sense of what it feels like to have a classful of leotards staring at you clutching your boobs to your chest? Of course not! She had segued to Brazil '66. Suddenly, twenty-three women fell to their knees . . . then jumped up! They all (including me) knew the routine. Three arches and two leaps for the roof which meant we were into the sixth minute of the noon workout.

Time for the Modified Poodle. I touched my toes, glued palms right where they dropped, then ever so carefully my left leg went into near-orbit, first kicking . . . now circling. Every tendon cried.

"Know how good pain can feel!" Ozelle yelled. "That's when you know you are *vorking!*"

I feel it! I feel it! My right knee just collapsed under the strain. Still, I didn't fall, not when my gymnast's pride was at stake. Ozelle was screaming, "Stay with it, girls!! Just six more!" and, like she was Zubin Mehta, I followed her lead. My head popped from my neck . . . my eyes searched the mirror. Everyone was following Ozelle's lead. Twenty-three pairs of legs had bisected the air. Twenty-three women were standing like mandrills supported on all fours. We were the missing link(s)! In a flash, it hit me. The Ponce DeLeon Health Club looked like a monkey house during mating season. . . .

I turned to see if Peaches had, by some long shot, wandered in yet. Instead I caught a glimpse of Marcie straining but keeping up. Three veins carved a road map into her brow. Her face was as puckered as a raisin. Still, she wasn't about to let up. Marcie's left knee struggled to keep up with the beat. Hatred! How could anyone be that thin? You could use Marcie Laster's rib cage to play a marimba, maybe in a pinch even to scrub out lingerie.

Then there were *my* ribs. The only thing they were good for was holding up *los pectorales.* And even at that, they could use a refresher course. You couldn't very well not notice the ever-increasing atrophy of the Florida Burns abdomen. At the Ponce DeLeon that mirror as big as Times Square relentlessly reflected every anatomical flaw.

28

Now I was laid out on the floor, slicing the air with one hamstring in perfect turnout. I was propped on my elbow, which meant that one breast would try to play dead. I let it flop, then watched it hover somewhere along my upper arm. Only the man with the seeing-eye dog and the tin cup wouldn't notice that Florida Burns had far more than her share (upstairs).

Breasts. I have a few words to say about big ones. You think you've got problems, well . . . try adding an "ample bosom" to your list. I'm not just concerned with Edith Lance's custom-made "flattener" fittings, or a monthly swell to honeydew-melon size. I'm talking about something much, much more. Take the problem of "C.J." Flournoy. Anybody with a D cup has had a "C.J." Flournoy in her life. A pimpled, pockmarked, duck-tailed greaser. A creep who grew up on the wrong side of the tracks. A night crawler let loose during the day where he clung like fungus around the hallways of Lomitas High which was (and is) in Austin. That's Texas. And he gathered spores, waiting for each day's highlight, its magic moment. Which was when Florida Burns cruised into Honors Algebra. Hidden behind a maze of steel lockers, a voice out of nowhere would boom, *"Hey Big Boobies, Hey Big Boobies!"*

Of course I died. Then I would skulk into Honors Algee and chalk my equations up on the board. They always sang. Florida Burns never made less than an A.

You couldn't, if you were a 34D. There was too much to compensate for. Nobody looked sillier than girls with big tits. Nobody could look more like wind-up bimbo dolls with cherry red lips than those who were (in that quaint vernacular) "built like a brick shithouse." Sounds ideal? Hardly. Some people might have wanted to wear micro-miniskirts and get felt up, but not Florida Burns. Even then, even in Austin, Texas, I had too many plans.

Besides. I knew how someone really smart was supposed to look. Flat. Well-scrubbed. Androgynous. *Like a man.* That's how one could tell the bright girls from the dum-dums, by the size of their bra. And by the men they were with. Boys from Choate or the Harvard B. School may jerk off with *Playboy* centerfolds, fantasize about a fifty-two-inch chest. But when it comes to getting down—really getting serious—the 32B will get them each and every time. I'm living proof.

And what does that leave me with? Construction workers? Hoods? The "lower middle class"? C.J. Flournoy! Some selection. This group was into knockers in a big, big way. And them I certainly didn't want. To be called "Earth Mother" was not my idea of a turn-on. I wanted to be appreciated for only one thing. My brain.

And I was, sort of. It was like the old cliché. I forced myself to be smarter and funnier than everybody else; to work harder; to know more dirt. I made myself the center of the action. I just knew that if people felt that organic need to be around me, even if it was just for entertainment, they would see my true qualities, whatever they were.

Don't get me wrong! I have plenty of good qualities, a darn sight more than my share. And some (including me) might even consider this pectoral endowment a quasi-asset. It's just that I never fit in with the Haight-Ashbury free-to-be-me-and-thee crowd. Yes, Florida Burns is a child of the 1960s, but that was just a chronological accident; no way was I part of the Decade of Love. Florida Burns never wore love beads or popped any kind of electric pills. Florida Burns never stormed the Pentagon or looked to the media to supply her with a culture queen. Nobody was going to label me a super-feminist like Gloria Steinem or a whining loser like Sheila Levine. So who am I? I wish I knew. That's the problem. What Florida Burns is, is confused. Everybody says to me, "What are your needs, your wants, your drives?" They say that self-obsession ("awareness," as they call it) should be the watchword for modern feminine youth. I agree! There's just one catch. When it comes to gauging Florida Burns, will anyone besides the subject herself ever care?

Here's what I'm trying to say: when you grow up with *Playboy* and *Cosmopolitan* stuffed down your craw and everybody around you is ordering the Mark Eden busterama course or rubbing in snake oil and talking about IUDs and morning-after pills, what do you do? If you're Florida Burns, you feel guilty about getting felt up at age sixteen. If you're Florida Burns and the sentence "God you have fantastic tits" hangs in the air, you want to crawl into the woodwork and die because you weren't blessed with what Peaches Rosen has: absolute linoleum. So when the day comes that Mr. Anonymous is reaching his hand up under your sweater, trying to crawl under the wire that is holding you up, *way up,* and he's getting his hand cut to slivers, but still he's trying . . . then he says, "You have such great breasts, Florida. Why can't they get hard?" The fact is, they lie there like water balloons. You want to tell me what's sexy about that?

I know what *is* sexy in this modern age. Brains are sexy! Accomplishment is sexy! Doing things is sexy! Piano. Ballet. Debating tournaments! (Does anybody besides me remember the J. Weston Welch guidebook for "Resolved: that Section 14B of the Taft-Hartley Law should be repealed"? What I would do now—a decade after that high school triumph—to meet a labor lawyer! By dessert we'd be picking out the shell-and-scroll pattern at Tiffany's.) Then there were the fencing lessons at the Austin Jewish Community Center, clicking foils with Chuckie Mayerson. Nobody could tell me I wasn't *his* equal. And-the-tennis-and-the-tap-dancing-and-the-pottery-and-the-Girl-Scouts . . . *Merit badges!* I got every single one. Every single one? You bet. I cheated. By filling in the weaving and the camping and the basketmaking and the music and the art and the tilework requirements *myself.* Even at age ten I was convinced there was only one way to get ahead in this world: *make your own rules.* Why complain to the fates when one ounce of cunning could arrange for tiny green embroidered badges to cover my scarf? Anyone could be all-city, all-state. (Only later would I learn that this was the way the Boy Scouts behaved.)

Anyway, I'm still in the Girl Scouts, only now it's called the Ponce DeLeon Health Club. Body awareness or weaving baskets; only the conversations—not the level of competition—have changed. We are a microcosm of female singlehood in urban life. All of us in a constant state of before and after; all of us in the final stages of Growing Up. Wasn't taking care of one's flab a sign of mental maturity and emotional health?

Of course. Extremism in the defense of liberty is no vice. I knew—we all knew—what could set you free. A perfect body! So who could blame my twelve o'clock class for being compulsive fanatics? We were contemporary women, a high-energy brigade. That same zeal we applied to our jobs we focused on our waistlines or our pet neuroses, at least in the middle of the day. Marcie Laster's three-pound ankle weights and plastic cleaners' bags wrapped around her thighs (under her tights) to make her sweat are nothing, really nothing. Not when you compare her to Lana; Lana's level of anxiety wins her the award of the Ponce DeLeon's professional *kvetch*. Lana whines about her boyfriend, her job, and the fact that she's *huge*. (Lana weighs in at one hundred pounds.) Lana tacked up a clipping on the Ponce bulletin board: "Girl Loses 102 Pounds With Jaw Wired Shut." "Let this be a warning to us all," she had printed neatly underneath.

Then there's Randi, twenty-nine years old but already settled into *yenta*dom. In the sauna she casts mean eyes at my baby oil. *"Somebody could kill themselves slipping on that puddle of yours!"* Five thousand years of suffering smolder in her prematurely middle-aged gaze. Her focus remains fixed at my feet. And I'm guilty! There is the evidence—my personal puddle. What am I going to do, fight with her? She's probably been having a rough day. So I say nothing, but pull the *New York Post* over my face. This disappearing act fails. Randi calls in the towel girl, who gives me unadulterated hell. Next week I catch Randi crying under the dryer and all is forgiven. What can you do when the girl isn't well?

From then on out, Randi the Yenta keeps her mouth shut in the sauna, which is more than I can say for Fran, age twenty-five, but still an emotional infant.

"So when he calls me up, you'd think he could have made some plans, *but no.* I'm the one who had to think of everything we do! He says to me, '*I'm* in law school. *I* study all week. *I* don't have time to look at the movie page!' So I say to him,

'Well, *look*. Working at Bloomingdale's is no ocean cruise! It's all *rel-a-tive*.' " Fran checks out her captive audience in various stages of tuning out. "*I am so maaaa-aaad!* Then he starts picking on my hair, just because I got it whacked off. He says to me, '*Fraaa-aan.* Your hair is just *hore-ee-bell.* Fran, your hair is the pits. Why don't you let me buy you a wig?' That's how he talks to me! My very own boyfriend! Even in front of my mother!"

I ask Fran-in-the-sauna why she doesn't dump this very obvious prig.

"We're getting married in June. As soon as Malcolm gets his degree."

If nothing else, her loyalty inspires a sense of womanly camaraderie. Support! We'll all be there to gather around and nurse Fran through her marriage and probable divorce.

Then there's Jill, recently back from a disbanded New Hampshire commune. She's a naturalist, so we call her The Farter. Every gym has one of those. Let Ozelle start the isometric stomach paddle kicks and you'd think you were back in nursery school. Get trapped with Jill in the steam and you'd swear you'd been hijacked to a duck farm.

Only once did I give her a look.

"Bodily functions are nothing to be ashamed of," she'd said.

Still, you couldn't help wonder if Jill sits in her secretarial pool passing wind. Somehow I'd be surprised.

Ah, female kinship! Was there ever such a group of women as these, bound by much, much more than the mere dictates of body awareness? We were a cross-section of survivors of the sexual revolution; all of us were in various states of post-feminist despair. We were trying to find our way, trying to stay on course in a world where the only law remaining is: *Do What You Really Feel.* Pain! That's what I feel right now when Ozelle screams, *"Soles of the feet together and knees to the ground! Nothing is accomplished, ladies, unless we push ourselves to our limits!"* I feel my knees giving in, dropping like bombs, but my mind is protesting. We, the tattered remnants of a decade which aimed to teach us (among other things) that identity was paramount, have been stripped of our limits. We can do anything! Isn't that what we were taught by our mothers? I was anxious, my head kept bobbing toward the door. Peaches! Where was she? I needed my best friend like a fix, I wanted to make contact. She would like my tear sheets, she would make me feel that what I spent days on was surely worthwhile. Peaches was my soul sister, my buddy. Just like me, she wasn't afraid to take on the real world, *to get out there and show them.*

The difference was that Peaches Rosen had help, in masculine form. Even though I was sure that Peaches Rosen could have made A New Leaf a success on her own, you can't tell me that having a man to come home to didn't give her an enormous leg-up. She was free of the worries that the rest of us had. Peaches Rosen was taken care of. She knew that somebody besides fags and the girls at the gym would be there to listen, to care. Peaches Rosen had what is called "emotional support." Anachronism! She was the only woman I knew who could Sustain A Relationship. And the rest of us? Well, we had our fantasies and our ambitions; our daily workouts at the Ponce DeLeon and our lunch dates. Some of us had shrinks; some of us had a man (even two) hanging by threads. We were vulnerable, but busy; functional, and alone. But put away the Kleenex. Peaches Rosen, Marcie Laster, Randi-Fran-Jill, and every other female I knew all agreed on one basic issue: surely, Contemporary Woman was more interesting than any run-of-the-mill man. What we couldn't admit in our klatsches in the steam room was that we were still—all of us—véry much on the prowl.

Last stop, Jason Jaffe's! Peaches Rosen dug into her tote for the actor's familiar downstairs door key. How many women would give their *she didn't know what* to be in possession of this sliver of brass? His audience might think of Jason Jaffe as flesh and fire, but not the phantom doctor from A New Leaf. For her, Jason Jaffe hardly existed; she had met him only twice. He was a regular client, but he was never home. Peaches Rosen knew nothing about his theatrical life.

Damn, he was home. Wouldn't you know that this would

be the day that Lee Strasberg would cancel Advanced Scenes? Just when Peaches thought for sure she'd make it to the Ponce DeLeon in plenty of time for the noon class—maybe even grab a bite with Florida afterward—she would have to exert an hour's worth of effort on his minimal botanical needs. Frankly, he made her nervous, the way he looked at her when he walked with her for the first time into his East Side (but not plush) living room. She hardly knew what to say. Five years she'd lived in New York, and in all that time here she'd been in the audience of no more than a few hit plays. Hers was a world of movies and East Side dinners, of parties with young business types or with gay decorators she worked with who could bring along straight friends. Friends from college! Suppers at faded French boîtes. Because of her work, Peaches Rosen had grown used to being called the most eccentric girl in her social group.

Talk about *eccentric;* Jason Jaffe had written the book on it. Like the way he'd gotten her on the phone, after he'd seen her ad? "This is the Baron Dmitri Rostapovich Obolensky Romanoff DeRede," he'd shamelessly announced. "And I need your help."

The only way Peaches had known the actor's real name was from the label marked "Jaffe, J." on the downstairs bell. Anyway, she still didn't know much about "Jaffe, J." That he acted, had been in a few plays. That he was short, dark, and Jewish . . . a dead ringer for Dustin Hoffman. She'd told him just that, the first time she'd worked on his avocados.

"Why does *everybody* tell me that?" When he smiled in response, his face changed to Al Pacino.

"Because you do." Flushed, she had turned back to his satiny seeds. Avocados! How could he mess up seeding an avocado, especially when he was so obviously obsessed with making them sprout? Jason Jaffe had first called for A New Leaf when after three months, not one of his twenty-two seeds had even a hint of a root.

It had taken Peaches mere seconds to solve what was wrong. "Too much light!" She moved twenty-two jam glasses away from the window sills and docked them above his sunless sink.

Now Peaches Rosen had been employed to take care of his baby trees. Moving them from dark to light and back again; feeding them, watering them, nurturing them, humming soothing Ella Fitzgerald-type sounds to them. Three times a week she'd let herself into Jason Jaffe's two rooms; she could chart every quarter inch of the avocados' growth. And she could be . . . alone! Unbothered by Jaffe's aura, Peaches could zip in—use the bathroom, make phone calls, steal a cookie or two—then zip out, refreshed for her next stop.

But today Jason Jaffe wanted to talk. He offered her coffee, then commanded her to sit down. "Why are you so quiet? You're like some invisible shadow I can't figure out in my life."

Startled, she looked up at him. "What do you want to know?" She knew that if she sat down, she would blow not only Ozelle's noon class but also the steam room and her twice-weekly catch-up lunch with Florida. Tentatively she arranged herself on the actor's Moroccan floor pillows, then thanked him for the steaming mug, which she held onto as if its destiny had always been her hand.

He was a man of few words, but his instincts were gut-level superb. "Do I make you uncomfortable?"

"No, not really. . . ." Her eyes darted away from his face.

To help her relax, he began to ask questions, about where she'd grown up.

"Down South. . . ." Only when pressed did she tell him specifically where. He was giving her that but-what-happened-to-your-accent look. Unconsciously the candied edges of her long-lost drawl crept back into her speech. As a child she had only been too glad to give it up. She was sure magnolia syntax was a bellwether of ignorance. Peaches wanted to sound "cosmopolitan," always to be set apart. But now she found herself dripping honeysuckle as if she'd never even practiced speaking with marbles in her mouth. She would have been shocked if she could have heard herself, but she was begging him to call her "Peaches," opening up like a tulip, telling him how she'd gotten started, in the most dulcet tones. "I guess when I first came to New York, I didn't know what I wanted to do . . . so, I

36

wound up in an advertising agency . . . as a secretary to an account executive for Delta. . . . I couldn't even type thirty words a minute. . . ."

Excruciating! They both agreed.

". . . and this man was so darn intense, I swear, I thought I would die. I used to go home from that office with the absolute . . . shakes! I'd never heard so much . . . *noise.* Telephones ringing every second and . . . screaming, like you wouldn't believe!"

"Hey. He sounds . . . just like *me.*" Jason Jaffe smiled.

"Well, you're an actor. You all are supposed to be . . . different. But when I would leave at night, I would have to walk all the way up to 96th and Madison . . . just to relax. And that's how I became a plant doctor." Peaches leaned back in her pillows, delicately she sipped from the mug gripped in both hands.

"Huh?"

"Well, *that* wasn't how I became a plant doctor. It was because I walked past that shop called 'Green Stuff' . . . up on Eighty-seventh Street? Do you know the one I'm talking about?"

Like a reflex, Jason Jaffe nodded . . . yes.

"Well then, you know, how special it is!"

His understanding caused her to glow. "So, you know! You can get lost in there in the calm . . . It's so peaceful. Every night I'd walk around it just . . . breathing, looking at plants. And you know Bob?"

Jason Jaffe frowned, then shook his head no.

"*You know,* with the beard . . . the one who runs it?"

"Oh, yes. *Of course.*"

"Well, you know how wonderful he is. And he would just talk to me . . . every night! Even if I hadn't bought anything."

"I would have done a lot more than *that.*" He was stunned when he saw Peaches blush. Did women still do that? He had been sure that that was a feminine trait lost to the past.

"Well, anyway. I had one *huge* fight with that monster at Humboldt and Jackson and . . . that's all I needed."

He would ask her. "What about you and this . . . Bob?"

37

"What do you mean??"

"I mean . . . is it a thing?" It was Jason Jaffe's turn to squirm.

"You mean . . . a romance? Me and Bob from the plant store?" Her laughter rang through the room. "I don't even know his last name!"

"*Oh.* I see. *Hey,* that's great."

Now Peaches was really nervous, but she didn't want to let herself find out why. Restless, she stood up to go.

"*Hey.* Where are you going? Don't . . . I mean, can't I make you some lunch?" Again, he flashed her his Al Pacino smile, its little-boy quality usually did the trick. (He had first developed that exact smile in high school, A White Plains production of *Our Town.)*

"Oh. That's su-weet. But I really do have to go. . . ." Peaches Rosen looked down at the floor. "Maybe . . . you'll be here on Friday. . . ."

"I never know where I'm going to be. Or when." Annoyed, he heard his voice snap, then he softened. "I mean, I really like you. I thought we were getting to be . . . *friends.*"

She was passing him, negotiating the narrow theater-poster-covered front hall. Awkwardly, he followed on her heels, which caused her canvas sacks to bump against the walls. Suddenly she turned. In the small foyer, they were inches apart. "I really hope I'll see you on Friday. . . ." Jason Jaffe could hear the fragile blonde breathing. "I mean, I really enjoyed today. . . ."

He found himself thanking her—and meaning it—as she slipped out the door. *Christ.* He would have to change his rehearsal times . . . what would this do to his professional life? What if Peaches Rosen was already involved . . . even somebody's wife? He couldn't remember if she'd been wearing a ring.

The minute I walked in, the phone had started to ring. Angry! It screamed off its hook. That meant it could be none other than Brian Milman, Tower Syndicate New York Bureau

Chief, and my editor. It was a few minutes past three, which meant it was time for us, in Milman's words, to "touch base." Time to hear: "Tower to Burns! Tower to Burns! WHERE IS THE . . . COPY?" The density of The Milman Sound could only be compared to a sonic boom. And the level of the noise would be a healthy indicator that the Afternoon Screaming Session—the AS², I called it—had begun. I decided to let the service pick up. Twelve rings later, the phone was still screaming. On the thirteenth, I grabbed it. Forty bucks a month Exec-U-Answer cost me, and for what? So Brian Milman could find me on demand? I couldn't wait to get my hands on them.

"Florida?" The voice was passive, soft. No way was this Brian "100 Decibel" Milman.

"Yes?"

"Hi . . ."

"Hi . . ."

"How are you?"

I hated games. "Who is this?"

"Howie Leon."

"Who?"

"You don't know me."

"I know."

"I got your name from Dina Bellamy . . . over at the *News*?"

I paused. This might be interesting. "Dina Bellamy gave you *my* name? Is she a friend of yours?"

"You could say that." The caller waited for what seemed like a year, then he went on. "She's told me all about you. What-a-fantastic-writer-you-are."

"Really?" This was hard to believe. Dina Bellamy was A Media Star. She had been quoted in *Time* and *Newsweek*; I hardly knew her. I brightened. Maybe I was more respected than I actually thought. . . . "Dina Bellamy is one of my best friends. I love her. I'd stick my hand in the fire for her."

"Have you read her article in the paper today?"

"No . . ."

"May I tell you about it?" Howie Leon didn't wait for an

39

answer. "It's about single women. Single men. Their problems . . . like forming relationships, making them work, how they cope with loneliness. . . ."

I laughed. "*That* again?"

Howie Leon was silent. The midday light filtered through my windows; shards of sun like golden threads danced around spider ferns suspended from coat-hanger hooks. "That's not what I meant, Florida, you're not listening. It's *not* about 'swinging singles.' It's about men and women, like you and me."

"Oh. I should read it, huh?" I began to flip through my mail.

"Yes. You might learn something. Dina's told me how bright you are. . . ."

"She's not objective. Maybe she thinks I read all her articles. . . . Don't tell my secrets."

I heard him breathe. Then he spoke: "All right. But she *has* told me all about you."

"Oh? Like what?" Another bill from Bonwit Teller, when were they going to get my account straightened out? I had closed it months before. I ripped open the letter, not caring if Howie Leon heard.

"That you're really sharp. I already told you that. That you know everybody, that you have an unbelievable body. That you live in the Dakota. That's pretty expensive, isn't it? Living there? Isn't that where Lauren Bacall lives?"

"Yep. But don't get the wrong idea." I allowed myself a laugh. "My apartment is the size of a . . . coffee cup! I don't even own it! It's a sublet."

"Still . . ." He sounded disappointed. There was an awkward pause. "I'd really like to meet you, I think we could really give a lot to each other, help each other out. Let me explain. I have a radio show, I interview all kinds of people all the time, a lot of singles, too. I'd like to put you on my show."

"But you don't know me."

"But I feel like I do from Dina. She's one of your greatest fans."

I tried to sound modest. "And I'm her biggest. . . ."

40

"When are we going to get together? I think you might learn some things from my group sessions, I run them on the radio."

"Group sessions? You mean like T-groups? Encounter stuff? Are they still doing those boring things?"

Howie Leon's voice became a shade softer, even tense. "Yes. 'They're' still doing 'that stuff.' Only now, it's no longer fad. Now it's part of the real world. It's *substance*."

"I see." How could Bonwit's keep insisting that my balance was $658.73?

"*Look.* Do you want to get together or not?"

"We-e-elll . . ." *Ease up, Florida,* my inner voice was saying. *You can never tell what a Howie Leon—what any man—will turn out to be like. This could be the one. Prince Charmingstein!* He had a radio show, didn't he? "I'd love to, but . . ."

"But what?"

"I'm on deadline. You know, my column?"

"But I could *really* help you. If you would just . . ."

"You could help me? How? Do you know any gossip? *God.* Do I need items."

"I don't mean *that* way. I could help you get into a new space. Open yourself up. Clear your head out."

"An anti-histamine, I don't need. Now a good 'leg man,' that's something else. Even a secretary . . ."

"I guess I'm not getting through to you. Maybe it takes more time in your case. Look. I'm free tonight. Are you?"

I waited. Debated with myself. How bad could he be? He was a friend of Dina Bellamy's, wasn't he? Who knew? Howie Leon could turn out to be a young Dick Cavett. Of course I said, "How's eight o'clock?"

Then I went crazy. Only five hours to whip the Florida Burns Show into high gear. Only five hours to rush to the florists, pack in dozens of chrysanthemums, pick up the Chablis and the brie. Was my flowered bra clean? A Blind Date! I was best at blind dates, opening night was (is) like a command performance. I keep each one of my anecdotes ready, polished to high gloss. Spontaneous Delivery! I had one that Mel Brooks

41

would die for! Practice makes perfect. I'd run through my "after-dinners" hundreds of times. Between gigs, I stored them like bibelots, high up on a shelf. Only for special occasions would I dust them off, bring them down, give them a workout.

Tonight would be one of those occasions. I would work on my David Merrick and Elizabeth Taylor story this afternoon. In the tub, I might work over the Faye Dunaway and the Bertolucci. This was indeed a special night. So special, I put in three emergency calls to the *Daily News.* I was desperate to find Dina Bellamy, desperate to get a report, desperate to check Howie Leon out. I wanted to know exactly how I should behave, *what he would expect.* What he would like. I wanted Howie Leon to fall in love with me. I wanted *someone* to fall in love with me, somebody decent. Who was I kidding? Just about anyone would do. In point of fact, I wanted A Man.

What a thing to admit! That I don't give a damn about this ridiculous "career," that if it came to picking self-expression or female regression, Florida Burns' choice might set the crowd at *Ms.* back twenty years. Oh, I know what they'd say: "How dare Florida Burns still think men radiate power, that men are where it's at." But dare I do, and more: if one needs to sacrifice work for love, then it may be gross, but here I am. Even worse, I'll come right out and plead. Desperate! You bet, but I was at the end of my rope. Believe you me, alone and functional is no way to live. Wasn't I already proof that you don't need a man to get ahead?

Yes, I was plenty "functional." There was my column. Tell Me Everything . . . need I say more? Twelve newspapers in the Tower Syndicate subscribed to it, a thousand dollars per was the price a year's worth of TME could demand. I dotted the Northeast and pronged into parts of the South.

This meant: *The Fayetteville Eagle! The Winston-Salem Beacon! The South Orange Outlook! The Charlotte Sentinel!* (76,000 readers right there). Let's not forget Pensacola; they call their paper *The Pilgrim,* circulation: 9200! Or the *Arnold* (Maryland) *Bugle* (my best friend from high school must read me each Saturday!). I was in Key West's suburban weekly and

Sioux City's *Northside News.* Eclectic! The only thing this mix had in common was . . . you guessed it, me. And their umbilical link to the Tower Syndicate, the news giant servicing any daily or weekly with a circulation of five figures or less. The Tower and I had plenty going for us in terms of readership appeal. Take our cost. The Tower undersold not only the Associated Press and the *New York Times* Wire Service, but the *Washington Post/L.A. Times* and the UPI as well. But that's not all. We were a lot more fun to read than any of them (including Reuters). Just ask anyone who knows media, they'll tell you all that.

I know it's not big-time, but I still had my dreams. I might have an income of $12,000 a year and I might call the Dakota my home, but I wasn't slowing down. Besides a husband (even a boyfriend), the only thing I had my sights on was: The Big Plum. In media terms, that meant a toehold on the *seaboards*— recognition where it counted, where *every* trend (so they told me) was set. Los Angeles! New York! Boston! Washington! San Francisco! I wanted to take my place with the cultural greats: Rona Barrett, Suzy Knickerbocker, Earl Wilson, Liz Smith, even Cherie Rivers, Manhattan's local (Channel 8) Rona knock-off on the ten o'clock news. I'd look at that dimwitted blonde every night that I could and I'd think, How did she get up there in front of millions of viewers? Had Cherie Rivers gotten her gig the way I got my own byline planted on Tell Me Everything? Because if all you had to do to get your own six-minute spot was march into Telemedia (the way I had into the Tower Syndicate) in response to an ad for "Gal/Guy Friday JOURNALISM $140 wk." and then just sit tight for a dull year, maybe two, until you were promoted, who said one had to grow up one-track-minded, like Rona Barrett? Rona had spent her childhood years planning her gossip career whereas I, Florida Burns, was a college-trained reporter and a potential TV star. Tell Me Everything was the faltering first step on what I hoped would be an abbreviated road to a fabulous career. I might not be Barbara Walters, but I knew that given half a chance I could give Cherie Rivers a run for her money.

I know gossip is thought to be smarmy, not something that

43

should interest a nice, refined girl like me. For me, gossip was A Science, an exacting form which demanded that one draw conclusions about the sociological bottom line. Edith Wharton and Thorstein Veblen weren't embarrassed by their trades, so why should Florida Burns not be able to hold her head up proudly in classy drawing rooms? Lay analysis is what I've been best at ever since I first drew breath. I was a born expert at being part of The Action, knowing and *understanding* what was going on.

Men are something else again. Them I wasn't so good at, but I knew, in time, my *career* would be the turn-on that would put a really "top-notch" male on the line. I was still a veritable apprentice at this partnership game. Make no mistake, though, I've had dozens of boyfriends, a few have even had the barest toehold on real fame. *But* (and there's always a "but") none have ever really stuck. Or I haven't wanted them to stick to me. That's no unfamiliar story, but the last thing on earth this cookie intended to be was a mere cliché.

The point is, blind dates—like Howie Leon—are crucial. The right one might mean escape, an early retirement. Then I wouldn't have to hassle going for the Big Plum at all. Even if he wasn't Mr. Wedding Bells, Howie Leon could hold promise. Summer was in the air and there was no way I was going to be marooned (again) grasping at weekend invitations to the beach. Riding that train which is so ancient the windows don't budge. The dust piled like cat fur in great heaps upon the floor. Maybe Howie Leon had a place in Southampton (or even a share). It might only be April, with spring winds kissing bicyclists gliding down Central Park West, but I knew what was coming: the sewer-steambath of July. Alone-and-Single in New York during dog-day afternoons. Everywhere you looked would be fetid humanity in fishnet T-shirts, rancid garlic wafting from their collective underarm. You'd have to be nuts to want to spend yet another summer like it.

So, what was a deadline, when this blind date could mean a chance for love? If I hurried, I could get in *another* double class, maybe even take a little steam. For Howie Leon, I wanted to look and feel like Absolute Perfection.

"*Nope.* Boring! I hate it." Mike Markman's leather sneaker crossed his leg and kicked at the air. "Taupe just ain't gonna do it for me. I thought we agreed! No chi-chi colors. Bright ones! I want the room to have . . . a fiesta atmosphere."

Mike Markman's architect brushed golden bangs from her eyes. "But *Michael.* For what you want, this 'fiesta atmosphere' . . . monochromatic is really considered to be more effective. *I promise.* I've read studies. Just because a spectral shade might be subdued doesn't mean its connotative emotional value is negative." She folded imperceptibly into her architect's stool, quite aware her client was staring at the endless expanse of her dangling legs. She was glad short skirts were back in style. Fresh out of Yale Architecture School, Brook Nicholson had hustled and landed a spot in a top firm. La Taquita (planning its New York East-Side-location look) was her third client. She and Mike had met at a dinner party, talked design-design-design till he asked her to bed. Graciously Brook Nicholson had turned the young entrepreneur down. She had too much at stake to let sex get in the way of landing her La Taquita account.

So now she had it, but not him. Michael Markman was driving her, keeping her agitated over every light socket, every doorknob. Day and night she got calls. She wondered if he was punishing her for turning him down.

Like now. Perfect example! A simple issue like monochromatics and Michael's response had been, *"Come again?"*

"How a color affects the occupants of a room. How different shades make people behave. *Michael.* I can show you statistical proof that customers in subdued surroundings *linger.* That bright colors have the effect of driving them away."

"Exactly my point!" Triumph floodlit his eyes. "I don't want them lingering. This is fast food. Quick service! Not La Fonda Del Sol." Mike Markman surveyed his architect's office. Thank God he hadn't gotten involved with her. The cerebral coolness of charcoal flat-weave rugging covered every square inch of space. Brook Nicholson, with her disciplined body and mind, obviously thrived in functional steel surroundings that cried,

less is more. The slate-gray carpet crawled over floors, walls, ceilings, and platforms that she'd built herself on the floor. As a concession to comfort, she'd scattered some overstuffed pillows (also gray), installed a few tractor-seat chairs. An elongated snow-white Parsons table and two matching Breuer chairs provided the only color.

It was over this table—littered with swatches of fabric, sheets of plans, tubes of sketches—that Mike Markman and Brook Nicholson huddled, arguing, most afternoons. Like today. He had wasted hours of April sunshine fighting over function and form; he couldn't let a detail pass him by. Not when the future of La Taquita was at stake. Well, yes. When he felt that spring air, Mike Markman had momentarily thought about canceling (for the first time ever) his one o'clock bubble slot. Now he wished he had. Brook Nicholson had tracked him down, shattering his concentration in the middle of his first set.

"*Michael.* Could you come down? With any luck, we could bolt down the last of the prelims on the exterior budget design." He never knew such an educated voice could have such a subtext of pure whine.

After he'd hung up, he'd been slaughtered six-four. Mike Markman hadn't had a chance. Not when he found himself thinking about his expansion plans, what he was going to risk, not when he was smashing a fast lob to the rear court. *Out!*

$400,000! Just about every cent he had, borrowed or cajoled. *But if it worked, if La Taquita scored at Sixty-fourth and Third . . . if fancy fast tacos could make it in the Big Apple . . .* A smile crinkled his eyes, pushed at the corners of his mouth. When Mike Markman caught Brook Nicholson's stare, he forced his face into a squint. He picked up a silvery swatch, then his foot counted off the seconds like a metronome hidden under the table.

"What about this one?? This gray's not so bad. Maybe with a lot of plants. Yes! Hanging plants everywhere you look." Mike Markman clutched the square even tighter, admired the smoky shade. *Yes, this one had character.* Unbelievable! It was almost warm. Maybe it was even close to the color of his hair.

Yes. The jeans had been the right choice. I knew it the second Howie Leon pushed through my heavy oak door. "Sorry I'm late," he said, half-smiling through golden wire rims.

"Oh, are you? I hadn't noticed." For an hour I'd been ready and waiting. Well, what the hell? It gave me the edge. This Howie Leon didn't look bad. In physical type he was Basic Overgrown Brandeis: chunky, curly, and tweedy. Faded denims completed the look. I smiled. "Would you like a drink?"

"Wine would be great . . . do you have any?"

I nodded, but I knew what Howie Leon had on his mind. An L-shaped studio with a loft bed in the Dakota . . . how did she ever find it? That's what everybody thought the minute they caught a look at my place. Then they studied The Wall: bottle green and papered with lithographs, posters, etchings, water colors, silhouettes, special photographs, two clocks (only one kept time), a smallish tapestry, three batiks. A matched pair of antlers speared a feather boa, then hooked a brown felt derby.

I was right! I turned just in time to see Howie's eyes move from wall to floor. Hundreds of books supported a low-slung marble slab. *Yes,* it was my coffee table. *Thank you.* I liked it too. Everywhere he looked was the good kind of clutter. Pillows piled around wicker baskets! Wine racks stuck on top of metal files! You could work miracles with a twenty-foot ceiling. Stuck in a corner was my oak table and Olivetti. My kitchen? Right there, *yes,* in a closet. It was perpendicular to the bath.

"This is a great place. *Terrific.* What's that stuff upstairs? Those streamers or . . . ragged . . . Scrap paper?"

I walked over to where Howie was standing—"the conversation pit," I called it—and flopped down on my yellow and green Salvation Army special. With my wine glass hugged close to my chest, I propped my size nines up on the marble table. I was relaxed, sort of. "That isn't scrap paper. Those are my columns! *See, I glue them to the ceiling. . . .*"

Howie Leon looked at me. "You've got your bedroom up there?"

47

"Don't get any ideas." We both laughed. "I keep all my *Close-Up* stories there as well. That's our Sunday magazine. Have you ever heard of it?"

Howie Leon was standing in an opposite corner, straining to see. "You'll have to show me. All I see is a bunch of rotting newsprint. I'll need a . . . private tour."

"Well, maybe sometime."

"Maybe tonight." He flopped down in a rattan chair. Beneath his weight, it sagged like an old woman. "I really like your apartment. The vibes are happy . . . wow! Your head must really groove in this place. How did you find such incredible far-out psychic space?"

I paused. "*No.* Actually, I got it from an ad in the *New York Times.* Just like on the bus cards."

He frowned at me or maybe I imagined it. "Are you an Aries?"

"No. Why?" *Oy gevalt.* Astrology! I forced myself to be polite. *Keep your mouth shut, Florida, maybe he's nervous. Give the man half a chance.*

"You seem like the type."

"Thanks . . . if that's a compliment. Are you into the occult? All that stuff . . . numerology? Rising signs? What should I ask: where's your moon?"

"Scorpio. And my number is five."

"Aha! Now I know your whole personality. A Scorpio moon and a five, huh? I suppose that means we get along."

"Not till I know where *your* planets are."

"Let's stick to numbers. How do you figure those, from last names?"

Howie's reply—"First and last"—was curt. He was too busy programming "Florida Burns" into his cosmic computer. I sat quietly, ignored in my own living room, while Howie added up my score. "Two," he finally announced. He seemed pleased.

"Great," I said without enthusiasm. "How do fives and twos get along?"

"What if five's not my real number?" Howie moved toward me, pouring more wine.

"What do you mean? You figure it on the basis of your name, don't you? So Howie Leon's your name and five's your number. What's the big deal?" Howie didn't say anything. "Your name is Howie Leon, right?" Silence. "Hey, are you in the wrong apartment?"

"What if I changed my name?" Howie smiled, his eyes shining beneath his glasses. He was beginning to bother me. I stiffened.

"Did you . . . change your name?"

Skin glowing, he purred, "Sure, I changed it. Leon is from my sign. Leo the lion. I wanted to signal the world that I have the lion's most basic characteristic—boldness." I nodded, *brilliant, what a clever idea,* but Howie wasn't looking for agreement. "Strong-willed, outgoing, popular, a Don Juan," he continued. "And I always get my way."

"How lucky for you. In my next life, maybe I'll have a shot." I sighed. This was going to be a long night. I didn't even know him and we were fighting already. He probably hated me. I looked up. He was staring. Nervous, my words came out way too fast. "I guess what I'm really trying to say is that astrology—at least for me—is just a way of ducking the real world. I don't know, I've never been into it. But I read the paper, I always look to see what my horoscope—"

"Why are you afraid of me?" Howie reached for my hand. I looked at his face, now even closer. His forehead was pink and oily. If it weren't for his eyes, he would have looked almost naïve, like a piano teacher, or a graduate teaching fellow.

"I'm not. Why do you think that?" I looked down. Where his thighs met there was more than a gentle swell; maybe it was just the way his pants were creased. Was this the way boys looked when they weren't wearing any underwear?

"Fear is often sexual. Do you know that?"

"You'd have to be pretty stupid not to . . ."

"Fear is often little more than the anger we feel at unexpressed—even latent—desires."

I hesitated. "Not in this case."

"In all cases."

"Besides, I'm not afraid. Why should I be? Of what? This

49

is silly. . . ." I pulled my hand away, used it to reach for the wine. I took a long sip, continued to hold my glass. What was with this guy? I was beginning to feel awkward. Like a fifteen-year-old on her first car date.

"Look. I know all about these things. I do a lot of work with girls like you . . . women, I should say, and I can spot someone in need a mile away. Men have been really shitty to you, haven't they?"

I bristled. "No!"

"Florida. Why are you so defensive?"

"*I'm not* . . . I'm not at all defensive, I'm just saying . . ."

"Look. Being a sex therapist is what I do. I help people."

"I thought you had a radio show."

Howie Leon's words tripped over each other. "I do! I do have a radio show, that too. But I'm also a trained shrink—a psychologist really—Brandeis. I do a lot of sex counseling. A lot of work with singles."

"Oh."

He seemed to relax. "You can't believe what they're turning up in research, the kinds of techniques patients are responding to. Wow. Therapy has really put some people into some far-out spaces, really turned some heads around. Especially the ones whose sexual heads were in bad places. You know, just about all my patients are fucked up . . . sex-wise, I mean."

I tried not to seem too interested. "Really?"

"*Of course.* I mean, you should just dig some of the ways I try to acknowledge what is, *is,* with these guys . . . how I try to help them open themselves up."

"Is that how you met Dina Bellamy?" I laughed, pleased with my little joke.

Howie glared, cutting my giggle short. "Do you make a fucking joke out of everything? Is that the way you deal with stress? Is that the way you create negative space? With bullshit laughter? *Fuck.* Florida Burns. You're like every other cunty woman in this city." Anger froze in his eyes, then in a flash, his face softened. Once again he seemed benign. "Look. I bet right now, some man has got you in a really bad place. I can read it all

50

over you. You're programmed. You're hearing all those bullshit voices in your head. I can tell." His voice dropped back to a ripple. "Tell me. Trust me."

"I don't know. . . ."

"Hey. Look. We're friends, man. I mean, aren't we digging each other?" Howie Leon wrestled my hand back into his lap.

"Why not?" I fluffed my afro out, shook the curls in the air, hoped he was cooling out. "After all, we both share Dina, don't we?"

He didn't answer. "That's more like it. Who is it? The guy who's playing with your head . . . running weird numbers on you. What is it? Does he have a wife? Is he into faggot sex? What? You wouldn't believe the fucked-up assholes in this town. I hear about them on my show, even get a lot of them . . . as guests."

"Oh?" This was getting more interesting, at least more interesting than the stars. Who knew? Maybe Howie Leon programmed celebs on his show, there might be an item in it. Or maybe I could, at last, get some *professional* advice about Ezra Matthews, my life's number one question mark.

"I could really help you, Florida. I help women like you every day of my life. *Trust me.*"

He seemed so sincere. "*Well* . . . there is one. But I don't know, it's so stupid to talk about him, since he's not really 'real' . . . I mean, at least in terms of *my* life. We see each other, but it's not a thing, do-you-know-what-I-mean?"

Howie nodded that of course he did.

I began to relax. Marcie Laster had been telling me for months that my problem was I was too "closed off," that I needed to have my feelings "let go." *Okay.* So, now a real doctor is sitting in my living room, gratis.

I decided to take the plunge. "Look. I don't knew where to begin this story, but there's . . . this man." I cleared my throat. "Actually, I hardly know him. I just interviewed him once. He's thirty-seven."

"Is age important to you?" He was encouraging me with an analyst-type smile.

51

Why was he asking me that? Interrupting me just when I was warming to the topic of Ezra Matthews? "Age? Not really. Well, I take that back. When a man is thirty-seven and he isn't married . . ."

"I'm thirty-seven." A dot of light appeared in each of Howie Leon's eyes.

"You are? You sure don't look it. *No*. You really don't." I tried one last time to get my foot out of my mouth. "Besides. You're a shrink. It's a whole different thing."

Howie's arm slid over the top of the sofa, then he asked me to fill him in on a few crucial details.

For some reason, I stumbled over more than just Ezra Matthews' name. I tried to recoup, to organize my thoughts. "Anyway . . . what can I tell you? I met him through this interview . . . not *this* interview, another one . . . but, never mind. That's boring, how we met. Forget that. But that's really it. We just met—we had one long lunch at Madrigal—and we . . . What I mean to say is: we don't see each other. I mean, I want to, God, do I want to! But Ezra is always traveling. He's always so busy. Isn't it unbelievable how all the good men never have time to get involved?" I could see Howie Leon looking at me oddly. "Look. I know I sound nuts, like I have a fantasy or something, but have you ever had an instinct that someone was just perfect for you? That's what I've got! The time we had lunch together was *unbelievable* . . . we had so much fun!" I couldn't stop myself from blathering on. "But then—at the end—he did something really *weird*. He treated me just like . . . *a reporter!* Like all he cared about was the story? Can you believe that? So I said to myself, 'Get it together, Florida. Maybe he's *involved* with someone. Maybe he's married to his job!' I even almost talked myself out of this infatuation . . . but you won't believe what he had the nerve to do!" I didn't wait for Howie Leon to press me. "Postcards! He started sending me postcards from wherever he went. And they were . . . *friendly.* Like the two of us were having a thing or something. So what am I supposed to think? That it's me he's sending postcards to or . . . is he sending them to Tell Me Everything? What a *downer*. He's absolutely perfect for me." Talked out, I let the enormity of my sadness propel me back against the sofa.

Howie Leon picked up on this last fact and popped an eye open. "What makes him so 'perfect' for you?"

I laughed. "Well, for starters, he's Southern, rich and . . ." I grasped for the right word. "*Jewish*. Not that being Jewish is so important, I mean, where I'm from, I'm like one out of seven and most of us are somehow related to each other. . . ." I saw Howie Leon start to say something. "I mean, Texas Jews! We're like *Wasps,* only smarter, if-you-know-what-I-mean." I laughed, hoping he would as well. "But just because I've never been to a Jewish wedding doesn't mean I don't want one for myself. Besides, the point is, Ezra Matthews is like *me*. Same background. *Smart*. He's a catch! But the only way I can think of catching him is to throw myself at his feet. Only then he might think I'm desperate. Which—of course—I'm not. I just . . . I don't know. I guess if we just knew each other better—me and Ezra, that is. God! I hate thinking about him! I hate hearing from him! Either he should marry me or get completely out of my life! I can't deal with ambiguity . . . why can't he learn to leave a girl alone?" My tone horrified even me.

Howie didn't seem to mind. He squeezed my hand and asked. "What does Ezra Matthews do?"

"He's a lawyer in the city's department of cultural affairs." Howie didn't smile. "A lot of bread?"

"*Yep.*"

"How is he in bed?" Now both eyes were raised to half-mast.

"Who knows?" (Could he see me flinch?)

Howie ran his palm over his hair. For the first time I noticed it was dirty. "Hey. This is my *work*. I take it seriously. Could you?"

"If I did, I'd kill myself."

Howie ignored me, but asked me if Ezra Matthews saw anyone else and, if so, why hadn't I done something "real" about it. He had a confrontation in mind.

I thought about it. "You know, I don't think my case is

strong enough. . . . What would I say? He's just another messed-up super-bastard." What was I going to say? Was I going to admit that Ezra Matthews had never even taken me out? I sank even deeper into my corner of the couch.

"Well, Burns, *let's show him!*"

I said *great,* then asked exactly how.

"By getting even . . . *just like this.*" His arm "slipped" from the sofa where it had been propped, then he pulled me to him. For the first time I noticed he was strong.

"*Hey, man.* Give-me-a-break, okay?" I readjusted turtleneck over jeans, after pulling away. What kind of professional turned a consultation into a mash scene?

"I said, 'WE'LL SHOW HIM!' And everybody else too . . . whaddaya say?" Deep laughter wracked his body. He seemed out of control. Eyes closed, he pulled me to him again. The force knocked his glasses askew, sent them skittering down his nose. He ignored them, stretched his arms out. "Just trust me, that's all. *Trust me.*"

Then I felt sorry for him, at least for a moment. *Of course I trust you,* I wanted to say, but I let him kiss me instead. His lips were soft, like chamois. Again he tried to pull me down. His hand reached up under my sweater. "*Hey! Howie . . . Come on . . .*"

"*What is with you?* Tease! Pull away. *Tease-Pull-Away-Tease-Pull-Away!* God damn, you are *fucked up. . . .*" He was staring at me hard, his eyes had turned to stainless steel.

"Why don't we go have some supper? I'm starved."

Howie Leon kept on. "Didn't I tell you that we could show them? Together! Burns, we can show them . . . Ezra Matthews, all of them. . . ."

"All of whom?"

"Anyone who's laid a bummer on your head . . . anyone who's mind-fucked you . . . who's mind-fucked me. . . ."

"Who? Who's hurt you, Howie?" I saw a wedge.

"Lots of people . . . women . . . more than you would want to hear about. . . ." I followed Howie's gaze out across the courtyards where a light was glowing in a downstairs window.

"Try me, tell me about one."

54

"Lay off, okay?"

"Come on, I opened up to you. Fair is fair."

He seemed as if he wanted to talk. In the silence, I smiled, hoping it would encourage him. Anything to keep him away from me. "It was a bad scene. . . . Ten years ago, almost ten years ago, in the fall. I was doing the whole marriage trip, the ring, the flowers, the whole rap. . . . That's all. It's over. What more is there to say?"

"Just about everything."

For a moment, he said nothing, I thought he was going to come after me again. Then, he relented. "Okay . . . this chick, this woman, she was a painter, Laurie was her name. I loved her. I really did. I had everything all planned: marriage; when we'd finish grad school; living in Boston. She would have painted while I'd see my patients. Everything was set and . . ."

"What happened?"

His eyes blazed. *"If you would let me finish, just don't interrupt me. . . ."* Then he seemed to relax. "A month—one month!— before the wedding, Laurie drove her car into a tree. A day later, she was dead. . . ." He looked down, "Do you know what that means? It means she killed herself, committed *fucking suicide,* just to spite me. All we'd had was some stupid fight, a nothing fight, the kind of fight that the next day nobody remembers or even cares. . . ." He had looked up, through me, past me, as if he had no idea where he was. "And just to prove a point that *cunt* had to go kill herself. Just because *I* had been right! I've hated her ever since. I wouldn't even go to her funeral. . . ." He was defiant, so he grabbed me. "BURNS! Let's get them! Ezra Matthews, Laurie . . . all of them. LET'S GET THEM!"

He was serious. He grabbed at my turtleneck, tried to rip it off. He was pulling me down hard on the floor, scraping my arms against the marble slab. *"Leave me alone, what-the-fuck-do-you-think-you're-doing,* STOP IT! I was yelling, clawing at his stomach, kicking him. . . . GET THE FUCK OFF OF ME! Over and over he'd scream, "LET'S GET THEM!" while I drilled my nails into his back. Anything to get him off me. But he ignored my nails, pretended he couldn't hear my shouts.

Then for a second, everything stopped. The screaming, the clothes being ripped off. I relaxed my hands. Beads of sweat covered his face, prongs of dirty hair stuck into my chest.

"*Howie.* What would Dina say? She wouldn't approve." I laughed, squirming underneath his weight, hoping he would laugh too and drop this bit.

"Dina wouldn't say a fuckin' thing." He was glaring down at me, a drop of sweat fell from his brow. It landed on my face, running down my cheek like a tear.

"Of course she would. Dina wouldn't like it. Attacking her good friend, and on the first date, yet." I struggled to get up. He had me pinned. "Get off, okay? Before I squeal on you to Dina."

"You can squeal all you want. I don't even know her."

"WHAT? I thought you said . . ."

Howie shook his head.

Now I was really frightened. The joke was over, but the scene had yet to play out. My stomach felt as if I'd eaten rotten oysters. I hoped it was from Howie Leon's weight, not my fears. I didn't know what to do, so I did nothing.

"Look. I called you this morning. I said that Dina Bellamy had given me your name. Nothing more, nothing less."

"You told me you were friends. When I kept mentioning her, you pretended that you knew her. You played along!" I could feel my voice rising, filling up my tiny studio. "What are you, one of those sickos that get written up in the papers?" I tried to sound firm, but more important, to stay calm. It wasn't easy to keep your sense of the ridiculous when one hundred and eighty pounds of sweating humanity had you clamped to the floor.

"Sick? Me? Any more than anybody else is?" As he looked down at me, one fingertip found its way to my breast. He traced my nipple till it exploded like a tiny gun shot, then hardened at his touch.

"Could you let me up . . . please? *I'm really getting upset.*"

Howie Leon wasn't listening. "You have great breasts, you know that, Burns? Lovely, huge breasts. . . . Calm down, calm

56

down. I'm just having a little fun with you. Just playing around a bit, what's the big deal? Isn't Ezra Matthews into tits?"

I was numb. Where Howie Leon was straddling my waist, my nerve endings had died. I felt black and blue. I could hardly talk and I was terrified. But something much worse was happening. The fear was exciting me and the possibility of becoming turned-on disgusted me even more. "Why did you lie about Dina, Howie? Why did you lie?" My question never rose above a whisper.

He began to shout. "GOD DAMN IT, YOU STUPID CUNT. DO YOU THINK DINA WOULDN'T HAVE GIVEN ME YOUR NUMBER IF SHE HAD KNOWN ME? DO YOU THINK I'M THAT REPULSIVE? YOU THINK IT'S SO SACRED, GETTING YOUR FUCKING NUMBER? ALL I DID WAS CALL YOUR LITTLE FRIEND AND TELL HER I WANTED TO KNOW MORE ABOUT SINGLES—HER ARTICLE WAS TOO SHORT—AND SHE SAID, 'CALL FLORIDA BURNS; ONCE IN A WHILE SHE WRITES ABOUT BACHELORS.' . . . DINA WASN'T SCARED OF ME, SO WHY ARE YOU?"

His face was florid, a muscle twitched in his neck.

I didn't have time to answer. Suddenly, he was all over me, holding me down, pulling down my blue jeans, shredding my sweater . . . *screaming!* "I COULD BE ANYONE, I COULD KILL YOU." His head had pumped up to basketball size. *"Anyone could get your number . . . anyone! Someone who is really sick could come in and . . . murder you! Burns! Burns! Let's get them, let's really get them. Just the two of us. . . ."* He was pulling himself out of his jeans, keeping me in a hammer lock. I still wasn't sure he was serious. If I had been, I wouldn't have known what to do about it, how to handle him. And I almost started laughing when he popped out of his fly, all gawky; a veined, bruised, pastel cucumber was coming at me, coming in me. I looked up at the ceiling feeling his weight, but little else. Why do men think their cocks alone cause any sensation? The only thing about Howie Leon I could feel was his bulk. His cock didn't exist and I couldn't breathe. I listened to him grunting; finally he rolled off. I looked at the wall clock. Three minutes had gone by.

Neither of us spoke. I pulled my jeans back up, the sound of the zipper punctuated the silence. I sat up, still on the floor,

57

feeling dazed and unable to focus on the man who'd just raped me. I think it was rape, I wasn't sure. Had I seduced him? I was trembling. I wanted to be alone.

Finally Howie Leon spoke. "You're not mad at me, are you?"

I looked at the wall, praying he'd leave. My voice was so soft, it was barely a whisper. "No, I'm not mad. Just tired. I really would love to go to sleep."

Howie smiled at me. Once again his features were in repose, his face relaxed as if nothing had happened. He seemed to be struggling for something to say. "Look . . . I know I forced you, that you didn't want to. . . And I'm sorry, I really am. . . ." His voice trailed off. "Why don't I stay with you—overnight, I mean—and you'll feel better in the morning. . . ." He reached out to touch my arm.

I pulled away. "I really need to be by myself." What I actually was thinking was: *Please, get the hell out of here.* I was trying not to break down completely.

He wasn't making it any easier. *"Let me stay,"* he said, *"Wasn't I good enough?"*

"Of course you were, of course, I'm just tired, that's all." Once I'd read somewhere that the idea with mental patients is to stroke them, soothe them, make them feel loved, then they'll leave you alone. I tried. God knows I tried. What difference did it make if I told Howie Leon—pathological rapist—he was the best little boy in the world? Women are always selling somebody out (usually themselves) because of sex. I never knew what was so special about it anyway, unless it lead somewhere, unless you were blindly in love. As far as I can see, if an experience like this is any measure, it was just something to get through. To get around. To get out of. Which is what I had to do with this psychologist, get him out of my apartment, I mean, before the evening turned into a real horror show and maybe headlines tomorrow. This was a big city, anything could happen.

An hour had passed, maybe two, but still he wouldn't leave. Now he was sitting on the floor telling me about his childhood. If I didn't hate him, if I wasn't afraid of him, I would have laughed. Howie went on and on about his mother, how he hated her, hated *all* women till Laurie, then he'd wound up hating her as well. It was a textbook case, the story Howie wove. To think that this guy saw patients, told *them* how to behave. Life sure could be weird.

But not as weird as having a rapist in your living room babbling about his overpowering mother. Finally, I got an idea.

"*Hey.* It's midnight. I'm starved. Why don't we go get something to eat?"

"Don't you have anything in the house?"

I walked over to my tiny fridge. "Yogurt. Dijon mustard. An apple with six brown spots. Some wheat germ."

"Yech."

"Exactly."

Howie sighed and stood up. Then, like Mr. Universe, he puffed out his chest. "I'm disgusted with myself," he confessed.

"Why's that?"

At first a navy wool cocoon muffled his voice, then Howie's head burst through his sweater. "I've gotten so chunky, I hate myself." He emerged, swiped at a clump of hair orbiting his neck. All the while he was walking toward the door.

I was an inch behind him, trying not to seem relieved. "You don't look bad. I think husky men are sexy."

Howie pivoted. "What do *you* know, with those enormous breasts?"

We were silent the whole way down in the elevator, even when my friend David the Novelist got on at the fifth floor to take his bulldogs out for a stroll. The three of us walked through the courtyard, the sound of dog claws on cobblestones hardly breaking the stillness. When we got to the gate I banged it shut—with Howie and David outside. Through the iron-work, I announced, "Howie! I am so stupid. I left something upstairs. I'll be right back. . . ." The echo danced over the emptiness, dissolved into the night.

The next morning, Angel the doorman told me that the señor had waited no more than an hour before he headed toward the park. For three days my phone stayed off the hook, in case Howie Leon tried to call me for another date. I wouldn't have known how to turn him down.

The only place to escape was the Ponce DeLeon. I went early—Ronnie's 10:30 Body Jazz—glommed onto a spot in the back row, way in the back. I thought I would have a football field to myself, then I remembered Simone Ravitch. The back row was her territory, but it was too late to move.

"CAT. HORSE. CAT. HORSE. CAT. *Breathe,* don't forget to breathe. . . ." Ronnie threw an auburn mane over her shoulders and gasped for air. She was on all fours, warming us up. "COME ON, LADIES. ROUND YOUR BACK FOR THE CAT. ARCH YOUR BACK FOR THE HORSE. REALLY FEEL YOURSELF BECOMING *A CAT.* NOW ARCH YOUR BACK INTO THE HORSE. *Cat. Horse. Cat. Horse. HOLD THE CAT FOR ONE-HOLD . . . TWO-HOLD, THREE-HOLD, AND FOUR. . . . Horse.* Ready for the stomach? Are you nice and warm, ladies?" Ronnie rolled over, her legs waved in the air. "LYING SCISSORS. Let's see some energy in those kicks. Come on, backs flat! Think about your legs! *Concentrate!* Nothing is accomplished unless you keep your concentration! If you don't feel those muscles burning, then you're not getting any benefit!" Her voice blasted through the gym. "Ready? *Open legs* . . . wider-wider-wider and close . . . sharper-sharper-sharper-sharper! *Your legs . . . Your butts* are t-i-g-h-t!" She yelled that we were going for twenty-five, then started to count. "Is everybody ready, 'cause if you ain't, you're gettin' left behind!"

Ready? Are you kidding me? The way I felt, it was all I could do to hoist my trunks to forty-five degrees. God knows I was trying hard. Nothing like physical therapy to make you forget a night of bad sex. But this was Ronnie's killer! And I had turned this mockery into a travesty by strapping Marcie's three-pound sandbags right below each calf. I hoped mental energy alone would carry me though the last dozen Lying Scissors left in this set.

"Hey. Will you keep your dirty feet out of my face? *Hey!* *Watch your goddamned feet!*"

I cranked my head up. Simone's head lurked precariously under my toe. I nearly knocked her nose off.

Yelling, she sat up. "*God damn.* Just *God damn.* Can't you get that I don't want your feet flying in my face?" Simone's face flushed. She was angry.

"Look, I'm really sorry. It's crowded, I'm . . ." I turned around to see who was staring.

Only Simone looked back. Neil Diamond belted out his third *Hol-lee—Hole-lee,* which meant we were down to number twelve. I had missed over half; still, I waited for Simone to say something more. Her leg whipped through the air. "Just watch your feet, that's all. . . ."

But there was no way to watch my feet. Not when looking down also meant spotting the vibra-belts. I couldn't believe it. Two hundred twenty-five pounds of green leotard—who knew Danskin made colored sizes that large?—was strapping herself in. "Absolutely No Machines During Exercise Class" a sign screamed over the whirl-a-bikes. Oblivious, the lime-jello mountain flipped on the switch. Two hundred volts sent tremors through the mountainside, the machine roared like a Harley-Davidson. Ronnie's head jerked toward the noise; Simone, Fran, and Randi all turned, froze in their spots. Now Ronnie was angry, she bounced the needle off Neil Diamond and yelled from the platform, "*Ma'am. Ma'am. ,Please. Not during class.*"

The Green Mountain didn't move, not even a hair. Again Ronnie tried, then again. Still no response. Dozens of leotards squirmed with annoyance. *How dare she? Somebody do something,* buzzed through the room.

Simone was elected: she pulled herself up, tiptoed to where the mountain stood, eyes closed, inviolate. Then she bellowed, "COULD YOU CUT THE GODDAMNED MACHINE OFF DURING CLASS? PLEASE?"

The electric harness slipped from her waist. The woman half-pivoted, the belt vibrating wildly in the air, glancing her knees. Everyone stared. "Oh my *Gat!* I couldn't hear! I'm deaf!

61

I couldn't hear! I'm sorry! *I'm so sorry. . . .*" Tears formed in the corners of her eyes. She fled, stumbling on the avocado shag.

During chin stretch I escaped. I prayed the sauna would be a friendly haven. Luck! Marcie Laster sat embalming herself with plastic bags on the lower bench. Marcie was the kind of friend who could be counted to pull through in a sexual crunch. She was a human grab bag of how-to books and good advice. Maybe because she was a professional reader, she could make you feel that whatever had gone wrong was a widely analyzed slice of life.

"So? How was the date?" She tucked a loose corner of plastic into her cummerbund, studying my face as I oiled down my thighs. "That bad, huh? I can always tell."

She clucked sympathetically after I announced that I hated *all* men.

"You fucked him, didn't you?"

My head snapped to double-check that nobody was around. A little too quickly I asked her to give me a break.

"You did, didn't you? I can tell, it's written all over your face." With both hands Marcie was stuffing her plastic-encased flesh into tights. Her breasts were like two fried eggs; as she stood up they came close to my face.

I rolled over onto my stomach, anything to avoid meeting her eyes. I wanted *help,* not true confessions. I wanted some happy blend of Fritz Perls' illogic, shot through with the flavor of *Cosmopolitan.* Should I tell Marcie the truth about what really happened between Howie Leon and me? Beads of sweat broke out on my neck, then took off like a ski team racing down my chest. I slipped down to the lower bench, hoping the heat wouldn't attack me quite so fast.

Squish-squish-squish. The sound of Marcie's shifting Handi-wrap caused me to laugh. "What are you doing?"

She was running in place. "You laugh, but I can lose three pounds in fifteen minutes with this number . . . three pounds! The bags make you sweat under the tights."

"Well, it's just water."

Marcie continued stomping on wood. "Three pounds is

three pounds . . . you know what I mean? It's all in your mind. Seeing that number drop on the scale . . ."

"Don't you ever wonder why we even bother? . . . I mean, really. Who the hell cares?" I crushed the Johnson & Johnson plastic bottle in search of the last spritz.

Again Marcie stared, again I looked away. "We all care. That's why we're here . . . on a Saturday. At the Ponce DeLeon."

What fell between us was an easy silence with an edge of gloom. I could tell Marcie was dying to say something to me. I hoped she would resist.

She wouldn't. "Listen, Florida. This happens to *everybody.* . . . What happened? *Let me tell you.* You're making out like two high schoolers and all of a sudden—whammo!—it gets away from you and becomes a semi-rape?"

She was trying to be helpful, but a fine line of pain wound its way down the back of my head. Any second I knew I would have to get out of there.

She read my discontent. *"Don't go.* Stop avoiding! That's your whole trip. What can I say to make you feel better about yourself? To stop doing such a number on your innocent head?" She didn't wait for me to answer. "Listen. My shrink says this whole guilt trip that women our age get into because of a night of pure sex . . . is nothing but approach-avoidance. In other words, we follow our instincts, right? And our instincts tell us we're red-blooded, so we'd like to fuck someone with the kind of abandon that a man always had had. So then what happens? We do a big self-destruct and self-hate number the next day . . . and we think that we're never going to get over being fucked up. My shrink says, 'Is it so much to admit we might want what was in *Fear of Flying* . . . remember the 'zip-less fuck'?"

I sighed. "There's no such thing, Marcie. *Sex isn't calisthenics, at least not for me.*"

"Well, maybe it should be! You want to think this guy raped you—forced you—then fine. If it makes you feel better about yourself, go right ahead. But maybe you should take a

63

look at why you can't just say, 'Slam-bam, thank you *man.'* Turn the fucking tables for once! This is the seventies! You're the one who's creating your problems, you're the one who's doing the self-abuse number on your head! *Stop overcompensating.* You're too special to still be hung up on a little thing like . . . *sex.* Besides, at least this guy is *someone.* At least this guy is no *Ezra Matthews.* Howie Leon could be a bird-in-hand." Marcie's nails tapped on the redwood slats. "Anyway. A bad one-night stand happens to *everybody.* And all the time. It's like getting your period or something, just a fact of female life. Monday you won't even remember it . . . not even the guy's name."

"I will never *ever* forget Howie Leon. I can assure you that in my date book both his name and April 3d will be forever etched in black."

One perfect puddle had formed under Marcie's feet. She had no time for my theatrics. Stopping to listen might make her late for Ronnie's second class. "Look. One parting shot. *Just forget it.* I can assure you that Howie Leon already has."

Forget it? Just like that? Naturally Marcie would have some well-intended parting shot to tell me exactly how to turn tragedy into nonexistence. Swill! If only Marcie's homilies weren't culled from the half dozen human potential cribs she'd groveled in. She wasn't sure which swami her life-saving wisdom came from, but she *thought* she was quoting the gospel according to Werner Erhard: "The truth is what's so. Not so obviously, it's also so what." In other words, Florida, let it be. Obviously.

But the only obvious fact to me at that exact moment was: drop all that. *Suicide* was the only solution for such abject debasement as I felt.

Of course I'd brought it on myself. Whatever the insanity of her gurus, Marcie was absolutely right. If I'd had a brain, I'd have waited till Dina Bellamy called me back. I would have waited to check this Howie Leon out.

Anyway, that's what somebody balanced would have done, how someone with an 800 SAT would have behaved. But not me. All I knew was that there had been a man lined up in my sights and I had pounced like a pack of police dogs let loose on one stinking filet. Florida Burns couldn't have let the moment pass.

Filled with self-pity, I reeled up Seventy-second Street sickened by everything around me. People were smiling at each other, jostling into boutiques. Couples walked hand in glove through the spring air, peering at antique clothes in proud windows. A kid on a tricycle dripped ice cream all over the sidewalk. The nerve of this display! Didn't they realize that only a dozen hours ago, Howie Leon had pinned Florida Burns underneath him? Didn't anybody understand or care about what I was going through?

Apparently not, but I knew why. It wasn't like I was Raquel Welch. Or was I? I watched myself walking by in every passing window. At the same time, I checked out the pizza, the pastrami, and the trays of blintzes. Candied orange rinds! This was no exercise in blind narcissism. I was not Raquel Welch: Peaches might say I was a size nine cross between Barbra Streisand and Jackie Bisset, but I knew better. I was a neon Hedda Hopper, the young set's Queen of Dish. And I had my work, always my work, to pull me through. Thank God. *There was so little time and so much to do.*

I began to enjoy the New York street scene. There, just a block from my home, a man in a battered leather jacket had spread out his wares. Spoon bracelets! Dollar necklaces! And he had as a customer, a medium-height boyishly built (from the rear) hunk, topped with salt-and-pepper hair. *Ah, yes.* It was the new neighbor . . . *Markman,* was that his name? I was walking closer, trying to carry off simultaneously hiding and checking him out. I sighed. The new neighbor had an aura. Even from twenty feet off you could tell he was a high-energy, totally confident, and very married man. Why married? In his hand was a necklace, he lived in the Dakota, his hair was silver; I was sure my columnist's instincts were, as usual, right. But I was coming ever closer, just a few feet away. I smiled, hoped to catch the New Neighbor's eye. *No way.*

65

This ideal side of male flesh knew in an instant I wasn't his type.

Get off it, Florida. Your sense of fantasy is completely absurd. Self-delusion! Why did I think everyone had to react to me, that I was anything more than a speck, just another city face?

I turned around to get a last look. The New Neighbor had disappeared; within seconds the city crowds had swallowed him up. Maybe I had imagined him, maybe Apartment 87 was a figment of my self-abuse, a dirty unfair optical illusion.

I kept moving. The street was a carnival, a vast impersonal circus. Anybody who was anybody would be at home, getting stoned on the *Times,* making phone calls, planning some kind of fun. The streets! Out here I was anonymous. One more miserable wreck. I needed to be rescued. I needed to retire. Maybe if we'd waited till the second date. . . .

Something would have to make me feel better. I was wretched, vile, and boring, especially to myself. I continued to walk. Then I smiled. *Aha.* The answer was so simple. Carbos! Over a dozen hours had gone by since my last major hunger attack. Food is love! I don't care what anybody built like Marcie Laster says. Even when you weigh 127 pounds stripped, once in a while you can be allowed a couple of hours of undiluted pleasure. *Oral love!* Life can't be all broiled chicken and cottage cheese.

Not today, anyway. I had died and gone to pig heaven, which meant that Seventy-second Street—and its endless bakeries, delis, candy kitchens, and nosh cities—was my reward.

Blood-red tarts screamed at me from Cake Masters' window. Almond crescents so sticky-crispy-chewy that you wanted to *plotz* on the spot, particularly after you let your eyes fall on the 100 percent bittersweet milk chocolate hugging each tip. I took a deep breath and kept going. Past the Sacher tortes and the fresh pecan taffy. Past the hundred jars of penny candy and the raisin *kugel.* Past the Kentucky Fried and the Oscar's Fish 'n' Chips. I knew what I wanted; I had made up my mind.

Nothing was going to stop me. Only one problem

remained, but I wasn't yet sure how to resolve it. Which was the right one to choose? I stopped dead. *Meditation time.* Which would it be: the Yum-Yum, forty-six flavors, and only three steps away? Or Baskin-Robbins' "31"—across two lines of traffic—a veritable continent away. Some choice! Head bowed, I pushed open the door of the Yum-Yum and hoped nobody had seen. I was giving in. *Fuck it.* I deserved this reward.

But I didn't think *he'd* be standing in line. Over six feet of gorgeous blond older-man, a Dunlop Imperial racket hanging regally by his side. Better! He was exposed. Endless skinny legs stood naked in the wind, white shorts, and Brooks Brother cable-knit sweater were all that protected him from a draft. His back was to me, but even from the rear he looked . . . *familiar.* Was it someone I knew?

Then I heard the voice. *Coffee Fudge!* Gloriosky! It was John Lindsay himself, standing inches away. John Lindsay, *half naked* in the Yum-Yum. Was I the only one who noticed or who cared? I tried not to stare overtly.

Maybe I was imagining hizzoner, maybe this was just an imitation neighborhood-type WASP. I came up behind him, beamed my gaze toward the list of flavors beyond his noble brow. Butter Brickle! Cherries Kijafa! Turkish Delight! Creme Carmel! Mocha-Royale-Pineapple-Passion-Raspberry-Cheesecake. It was John Lindsay all right. A thousand gentiles could have those legs, those sinewy elastic thighs, but only *le roi soleil* could have that special face. Electric blue eyes, just beginning to fade. Furls of gray-blond-red tutti-frutti hair. Cheekbones so sharp you could use them to open letters with.

Stay cool, Florida. Try not to pounce. I forgot Howie Leon. I forgot what flavor I always choose. I forgot that I had moved so near, all John Lindsay would have to do is pivot and he would trip over me. I even forgot for the tiniest instant that I was Florida Burns of the Tower Syndicate, that I might be able to use this moment to latch on to Lindsay for an interview. Even an item would do. How did his novel sell? Would he run again for mayor?

I was star-struck, lost in memories. I had blocked out the

gallon ice cream drums, closed my eyes to the fluorescent lights, throttled the sound of piped-in rock 'n' roll. Somewhere beyond the Yum-Yum, past the crying babies, I heard a voice say, *Excuse me,* felt naked legs brush by.

Swimming in nostalgia, all I could think of was the first time I'd met The Mayor. *Two years ago,* spring. Just about this time of year. Florida Burns, right out of journalism school, new on the job, sent by the Tower Syndicate to cover An Event.

And what an event! Three hundred Women of Achievement fighting over jumbo Louisiana shrimp. Betty Friedan had red sauce dribbling down her chin. By the far wall, Gloria sipped club soda, talked with Tuesday Weld. Flo Kennedy! Barbara Walters! Marya Mannes! Bella! A tide of peasant skirts and suede, N.O.W. buttons and French jeans swirling in a baronial hall, hobnobbing under gold-leaf ceilings.

Mademoiselle, I'd been told, always gave out awards to Women of Achievement. Always at the Carnegie Mansion. Always in the spring. Always packed in the same crowd, year after year: writers, architects, musicians, editors, politicos, painters, city planners. The literati turned out in droves. Months later I realized they'd go anywhere for a free meal, even some chopped liver on the sideboard. A few potato chips.

Panicked, I huddled by the cheese board. What was I doing here? Brian Milman had said, *cover it,* but no J. School teaches you how to ambush Barbara Walters to get a juicy quote. I didn't know anyone, so I did the only thing anyone could do. I eavesdropped.

It wasn't hard. Nearby, a tall girl—her head swathed in Indian paisley—was screaming at her friend. "Look. You want to sell books? This is what you have to do. Jackie Susann memorized the names of the kids of the fucking bookstore owners . . . she had it down cold! And what did it get her, if not a premature grave? So you want to be on the best-seller list, who doesn't? But what are you going to do? Schlepp a steel file box everywhere you go?"

Her friend had closed in on the brie. "Is this yours?" She

was looking right at me, holding a soggy notebook. My soggy notebook. I'd put it down where someone had spilled a drink. "Oh, *no!* Yes . . ." I grabbed it, squeezed out the gin and tonic. "I never should have set it down."

"Sorry . . ." For a second she smiled, her eyes pulled into a line. Her head was stretched tight by her pony tail, her forehead looked like a kettledrum. Around her neck were two cameras; expensive ones with lots of lenses. For a moment she looked . . . guilty. "Well, I *found* it. Right here. . . ." Where the photographer had fished out my notebook, six half-empty plastic glasses fought for space. A clump of cigarette butts added to the effect.

"It's my own fault for laying . . ."

She ignored me completely, then almost knocked me down grabbing one of the Nikons. She wheeled away, screwing in a thermos-sized lens, aimed it across the room. "OHMYGOD. Is that Julie Nixon? What is *she* doing here? I can't see . . . *it* looks mousy enough. And *it's* wearing one of those awful mint-green dresses. Christ. With any luck, I can sell this shot to *Newsweek*. . . ." She clicked away over my head.

I looked over the crowd just in time to see a Julie-look-alike turn full face our way. The look-alike had a hook nose. I was trying to be helpful. "Maybe Tricia is here. . . ."

"Please. She is. . . Anyway, I'd never photograph her. No bones. Impossible. She comes out looking like banana marshmallow ice. . . ."

"Steinem is here. . . ."

My new friend turned away. "Gawd. Where isn't she? *Gloreee-ah* would go to the opening of a door. Of somebody's sinus passages! Anyway, she's *over*."

"Bella?"

"Are you kidding me?" She continued inching away.

"Well, who's supposed to be here? I'm covering it for the . . ."

"*Oh . . .*" The photographer stopped. "Are *you* a reporter?"

I smiled. At last. "Yes . . ."

Her hand came out like a crane. "Leesha Silver . . . so glad

69

to . . ." She fumbled in her carry-all, smoothed down her hair. "Here's my card. Please use me. I'm friggin' *desperate.* Also damned good, ask anyone. Tell your editor. Are you with the *Times?*"

"No." I took her ecru and ocher card. *Leesha Silver* was engraved in script. In the lower left—in tiny type—the word *photography* was barely visible. There was a phone number.

"Oh. I thought the *Times* was here. They usually send someone. Everyone else sure is. *Women's Wear,* the *Post,* you name it. This town. What's with all these writers? Spit out any window, you hit six reporters. It's not like anybody reads any more, anyway. I sure don't."

"Yeah. I know what you mean." I was just getting ready to brag to Leesha Silver that I was with a wire service—a syndicate, even—when suddenly the room turned upside down. Hundreds of women had been talking at once, dozens of conversations had collided in midair, thousands of sentences, slipped metaphors, shuck 'n' jive hyperbole, tinkling laughter, shrieked hellos, all converged. Under the muraled ceiling, everything stopped short. Three hundred women had found a focus.

John Lindsay had arrived.

Not that anybody pretended to notice, not consciously anyway. A few women fiddled with their chain belts, tugged ribbed sweaters over hips. Shoulders were hunched or straightened, leather feed bags were switched to opposite arms. Dozens of fingers tucked stray wisps back into place. And as if no drama were unfolding, everyone continued to talk.

But I noticed. And so did Leesha, who raced from my side. But Lindsay was flying high, working the room, oblivious to us all. He had one arm around Gloria, he smiled at an editor from *Mademoiselle.* He might have looked the other way when Bella steamed toward him, but even so he towered over each and all.

I froze. You see, I'd always had this fantasy about Prince John. I'd always imagined that someday I'd get to meet him— maybe even have lunch—that we would talk, really talk. I

70

thought that maybe he might think I was cute, that I had a few things to say.

What I didn't count on was that he would be hungry. He cut through the crowd, walking right toward me, his face lit up like the moon. Wow. His eyes were really blue.

"How nice to see you. Lovely to see you. . . ." He was chatting with Leesha Silver. How did she already know him? Wouldn't you know she'd avoid introducing me, knowing that I was an up-and-coming competitor, a member of The Press. My inner voice saved the day: *This is your big chance, Florida. Show what you're made of! Push!*

I'm pushing, already. Through streaked shag cuts and brunette curls, past the plastic cups and leather bags with crossed G's, stepping on toes. *Pushing.* Right up to the exact spot where Leesha Silver was click-click-clicking more pictures and, *just one more,* of the Mayor. She was jumping all over him like a dog while a sanguine John Lindsay suddenly began to look as if it might be time to run back to the mansion to flip on the ten o'clock news.

But not before I would catch his eye.

Mirabile dictu! He caught mine first.

"How nice to see you. I'm glad to see you again." Hizzoner was looking straight at me. I turned my head around like a top, who was there? Nobody! John Lindsay was talking to me?

Yes. "Nice to see you, Mr. Mayor."

He checked out the steno pad dampening my hand. "Are you a writer?"

"Yes-Florida-Burns-Tower-Syndicate. . . . But what I really wanted to ask you was . . ."

"Could you move just a smidge, you're right in my light . . . thanks-so-much." Leesha Silver had me by the turtleneck. Hammer lock! She was pulling me away from J.V.L. Oblivious, he continued to smile. I never knew anybody could have so many teeth.

He rescued me. "Did you want to ask me . . ."

"Yes." Then I panicked. What *did* I want to ask the Mayor? My business was gossip, not city charades. I was stammering. "What I really wanted to ask you is . . . was . . ."

71

"That's *all right,* take your time." Lindsay's smile was a freeze-frame on his face.

My mind was going blank. I was forced to free-associate. Kathy Lindsay! The mayor's Florida Burns-age daughter! I'd wanted her to pledge Sigma Delta Tau when at Penn, but "The Greeter" at Kappa Kappa Gamma (along with some help from Penn's Hollywood Kappa alum, Candy B.) landed the Lindsayette instead. Hah! By graduation day, she had deactivated and become engaged to a Jewish boy.

By now, Lindsay was ready to take off, looking over my head, scanning the crowd.

In a burst, it came out. "What-I-really-wanted-to-ask-you-was-how's-Kathy?"

"You mean . . . my daughter?" Did I detect a note of fear in those widening eyes?

I had better explain. "Right! We-went-to-Penn-together."

His face relaxed, the words rolled off his tongue. "Couldn't be better! She and her husband are living in Brooklyn. He's an architect . . . she's modeling. They're in . . . *Brooklyn.*"

This was a conversation! I was cranking up to ask John-baby about the sanitation workers, the concerts-in-the-park, *anything,* when he turned to me, said goodbye, and let himself be whisked away.

"I'll tell Kathy you said hello. I-know-she'll-be-so-*pleased.*"

His phrase would haunt me all through dinner. Some reporter! I get a chance to talk to John Lindsay and what do I do? Yenta! Make small talk. Anything to win his approval.

A voice played in my ear. *"So unprofessional. An outrage . . ."* Had Brian Milman been standing next to me, no doubt I would have been canned on the spot.

I could just hear him. "What did you think? Lindsay was going to ask you over for supper? *Climber.*" He'd hardly be able to disguise his utter contempt.

And would he be so wrong? In two years I hadn't learned a bloody thing. I had blown it completely. Lindsay ran out of the Yum-Yum before I could nail him, once more he'd slipped right through my hands. While my back was turned, he'd made good his escape. Obviously he'd recognized me, remembered who I was.

Would Hizzoner have run from Earl Wilson? Suzy Knickerbocker? Rona? Even Cherie Rivers? *Of course not.* With me, he knew he wasn't in the presence of one of the greats.

Marcie Laster had tried everything, but *nothing* worked. She couldn't believe it! She had run the entire gamut of human potential movements and psychological playpens and there wasn't a tip or trick from the literature of self-improvement that brought her any relief. Her whole life was flying by, she was on edge all the time. She had meditated, looked at barriers, memorized mantras, been dunked in simulated womb tanks, primaled her lungs out.

Still her days were melting into each other; each two dozen hours was the identical sodden twin of the brother that was born before it . . . of the brother that would surely follow.

She had never heard from Bruce Firestone again. She had tried to convince herself that he didn't deserve anyone with her unique abilities to please.

She had slipped back to her routine: office-gym-home-office-gym. The longest she'd ever gone with a man, any man, was a piddling three months, and that had been over an eon ago. But why? She had those Ali MacGraw looks and she was an encyclopedia of Hollywood lore. There was nothing Marcie Laster couldn't tell you about who was making which deal with whom.

Now she was counting the passing seasons in a different way. A novel she had read in manuscript would appear in hardcovers nine months after it first crossed her desk; one year later she'd walk by and see it leering at her from a paperback rack. Her eyes would see titles and she'd realize that since she'd first synopsized them, almost two birthdays had slipped by. Her life was caught up with lunches, titles, authors, how much Bantam Books had laid out for paperback rights, was the Literary Guild going to make it an alternate or main selection. "How wonderful!" somebody had said to her once, "you get to live in literature. You get to read! Everything that's published! What a great life!"

Hardly. Marcie Laster was allowed to read only fifty pages and the cover lines; probable best-sellers were sent to the Coast. At the end of the day, about the last thing she wanted to do was curl up with one of her 4367 publishers' promotional copies. Then, all she wanted to do was close her eyes. Or get drunk.

Still, she had thought that this day might turn out a little differently. Troy had sent her on a secret mission! She would get reimbursed for her cab fares—$25 worth. It was a long way to Brooklyn Heights. Once there, she had been locked in a room for hours; all she had for company was a six-hundred-page manuscript, a green overstuffed armchair, and an ancient cat.

Who could blame her for being on edge and madder than hell? But there was no salve for her vengefulness. Troy Younger had ducked out of the office before she could tell him exactly what she thought of this latest offense. Because of this expedition, Marcie Laster had missed Ozelle's class and a boot sale at Bloomingdale's.

She crammed a piece of rag bond into her typewriter. It answered with a roar like the downtown express. Which was just how she liked it. Marcie Laster had demanded the IBM man take the mufflers off her machine.

"I like to hear myself work," she had told him. "The more noise it makes, the busier everyone in this office thinks I am."

If only anyone kept late enough hours to hear her! She frowned, then relaxed. She liked working late. Let them have a good dinner, a good rest, because *tomorrow* her angriest memo ever would await them on their desks.

TO: TROY YOUNGER, ARNOLD SCHILL   April 5
FROM: MARCIE LASTER   RE: CARMINE by
                                             Joey Maltavese

This time you really did it. At *your* suggestion, I trekked over the Brooklyn Bridge and spent three of the worst hours of my young life, sitting on Dorothy Meyer's very uncomfortable sofa, leafing through 765 manuscript pages of Ms. Meyer's closely guarded tome of CARMINE by Joey Maltavese. Could you guess it was a portrait of gangster Carmine DeLangella??

Why do I get sent on these wild gooses? Like Descartes to DeHorse doesn't it follow that any literary agent who summons a mere "Junior Story Editor" can't have more on her mind than a lot of high-blown fantasies about Hollywood and the desire to have a little company on a spring afternoon?

Out of politeness, I remained at Ms. Meyer's apartment for three excruciating hours. Also because she's one of those intimidating agents who make you feel honored to get so much as a *peek* at her wares. From the outset, she came on like a White Russian—cautioned me not to put my feet on her antique furniture—and removed me to a back room with only one bottle-green chair and moth-bitten cat. After several hours, La Meyer served me tea, along with a separate cup for my teabag.

I'm not through yet. After alternately dozing and laughing over the overly long, stilted, and, at bottom, worthless manuscript, Ms. Meyer popped in. I was halfway done. She said, "Of course, you're going to read it all the way through." I mumbled something about 300 pages being long enough to judge by (the thing was, as I stated, 765 pages long) and she seemed very offended. "But the whole impact comes in the second half," she said. She sounded so positive that I skimmed the rest, but do I need to say it? I didn't find any impact.

Later, she asked me if I'd ever heard of "The Godfather." When I nodded, she looked meaningfully at the manuscript and raised her eyebrows. I think that was supposed to convey that she held the reteaming of Al Pacino and Francis Coppola in her wizened hands. *No way.*

M.L.

Florida dear:

As you know, honey, you're not getting any younger. So I must tell you I was more than a little upset when Elsie told me that when her friend Ruda's son called you for a date, you gave him the brush. Just because he's in medical school, you told him (Ruda said) you don't go out with "grad students."

GRAD STUDENTS?? Is that your idea of a joke? Well, it isn't funny.

I know you think you're better than the old cliché about the Jewish Princess and the Doctor, but let's not get too impressed with ourselves just because we have a fly-by-night column in a few weeklies that nobody sees. I mean really, Florida, you're 26! To my eye, you're just wasting time.

But I have a *great* idea for you. Why not do a column or two even a book—about *bachelors.* Where they are and how to get them. All these women's libbers running around without men, it would sell like sure-fire hotcakes.

See, I got inspired. This morning Ruby dusted books I was planning to give to O.R.T. and as I was sorting them afterward, I found that old paperback "Where The Girls Are In The Ivy League." Only yours shouldn't be about the Ivy League. It's much, much smarter to write about Bachelors in Texas. Concentrate on the Big Three—Dallas, Houston, San Antonio. In the process, not only will you find a husband, but you'll have a book under your belt as well.

All our love,
Mom

Mamma, I'm trying. Really I am. I swear. Look, I admit it, don't I? Mea culpa, mamma mia, mea culpa. I was snippy to Ruda Dahlberg's son. You would have been too if you'd heard that nervous-nasal voice on the phone. Ten minutes he spent telling me about his Gynecology Clinic. Fetuses he was throwing out in medium-sized baggies. Baggies! *Do you call that class and breeding?* I hadn't even met this acne-faced creep and he was telling me about thirty-six hours of abortions! "Whoever knew I'd get to intern where they were legal?" he said.

Florida Burns was bred to have The Best. That's what you always told me. And Daddy agreed. I don't consider Marty Dalhberg (who sounded like he had a sock wadded up his nose) The Best. Mamma, you would have hated him, I'm positive! You know that word you always use, *vitality?* Well, Marty Dahlberg wasn't vital. No sex. *(Of course I didn't!* I don't mean it that way.) I mean, as you would say, pas de joie. So why should I waste my time meeting someone who has pas de joie? All he'd do is take me to some third-rate Italian restaurant. I'd be tempted to have a whole basketful of garlic bread.

Help me, Mamma. Because I really am trying. But nobody

has *dates* any more. Casual dates, real dates, let's-go-get-a-coke-maybe-take-in-a-movie dates. All my friends gave that up in college. It was much too demanding. Romance is dead. Mamma, men are crazy. They're all fags. Or if they're not gay, they think you're frigid if—you're going to hate this—you're not *sleeping with them* on the third date. I swear to God that's how it is. And *bachelors!* That concept died with Carol Lombard. Look, what I'm trying to say is, you either meet somebody that you want to have a relationship with or you go out with your friends. At least with your friends, the platonic ones, I mean, there's never any hassle. And from what I hear, the minute you get into A Real Relationship, that's when the problems begin.

Mamma, you were so lucky. At least you knew what you wanted by the time you were twenty-two. A Man. Macho-Jewish-Rich-Integrity-Handsome-Brilliant - Driven - Captain-of-Industry-Loves-Children-Never-Strays. Let's not forget generous. You knew what you wanted, damn it. But that's what I want too! So why did you get one and not me?

I know why. And don't tell me it has to do with you know what. The six curds of cellulite you spotted on my left thigh. Didn't I promise I'd squish them out every night with a rolling pin? I told you I was drinking the goddamned grapefruit juice, didn't I? Well, all right. Just cool it about those lumps. It's not like I'd be caught dead in a two-piece anyway.

I'm getting side-tracked. I know why you got Daddy, got him to marry you, "Snagged him," you call it. And I know why it will never work for me. Why? Because men are different now. They're all assholes. Sorry about that word, but truth is truth. Women are different too. If you ask the men, they say we're all ball-crushers. Maybe they're right.

I don't think I'm a "ball-crusher" though. Mamma, am I? I think, well, this is going to sound terrible coming out of my mouth, but you'll know how I mean it: I think I'm just too smart for most men. Too *cognoscente*.

Don't call me ridiculous, okay? All the evidence is there, it's not like I invent this stuff. The point is, Mamma, I deal in news. Hard news. I'm always learning from everyone I meet.

77

And I think that intimidates most men, hearing my high-level conversations across a pink tablecloth. You know what I mean. How a studio like Metropolitan had settled $2 million on a professor at some school like Marquette because one of their writers had ripped off his book for a movie-of-the-week. How Paramount laid a block-long Mercedes limo on Francis Ford Coppola when *The Godfather* broke the $50 million mark at the box office. And how, a little further down the pike, when that movie had smashed $100 million and Coppola had his own jet, the big honcho who brought the project to Coppola ended up asking his young director if he could borrow his plane some free weekend. That's the kind of story I tell at the dinner table; you can see why I might scare a few of the less-sophisticated away.

Because if these men (and I do use that term loosely) can't keep up with me, then to heck with 'em. You heard me, just to heck with 'em. Sophisticated, they don't need to be; but *smart?* Of course. At least, smarter than me. Show me a "companionate relationship" and I'll show you the door. I want a man who I can respect and, at my level, that means only one thing: Mr. Florida Burns has to be a real pistol.

So how do I meet this pistol? I used to think, become a columnist, do interviews for *Close-Up,* and I'd have it made-in-the-shade. I could meet anybody that I wanted to, even a husband. I would just call them up and tell them I wanted to interview them, use the old "I want to do a piece on you" trick.

Did I have a lot to learn! Mamma, the point is: I tried, I really tried. Daddy always told me, you have to make your own opportunities in this world. That just because I might have been lucky enough to have been born the only child and sole heir to Burns' Food Kings this did not mean I could relax. Or expect to grow up—in that tired old phrase—a Jewish-American Princess. What kind of JAP ever grew up playing "army" on a Rockefeller-like allowance of fifty cents per week? What kind of a JAP was disciplined by the demerit system and was forced to read books, never allowed to watch TV? What making my own opportunities translated out to in the Lomitas High days was working every single summer at one of nine

Burns' F.K.'s around Austin. How I Spent My Summer Vacations: wrapping packages, taking money at the register, cleaning up the stock room, putting cans up on the shelf. Inventory! *Mamma.* Every frigging summer. Did I get to go to Europe like the Levine twins? Did I get to go on the Experiment in International Living or to Harvard Summer School? No! Never! I'm not complaining! I learned to take care of myself. Give me a rubber check with a bogus signature and I'll have it collected within twenty-four hours. Tracking down latex checks turned me into A Reporter! The absolute, unquestioned best information-gatherer in the business! I learned to cope! With little things: like how to spot if somebody's sticky-fingering the goods, what to do if someone has a stroke in the "Five Items or Less" checkout line. Anyway, Papa's little parable has always played in my ear. "Make your own opportunities." Stanley Burns practically had it tattooed on his chest: "Shirtsleeves to shirtsleeves in three generations . . . *or less.*"

So that's how I met Ezra Matthews. Making my own opportunities. I put Tell Me Everything to work. This was the way I figured: I always knew that a career was only for one thing—to catapult oneself into a league with the contenders for a super-husband. And you only did that one of two ways: have a face like Princess Pignatelli or be as brilliant and aggressive as yours truly, Florida Burns.

Brilliant, me? Try this. I followed your advice, mother. I did all the research—I was a reporter/columnist, wasn't I?—scanning copies of *Fortune, Business Week, Barron's,* the *Wall Street Journal,* searching for Mr. Right. I made a list, candidate after candidate, each and every one on the verge of being great. I even bought a new tape recorder, thinking that would make me look mòre real.

When I spotted Ezra Matthews staring out at me from the *New York Times,* I thought I had it made! You know what? For a moment I almost unbelievably did.

"Cultural Affairs . . ."
"Ezra Matthews, please."

"May I tell him who's calling?"

"Florida Burns. Tower Syndicate."

"I'm sorry, Florida . . . and what was the last name?"

"Burns-Tower-Syndicate."

"Tower Syndicate?"

"That's right. Tower Syndicate."

A pause. "Will Mr. Matthews know what it's about?"

"I don't think so."

"Might I tell him?"

"I'd rather talk to him directly, if-you-could-be-so-kind-as-to-let-him-know-I'm-on."

"I'm so sorry. Mr. Matthews is a very busy man. Could you possibly tell me what it's in reference to? It would be a great help."

"Look. *Could you just tell him I'm on, please? I'll hold.*"

"One moment . . ."

Five minutes later, the voice returned. "Still there?" It didn't wait for me to answer. Trembling with victory, the voice announced, "Mr. Matthews wonders if there's anything I might be able to help you with."

This was getting boring. "I really do need to talk with him. Thanks-so-much."

"Well . . ." the voice cleared its throat. "We'll try to get back to you, but unless you're willing to tell me what it's in reference to . . . I suggest, perhaps you might be happier writing Mr. Matthews a letter."

I was trapped. "Tell him it's about . . . a story. That I'd like to do a story on him."

"*Oh.* Hold on please."

Within seconds, she was back. "Mr. Matthews wonders . . . what's that? *Oh.* He'll be right with you! Please forgive me, Miss Burns. This just isn't my day. What was the name of your publication? For my files?"

"The Tower Syndicate. We cover the South . . ."

"I see. Could you hold?"

I wasn't sure a boyfriend was worth all this trouble. "Why not? I've come this far."

"How patient you are. . . . *Ah, yes.* He's just getting off long distance, Miss Burns . . . it was Burns, wasn't it? He'll be right with you."

Four minutes after Ezra Matthews said, "Ezra Matthews, here" into my receiver, we had made a lunch date for the following Tuesday. 1:30. Algonquin. *My secretary will take care of the table.* On the Friday before the following Tuesday, Ezra Matthews' office called to say that Mr. Matthews would be in Boston for the day and could we push our luncheon appointment up to Tuesday week. 1:30. Algonquin. *Thanks so much.*

It took only three more days for the executive assistant to ask for the subsequent Friday. Could you make it by any chance at one, in the Oak Room? We'll make the reservations.

Almost three weeks had gone by before I rushed into Le Madrigal at 1:45, fifteen minutes late for my luncheon with Ezra Matthews, a year ago this spring.

At 1:58 Ezra appeared at the door. He greeted Bruno, then looked immediately to his left. A buffet of cold salads was displayed like Fabergé eggs. On the fish platter, a dead eye stared up from a parsleyed grave. "No more sea bass?" Ezra Matthews asked.

The maitre d' shook his head. "At this hour?" Never . . . meesi-your Matt-oose."

Ezra Matthews looked disappointed, but instead scanned the room. Just your everyday lunch crowd.

Lena Horne nibbled at crayfish mousse while Helen Gurley Brown smoked cigarettes and stamped them into Madrigal's pebble-sized porcelain ashtrays. Lillian Hellman held court a banquette away. I stared at her while I waited for Ezra to find me. What a face! Not like a cosmic herring at all. I read that once some reporter had described her in those unflattering terms. And it bothered me. I thought, what would I do if somebody—in print—called me "A cosmic herring"? Lucky me! That's what I'd think. Then I'd probably lay some flowers on the kid.

While Ezra took in the room, I took him in. He was in

81

three-quarters profile, his rusty hair caught the light. Green tweed was good with the freckles, too bad his bald spot was as big as the Ritz. What did he look like? Like the gifted son of a Detroit rabbi (which he wasn't). Or like the author of his first (and only) tome. *Beyond Ethnic* was its title, then it was subbed: "A History of Neighborhood Reform." In hard covers it had sold 3500 copies; it had never made it to soft. I'd checked it out in *Publishers' Weekly* before our lunch.

Suddenly Ezra was smiling, waving. "Ah'm so glad to see you," he yelled across the room.

I smiled, ready to yell back.

"Ezra . . . hello!" The voice came up from behind me, modulated, with a hint of lisp. "Come say hello. I'd like you to meet . . ."

I spun around, then I died. Barbara Walters on a diagonal—right behind me!—two tables away. And she was talking to Ezra Matthews! Barbara Walters! Ezra Matthews and Barbara Walters were on first-name terms? I wanted to rocket out of Le Madrigal. I wanted to crawl into its French porcelain bathroom and flush myself down a toilet or stay in hiding all afternoon.

Barbara Walters! My generation's Joan of Arc! Her show had chaperoned us through every major cultural shock; at age ten, there was the space shot, before school I gaped at the tube. At thirteen, I was sobbing my eyes out with it when John-John saluted the funeral cortege. At sixteen, I watched Daley detonate a militia of kids. At twenty, I watched her get turned on—on the air!—by the wiles of Henry the K. At twenty-four, the Watergate mess. We spent every second glued to those blessed TV sets. Now, she's been through a marriage, divorce and new job and I'm twenty-six. Scavullo takes her photographs. And I'm still asking: isn't there a message here?

If only I knew what it was. Meanwhile, what would I say to Barbara Walters? What if Ezra introduced us? I would have to say something (should I smile?) to be polite.

Or should I say, *Watch out, Barbara-baby, because someday you're going to be watching Florida Burns with heads of state! With*

82

Warren Beatty! With Teddy K.! Someday, none other than yours truly will be warming up your seat!

"Sorry . . ." Ezra Matthews flopped down at the table. Since he'd meandered in, six minutes had gone by.

"That's okay."

"No. It's not okay. I reel-lee apologize. I hate being late . . . making people wait for me. I really do."

"Me too."

Silence. Then, he spoke. "I'm Ezra Matthews. I'm real glad to meet you."

"You might not be after I get through with you." I smiled, hoping he'd catch the joke.

He didn't. "What do you mean? Are you going to write a 'hatchet job' on me? Am I going to have to watch every single thing I say?"

I nodded. "You bet. You're going to have to watch every tiny little word, every comma, every adjective, every metaphor, every adverb, every participle. . . ."

Ezra Matthews began to smile. "Even for the . . . what syndicate? What was the name of that wire service?

"The Tower Syndicate."

"That's right. I mean, why would anyone want to write about . . . me? How'd you even find me?"

"You wouldn't believe it, it was so complicated. All I can tell you is that I found you in a really obscure place. I was just lucky, I guess."

"You were?" His eyes sparked. "Well, what was that 'obscure' place?"

"I'm not sure I can tell you. . . ." Barbara Walters' eyes drilled into my back.

"You've just got to. *Please.*" From underneath his lids, Ezra looked up at me. The wine list lay open in front of him.

"I can't. You understand how it is. Reporters and their sources? The confidentiality shield?"

Ezra flipped pages, skimmed *rouges* and *blancs.* "You must. I'm desperate to know."

"Well . . . no. I can't. Really." I let the suspense build.

His finger was running down the Puilly Fumé column, his attention had wandered to the *vin.* I would have to win him back quickly.

"*Oh . . . all right.* I'll tell you. But swear you'll never repeat it."

He glanced up. "You have my word."

"Promise?"

He nodded.

I took a breath. "The *New York Times?* Front page? Last week? Your picture, remember?"

We both laughed. "That calls for a drink."

Two bottles of *vin ordinaire* later, I was hopelessly in love. Especially after Ezra told me that his father had been the first New Orleans Jew to be appointed Louisiana's trade representative to Costa Rica. That title, in certain Southern Jewish circles, he'd said, was more coveted than a diplomatic pass to anywhere, even the court of St. James. Aristocracy, his family was. I could tell. The Matthews were obviously in the Jews-who-fought-in-the-Confederacy league. Nobody in Belvedere Heights, Austin, Texas, could boast of *that.* But Ezra, like most of his class, was modest. He didn't let on just how elite his Southern Jewishness was until he confessed. "Growing up," he was looking smack into the centers of my eyes. "I always felt like I didn't belong. Like *an outsider,* you know what I mean?"

I nodded. Even in Belvedere Heights, among the assimilated, that syndrome had a name. "Sounds like your basic Southern Jewish alienation phobia. . . ."

"Really?" He was encouraged, he would open up. But not before Ezra Matthews told me about his more recent triumph-laden years on the "inside of things," that is.

". . . Kennedy! From there I went on. . . . Bobby and I had met in Washington in the early Justice Department days, so I sort of helped out with his campaign—did what I could—nothing major, just kind of ran the whole Southern strategy . . . but, I don't want to give you the idea that *Ah* was important. It was really nothing. So, when Bobby was assassinated . . . *My God.* Florida, *Ah,* was in L.A. when it happened. . . ."

I hoped Ezra Matthews noticed my eyes filled with tears. He didn't seem to. ". . . *Ah* was at the Ambassador Hotel, *at the time.* My God, I was the one who had to go and pick up Caroline and little John. . . ."

"Were they there?"

Ezra Matthews was curt—"At the Beverly Hills Hotel"—and then he continued, almost without dropping a line. "So. That's when I thought. This is it for me and politics."

For once, I kept my mouth shut. I was too busy scribbling down *everything* to say a word.

"And then I came back to New York."

I asked him, *then what?*

Ezra stared down at his plate. "Well, that was June of '68. . . ." Three fingers of poached salmon were left. "Are you sure you're interested in any of this? I bet you were a kid . . . in high school then." He looked visibly depressed.

But maybe he could see that I was mesmerized, enthralled. I had never met anyone quite this close to power before.

He went on. "So . . . that was a real strange period for me, Ah guess for everyone connected to Bobby. So hard . . . for all of us to adjust to his being gone."

"You mean . . . the loss of power? Letting go of all that? . . ."

"No! *Not the power.* The feelin' that you were really doing good for people. That something you did mattered. That *the good* we were doing would somehow never come together like that again. . . ." For the first time since our lunch had been served, Ezra asked *me* something. "Haven't you had that feeling . . . that group chemistry when everybody is committed to *really helping* others?"

"Oh yes." I took a sip of my wine.

"Then you know! It must be like writing a really great story. In a sense, *Ah* guess that's what you writers do . . . you give people pleasure when they read."

I opened my mouth to answer, but then I was cut off.

85

Another country heard from. *"Her give anybody pleasure? What are you . . . kidding me? Florida . . ."* Standing over us, Harvey Kaplan had paused to take a look at his watch. "And pretty that it is now quarter after three and I was due at the analyst's ten minutes ago. . . . What am I doing standing here when I've missed ten dollars' worth of the session and I'm still seven blocks . . ."

Now I cut *him* off. "Harvey Kaplan? Ezra Matthews! Ezra Matthews? Harvey Kaplan! You-all will just love each other. You're both from the South."

Harvey's lips twisted into a smile. He detached the finger that was compulsively twirling his forelock and used it to shift his attaché case from one arm to the other. Only then did he shake Ezra's hand. "You're from the South? *Hah!* Then you'll understand why I'm on the way to the anaylst, why I go four times a week. . . ." Harvey's laugh reverberated over the late-lunch hangers-on.

Ezra Matthews looked confused, but Harvey Kaplan was long gone out the door. His raincoat would be a sail behind him, but even it would not propel him fast enough. By the time Harvey Kaplan had hit the street, he would have greeted eight different friends and/or clients. By the time he settled onto the couch, his session would be almost over.

And we would still be lingering over our demitasse. Ezra took one delicate sip. "Who was that man?"

"Harvey? He's *fabulous* . . . one of my absolute best friends. . . ." I let that sink in before I told Ezra Matthews that Harvey was a true genius in his field, which was "p.r." I hoped he was impressed that I too knew someone lunching at Madrigal. I reiterated Harvey's absolute brilliance, Ezra said something about his seemingly unique energies.

"He's *fabulous*. One of the most original minds in the business . . . *really.*"

He had sipped the last of his tiny after-luncheon drink. *"You press stars.* All of you all, *all* . . . you journalists! You investigative reporters! Isn't it chic these days to be 'in media'?" He looked over toward the middle of the room, his gaze resting for a moment on Lena Horne. "I'm really enjoying this . . .

this being interviewed. I never knew it could be so much fun."
He smiled. "I'm not even tired of talking about myself, not
when I can look across the table . . . at you."
I thought I would have to be scraped off Le Madrigal's
tangerine walls.
"Ah'm serious. *You know that.* You're much su-weeter than
Ah had any right to expect. . . ."
I protested that that wasn't so.
"Listen. Why are we sittin' here anyway in this dingy old
hole? You don't want to spend this whole afternoon *here,* not
when we could go walking and talking in the sunlight all
friendly like. . . ." He explained that he didn't like being made
nervous by too much exposure to the press.
It's just that he couldn't help it. I mean, how else do you
explain it, when my simple question, *tell me about your social life?*
makes Ezra Matthews turn—in the middle of Central Park—
and yell, "*Girls,* you mean, *girls,* do I like girls, what girls do I
go out with? Is that what you're asking me?"
"Exactly." I pulled my hand away.
"Florida . . ." Ezra grabbed it back. "Does Macy's tell
Gimbels?"

No. And as it turned out, Macy's wasn't big on seduction
scenes either. For a minute though, I had my dreams. We came
upon the Dakota riding the crest of Central Park; we came
upstairs, he admired my loft, I poured him some wine. Then
he seemed nervous, what was he doing there? "Do you know
any girls for me?" Ezra said after his first glass was gone. "I'd
really like to meet some new women. Reporters. Media types.
They're usually . . . sleek."
"Absolutely," I said. "I have the perfect one: *me.*"
That was a mistake. Ezra laughed. Then he kissed me—
not a bad kiss, either. Then he pulled away. I understood why.
It's one thing to go with a reporter to her loft, play shy, and get
your hands on her breasts. But going all the way is something
else again. I see what went wrong. If I were Ezra Matthews and
Florida Burns came around to interview me, would I have
behaved differently? Of course not! Not if I were number-

three man, General Counselor, and Tax Adviser to the New York City Department of Cultural Affairs. A job like that—with real responsibilities—you had to be careful, watch the way you behave to The Press. How was he to know this was just one of my little masquerades?

So I understood it, I understood it, but that doesn't mean I had to like it. I knew that professionals had to make sacrifices, like not letting naked lust come in the way of The Story. But I had lined him up for *me,* not The Tower!

And he was fooled. So I'd even come to terms with my prize specimen walking out the door without so much as a hint that he'd call.

What I hadn't come to terms with were the prize specimen's parting words: "When you get done with the piece, why don't you give my secretary a call? I'd like to read over my quotes. I mean, we are friends, aren't we?" Ezra Matthews smiled, then patted me like a cat-hater fondling a prize Siamese. "I've had trouble with you reporters before."

She was soaring, she was limp . . . they were swimming like fishes through a molten sea . . . rising, rising like the sun until . . . "OHMYGOD . . . YES!" shattered the quiet of the shuttered room. For the briefest instant, Peaches Rosen felt sure she'd passed out. The tiny pale horse tightened her grip, the dark rider responded in kind. They were frozen, locked to each other, eyes shut like doors. Each blessed their mutual fate.

Some April this had been. The Friday after the first Wednesday, Peaches Rosen had dressed with special care. Toenail polish! She had made sure hers didn't have a chip. A girl never knew, but then again . . . girls always do. Still, she'd had a bad moment. When she walked in and waited (but for what?) by the front door, the silence in Jason Jaffe's floor-through was worse than a morgue. She felt herself visibly sag. Then she heard her name called and the sound of water running in the bath.

Thank God! He was home.

"I'll be out in just a second. Sorry!" Jason Jaffe was yelling from the naked sanctum of the tub.

She found that strange . . . taking a bath in the middle of

the day? It was Friday. She always came before noon, how could Jason have forgotten? For comfort, she turned to the kitchen and her baby trees. Today was the day she must check them for any sign of root disease.

Nervous! Since Wednesday her stomach had been in perpetual uproar; and the fact that Jason Jaffe was nude wasn't helping, not when he was a few inches away on the other side of an oak door.

Only he wasn't. He had slipped out, wrapped in a towel, just to say hi. He was still wet, tiny beads of water winked in his hair waist to neck. He was standing so close, a touch away, and he was relaxed, at ease, as if he greeted her like this every day. Jason Jaffe might be fine-featured and small-boned, but now she understood why his casting type was pure DeNiro, violent, against the mold. He had the most powerful body Peaches Rosen had ever seen. He was in repose, but he was lethal, every pore fairly screamed. She felt herself lean against the kitchen sink, take in a breath. She wondered if Jason Jaffe could see her face washing with crimson, her hands start to shake. She had always lived in a secret inner make-believe world, weaving fantasies for herself as a child. But now she had grown up and her daydream was real . . . and he was carrying her away.

It was only then, that first time over a month before, that Peaches had found herself folded like a rose in the crook of Jason Jaffe's arm. Only then had she allowed herself to open half an eye. She had been surprised to notice that Jason's library table in his bedroom had been cleared of every script. Upon it had been arranged a pottery and crystal luncheon setting for a romantic *deux.*

She had confided to no one about their Last-Tango-like affair. That would take the fun out! This way, MWF, an extended ten till four, Peaches Rosen was playing out a secret dream. She was gliding, falling into love with Jason Jaffe, or was her attraction to his stardom, Jason Jaffe's public mask? For the first time in her twenty-seven and three-quarters years, Peaches Rosen had started reading *Variety,* asking Florida so many questions about actors and the theater that her best friend had been moved to say, "Hey, what gives?"

89

It had taken every shred of self-restraint for Peaches not to tell her best friend the news. Superstitious! She was afraid that once the words formed in the air, Jason Jaffe would dissolve into little more than myth again. Infatuated as she was, she wasn't about to let Roger Rausch slip from her grasp, not till she was sure that with Jason she had safely burrowed in.

She felt silky, feeling more like her nickname than ever before. She was in half-sleep, she was awake. . . . Was Jason showering? Should she join him? Or was that running water for something else, maybe a shave? She opened her eyes, stretched, then looked around the room. Chocolate walls! His bedroom always seemed like a mausoleum, even on these glorious April days. Fitful, she sat up; she suddenly felt alone. From the bedstand, copies of *Newsweek, People,* and *Time* caught her eye. She stretched, then chose *People;* that was what she needed, lots of pictures and gossip—nothing taxing to the mind. She flipped past Marisa Berenson and Susan Ford, skimmed Michael Caine and James Michener. Bored, she turned to the last page. Two familiar names up and punched her clean off the page. *Pamela Rosen!* When she realized that was *her* down in cold print, she wasn't sure whether to laugh or scream.

ITEM: PEOPLE MAGAZINE
"CHATTER"

Love-in-Bloom: When Manhattan plant doctor Pamela Rosen, age 27, knocked on the front door of Broadway actor Jason Jaffe over a year ago, few would have guessed that the actor's avocado collection wouldn't be the only seeds that might sprout. Now Rosen, a petite Atlanta-born blonde, has replaced actress Mimi Martin, Jason Jaffe's frequent date. The hot-house romance bloomed in secrecy for months, but last week the pair was spotted snuggling in a back booth of New York's Maxwell's Plum. "I still don't get a dime off my plants," the Tony Award winner ("Day-Glo!!") said, when asked to comment on his romance.

She opted for screaming, and nothing Jason Jaffe said could calm her down.

90

But he was trying. "It was *Harvey*. Harvey Kaplan! God damn him! I told him . . . to lay off. I told him that—"

"But how did he know we were even . . ."

"In love?" Jason Jaffe grabbed Peaches, then pulled her down, hoping a physical display would lighten her mood.

"In love? *Please!* Having a . . . thing." For the first time, Peaches Rosen pushed him away. "How did Harvey Kaplan know, Jay? He's your press agent, not your best friend! Didn't we agree not to say anything to anyone? *Damn.* If he's your best friend, wouldn't he tell you that he was going to do it first? Bastard!" She jammed a cigarette into her delicate shell of a mouth.

"Hey, *babe.* Harvey Kaplan is my press agent . . . which makes him a close friend. This is what he gets paid to do. *So accept it.*" He paused, feeling Peaches' mood deepen; his sparks faded in the air. "Look. You're not really upset, are you?"

"Oh no. Nothing like that."

"Crap! What are you upset about? That this'll wreck your cozy set-up with that putz you keep for insurance . . . at home?? IF SO . . . THEN JUST DENY IT! That's what stars always do. . . . Just say it's a lie. *A media distortion!* Who's to know? He knows you look after my plants, so? Just say somebody spotted you coming out of the building . . . and, *isn't that ridiculous?* Tell him it's bullshit! Tell him I'm gay! Tell him I'm a raving queen for all that I care!" Jason Jaffe stormed through the room.

"He'd never believe that."

He swiveled too quickly, was she being snide? But Peaches had moved on, so Jason Jaffe brushed his moment of doubt aside.

"Tell him it's a lie? Then what? Sneak over here same as always? Do you want me to pretend that *nothing* is going on? Then what? We're to go on, *same as always* . . . Roger Rausch and Pamela Rosen making plans to visit his parents in June? *Is that what you want?"* She paused just long enough to ignite another Virginia Slim. "And it's not only Roger . . . fuck Roger! Him I can take care of! But have you ever stopped to

91

consider that my best friend, my almost sister, knows *nothing* of this? It's fine to blab to your best friend who just happens to be a press agent, but when it comes to me, being able to confide in my best friend! *Well.* At least, if Florida was going to fuck *me* over, she wouldn't do it on quite so national a scale!"

Jason Jaffe felt his anger beginning to show. "*Wait.* We're talking about your friend . . . the one who writes that column?"

"That's it."

"Well . . . *Forget it! Harvey Kaplan, I trust. But a gossip columnist?* NO WAY, man! JUST NO WAY! *I wouldn't let her within fifty yards of this house.*"

Peaches Rosen thought for sure she was witnessing a mental aberration; Jason Jaffe taking a flyer, going out of his gourd. Then he told her a story that he swore to be truth: Suzy Knickerbocker—last year?—had quoted him at a dinner party making some stupid crack. Quite rightly, the *crackee, Day-Glo!!* producer Sherwin Sunneson, theater's number-one prick, had decided to come back and fight the good fight. Paradoxically (and unfortunately) Prick Sunneson's signature could clearly be read on the bottom of Jason Jaffe's paychecks of the time. Next: they had *words in rehearsal!* Then, published reports of their tiff. All of which led to Sherwin Sunneson on the talk-show circuit calling him a "hiring risk." And, as Jason was pointing out, it's one thing to be dumped on by a Joe E. Levine or an Otto Preminger, former Hollywood heavies now lost in the minor leagues, but to make number one on Sunneson's shit list? For New York's "Quality Actor" (as he'd once been referred to by the *Times*), that was the same as being buried alive. Sunneson was bigger than David Merrick, as creative as Hal Prince. In a slow season, he could stage three productions a year.

Now he wouldn't return Jason Jaffe's phone calls, even though he'd won a Tony for *Day-Glo!!* Sunneson was determined that his career should go "cold."

All because of Suzy Knickerbocker at a party distorting something stupid he'd said.

"Well . . . what *did* you say?" Peaches forced herself to ask.

"NOTHING! That's the point! That's why your friend Florida—hey, what-the-hell kind of name is that, anyway, *sounds like a maid!*—ain't comin' around this place. Ever! I know all about these people! I don't care how close a friend she is . . . *nobody can tell me!*"

Peaches felt herself take a deeper-than-usual breath. "*Well.* What did you tell Suzy Knickerbocker that was so bad?" Something told Peaches not to let it go.

"I TOLD YOU! NOTHING! I never even laid eyes on her. . . . She wasn't even at the *party-in-question!*"

"*Oh.* You mean *someone* made up the whole thing, like they did with me having been 'spotted snuggling at Maxwell's Plum'?" Had she stumbled on some subtle show-business truth?

"RIGHT!" Jason Jaffe looked at her from the sides of his eyes. "What are you driving at?"

Peaches shook her head, then whispered, "Nothing." She wasn't sure exactly what she was getting at. She was a behavioral phi bete, an unschooled savant. Twenty-seven years of vicarious observation made her understand that in this encounter, she would be backed up against the wall.

It was time to back and fill, time to get her priorities staright. But what were they? Ending this mind-boggling sexual mess, that was number one. She couldn't deal with two lovers; for that matter, she had a rough go with ambiguity of any kind. She had to decide whether she wanted to be with Roger Rausch (not very much) or with Jason Jaffe (oh yes). A double life? No way. She might have cherished her daydreams, but this was a *coup de foudre.* She was, after all, a man's woman. She liked to run straight from one pair of masculine arms to another. The present situation reeked of duplicity. She was a product of Atlanta's Northside High and Camp Blue Star. Hers was an upper-middle-class sensibility that allowed her little moral leeway. *No.* A secret life was not to be thought of. She had her fingers on the Big Plum, but she would give him up—run back to Roger—if it meant she would have to masquerade.

She placed a delicate hand on Jason Jaffe's lower back. "I can't lie to Roger, Jason. I just can't."

She flinched from the subsequent roar. Jason Jaffe was up, he kicked the covers from his bed, a frown creased his brow. He tried to force his features to relax (a trick he'd learned from Uta Hagen), but he wasn't prepared for what would come next.

"Would you like for me to lie to *you* someday?"

His voice exploded, leaving her eardrum vibrating like a hula hoop. "SO . . . WHAT DOES THAT LEAVE ME TO SAY? ASK YOU TO LEAVE HIM FOR ME?"

She was cashing in her every chip, her voice barely rose above a sigh. "I guess. . . ." She collapsed into pillows, closed her eyes. *Please God,* she was thinking, *please make him let me stay.* The last thing she was thinking about was Florida Burns. Friendship was one thing, but what she had (potentially) with Jason Jaffe was paradise. Besides, once she was part of the household, had a say . . . well, no actor was so crazy that he'd cut off every aspect of your former life, or keep a best girlfriend away.

For what seemed like hours, Jason Jaffe was stone-quiet. He had fought off relationships ("commitments") since he'd started on stage. He liked few people and trusted even fewer; like most of his ilk, Jason Jaffe had been able to coast through life without hassle or reward, without long-term strings.

But Peaches was *different.* Trite, but she made him feel like a man. And she wasn't in "the business," so there was never any talk about agents and scripts (except his). Noncompetitive! Feminine! He'd never call her that to her face . . . she'd be insulted at the choice of words. Didn't anyone call the gentle sex gentle any more? How could they? For the past few years, he'd met a bevy of ball-crushers; he called them "urban mutants." In that group of desperate characters, ambition was used like a gun.

Not that he minded hard work; *hell,* he knew all about that. Peaches worked hard, but she was still . . . girlish. That

94

was it. She was what the last generation used to call "piquant." He wondered if her ingenuousness had been distilled in the South, then he thought of the corollary: was her dewy knowhow masking a born little fox? Well, he'd always gotten along with Southern women. He let himself look down at the slim vanilla streak thrown against his mocha walls, his blow-ups of both Broadway triumphs: *Jacaranda* and *Day-Glo!!* Peaches Rosen looked helpless and a little sad, as if she felt she might never be in that bed again. He wished he had never met this Peaches Rosen, his almost identical physical twin. She was the matching book end to his looks (with the coloring reversed). He cursed those avocados and their fucking stunted sprouts. He cursed having to deal with this problem, being forced to walk a line. He was in turmoil, but he was a realist; the prospect of never seeing his matching zygote again left him inexorably sad. He swallowed a whole Gulf Stream of air. He'd made a decision, arrived at the bottom line.

Then he tried to smile. Without touching his new roommate, he asked, "Would it take you very long to bring over your things?"

"One moment for Roger Rausch, *please.*"

Oy. This was the call I'd been dreading for days. I would try to sound light as a lemon soufflé, but I hadn't been able to get through to Peaches Rosen all week. Strange! It wasn't like her to pull a disappearing act, not at least without telling me. But she hadn't even called. I hoped that Roger could tell me something more.

He wasn't a man to waste time with hellos. "Have you seen it? Have you seen *People?* Have you talked to her?"

"Who can find her! How about *you?*"

He was more than a little agitated. "I came home, a note was on the bed. . . . A note! She had written two lines . . . something about sending a friend for her things. I was hoping *you* were that friend."

I was sinking from ignored to betrayed. "Me . . . that friend? No! I wasn't, but if it wasn't me . . . who could it—"

95

"But why? I mean . . . doesn't she owe me an explanation after six months? To leave, just vanish without a note? Doesn't she owe us more than that? Who is this Jason Jaffe anyway?" Roger Rausch leaned back in his chair. On a clear day, from his window on Wall Street he was able to see all of Brooklyn Heights, tugboats churning out to the Atlantic, a horizon away. But today he wasn't looking at boats, he was too upset to see or do anything. His tie sagged and was dangling from his collar like a broken arm. He didn't understand why this was happening to him, what he had done to bring disaster on.

"Yes. She owes you more than a note. But at least you got . . . a note. What did I get? Not a note . . . not a phone call . . . *not one stinking thing! Nada. Zilch. The Big Zero.* Talk about upset! You all may live together, but what am I, *chopped liver?*"

Roger Rausch and Florida Burns weren't the only ones with complaints about media burn. Seconds after I'd detached Roger Rausch from the line with a promise of "The minute . . . *the very minute I hear something, of course you'll be the very first one I'll call,*" the Florida Burns "hot line" began to chime like cathedral bells.

"So . . . how's my favorite columnist this morning? How's the Queen of Dish?"

Double oy! Brian Milman! I wouldn't let this conversation bog down in amenities. "I know you've seen *People,* Brian. I'll even save you the words. I bet right now you're thinking something along the lines of, 'If Florida is so smart and such a great reporter not to mention the best friend to about half of New York, then why is it that *People* got what could have been a four-color exclusive for *Close-Up?* Or indeed will be, without fail, plastered all over the newsmakers section of both *Time* and *Newsweek?*' Am I right? Would you like to kill me?"

"In a word . . . *yes.*" His sigh, ten seconds of death rattle, blew from the Tower offices right up to the Dakota, ninth floor, where it landed and hung in the air like a bad smell. Nobody had to tell me that Brian Milman was angry. Worse! He was in a dead rage. So much so, he was trying to hide it, always a telling sign. His voice softened. "I'm just worried about *you,* that's all. I'm thinking about your reputation as a *columnist.* What those who respect Florida Burns 'nose for hard news' will say . . . once it gets out that you protect all your friends."

I tried to explain to Brian Milman that I learned about Pamela Rosen the same place he had.

"*Look.* You've been in this business a long time, so let's talk like 'professionals,' okay? *I know* you've spent time with them, *you know* you've spent time with them. I'm willing to forget this journalistic slip-up if you can just . . . *get on with it.*"

"*Get on with what?* Peaches won't return any of my calls. I haven't seen her in days."

A long pause. "Listen. Find her. I know all about Jason Jaffe. They're not going to hate you if you pester them for something simple . . . a few pages—how about ten?—with a color layout . . . baby pictures, high school. How they met! Peaches in her shop! We'll make them America's sweethearts! The most private actor in the world and the lady with plants! *Cute.* That's how I see it." I heard Brian suck on what I assume was one of his ubiquitous Kents. Then the squeal which was the next thought-gathering step. Brian Milman was leaning back in his chair. "Yeah. I sort of have a vision of this thing. It might be *kinda* great if we could pull it off. I'd love to get some of that rack space away from the *Enquirer* . . . at least in the South. *So,* toots. Your job: *aim for a cover!* Develop it along the lines of little-girl-nobody-from-Atlanta meets Broadway-hotshot. If they won't see you, *fuck 'em!* Write it just like fiction."

"Well, I'll have to because . . . fiction is just what it'll be. Peaches Rosen, a nobody? She had a Cutlass convertible by the time she was sixteen!"

"SO WHAT! Who cares about 'specifics'? Just get it *in.* Pictures—gets lots of pictures—flesh out the rest with some text. Don't try to *write* . . . forget about *style!* You know what I mean, just stick to the facts, even if you have to make them up. I know that's what you do most of the time, anyway . . . so what else is new?"

97

So much for Brian Milman's ethics, journalistic or otherwise. Stick to the facts, only make them up. That was real internal logic for you. Symmetrical speech patterns if I'd ever heard it. To win back his favor, as a parting shot, I told Brian a story I'd heard about Jason Jaffe, his proclivities for certain kinky sexual treats.

"That's my girl!" he yelled, "Print that! Now that's sounding more like Tell Me Everything's Florida Burns!"

I explained to Brian Milman that under the libel laws, to print that non-specific little stinger would cause this reporter (and publisher) to wind up doing time in the pen.

"Nonsense! Tom Wolfe would be able to find a way to work it in!"

I was manic, uptight. I reached for the phone. I had known from the beginning that journalistic ambition, unfettered, out of bounds, would someday lead me to this very issue: where do one's loyalties lie, with naked self-interest or with protection of friends?

There had to be a way to achieve the best in this treacherous world, but to find that ideal path you had to have help, and what are you going to do if nobody answers after you'd tried calling your best friend nineteen different times (in one day)?

You do the next best thing, that's what you do. In this case, that meant Harvey Kaplan would have to get dialed.

"Listen, Harvey. This is it. I have had it with this dumb show. I know you know exactly what is going on and I'm telling you that you'd better level with me—and right now!—because you know why Peaches is not returning any of my phone calls and were-you-the-one-who-planted-that-lie-in-*People?*"

There was a pause. "Who am I speaking with?"

"Harvey, come on. It's Florida."

"This is one of the sickest, sickest phone calls I have ever gotten in my life. What are you talking about?"

Harvey's tone slowed me down, but not for long. "*People* magazine, page fifty-two? Pamela Rosen and your client, Jason Jaffe?"

"What about them?"

"That they're . . . an item. That they're . . . come on, Harvey! I know you planted it! *Jesus.*"

"Are you crazy? What do you think I do? Go around inventing this sick, sick dreck? Do you think I care about who the fuck my clients see in their private lives? That it matters to me? I'm a businessman, not some sick, drecky little columnist who happens to write an equally sick and drecky column that nobody sees for twelve sick weeklies. And just because that drecky columnist happens to have a friend who gets her picture and her name in a national magazine . . ." Harvey's voice suddenly sagged. "When are you going to grow up? Why don't you go get analyzed, I mean with a shrink. You sure could use it. *I'll even pay for the first session.* Anyway. About your sick, drecky question? I don't know, nor could I think it was less important whether anything's going on. They probably don't even know each other. . . ."

I had pushed Harvey over the line, now I would have to take a giant step backward. I chased my words back into hiding and ended with a line like "Of course I trust you," hoping that would do the trick.

It did. "That's better. I mean, just use your head! Wouldn't that be absolutely, absolutely the most self-destructive thing I could do? To lie to a gossip columnist? About my client? Besides, I mean . . . Florida! Forget the working relationship you and I have. Don't you understand that *nothing* can come in the way of our friendship? Certainly *that* means more to me than any piece of dreck actor, even if he's a client, okay?"

"Alright-alright-alright! I'm getting the fact that she knows, but the question is . . . how does she know?"

Within seconds Harvey Kaplan had placed the call. "Well . . . I think *People* magazine, that's for starters."

"But you were supposed to deny—"

"Listen. Florida Burns is not dumb. Manic maybe, but not dumb." Harvey's index finger was twirling his forelock. "It is so, so unimportant. Such boring dreck! I really don't even want to talk about it. *But* I think we did the right thing. Both as your press agent and your close, close friend, I think we did the absolute, absolute right thing. But if—"

Jason Jaffe put his hand over the receiver. "*Peaches.* Darling. More than anything in the world right now, what I would kill for is some coffee ice cream. . . . Is there any left in the kitchen? God . . . that is the nicest, nicest thing you could possibly ever do for me." Jason Jaffe took his hand away from the phone, refocused his attention back into the receiver. "I'm sorry, Harvey. What were we talking about?"

Everything had a first time and this was Peaches Rosen's primary experience of being shut out. She paused in the doorway, a light from the hall shining off her luminous, endless saffron surfer-girl hair. She was only too happy to service Jason on these little things, rather than acquiesce to the big. Still, this scene was a classic—actor and press agent—like on the late show. She couldn't resist the temptation to say something, to assert herself. She opened her mouth: "Do you know that you're beginning to sound 'just-just-just' like Harvey Kaplan?" She poised waiting for some sign that he'd heard her, but getting nothing, her footsteps drummed staccato hammer blows in retreat down the hall.

Only then did Jason Jaffe truly relax; a tone of studied annoyance crept into his voice. "Well, *nice work.* This little 'career booster' of yours in the form of that favor to your friends on *People*'s last page has gotten me . . . a new roommate. . . ." He lowered his tone, sneaked a look at the door. "No-no-no, I'm not complaining . . . *of course not!* It's just I wasn't planning making this kind of heavy commitment so fast, right at this moment, you-know-what-I-mean?" Whaddaya mean it was *my* idea? How the fuck did I know her best friend is a columnist? How the fuck did I know that she would explode! What am I, Jesus Christ? . . . that I should know she wouldn't go along in a lie with her 'ex.' Listen, smart-ass. Whaddaya say when somebody turns those baby greens on you and says, 'How would you like it if I lied to you someday?' I mean, you wanna tell me how to argue with that?" Agitated, Jason Jaffe swung his legs over his desk; for the most cursory instant, his eyes seemed to mist over. He plucked a long blond strand from his bedspread and wound it around his fingers, feeling it stretch. "The point is, *Harvey.* What do I pay you five hundred bucks every month for, if it's not to protect me from both *myself* . . . and *the press!*"

The two middle-aged Atlanta matrons had presented to their only customer a wall of solid back. This might be the nineteenth Brandeis University fund-raising secondhand book sale, but in front of Sylvia Rosen and Rose Matthews (along with 6798 used books, dozens of *National Geographics,* towers of defunct copies of *Life,* scores of *Colliers* and World Books and an already-sold first edition of *An Exhaltation of Larks*) was the most recent copy of *People* magazine, turned to page fifty-two. On the mall at Atlanta's West Pace's Ferry where crates of volumes stood begging for tags, the financial needs of Brandeis U. had been shoved to the back burner.

Sylvia Rosen couldn't stop nodding her head. "My Peaches! She'll do *anything* to promote that little business of hers."

Rose Matthews stared at the glossy copy, the black type. "I don't know, *Syl.* It sounds like our Peaches might be . . ."

"Nonsense! She would have said something. *Ah* know it."

"Well, of course, *I* don't have any daughters." Rose Matthews smiled, revealed her teeth. Behind her butterfly lenses, not a crease wrinkled her eyes. "So, naturally I don't want to say anything, *to interfere,* but I imagine this is the kind of thing a daughter would *not* share with her mother. Course *I* wouldn't know. Anyway. That Peaches! She always did like a . . . different type. I said to myself, '*Rose,* once our Peaches moves from Atlanta why, that will be it!' Peaches was always so . . . *unusual. So interesting,* especially for a Jewish girl."

Sylvia Rosen dipped into an open crate. "How's your nephew, Rose? The one who isn't married . . . what's his first name?" Almost to herself, she smiled, then handed Rose Matthews a tattered copy of *The Serpent and The Rope.*

"My Ezra? Couldn't be better, that's-so-*su-weet*-of-you-to-ask. *Ah* don't know how he finds time to do everything he does! He told his mother that since his picture was on the front page of the *New York Times,* his phone just *rings* off the hook. Why, you know what he told his mamma?" Rose Matthews neatly printed "75¢" in the upper right-hand corner, then snapped the book onto a pile. "That he feels like one of those *Cosmopolitan* magazine bachelors-of-the-month . . . isn't *that* just wild?" Rose Matthews hardly took a breath. "Such a shame he and Pamela have never gotten together up there. Ah just wish that nephew of mine had more time."

"Ah know. It's a *crime* they haven't met. I tell Peaches not to turn her nose up just because Ezra's *what,* thirty-six?, and never found himself a . . . but you know Pamela, she's as stubborn as her father's side of the family. Why couldn't she have gotten my Weintraub temperament?" Sylvia Rosen made herself very busy with her hands. "But how nice for him that he's so popular just when he's almost middle-aged."

Rose Matthews took a step, her polyester pants legs hung neat as swords. With a flourish, she wrote "95¢" in the lower left. "You are so right. That boy is fussy. He's old-fashioned . . . looking for a girl with *character.* You know, when they made my Ezra, they threw away the mold."

"*Harvey? Me* again. I gotta talk fast because Peaches is in the shower. Forget doing anything! I took care of it. . . . Whaddaya mean, 'What did I do?' What-the-hell-difference-does-it-make? *I took care of it.* She makes her demands on me, I make my demands on her. That's all. The point is, I got her to agree about her friend, what's that columnist's name? I said, 'No way, baby.' After Sherwin Sunneson, I ain't takin' no more chances with *this* career. I told her . . . *straight:* no publicity people in this house unless it's under strict Harvey Kaplan control. . . . *Hey,* is that funny? *So?* Why are you laughing? *Look.* I'm calling to tell you that we're splitting, just for the weekend, we need to get out of town. So . . . you want to get me off my gig on 'Mid-Day Live'? Twenty-three minutes to push Actors for Animals with Cicely Tyson, I can really live without. . . ." Jason Jaffe was impatient.

He hadn't been out his house all day, not even to take some steam. "*Nope.* I ain't telling you where we're going because . . . I don't want *you* or anyone else to know. *Come on.* Emergencies? There won't be any . . . *emergencies,* give me a break." For the first time, he laughed. "I don't care what Bart-Palevsky are offering DeNiro, *I told you,* I ain't about to ask *them* to send me a copy of their script. *Fuck 'em. I got too much to do.*" Bored, Jason Jaffe—phone in hand—crossed to the center of his room. He stumbled over a bearskin rug nestled at the foot of his bed, then quickly recovered himself by whirling into an impromptu *pas de chat.* He landed with a thud. "*Shit.* What? Nothing . . . that was *nothing.* Anything else to tell me?" Jason Jaffe sat motionless, listening. His burst mocha walls blocked out the last few rays of sun. He heard the sound of water running in his bathroom and it comforted him. Then he thought, *what is she doing in there so long?*

Was this what living together was all about? He was afraid and alone, unable to hang up, to let go of Harvey. He needed a friend. Six Jason Jaffes with heads the size of Gulf signs stared down from his walls. *Presenting . . . Jason Jaffe:* Laughing! Crying! Scowling! Grinning! Threatening! Jason Jaffe in *Streetcar!* Jason Jaffe in *Jacaranda!* Jason Jaffe in *Day-Glo!!*

The *Day-Glo!!* poster was still his favorite, not just because that production had brought him his first (and only) Tony Award. He liked to look at it when he was thoroughly depressed. Eight feet of Jason-Jaffe-as-leather-biker could usually perk him up. Eight feet! He stared at his visage. Critics (and friends) had for years compared Jaffe's walnut eyes and hair to the Hoffman-Pacino Intensity School. At first the analogy had greatly pleased him, but now he was annoyed. He was an original, he wanted to be more than just some smoldering stand-in. He often wondered what it would feel like to be tall, even for a day. Jason Jaffe was five feet seven. He was described (universally) as "wiry-intense-lithe." Just once he'd like to be called "massive-monumental-towering," and have them be talking about his physical stature, not his personality type.

Still, he'd won a Tony, hadn't he? And, *just to show them,* he'd stuck it in there, right over the bowl. On Peaches' second visit, she'd potted it in with the ivy, without saying a single word. She had inserted herself into his landscape; he admired that kind of subtle nerve.

He dropped his voice. "*One more thing,* Harvey. I'm not te¹ling her about . . . *that's right.* Not yet, anyway. It's too soon. So, lay off the little jokes when you see us, okay?" Jason Jaffe flopped on his bed. In the dimness, he gestured at some unseen interlocuter, receiver clamped to his neck. An orange spark from his cigarette momentarily beamed a flame at his face. "I know, *it's not* honest . . . tell me about it, okay? After twelve thousand dollars' worth of therapy, you bet I know what's honest and what . . . *isn't.* . . . *What? You're outta your mind. She'll never figure it out. Never.* Trust me. I know, that's how. I'd stake my Tony on it, but you know what? Even if she found out, she'd never believe it. . . . And *if she believed it,* she probably wouldn't care." Jason Jaffe laughed, then spoke even lower. He thought he'd heard the faucets being shut off in the bath. "Why? Why? My very own press agent has doubts about my powers? *Schmuck!* Why do you think? The first night we were together, I must have fucked her a dozen times." He smiled at the memory. "And you think *that* was something, *that* was bupkes compared to the second act!"

LA TAQUITA NYC PLANS ANNOUNCED

New York—La Taquita, Inc. of Baltimore, Md. announced yesterday that it had reached an agreement in principle for two undisclosed Manhattan locations. La Taquita, which operates 14 Mexican specialty food stands, reported a profit of $123,000 on sales of $3½ million for the year ended last Jan. 31. The company said it expected sales in this fiscal year to be much higher, even after an estimated outlay of $600,000 in construction and start-up costs. The company's existing locations are concentrated in Virginia, Maryland, Kentucky, and North Carolina. Manhattan sites and projected opening dates will be announced by the end of the current quarter.

—Franchisers' News

TO: BRIAN MILMAN
FROM: FLORIDA BURNS

SUBJECT: *NOTES FROM THE THIRD GENERATION*
(Or: What Feminism Means to One Twenty-Six-Year-Old)

1949 was quite a year for my parents. Married three years, they were taking their first winter vacation. So it was in Boca Raton, Florida that, by coincidence, I happened to pop out. I was six weeks premature. "Get us out of here alive and I'll name her after the state!" Margie Burns (supposedly) shouted just before she went under the gas. She never considered for a moment that she might be giving birth to a son.

1949 was quite a year for a few others as well. Simone DeBeauvoir had just given birth to *The Second Sex.* Arthur Miller was surprised when his *Death of a Salesman* became a Broadway hit. Later he'd describe 1949 as "the last postwar year . . . when the basic illusions of the era were exhausted."

But not everyone's illusions were exhausted. Betty Friedan was buying a pressure-cooker and reading *The Joy of Cooking.* Alice Matlock, my mother's kid sister, was defending the Ingrid Bergman-Roberto Rosselini love affair to Margie Burns, who, at 24, was almost twice her age. Alice was trying to understand Kate Chopin's *The Awakening* that year; my mother was keeping her mind active with articles from *McCall's* ("Women Aren't Men," "Isn't a Woman's Place in the Home?" "Half the Women in *Who's Who* Are Single"). Alice and Margie disagreed about everything. Was it any wonder? They were a spiritual, not just chronological generation apart.

Twenty-six years later, Alice is a forty-year-old (divorced) clinical psychologist, living in Los Angeles. Her thirteen-year-old won't wear shoes made of leather, her ten-year-old works with underprivileged kids. When Alice and I get together (which isn't often), she looks deep into my eyes and asks, "Are you happy?" I never know what to say. So we tread neutral conversational waters, talking about books and her favorite writers—Erica Jong, Alix Kates Shulman, Anne Roiphe. I don't get their women-as-victim mentality. Alice always explains, "All women are victims. We're programmed that way."

I don't see myself as a victim. And I know my mother wasn't victimized in 1949.

Maybe in New York, apartments were hard to find, but in Austin, you could find a fine three-bedroom house for

$16,000 or a duplex apartment (with a view of the Capitol) for $150 a month. That was in the best neighborhood, too—"The Georgetown of Austin." Margie and Stanley Burns could be happy there; they were settled and away from the East.

They'd met in Washington, at the end of the War. She was a secretary at the Pentagon, he was a Captain in the Navy, something to do with supplies. They intersected at a Jewish Community Center dance, just off Dupont Circle. (She used to tell me about it, the two of us sitting on my bed, drinking coffee and smoking cigarettes like college girlfriends: "I knew it would be a special night for me! I was wearing a beautiful ice blue slipper satin gown! That dress, I still remember it. From Ann Barron's in Brookline. It matched my eyes, so I splurged a week's salary since I'd just lost five pounds.") Though she was immediately attracted to Stanley Burns, she was also a little afraid. The way he looked in his uniform: "Tall, husky, *like a man*." His thirteen years on the far side of her age fueled her fear-attraction, as did his leathery, exotic Texas syntax, which hadn't changed much since his boyhood in New Braunfels, where Burns' Groceries (as it was called then) first started. While Stanley was at the Wharton School (Class of '34), his father had expanded into the hill country and moved to Austin, where he was accepted as solidly middle-class. So when my mother, aged twenty-one, married Stanley Burns, she was Making Good.

Her older sister wasn't sure. "You really want a man of such years?" Ruth had asked. Mother wasn't intimidated by Ruth's status as a staff writer for the *New Republic*. "Of course," she explained. "He'll take care of me." Naturally, she was right—Ruth didn't marry until she was 34, and then, as Mother says, "she had to settle." Her husband, a rewrite man on the *Trib*, used to laugh at my father and call him a "killer capitalist." But as soon as the *Trib* folded, he and Aunt Ruth got divorced.

The update, of course, is that Aunt Ruth and Aunt Alice think they're "modern"! They brag to my mother that while she doesn't understand me, they *certainly* do. But I feel as awkward around those two stereotypes as I do around Margie Burns. Because it's really the same game—guilt—that all three are playing. The aunts make me feel guilty about wanting a man. My mother takes off on my career. "Honey, if you get too successful, you'll scare all the men away," Margie says. Then she lays on her pearl: "Look what happened to my sisters, do you want that to happen to you?"

And all I can ever think to say is, *"When will anything happen to me?"*

Because although I was brought up to be a Real Person, no one said that meant you'd have to be independent and self-reliant forever. Catch-26! That's when you start to see how age is gripping you by the throat. No matter how "rich" you become, the final step is still just a husband away. Meanwhile, we had our "tools"—developing those inner resources, keeping busy with careers and graduate degrees. I did (we all did) these things. We sailed through a million "changes." We developed, studied, were stimulated, and thus . . . we evolved. So where's the payoff?

We've been waiting in line a long time. I'm sick of waiting in line. Oh, I would like to *retire,* to marry and rot for a while. But Stanley Burns' childhood lectures still rule my mind: *Sink or swim, toots,* forget about running Burns' Food Kings.

So I followed his advice, swam to New York, and began to put my plans into action—with thirty-nine pairs of pastel Pappagallos in tow. Saturday, August something, six years ago, Fifth Avenue beckoning . . . I flew through Central Park. It was the perfect day to arrive. Thousands of women marching arm in arm, blue-jeaned waves of womanhood surging through the streets—it was the first NOW parade! I stood on the sidewalk with the dispassion one would reserve for dim-theater viewing of an old Movietone newsreel.

And there he was! I woke up in a hurry. Navy Lacoste shirt, Sperry Topsiders (without socks). Well, enough was enough! Twelve hours later, I was no longer a virgin.

I only wish I could remember Mr. Boat Shoes' name. I'd like to thank him for taking my virginity on National Female Victimization Day! He did me a real favor, that's why I want to thank him—I awoke with no romance, no mystery, no promise of roses, no mess and fuss. I had a headache and a sense of relief. Twenty years old and fresh off the boat, I'd had my wants and needs taken care of, thanks to NOW. To the victor went the spoils, the con sliced both ways.

"Well?"

"You have got to be kidding." Brian Milman leaned back in his antique desk chair, allowed one riding boot to rest on an open drawer. "I mean, you're not serious, are you? *You couldn't be."* He threw "Notes from the Third Generation" down on his desk, heightening the drama. "The Tower could never run this. *Ever.* Sorry, kid." He watched my face for the first sign of tears.

He would get them. Brian Milman was one of the few who could get me in seconds, way down deep where I live. But first, I would further seal my own coffin, ask for more Milman-inflicted abuse.

"But why don't you like it??"

"Because shit is shit. I don't care how 'sincere' it is. There's no place for feelings in this business. Get it together, Florida. Toughen up."

I was on my Ezra-Matthews-inspired "soft-pink-and-fluffy" campaign and toughening up was the last thing I intended to do. I would try to be nice, to understand where Brian Milman, my sometime good friend, was "coming from."

Brian Milman. His very name gave it away. Forty-two years old and super-professional, a fact that he wouldn't let me or my co-worker, Andy Marks, ever forget. Brian Milman swore that he'd gotten everybody started; that he'd known Jimmy Jones when, gotten drunk with Irwin Shaw. He was the Mayflower of the post-World War II literary generation, and Andy Marks and I were never allowed to forget *that* either. I flipped open a *Hollywood Reporter* to stall my inevitable tears, tried to make chit-chat while I let his insults soak in.

I stared at the back of his head. The hair was dark and closely cropped, a threateningly chic camouflage for an enlarging bald spot. Mod! He had to keep up, you couldn't let yourself go when you'd been an editor for almost twenty years. He was abrasive, but sadness clung to him like a warm summer fog. Lately, he seemed exhausted all the time, but maybe that was because he was a "hardened professional" (those were his words, not mine). I'd heard his wife left him, but I couldn't confirm that it was true. He might be on the attack with me, but I wouldn't fight back. Florida Burns would never consciously cause *anyone* pain.

I braced myself as Brian tore into "Notes from the Third Generation," winced when I heard the word "boring" collide with "egotistical," "stupid," and "selfish" more times than it was necessary to slam the point home to a female of my sensitive ilk. He ended with a devastating crippler of a line. "Write what you're good at: *gossip!* Forget all this swill. Earl Wilson ain't

Hemingway, so think about your loyal readers! They don't pick up Tell Me Everything to get third-rate Anaïs Nin."

This was too much. I started to wail like a babe. "My readers don't count! They don't even know me . . . way down deep! They have no idea who I really am! And I bet they don't care! As long as I keep bringing in the goods on people like R. J. Wagner and . . ."

"That's the point. You'll tell them 'everything' about Natalie Wood."

"But that's just what I don't want to do. I want the readers of Tell Me Everything to understand that I might be more than some avaricious shallow media hound who goes around 'dishing the dirt' about stars. I want them to know the real me . . . the lovable me . . . the me with warmth, ideas, and feelings. . . ."

Brian's look—do I know this girl?—sent me into temporary retreat, but not before I noticed Andy Marks, my ally and Tower-rewrite-desk/general-copyboy, poke his head out of his cubicle door. He dissolved quickly, anything to escape this firing line, but not before I'd caught his eye. *This again?* was sympathetically registered all over Andy Mark's face.

Brian's gaze told me it was time to give in.

I ignored him. "Assign me something BIG, Brian. Get me off this crap. I hate it. It's ruining me as a writer, decimating my . . . creative urge."

"*Florida,* please. Save it for George Sand revival meetings, okay?" He anchored himself with his left boot and rotated counter-clockwise. "Look. You women with your great careers, *I know all about it.*" Brian Milman softened, he was attempting to be nice. "Keep doing these little essays . . . I think they're terrific . . . for *Ms.* They might even publish "Notes," though I'd be surprised, but just remember one thing. . . ." His eyes narrowed into slits. "You guys writing for me? You're all interchangeable . . . like toilet paper. And I can replace you—all of you—with dozens of *new* writers ready to kill for *your* spot. *Comprende, amiga?*"

I comprehended all right, you bet I did. I'd been comprending since the moment I'd walked up the stairs—fresh out of J. School—three years before. You had to, if you wanted to make it at the Tower Syndicate. And in those days, Florida Burns did. She really did.

But in the early days, at first . . . I wasn't sure I ever would.

Slouching toward the river on West Fifty-eighth, almost two score months ago, a casually interested visitor might have noted the following high spots: Walgreen's (where one should avoid the hot dogs); Albert's Hosiery (try their seconds on opaques); Bohack's (mind the rotting lumber still not hauled away since the fire). A & C Ice Company, where the polyglot of Greeks shoving pushcarts might temporarily retard your footsteps.

Have patience! Nestled at the foot of the block is a small, yet shabbily elegant brownstone. The Tower Syndicate calls its fourth floor its home.

Plush is not the word a precisionist would use to describe it. Nor do I mean to suggest that the bohemian aura of journalism-in-the-making made us rise to the "sweetly squalid" class. Indeed, only one word would fit our minaret of a city room and, I'm afraid, it would carry a negative charge.

In point of fact, the Tower was a dump. But it was a dump . . . with class. A page from Ben Hecht, what with the maple desks landscaped by mountains of crumpled lemon copy proof, army-surplus coal-colored phones, ancient Royal standards, tin ashtrays filled to overflowing. Empty Mayflower Coffee Shop cartons were littered everywhere one looked. It seemed as if in all these years nobody had changed the props.

Of course, my first day, I thought it was a Renoir. That was before I understood the ropes.

Since early that morning I had been sitting in my chair arranging and rearranging the fifty-two pleats in my so-far-spotless white sharkskin skirt. *Maybe it's a holiday,* I remember thinking, *maybe that's why nobody is here.*

Then I got paranoid. Maybe they found out, maybe my

cover's been blown. Could they have checked the *Mexico City News?* Discovered that I'd forged my clips? That I landed this plum job by a *scam?* I took yet another extended breath, only looking up from my misery when I saw a young man strolling through the door.

"Are you the new secretary?" He looked at me from underneath his bangs, which fell over the rim of frames. In his hand was a crumpled white bag, "Mayflower Coffee Shop" embossed gaily on its side.

"*No.* I am *not* the new secretary here." Piqued, I recrossed my legs. "How much do I owe you?"

"Excuse m-m-me?"

"My coffee? How much do I owe you?" I was getting annoyed. How could this jerk be sent around with deliveries? He was having an impossible time just slipping out an intelligible word.

The messenger continued to stare. A leather bag slung over his left shoulder was shifted to the right. He placed the Mayflower Coffee Shop bag down on the desk. I reached for it, then frowned. What the hell was this?? I didn't order two bran muffins, not Florida Burns.

"You'll just have to take this back. This isn't what I ordered. Not at all. They didn't even send . . ."

"But if I had known you wanted anything, I would have . . ." The messenger still didn't get it.

". . . I called. And I was very specific. A carton of cottage cheese, black coffee, 2 packets of sweet 'n' low. Now how did two bran muffins come out of that?"

Then the messenger laughed. "*Look.* I work *here.* I'm Andy Marks. I don't deliver, but if y-y-you'd like, I'd be more than happy to run out and get you something."

I was too embarrassed to answer. *Jesus.* What if Andy Marks had power? What if he took umbrage at being mistaken for a delivery boy?

I didn't have to worry. "So . . . what's your name?" He sat down to talk.

He was still there when Brian Milman made his entrance

111

over an hour later. Andy—by now we were best friends—had warned me, *the minute you're hired, that's when he turns off the charm,* but who knew it would be so immediate?

By the time Brian wandered in, the time was almost noon. "Well I see the two of you have met. Florida will be working for *me,* working with us, Andy." He smiled, then got hold of himself. "Where am I having lunch today?" I suggested a $2 neighborhood hamburger place.

"WHAT? Almost noon and you still haven't made my reservations? What the hell . . ." Brian Milman fell over me in his haste to find his appointment book. "What have you been doing all morning?"

"But, this is my first . . ."

"*Procedures.* A news service lives or dies, loses or wins on its . . ."

"*Rules.*" Andy Marks filled in the blank as he skulked into his cell.

"Where's my memo? Where the hell is the memo I left for you last night? I put it right here on this desk before I . . ." I panicked! What memo? I said I was in the dark. Any minute I knew he'd fire me. If he hadn't already seen through my act. Billiard balls ricocheted inside my rib cage, any instant my heart would inch its way out of my throat. I knew it would only be a matter of seconds till he would turn on me and yell.

"HERE! I FOUND THE GODDAMNED FUCKER RIGHT HERE . . . WHERE IT WAS ALL ALONG! I wish I knew what the matter with you people was. Obvious! Right in the most obvious place . . . the goddamned sports file in my third desk drawer." He let the sentence evaporate, then glared at me. Standing knee deep in scrap paper, he waved the epistle at me. "Another thing. I know this is your first day here . . . and all that. But if we're going to make it, Florida, you're literally going to have to read my mind." He watched my reaction, then quickly added. "Like it or not, that's what comes with the territory."

If only that was all that came with it. That first year, anyway. Hired as what they used to call a "cub reporter" at age twenty-two, I was quickly demoted to answering Brian Milman's telephones. But at least he never made me bring him coffee. He'd lost a wife because of the women's movement, he wasn't about to take chances with his secretary.

"So? I still don't get it."

I stepped back, watching the fuzzy white sphere coming at me. "I don't get what you don't get." Racket back, I was ready, but my voice got lost in the bubble.

"WHAT? YOU'RE GOING TO HAVE TO YELL, FLORIDA." Dunlop Imperial slammed into Wilson three-dot, three-dot cleared the net, skittered to rear court and dropped. "IN?" Marcie Laster paused. "I'm not sure. Can we take it over?"

I nodded. The white sphere arced over her head—a perfect toss—then connected with her aluminum racket. Tension locked my knees, I felt my socks begin to crawl down around my ankles. "LONG," I yelled.

"SHIT!" Marcie tried again. This time her ball pierced the service court, met my forehand. I watched the ball sail back to where she stood, legs apart, racket clutched like an inverted five iron. Her mouth was tight, then she swung.

Ping. It sounded perfect, I started running, my shoes slid in the clay, then stopped. Marcie's return had detoured into the net.

"*Marcie.* Pretty that you can't even hold on to the . . . racket," she screamed, berating herself.

I was glad nobody was around to hear. Marcie Laster was the female Bobby Riggs of the Young Career set. So we played at the Yorkville Bubble, where each court was divided off from its neighbor by a high wall of plastic. And a good thing, too. I wasn't so sure if Marcie and I could live through our twice-weekly tennis encounters, not if the Junior League or General Motors was on the next court listening. Tuesday morning was Marcie Laster's self-improvement day. Analyst at nine, spine cracked at ten, tennis at eleven. Then she'd go to her office.

"What do you tell Arnold?" I asked her.

"That I'm reading 'at home.' Everybody does it. You don't even have to be a full story editor." Saturday was our day. Eleven, tennis. Twelve-thirty, lunch. Burt could hardly wait to get to the table to start pumping her, this week's column was a disaster area.

Just like this set was for Marcie Laster. "Change sides?" she yelled. Then we passed at the net. "*Love* your dress. Just love it. It's darling," I said, taking the balls. She nodded. Marcie Laster was not big on losing, especially the first game, first set. Still, her dress was cute. Pink and green crocheted, you had to be a stick to get away with it. Marcie Laster was. I knew she'd crocheted herself this number just to bug me. Well, I wouldn't let it.

"First one in?"

"All right." Marcie's thighs tightened, her knees eased into a *grande plié.*

Warming up for my toss, I could see her cross court, rocking back and forth, dancing her *come and get it* Wimbledon Twist. I would not let her distract me from dropping a serve in. Rocket! I still couldn't quite connect with full arm velocity to the downward spin of the ball. I was desperate to beat Marcie Laster. I had to win. Otherwise, when we got to the lunch table, I knew she'd clam right up. But if I slaughtered her, she'd be contrite. More than petty pride rested on this toss. . . . My entire column was at stake.

I threw the ball. It arched. *Perfect.* Just like a cathedral window. I raised my racket, feeling every muscle preparing for take-off. *At last!* Centrifugal force was there. I was gliding, gliding in holy alignment, praying it would smash in.

Then I noticed the yellow ball come up from over the plastic divider behind me, whizzing by. I sagged. Wouldn't you know it? A man on the next court bellowed, "THANK YOU." . . . I'd have to stop everything, just when it looked like I had Marcie Laster on the run.

Mike Markman had been practicing the relaxation response, a little TM. A lot of deep breathing in the locker room as he pulled on his sweat pants. *I just won't think about it, that's all.* I won't let the morning ruin another game. Not when this court costs me $16 an hour, not when I'm playing with Bobby Stein.

Mike Markman only got to play with Bobby Stein, rising star of Lehman Brothers' corporate finance division (and number-two seeded player of the '67 Harvard team) once a week. That was Saturday, eleven o'clock. All week long, he looked forward to this game, Stein was the only one of all his partners who gave him a good run. Mike Markman liked to be in top emotional form when he took him on.

The game had started well. Mike Markman had found his center, shutting out the noise from the girls on the next court, shutting out the noise from his early-morning breakfast meeting. He'd won the toss, aced the first serve, thought about the Sixty-third Street Neighborhood Emergency Consumer Group, just as he was running for the second point. He focused his anger, smashed a cross-court spit ball, then smiled when it passed Bobby Stein's racket and fell like a snowflake just inside the line. It was his best shot, the hardest one to place.

"Lot of top spin on that one, huh?" Bobby Stein had yelled as he blew it back.

"You bet." Thirty-love. His next serve raced by the service court . . . *long. Get a grip, Markman,* he said to himself. *Get a grip.* He flipped the ball up in the air, got ready to meet it. He blocked out the morning faces—those goddamned divorced do-gooders—didn't they know that Mike Markman was no MacDonald's, that La Taquita had more than a touch of class?

Apparently not. They had served him with papers, petitions, even ad campaigns, all because Mike Markman wanted to bring one of his restaurants to their neighborhood. "Go back where you belong," they had yelled at him. "Save New York!" Was it any wonder their husbands had left them? Outside the coffee shop on Lexington Avenue, pre-adolescents carried placards. "STOP THE MEXICAN INVASION," one of them had read. That one hurt his feelings, what did they think, he was a goddamned hell hole? That he was Pup 'n' Taco? Mike Markman blamed it all on Contemporary Female Sexual Displacement.

He must breathe, force himself to relax. His entire shoulder pirouetted in its socket, it squealed, then came down upon the ball. Mike Markman's eyes narrowed, he felt his muscles flex. Like a cannon, his serve found its mark. Forty-love. Bobby Stein was scowling now, getting down to business. His lob crashed at Mike Markman's feet.

Forty-five. Server double fault. Ad in. Deuce. *Two* more points! What was the problem about two stinking points, particularly when he had him on the run? What a volley! Bobby Stein was running him from one corner to the other, dancing him, playing with him. Now a drop shot, now to the net. He was strongest at the net. He crashed his return at Bobby Stein's feet, sure that he had him, then he saw the lob. It broke free, soared high, gliding right over his head, but in control, so Mike Markman would have to return it. Sprinting! He lunged backward, his racket held high above him like a mast, his shoulder pivoted into place, the bases were loaded and Mike Markman was up to bat. Unbelievable! *Home run.* A perfect connection. He watched it lift, higher, higher, an infinitesimal streak against the bubble roof. *Drop in, drop, you motherfucker..* DROP IN. He knew there was no way. It sailed into the next court, where those damn girls were yelling.

Game, Stein. From forty-love he'd lost the game, the first game, the all-important psychological edge. His mental reserves were washing away, he felt them leaving at high tide. Suddenly, he felt tired. Very, very tired. "THANK YOU," he bellowed. Another deep breath, then lightly, oh so lightly, he tried to bounce across the court on his way to retrieve the ball. He frowned. Again, he yelled, *"Thank you,"* still there was no response. What were those girls doing behind the plastic wall? *Beginners!* Bad enough he should blow this game, but now he felt helpless, waiting for the woolen sphere before he could change to the opposite service court. *What was he going to do, continue standing here like a fool?* He would have to go get his ball himself. Angrily, he sprinted toward the back corner of the court, where the plastic and canvas divider hung. From Court Five he pulled the curtain back just enough to squeeze into the next court, but he hadn't been quick enough.

"BALL COMING!" The curly-headed girl on the far side of the net had been oblivious to his entrance; he watched the Wilson three-dot soar fifty feet into the air. Powerful! She had a forehand to rival both his and Stein's. Hidden in the corner, Mike Markman lingered to take a better look. *Not bad.* She was built just the way he liked them, energetic, but with sturdy (almost athletic) thighs. He wondered if he should introduce himself, challenge her to a game. *Yes.* He smiled and called, *"GRACIAAHHSS!"* hoping she would look up and smile back. *Too late.* She waved him off, her attention had refocused on her set. She was already jockeying for the next point. He turned his back and forgot about Court Four in his zeal to try to seek revenge on his real nemesis, Bobby Stein. Next game he would show him that the first game *never* told the tale.

How could I have done this to myself? Marcie Laster was halfway through her Coquilles St. Jacques and I hadn't been able to wedge in one question, not about anything that I was concerned with. Not about business, anyway.

My own fault, really. The score had been 6-4, she had gained on me in the last minutes. Now I was forced into submissive position. I had to listen. How Marcie couldn't believe it, but when she went to Bloomingdale's to look at summer clothes, she actually got into a size three pants. Polo, too. Marcie swore polos were always cut smaller, since they were so expensive. ("Rich women aren't fat . . . you know that.")

Did I ever have to listen. Walking toward Grand Central and the Oyster Bar, how I listened. What Marcie almost said to Peter O'Toole when she saw him sitting on the brown leather couch in Arnold's office. What the analyst had said when she said that sometimes she gets so depressed she spends an entire day getting stoned in her office when nobody's around. Why it was that everybody seemed to be getting everything they wanted but Marcie wasn't. How she had found this unbelievable diet in *Women's Wear*—avocados and crab meat—guaranteed to get rid of anxiety, strip away tension. What energy Marcie Laster had! How I admired the way she was always working on herself! I resolved that today I would try to really hear her, instead of tuning out everything but the items.

117

What I didn't bank on was that Marcie Laster would start grilling *me*. She started off easily enough. "So . . . you never finished telling me how you got your column in the first place," then absorbed my words the way her bread soaked up the cream sauce. How could anyone with that body eat the way Marcie Laster did? Innocently, she looked up at me, waiting to hear my answer.

That's when I told her about Danton Turbeville. A long story! How this queen who lived at the Royalton Hotel had been doing the column for a thousand years, only then he got emphysema and any moment he was going to plotz. How Brian Milman, in addition to my other duties—answering the phone, line editing, clipping the wire services, making his lunch reservations—made me ghost Tell Me Everything too. *After all,* Milman said, *Danton Turbeville is a sick old man. We need to give him all the help that we can.* That fact that Tell Me Everything was the most popular item on the Tower Syndicate service, he said, had nothing to do with it.

"But what made him think you could write?" Marcie asked me.

"He'd seen my clips."

"Come on. You told me you had never written before."

I stared down at my shrimp, four little pink pieces of flesh lying like infant's toes on a bed of ice. What the hell, Marcie Laster was a good friend, I could tell her the truth. "I plagiarized them . . . what do you think?" I watched her face change, so I added, "Look. I went to J. School, right? And nobody was getting jobs, not anywhere. So, what did I want to do, get sent to Albany? No way. I said to myself, Florida Burns, in this world you make your own destiny. And the way I made my destiny was by inventing myself. *Easy!* All you need are a bunch of clips from some obscure paper, without a byline, and just take credit for them. It's an old trick. I knew I could write as well as anybody else, so it was just a question of . . ."

"I wonder if *I* could do that. . . ." She twisted in her chair, checked out the menu. "Should we order dessert?"

"You go ahead." Now I really hated her. Bad enough she

would be so thin . . . but dessert? At lunch? She had to have a tapeworm.

Pecan pie and ice cream . . . she was trying to kill me. "So. This Danton-guy died, is that the point?" I nodded. "You're so lucky, Florida. You have such a power base. Your own column! And I don't have shit compared to . . ."

"What do you mean? With all those movie types in and out of your office all day long? I never get to meet anyone."

"So, what do you think? Gene Hackman is going to ask out a glorified secretary? He's married anyway." She seemed genuinely depressed.

It was then—watching Marcie Laster finish off her pie wedge—that I decided to give her the *zetz*. The Florida Burns pep talk. Anything to keep me from ordering the rum cake. I laid out the whole crash course: how everybody says the way to really make it is to begin at the beginning, but no way. How the way to really make it was just to invent yourself, start in the middle, what did you want, to be like Barbara Walters and wait fifteen years to have your own show?

Of course not. Then again, you could get lucky. Turn into Pamela Rosen, which is to say a sniveling, manipulative ingrate, a bitch on wheels who forgets who she owes what to the minute she's able to attach herself to everybody's dream: a Broadway star.

"You mean Jason Jaffee?" Marcie asked.

Yes, I meant Jason Jaffe and *no,* I still haven't heard from the bitch, but the point of it is, she got what she wanted and I'm the only one who knows how.

"How?" Marcie asked.

By selling out her friends, that's how. Which is to say, I told Marcie Laster, I'm basically a romantic at heart, a softie, a push-over, I'll do anything for anyone, so what did I do, anyway, to make my best friend turn on me?

Instead of answering me, Marcie Laster changed the subject back to her career. "*You have just got to help me.* It's a matter of my life! Let me explain it another way: say somebody came to 'a person' with a really great story, something that this

119

'person' knew was true . . . because like the person who came to the first person with the idea in the first place was somehow involved in it?"

"What *are* you talking about?"

"What I'm trying to say is say somebody, 'this person,' for example, unearthed an unbelievable . . . crime story. And that they wanted to write it. How would you tell them to go about it?"

I had sat at this table way too long. "I would tell this person, if she were the person who just ate about seven thousand calories at this lunch table, that if she wanted some help to come out and ask for it . . . instead of—"

Marcie cut me off. "The point is, Florida, *how are we going to make me a star?* You're a star. I want to be like you."

I paused, watched Marcie twirl her butter knife between her fingers. I hated these non sequiturs of hers, hated the fact that there was no barter, no items for all my advice, no information in return for my services as a shrink. Me a star, was she crazy? "You want to be a star like me? Call up Brian Milman, tell him I told you to. Maybe he'll let you do your big story for him . . . if it's so secret you can't tell me about it. *Jesus.*"

I watched her disappear into the bathroom; wouldn't you know she'd stick me with the check? Girlfriends! I fished out my wallet and thought about Marcie Laster for the briefest of instants. How lunches like this made me wonder why she and I were even friends. After all, we had nothing in common. I was the daughter of Burns' Food Kings. Marcie Laster's mother (her father had died when she was young) had held them together by finding her slot as guidance counselor/dorm mother-in-residence (yet) at St. Francis', a Connecticut girls' school with aspirations to be Dana Hall. As a daughter of faculty, Marcie Laster had been able to attend school for "no fee"; then had come the scholarship to Connecticut College. Marcie had never gotten over these massive financial insecurities. How she loved to think, look, and act rich! But somehow when she tried, it came out a beat wrong. Like someone wearing polished Gucci loafers with Levis, instead of Sperry

Topsiders. You know what I mean; she was trying way too hard.

I know what you're thinking! That Marcie Laster sounds like a cliché—the ambitious girl clawing her way to the top. Of course that's it! But so what? There's a little Marcie Laster in all of us (including me). And when it comes to choosing friends, it's a lot more fun to be around the ruthlessly ambitious; at least they're an endless source of activity.

It's just that today I had my own activities. So when Marcie Laster hadn't appeared by tip time, I went to find her. Seven expressos over a two-hour lunch can really do it to you. I thought if I sat at the Oyster Bar another minute, I'd scream.

Annoyed, I pushed open the bathroom door. What a fool I was! I'd shot my mouth off about Brian Milman, tooting my horn about how I'd lied. Dumb! I'd let Marcie Laster get away with *hondling* my connections. Worse: now she had something on me. I tried to smile, then prepared to face her.

Only she was nowhere to be seen. I called out. My voice bounced off snowy porcelain walls, died on white marble floors. How could I have missed her?

In point of fact, I was glad. Peace and quiet (and an empty bathroom) were what I craved.

This one was a morgue.

I let myself into a stall, bolted the door, relieved. I looked down at the floor. A pair of French brushed jeans wearing Italian loafers were kneeling over the adjoining bowl.

Then I heard the noise.

"*RAAHTCHAOUGH . . .*" Someone was puking her guts out inches away. "*RAAAHHHTCHAOUGH . . .*" The noise erupted again, followed by three small burps. A sour smell began to rise, my stomach began doing somersaults to greet it.

I knew I would have to get out of there and fast. Body wastes flying around like orange cottage cheese is a sight Florida Burns can live without.

So I stood up, again seeing the Guccis, the pale jeans.

Then I connected. "*Marcie.* Is that you?" I'd know those mulberry loafers anywhere.

"RAAAAHHHTHCHAOUGH . . ." was all I got for an answer.

"Are you all right?" I had visions of headlines. MOVIE EXEC CHOKES TO DEATH AFTER LUNCH WITH COLUMNIST—INQUIRY SLATED. I banged on her door. *"Let me in . . . It's Florida. Are you sick? Can I help you?"*

She didn't answer me, just threw up again. What if she'd taken in a rotten scallop, been done in by a pecan? "If you don't let me in this second, I'm I'm going to get a . . . MARCIE, OPEN UP! ARE YOU OKAY? TALK TO ME!"

Suddenly a voice. "ARE YOU OUT OF YOUR MIND? . . . *I'm . . . fine.* Just go away. I'll be with you in a second."

Again I heard her retch. And again. And again. What the hell was going on? Why wouldn't she let me help? Dizzy, I leaned against the wall, the glare, the smell, the oppressiveness of the bathroom almost did me in. Powerless, I could do nothing but listen to the sounds coming from Marcie's stall. Primal! Like birth or death. Marcie was ripping her esophagus to shreds, but why?

"All gone." She laughed, bounding out of her cell. "Hey . . . you look green, what's the matter?" She wiped the last bits of lunch from the corners of her mouth.

"Was it something you ate? *God.* Are you all right?"

"Yeah. Now I am." From her purse, she drew a toothbrush, then splashed water on her cheeks.

"What do you think did it to you? The scallops?"

". . . And the pecan pie, the rolls, the ice cream, the three Bloody Marys . . . and what else did I have?"

She saw I still wasn't getting it, so Marcie Laster laid it out. Her secret for staying thin. The two-fingers-down-the-throat-after-every-meal diet. She held them up to demonstrate, advising me first to drink lots of milk before I tried it. *Makes it easier, if you're a beginner,* she explained.

"You have got to be kidding. That's disgusting." I was repulsed, but fascinated.

"Listen. The point is, do you want to be liberated from food or not? Because why the hell not give yourself the space to be able to stuff your guts till you want to die, eat everything you

122

ever wanted? Tamales. Baskin-Robbins, blintzes, bagels, lox—well, salty foods are harder to throw up, I don't know why, but chocolate chips, Sara Lee, quiche, once I ate two whole pies, and what about . . . pizza!? Why deny yourself? Why run that guilt trip?" She paused, then started in again. "I know what you're thinking. You'll *die, you'll choke to death* . . . it's so *unhealthy.* Well . . . crap! The Romans did it. Actresses do it! At St. Francis' everybody did it, that's why WASPS always stay so thin. It's actually quite healthy. Like fasting, only you get to . . . *eat.*" She turned on me. "You mean you've never before met anyone who does it?"

"I haven't."

"Well, they probably just don't admit it. The dirty little secret . . . food without guilt, forever!"

In silence we walked up Madison till Marcie decided she wanted to take a cab. Almost as a throwaway, I said, "Let me know what happens with the story . . . you know, for Brian?"

She held the door open, then smiled. "*Oh. Right.* I will, I will." She bundled herself into the back, said goodbye. I began to walk away, then turned when I heard her call my name. "*Listen. Florida.* Do me a favor. Keep what you learned secret . . . about the you-know-what? *The food? Some people might not understand* . . . you know what I mean?"

I nodded. "Yes. . . ." But her cab had already pulled away. I watched the taxi fade into the Saturday traffic. Now I had something on her, but you know what? I would have traded this knowledge for the most mundane of items. Some things are better left private.

The deadliest mornings were Tuesdays and Thursdays when Slim came with her machines. At first Peaches had tried to get out of it, the having to work out with Jason and his exercise teacher (and reflexologist), but there had been no way. $35! And that Slim charged just for an hour. She always stayed for three, which meant Peaches had to as well.

Slim. The very affectation of her name made Peaches' skin crawl. The fact that she'd been in the corps of the American Ballet Theatre till her knees disintegrated only made it worse. "What was I to do? Sit home and cry?" Slim explained the first time Peaches met her. "*Of course not.* I said to myself, *Slim,* keep yourself busy. You can still *move.* I turned my accident around."

So now she was going door-to-door with her machine, a mechanical slant board that guaranteed perfect stretch, sinewy thighs. Peaches still felt like a klutz on it, but she knew why. Slim had had it in for her, ever since she'd become a permanent fixture. Little things, like her eyes focusing somewhere on Peaches' forehead; the way she would smile too brightly and say, "Not quite right, Peaches, shall we try it once again?" Then Slim would bend over with those protruding hipbones, lethal as weapons, and gently she would take Peaches' feet, rearranging them in the leather straps. Her hands would move toward Peaches hips till she held them firmly in her grasp, then her fingers would start to travel till they found themselves somewhere over Peaches' pubic bone, where they'd stop and rest.

"Keep it tucked in. The abdomen always ages first," she would say. For emphasis, Peaches' stomach would get a little push, but all the while Slim's eyes would be resting somewhere else: her gaze would focus on Jason Jaffe, working out across the room.

Frankly, she made Peaches nervous, all the stress she put . . . on concentration. She said that was all it took to get the best of the Slim Rich Method. Which meant the moment Peaches took her place upon the board, the small of her back flat, her abdomen tucked, really tucked, her thighs tight, every muscle snapped to attention; from that moment on, Peaches Rosen was under Slim Rich's control. For three hours, anyway. Well, her mind could drift and it did. Usually back to the Ponce DeLeon, where working out had at least been fun, where one could sweat and enjoy it, without being made to feel like an ox.

"I can tell you've gone to a health club," Slim had told her. "Your muscles are in *knots.*" She fairly spat the words out.

Maybe she was right, her muscles were in knots, but then again, so was her life. Or was it? Her legs had never looked better, whatever else you could say, at least her body was together. At least her exercise regime was an improvement over life chez Roger Rausch.

It had to be. Jason had taken a house at the beach, the season was upon them. But why an A-frame behind a dune and why in Amagansett? How could anyone call that "going to the country"? There wasn't a tree for miles. And it was hot, way too hot for June. The mornings were the worst: the sun so strong over the water there seemed to be no escape. She'd have to cope. Peaches had thought it out; she'd stock up on hats and sun screen, maybe move A New Leaf to the beach.

All in all, she'd burrowed in, even at the shore. Jason Jaffe loved the water, loved the feel of sand burning his back. He even liked that end of Long Island, where the crowd was lower-brow. Painters and writers (but the B group), a subdivision of singles on the make. Three analysts were in the next A-frame, every weekend they'd hunker down with six children and four cats. Peaches wondered who belonged with whom and why, but she never asked. Only once had the woman of the triad made a move. By chance, Peaches had come up behind her in the supermarket line. "Is that Jason Jaffe . . . the actor . . . is he your husband?" the woman said. "Yes," Peaches said, then plunked her Tab down on the check-out slab. She could feel the woman looking at her, at her bare feet and floor-length peasant skirt, trailing on the linoleum floor. Rich hippie, the analyst was probably thinking. *A childhood regression, a flower child.* Peaches forced herself to answer. "Why do you ask?" Her pale eyes fixed the doctor with a granite stare. The woman, middle-aged, tried to blink, then looked away.

"I don't know . . . I wasn't sure. He seems more intelligent-looking than . . . I mean. He doesn't look like an actor. Whatever that means."

Indeed. Peaches smiled, felt a secret rush of pride. Jason Jaffe didn't look like an actor, he was brilliant and arrogant, more like a politician than a star. He was charismatic. He might even go over in Atlanta, should Peaches ever get to bring him home. He had, after all, been born Jewish, only now he was guilt-free. Having an analyst hovering by him at the supermarket wouldn't faze Jay, he'd love the chance to take the upper hand. *Experience it out, feel it, let it be!* he would yell at her. She wondered why his face seemed so furrowed. He was only thirty-five.

Peaches was changing too, over the summer, even though it had only been two months. She was sleeping later, finding it harder to get up. Jason said, "It's because you've relaxed," but she wasn't so sure. *Of course,* he'd say, *you don't have to work so hard. A New Leaf runs without you.*

And he was right, well, almost right. Business slowed down in the summer anyway, most of her customers went away; for them, she had a special service. Wet Nursery, Peaches had called it, ha-ha-ha. Her shop became a jungle in the hot months, the doctor stopped making calls. Then there was Harvey Kaplan and his prefix disease: why couldn't he get the press to run her name, for once, without his labels? Plant-doctor Pamela Rosen. A New Leaf's Peaches Rosen. Green-thumber Peaches Rosen. The phone never stopped ringing, her customers had become the *Women's Wear Daily* crowd. She hated being an ingrate, but Peaches felt as if A New Leaf was no longer in her control; Jason had made her hire helpers, there was an accountant to take care of bills. Publishers were calling about book contracts, Vogue wanted to do a spread. But she made Harvey turn everyone down. *Give me the summer to think about it, I want these three months off.*

What she didn't want was to be big business, what she liked was the one-to-one. Since the photos and the items and the stories, the one-to-one was changing shape. Now she was an appendage, a satellite, a girlfriend to a star. New York had opened up to her, why was she happier before?

Come on, Peaches. You were never happy. Not like this, anyway. Her hands were clutched on the wheel of Jason's Fiat, she let the wind whip her hair into her eyes. She was free and it was summer, she'd never had a summer this good before.

But she'd had to cut the house calls because of the questions and the looks. The way they tried *not* asking her about her personal life. She always knew what was on their minds. How could you explain about mealy bugs when the only thing they wondered about was how Jason Jaffe performed in bed?

126

Because he was terrific in bed, the sex was the best part. Who wouldn't like waking up with a sexual fantasy? Who wouldn't like a transcendent, cosmic fuck? Jason Jaffe was larger-than-life! And it wasn't just his stage presence that was big. For years, she had swallowed the propaganda, *size has nothing to do with satisfaction,* but now she knew that too was a lie.

Size had everything to do with it, that and being aware of what one held between the legs. Cock consciousness, she called it, for want of a better term. Peaches wondered if she was a sexual prisoner, if she'd been turned into an orgasmic junkie. Somehow, she didn't think she'd mind. Jason's friends were now her friends, her other life had disappeared. She had new interests, like needlepoint, she even cooked. Absurd! Six months ago she would have called the domestic urge sexual slavery, but now . . . she liked staying in, she liked to make Jason happy. She wondered if that meant that she was in love.

Whatever it was, it was different from anything she'd had before. And she'd thought she was the reigning expert; Pamela Rosen was a man's woman, isn't that what her friends had said? She'd certainly had her share: Nick Panovsky, her Anthro 976 prof, she'd stayed with him a year. Who knew that a Duke University freshman could fall into such high cliché, but the moment she'd walked into his class, she knew, she knew, that he would be her first. Bells rang for both of them, there was no more to say. Except that he was forty-three, and she knew it couldn't last. There had been encore after encore, but she would leave Duke her junior year. After three semesters with Panovsky, she couldn't go back to Phi Epsilon Pi. So, Peaches transferred (nominally) to Finch. It was a way of getting herself to New York.

She wanted fun and she got it, loads of it. Her first two years she'd shared an apartment with two others girls from home. Three girls in two bedrooms! The first time someone had a man stay over she thought she would absolutely die. Peaches Rosen was proper, she always went to spend the night with the man. She was a romantic, an idealist, a throwback to another time. For a moment, she thought about having a heart (tiny) tattooed at the top of her left thigh.

Thank God she hadn't. The way men were these days, she doubted than any of them would be secure enough to understand. Certainly Marco DiFinitti wouldn't have; he was a young Roman banker she'd spent six months with. That had been love, *colpo di fulmine,* he'd called it, but Peaches had blown it. She'd tried to move in, too hard, too fast. She'd become so prissy, a typical *American,* all she could do (he said) was issue "demands, demands, demands." So he'd left her. If only he hadn't been three years older and seven inches taller, if-only-he-hadn't-gone-to-Yale, Peaches knew she wouldn't have taken the loss quite so hard. Only the way he'd broken off struck her as foreign, even strange. Three Gucci bags—a wallet, a shoulder strap, an overnight—were delivered to her door. The card read, "Buon Viaggio."

She'd cried for days, but it was *finita la commedia.* Still, luck was always with her. One day she'd answered the phone and lo and behold, there was Roger Rausch, warm-blooded, but American, safe-bet Jewish lawyer. She thanked the person who'd given him her name; this time she saw to it that she played it smart. Within weeks, Roger's shirts were hanging in *her* closet (Florida's advice had been, "To keep the power, always make sure the man moves into *your* home."). On their one-month anniversary, she'd had a cake frosted in chocolate, inscribed it with, "Peaches and Roger: The Real Thing."

But, *wrong again,* when would she ever learn? Roger Rausch was far too bland, far too square, just what her mother would have chosen should she have spotted him hanging on a rack. Roger Rausch was the navy crew-neck sweater in a row of floral body shirts; he was a place to drop anchor in the middle of a storm.

Jason Jaffe had changed all that, he'd come along just in time to shake her life like a tambourine. So she'd thought, at any rate. In the beginning, how she'd had her dreams! *This is the worst part, the looking for the sand driveway, which meant that you were exactly a half mile on the speedometer from the cut-off. Why couldn't there be a sign or a marker? Why was she expected to tell directions by telephone poles and giant steps?* Was this what she thought would be crashing waves and raw adventure? Was this Capetown to Rio by way of the Orient Express?

Yes, so it seemed. Whatever it was it was a lot better than what she'd had before. Even if she didn't quite have her sea legs. All she needed was a crash course in native customs, language, lore. Take the Bernsteins. *Lenny and Felicia.* "*Steyan!* As in *Stein*way! BERN-STEYENE! You called them *Bernsteeeen!* It's a long *eye.* How could you have goofed that up?" Jason had screamed his head off at her egregious faux pas.

Peaches had asked what difference it made, how you said it, as long as you were *polite.*

She was answered by his by-now-standard withering look. "It's *very* important to them that you get their fucking name *right.* The Bernsteins want everyone to understand they're not hung up about being Jewish; so get it right, okay?"

Now she just called him "Lenny," and she wondered, what would Florida or Marcie Laster, or her childhood friends back in Atlanta, think about that? Peaches and Lenny B. on first-name terms! She wondered how many people she'd grown up with had seen pictures of her with Jason punctuating the magazines' spreads of glitterati openings-first-nights-screen-ings-parties-shows. She had known just what to wear at their first public outing; she'd scooted into Halston and (off the rack) bought a drop-dead white naked-front number, posi-tively cut down to *there.* Pamela Rosen made sure that in her publicity she was considered more than Jason Jaffe's "walking stick."

She would tell Jason, "No more publicity," then be de-pressed when *Women's Wear* would sometimes slip and forget to mention her name. She was ambivalent and confused, filled with self-loathing when she admitted to herself what one of her primary motivations might be.

She wanted her high school class to think: is *that* the Pamela Rosen of the class of 1966? She wanted them to discuss it at their reunion, over dinners, over teas.

They were her barometer, her conscience, her inner

votive light, always on her mind. Especially tonight. Angry now, she flipped the Fiat onto the sand. The tires bleated, then quieted down. Parachutes of dust threatened to overcome her. She smiled when she remembered: Jason had just washed the car. Served him right for buying midnight blue!

Tonight was her main reason to be annoyed. Three hours they had to drive—all the way into town—and why? John and Yoko Lennon . . . a possible deal was in the air for Jason, *that's* right, with the Beatles, did anyone remember them?

Because Pamela Rosen hardly did. She'd slept through *A Hard Day's Night,* walked by *Yellow Submarine.* She was Southern, an innocent, a vixen; she was a junior Scheherazade. Besides she'd always had a crush on Marvin Gaye. Peaches couldn't care less about John and Yoko's ashram, couldn't feign interest in their experiments with Zen. She imagined that's all the Beatles would talk about, that and how their co-op maintenance payments were skyrocketing. She would have to grin and bear it; this was "business," after all, so she'd have to tag alone. Maybe if she wore a caftan, they might think she belonged.

She promised herself that she wouldn't have this fight with Jay, not again, but here she went, she couldn't help herself. Peaches Rosen hadn't meant to slam the closet door, didn't realize her silence would be the thrown gauntlet that would lead them into war.

"*Listen.* I get that you're pissed. I understand that you're pissed." Jason Jaffe thrived on confrontation, he couldn't let the moment pass. "And, *believe me,* I want to deal with this. There is nothing I would like more in the fucking world than just to be able to stay home and . . . relax. But . . ."

"I know. That's the price you have to pay, right?"

He said nothing, he didn't have to. Peaches could feel his anger zinging from one corner to another, bouncing up against the windows, hanging in midair. For years, she had never been able to understand how actors conveyed emotion just with their bodies, with one isolated muscle quivering in their necks. Now she knew. If nothing else, Jason Jaffe had taught her about living theater, how to read her cues.

130

Enough was enough. She came up behind him, put her arms around him, playfully she shoved him on the bed. It was their special language and it always worked. Within seconds they were kissing, Jason had grabbed her by the breasts. He was rough and he was angry, he was at his best. He grabbed her by the thighs and pulled her down. *Ride me, ride me,* he began to yell, but he didn't have to, Peaches knew her part too well. She would let it build, legs snaked around his hips, feeling him all the way through her, and just . . . there . . . she would begin to flex, at first the tinest little bit, then draw him in tighter and tighter, now releasing, now tightening, then letting go. Subtle! The way she could bring it up or cool it down, that's the way, just like that, he would whisper, till her muscles began to ache, till she didn't think she'd have the strength to ride him any more. She was only too glad to be flipped on her back, she was only too glad to play dead.

She wondered how men did it, how they kept their balance; she wondered where they got the stamina required to stay on top. She wondered how much of it was acting, how much of it was pretense. Her eyes were open now as were Jason's. His hair had curled into ringlets around his brow. Above him, a two-D Jason Jaffe seemed to laugh. His *Day-Glo!!* poster went everywhere he went, watching it seemed to give him strength. For the briefest instant, Pamela Rosen wondered if he might be possessed. But only for the briefest instant, because then they began to move; his head was snapping back and forth, *driving, driving,* she was turning like a key. Energy! Even when he held her by the thighs, then ground his thumbprints, making purple splotches of pain, she felt . . . fantastic! Somewhere way in the background, he felt her tingling. His instincts told him she was on the verge of exploding, on the verge of blacking out. *Now!* He yelled, *God, I love you baby,* then his hands relaxed.

It was all because of *In the Know* magazine, why I was breaking down. At least, *In the Know* was the final straw. Well, no, Arthur Mandelbaum was the final straw. That is, Arthur

Mandelbaum in *In the Know* was the final straw. That's not accurate either: if I hadn't locked myself into my one room at the Dakota, if I hadn't been down, way down, then I would have never picked up *In the Know*. And I would have never seen the seven-page layout and four-photo spread on Arthur Mandelbaum.

If. But there were no "ifs," only facts. And the facts were that in my mirror my face looked like suicide and death and my body looked like a Mercedes touring sedan. Hunter Thompson on a bender couldn't have been in drearier shape. I was unsightly, unseen, broken out. Overnight my eyebrows and legs had turned into Sherwood Forest. I knew if I dared show myself at Elizabeth Arden's the waxing department would scream, "Get out, you beast." Summers were not my beauty season, not Florida Burns' special time to shine. And this summer was the worst on record, this June was a complete mark-down. Thirty warm days could have been condensed into less than a page in my daily calendar. A half acre of white space was filed under month number six. My date book was crying out for company, any notation to fill in the lines. Boring! I was so boring, mostly to myself. An eggplant had replaced what I used to call my brain.

So what can an eggplant do but read *Modern Screen* and *In the Know?* How much TV could one eggplant absorb in a day? I was print-starved. But the only print I could digest were the fan mags; like an addict I gave up and inhaled them. Masochist! *In the Know's* opening section, "Parties-People-Places," contained a dozen snaps; I scanned the group for Peaches and Jay. Yes, now (to the outside world) we were on first-name terms, now to anyone within earshot I *tutoyered* him. Behind his back, that is. Being shut out was one thing, but maintaining my image was another. If only for her loyal readers, Florida Burns had her reputation to uphold.

But even my reputation was beginning to slip badly. The Queen of Dish was striking out. "What's the gossip? Tell me everything!" a studio exec would demand on the phone. Instead of answering, I would stutter. Instead of trading news, I would wind up making jokes or worse. I would tell my source

132

something he had already read in the trades. In defense, I took up the fan mags; them *nobody* read, and I knew why. Only someone in my precarious emotional condition would have the time.

There was Peaches, bottom row left! Just her name with no label, no "Plant Doctor," no "A New Leaf's," no "Botanist." I sank lower. Anybody who does what I do knows that the dropping of her ID meant that "Pamela Rosen" (plain) had been elevated to the status of a household word. She had made it, she was a star. She even dressed the part. Take what she was wearing in the photo: a decade-old Nehru jacket tossed over her jeans. Peaches Rosen was the only girl who could get away with taking somebody else's old *shmatas* and turning them into tomorrow's news. What style! Like her belt. Yards of silver mesh studded with coral cameos, obviously one of a kind, I could tell. How? Well, not because of my peerless eye. We'd been together when she spotted it—and it was already in *my* hand. Rather than fight, I'd said, "Let's toss a coin." I think you can guess who won. "Of course we'll share . . .," Peaches had said at the time, which was the last (till now) I'd seen of my find. What to do, what to do. I wondered if I cut out her picture and mailed it, if I scrawled across the bottom a plaintive "Remember me?" . . .

I wanted her to take off on the world's longest guilt trip, at that moment I wanted her to die. She was my best friend, my comrade, my sister-under-the-skin. She was my confidante, my fan club, my shrink. Now the bitch wouldn't return my calls. Angry, I glared down at the photos. Always the same faces! Always Ryan O'Neal! Always Tatum! Always McQueen, Nicholson, Beatty, Candy B., Sylvia Miles and Andy Warhol . . . Tony and Berry! Bruce-Dern-Marion-Javits-Kenneth-J.-Lane-Polly-Bergen. When would there be a new rite of passage? When would there be a changing of the guard? And when that time came would anybody even care about this mangy trash? Would I?

I gasped. Then I got scared. How could I question the basic validity of my stock and trade, how could I admit doubt? Any columnist would sooner die. Because when gossip queens start grappling with an issue that large, that abstract, there can only be one logical next step: to wallow in self-hate about what you do; then to turn your face away and descend to ex-columnist's limbo. I wasn't ready. Gossip! I'd built my career on it, thrived on it, nurtured it, created it. I lived on the phone, I had three lines. I had, I hoped, titillated more housewives and angered more stars than there were in the heavens, and why? So I could be reduced like a high school sophomore to asking, "What's it all for?" Was I going to let the fact that Cher's manager slammed the phone in my face send me into an identity *crise?* Toughen up, that's what I had to do. Which meant not letting little things—like letters, or the lack of them—get stuck in my craw.

Those letters could send me over the edge. Take the one that arrived yesterday from "E. E., Albany, Georgia." "Dear Florence Berne," she began (I knew it was a "she," they always were), "Could you find out for me where Barbra Streisand buys her wigs? There's $25 for you, if you do it in the next thirty days."

Are letters like that what Hedda and Louella used to call a "power base"? Does Rona Barrett have to stomach reader requests? But that wasn't all: it was getting tougher and tougher to fill eight inches, and I was forced to fall back on every scum-ridden trick of my trade.

Like *foners:* whoever dreamt Florida Burns would be reduced to relying on "foners"? "Would Ann-Margaret care to comment on her beauty secrets?" I'd demand of her press agent, her manager, even the maid, if that's who answered my call. Then I'd move on: I'd dial Joan Hackett, Margaux Hemingway, Cybill Shepherd . . . Glenda Jackson! Three days it could take to excavate these gems, sometimes even more. It took a week of solid digging to learn that Joan Hackett's beauty tip was a circle of rouge applied to the end of her nose. For fourteen days I waited on tenterhooks for Glenda Jackson's agent to confirm that she'd dealt with her varicose veins the only logical way: through the surgical blade. I ask you, was this what the daughter of Burns' Food Kings had been bred for?

Seemingly so, but even worse: I didn't know why I was lagging behind. My steppingstone theory of upward mobility was passing me by; my Five-Year Plan was under attack. It's one thing to stumble out of J. School and answer an ad for a bona fide reporting job only to find yourself with the mixed blessing of writing your very own column and securing a mini-media base, but it's quite another to find yourself seized by *anomie*. I was losing ground fast and floundering, I was starting to drown. Paranoid, me? Well . . . to paraphrase a cliché, even paranoids get persecuted, and I knew at the Tower Syndicate, my ass was on the line.

Brian Milman's lips were puckered for a Sicilian kiss, obviously any second the ax would fall. Ridiculous? Hardly. Every sign was there. Take the Tuesday before the previous Friday. A memo—by messenger, yet—was delivered to my door: "Mistakes and Inaccurately Reported Data in TELL ME EVERYTHING 6/7." I couldn't believe Milman's gall. On the memo were ten little slips so minor any right-minded editor would have passed over them.

So, of course, Brian Milman hadn't. How was I to know that Rita Hayworth wasn't sixty-three? How was I to know that Paramount had already announced they were canceling their Nazi-hunter bio? Was I to blame for reprinting an item about Minelli which *Variety* had run in May?

The heat was on. Milman was breaking lunch dates, cracking down on my expenses, not returning calls. This was what they called foreshadowing. I didn't have to be a prophet to read the writing on the wall he had me backed up against.

There was only one solution: *avoidance.* I snapped *In the Know*'s pages like elastic bands, past the columns and the profiles, past the sports stars and the authors, till finally something caught my eye.

I back-flipped, then I died. ARTHUR MANDELBAUM (Arthur Mandelbaum?) was smeared across *In the Know!* The headline screamed: "SUPER JOCK!! 34 YEAR OLD STOCKBROKER CONQUERS PADDLE TENNIS!" And there were photos: "Mandelbaum at his Manhattan racket club showing off his form"; "Mandelbaum jogging through Battery Park en route to his Wall Street office"; "Mandelbaum on telephone placing orders during a normal, hectic day." Unbelievable. It was Arthur Mandelbaum, all right, mismatched Adidas, rumpled hair, spare tire, and all.

Arthur Mandelbaum! I was having an acute attack of déjà vu; I was flashing back, way back, to the Museum of Modern Art, a steamy Sunday—just like this one—only four (could it be five?) years before. Those were the days when I made an effort, I'd go anywhere, do anything, that might lead me to a man. Courage? I had it in droves, my confidence soared.

Nothing stopped me. I was a pro at the pickup, a master of the artful eye. I knew from a distance that Arthur Mandelbaum was different; he may have looked like a schlepper, but something about him made me smile.

Take his clothes. Where his shoes should have been there were blacktops; for clothes a flannel shirt was shoved into cords—in July! But it was his lead-in, that was the killer: "I'm the number-three seeded racket-ball player in the world. Within five years, I'll be number one." What comedians, what kidders, these boys from the Bronx were! It had taken me all summer to convince him to stop putting himself down. The lengths he'd go, playing out his charade: he even had ratings books on his shelf that had printed his name inside.

"Explain that!" he'd demand. "And *that.*" Arthur Mandelbaum would be pointing to triumph after triumph on the Ivy League rating books' pages.

But I, in my own small way, was equally relentless and, in retrospect, devoid of charm. "There have to be two Arthur Mandelbaums, sweetheart. And I'm still waiting to meet the *other one*—with the duplex on Park." This was the kind of thing I'd say.

Up till this very moment, I had perceived our entire summer as nothing more than a frolic, a game. Fantasy! I let him have it, let him think he'd convinced me; *yes, of course,* he had a seat on the Stock Exchange! Let him think that he'd snaked me into believing that Mandelbaum the Real and Mandelbaum the Mitty were a hand and a glove. What did truth matter when I

136

was convinced that his eccentricities masked nothing more than an educated tennis-shoed no-goodnik Jewish bum.

So, all Arthur Mandelbaum and I had between us was . . . *fun*. And that we had in spasms, in loads. He was a thirty-four-year-old teeny-bopper, he was corny and crazy; like tourists we'd ride the Staten Island Ferry, we'd hit Reuben's for cheesecake before dawn. The late-night air would be thick as angora, making clothes stick to the backs of our thighs. Even the waiters at Reuben's could sniff the promise of sex that hung low in the air, but it was just that . . . a promise, nothing more. Complicity! They'd hide us in the restaurant's Siberia booth and we would neck (all night) like two kids: Arthur would spoon cheesecake in my mouth like he was coming inside me, then I would reach for him and grab him you know where. And the whole time I was thinking: this is what it means to be young and happy in New York, this is what they were talking about in *My Sister Eileen*. This is what the world must have been like pre-sexual revolution, this was how living single in Manhattan had always taken shape in my dreams.

I was losing myself—to say nothing of my column—in reverie. For hours, I could be happy locked in my room with just my mental Mandelbaum summer scrapbooks. But, this was no way to spend a life. Better I should find a way to salvage my career, better I should walk out the door and look for the bravado I'd lost, the raw chutzpah which had once driven me to victory. Instead, I was fixated on only one point, the life-shaking question: Had Arthur Mandelbaum and I ever actually gone all the way?

I stared at his crotch in the photograph trying to remember, trying to evoke more of that summer than a Reuben's cheesecake. Did we do it? Did we fuck even once? Because I knew if we'd done it once, there wouldn't have been a second time. At least not that summer, not when I still had my dreams.

Which were these: I wanted to be loved for me alone, not because I was a convenient and succulent walking side of meat. Was that what happened with me and Mandelblitz? Had I fucked him once, then in abject terror and anger run away?

Once he'd rid me of my last trump—if Arthur Mandelbaum had shifted the lines of power, turned the tables, and called me on my own game (all the while thinking the femme-fille had indeed been tamed)—then what?

All of this is hypothetical because what I might have done was positively freak . . . *and run!* Or I would have felt sorry for both him and me because with my rules—please-don't-fuck-me-if-all-you-want-is-fun—nobody was coming out ahead. Not me, not Arthur Mandelbaum; not a dozen or so other pretenders to the throne; not one of a list of top-notch candidates had ever passed the aforementioned Florida Burns Ultimate Test.

I remembered the truth. I had panicked and run when Arthur Mandelbaum began teasing me in a very (to me) personal and hateful way.

"My God, Florida. . . ." He would laugh, *"My-God-but-you-are-tough."* Ha-ha-ha, but we all know what Freud said, that's right, *there are no jokes!*

He didn't understand the real marshmallow cream-puff me; didn't understand that what looked like brass was only soft pink fluff. Wasn't that what it had been about?

This was Kvetcher's Paradise. Even I couldn't endure the throes of agony for long. So I flipped back to *In the Know,* determined to learn—if nothing else—how the fan magazine punched up its lines. I perked up. Maybe I could find Tell Me Everything a new home in *In the Know,* maybe I could fry Milman's ass before he had his way with mine.

Then I caught "Superjock!!"'s last paragraph. "Married seven years, wife Linda, also a stockbroker, teaches summers at UCLA."

Arthur Mandelbaum, a husband? Somebody else's man? That putz had asked me to marry him!

Another wave of self-hate washed over me, I was tumbled into despair right along with it. Florida Burns, girl-dupe. Florida Burns . . . fool! Just like the women I scorned; a victim. Even the good times had been fakes.

Only one issue remained; what was I going to do to get back at them? How could I retaliate against both Peaches and

Mandelbaum? Another woman would have pulled on a see-through top and hurried down West Seventy-second, looking for a convenient revenge one-night stand. Another woman might have reached into the dope box and rolled a giant joint. Or called seventeen friends in California, making the men who own the phone company beam. Not me, though. For the resourceful-but-depressed Florida Burns, for your basic fledgling household word, only one panacea would do.

Dial-a-Deli.

I reached for the phone and ticked off my order: a half spring chicken, potato salad, a side of chopped liver and rye, half a cheesecake. What about . . . the ice cream! The milk! Quickly, I dialed back, then I sat down to wait. For company, I summoned Walter Cronkite, adjusted the pink tones of his cheeks. *Plans.* For a placemat I would use *In the Know,* I'd drip poultry schmaltz all over Arthur Mandelbaum. My after-dinner entertainment would be smearing mustard and mayo on Peaches Rosen's face. Bring on the elephant gun, I was after blood. Seeking vengeance, I began to get iron strength. FUCK-'EM-ALL! I smiled, then I resolved, "Victim no more." Which meant no more complaining, no more whining, Florida Burns would become a master at her special way of fighting. I would call it: below-the-black-belt.

I threw open the window to shout my battle cry, turning back when I heard the delivery boy ring the bell. I brought in my orgy, then turned up the news *molto voce.* Tonight *was* my night! I'd learn how to puke with milk and sherbet, but I wondered . . . would the sounds from the newscast be able to muffle the noise of one overstuffed columnist behind her closed bathroom door?

About the only thing that Cherie Rivers wasn't annoyed with was her navy T-shirt. Her lead item on "Tinseltown Wrap-up" might have fallen apart, but she was sure of one thing: her navy T-shirt would mask any underarm stains. *Thank God.* She would need a lot of camouflage for tonight's taping. Cherie Rivers could feel her pits getting damper and damper, a trickle was beginning to form underneath her seamless bra.

Telemedia! What a name for a TV station, especially one this uptight. Take *l'affaire brassière.* Cherie Rivers prided herself on her body—she fasted, she dieted. She chain-smoked, but she went to jazz class from five to seven every night of her life. She was weightless, hipless, and breastless. "Two bee stings" was how her boyfriend described what Telemedia insisted she should stuff into a bra. Sexist! Since 1967 she hadn't met anyone who still wore a bra, but now her station was getting complaints. Maybe she should ask to be transferred to KPOP-LA. Maybe she'd like Southern California. She'd heard people were real mellow out there. In New York, nobody was mellow.

She was beginning to feel like a San Quentin inmate, particularly tonight, twenty-nine minutes before air time. Worse: she couldn't even get any sympathy, much less a replacement item. Not on a Saturday night in June, not when all her sources had left for the shore. *This was a first.* A Cherie Rivers broadcast with a hole like a picture window. Because Cherie Rivers—so the hyperbole went—never missed a deadline, would die rather than miss a show.

So now she was smoking True Blue after True Blue in her cell on the thirty-third floor, waiting for somebody, *anybody,* to return one fucking call. She'd made dozens of them, looking for dirt. Goddamn that Rusty Leibowitz! If it hadn't been for her she wouldn't be trapped in an airless cave watching her G.E. Big Ben ticking off the seconds. The minute hand was a machete plunging deeper and deeper into her innards, driving Cherie Rivers over the edge.

Rusty Leibowitz! Whoever thought they'd both wind up "in communications," who would have thought that Cherie (Rabinsky) Rivers and Rusty Leibowitz would ever see each other again after the closing day of the Class of '62 (Girls' High, Kew Gardens, Queens)? They had sat next to each other in yearbook meetings and that was exactly where their relationship stayed. Until a decade later. "Sherrreee Rabinskeee!! You look faaaabulous!" Rusty had screamed across the first floor of

Bloomingdale's the moment she'd laid eyes on the former fatty. But it had taken Cherie one beat longer to recognize Rusty, with her nose job and streak job and equally toned-down body. Thrilled! In their joy at bumping into each other they completely forgot an entire series of teen-age grudges which had once soured their friendship. The time Cherie had called Rusty "a cow" in the Girls' High downstairs bathroom. The time Rusty had grafted Cherie's head onto the body of a four-hundred-pound janitor for the yearbook photo collage.

Childhood rivalry, they would call it . . . should they even remember. They were way beyond that now. Both were working in the Entertainment Industry, Rusty as Executive Secretary and Girl Friday to Norman Weiss of Weiss, Kaplan, and Bell, the hottest of the hot, as show business press agents go. But Cherie was a star! At least her mother thought so. Cherie did too; she just wished that Telemedia had a larger share of the Manhattan audience. Up against the eleven o'clock ABC Newscenter, she was barely a 16 in the ratings, her share had only once risen over 22 percent. Still, people came up to her on the streets, mail poured in from all five of New York City's boroughs.

Hate mail too. Lots of nut stuff came in neatly tied sacks delivered to the Telemedia mail room. Once she'd opened a shoe box and a foot-long rubber flesh-cock had tumbled out. The card was typed: "A pair of balls like the prick you wish you had," it had read. She was always getting do-it-yourself kits. A douche bag with a note reading, "Take it and stuff it," likewise a Fleet enema bag. She wondered if Rona Barrett had a staff to protect her from these humiliations. Maybe there should be a columnists' union. If only there were more than three columnists, they might be able to band together, wield a little power.

She longed for the days of Hedda and Louella, she longed to be able to ruin careers. What fun they must have had! Cherie Rivers was sure that Hedda Hopper had never been stuck for a lead-off, nineteen minutes before the red light was switched on. If only Rusty Leibowitz had double-checked about Marlon Brando before she'd given her the go. So much for Rusty's "flawless" ear: she only heard scraps of conversations, just the tail bones of the real meat. Even scraps Cherie Rivers would kill for, now that her regular sources had fled out of town. So for this "exclusive," she'd blown two days in the sun. And what had she wound up with? An exclusive *nothing,* she was holding the bag.

Her own fault, really. From the first it sounded too good to be true. Brando doing another Indian? When would he stop running that Red Power stuff into the ground? It was so *over,* but Brando wasn't getting it. He had thought a studio would spring for $14 million. Within a week, all the majors had wired "no dice." So he was making the rounds of the independents, trying to get a deal at Homerica, Metropolitan, any place he could.

It just goes to show. Cherie Rivers' first instinct had been right: the slob will never get the project off the ground. Ever. But Rusty had sworn on the lives of her unborn children that Brando had closed a deal. Ha! She had written a long story— ninety-five seconds' worth—then she'd gotten the call.

"You're going to kill me," Rusty had started out, "but Marlon's left for Tahiti and the last thing he says to his secretary and housekeeper before he goes to the airport was '*Pass*adena!' Can you believe the nerve of that slob?" Then Rusty had paused. "You're not mad at me, are you?"

Cherie Rivers felt the blood spill from her veins. She'd have to fall back on her support flank. She looked down at her legal pad, covered with notes. How could so many tips be so wrong? How could this business be filled with so many liars and sycophants? She thought for sure she must know every one of them. Her eyes buzzed over names—check Carol Burnett's face-lift, a possible split for the Bob Redfords, a sex ring in a movieland spa—the list went on and on. Innuendo, rumor, whisperings, trash. And the worst part of it was, none of it was true. Not one stinking item rang like a gong.

But wait. She had heard something, but what? About Jason Jaffe? Or was it Pacino? The other night. She'd even made a note, on her spiral, crammed it into her bag. Furiously, she threw lipsticks and nail files, dumped everything in her wallet out on the floor. Aha! Dynamite! She found the paper;

agitated, she looked at the clock. No time to check it, but her instincts had never failed her before.

She was right! It was Jason Jaffe. Now she remembered. A producer had told her all about it. Her source was someone who knew him—as he'd phrased it—"terribly well." Drugs or booze, the man had said, it's no wonder his career, once so promising, had gone so cold. The producer had told her to check into it, explained who to call.

Desperate! She had just minutes to go. Cherie Rivers nibbled at the point of her tongue trying to think up a plan. She'd have to use fillers, recap Jason Jaffe's career. *Jacaranda* and *Day-Glo!!* would use up forty seconds, Pamela Rosen was good for another thirty-two. Her brows had crocheted into a scowl, she jammed the back of a press release into her machine. Relentlessly she began to type. *Caution!* She would have to say nothing and have it seem like "news." Dangerous waters these, talking about Jason Jaffe's self-destructiveness, his botch-up of a once-promising career. She had fifteen minutes to plug the hole in her show.

Cherie Rivers closed her eyes and sighed, then leaned back in her chair. She was spinning cartwheels on a tightwire, balanced somewhere between viewer boredom and libel. But she knew she could find a pristine comment, a nonmalicious quote. She could feel the lines in her forehead deepening, felt small balls of sweat forming on the back of her neck. Mitchum's; she'd have to rub Mitchum's back there in the summer, then buy Preparation H. Cherie Rivers had just heard that was the way models erased the lines from their face. She laughed, suddenly, all alone on the thirty-third floor. Preparation H for crows' feet! She couldn't wait to rush home and try it. Energized, she continued her attack. Fuck him, he was just an actor, which, in Cherie Rivers' mind, meant *what the hell.* On the last Saturday in June, nobody-but-nobody would be watching her show, she'd be lucky if "Tinseltown Wrap-up" would clear a Nielsen 10. Might as well shoot for the top, at least have some fun. Jason Jaffe rumored to be unhirable? Fine! She'd say exactly that. She began to relax, took out her powder and comb. Even more than going on unprepared, Cherie

143

Rivers hated looking shiny; she had a theory that someday somebody interesting might actually turn her on. For that moment alone, she wanted to be ready. With a matte-finished nose, she knew, if nothing else, she looked good, damn good, for her age. She was pushing thirty-five, why did her fortieth birthday seem to be no more than five minutes away?

Marcie Laster was in a rage. She was dressed—to the nines—in a fluted skirt, a sharkskin blazer. Her good lime silk blouse was tucked underneath. Real stockings and high-gloss-sling-back-thousand-strap pumps finished off the look. Fuckin' shoes were killing her corns, fuckin' acid from Jean Naté spray was staining her shirt. So she kicked off her shoes, ripped off her blazer, but nothing helped. She had overdressed and she was angry. Inside the cramped room—stacked high with files—there wasn't an extra ounce of air. Marcie Laster wasn't sure she could take it another second.

She was molting in the research stacks of the New York Police Department Forensic Crime Detection Unit. The temperature felt like a thousand degrees. No wonder cops are crazy, Marcie thought. How could she have let herself be roped into this? Detective Murray Sandler, NYPD, was standing guard outside, making sure nobody broke in to see her copying out notes. Already she'd started spiral number two, she'd been writing for two hours straight, she'd be lucky if she got home before dark. Murray Sandler had guaranteed the stacks would be empty; "You'll have them all to yourself," he had said. He hadn't told her it would be like a microwave oven; that Marcie Laster found out for herself. That wasn't all she was learning, though. His ten-inch file was marked "Confidential #654987," which meant that it was chockablock with names, vital statistics, case histories, dates of crimes. The fat files, Sandler had explained, contained cases in which no arrests could be made; these were the tough ones, baffling, unsolvable, held up in the courts. Rife with drama, thus perfect movie material. Sandler had promised that #654987 alone would knock the other eight thousand uncaught criminals stalking the Naked City flat on their collective feet.

Murray Sandler was hoping for a deal.

And he wasn't the only one. Since *The French Connection, Super-Cops,* and *Freebie and the Bean,* an epidemic had hit all the movie studios, a virus had spread to every producer. Suddenly cops were everywhere, dying to spill their guts, dying to cash in on an off-the-cuff story conference, for a small fee, of course. Marcie Lester had met a million Serpicos, each one hoping to have his palm greased. Seeing what the men in blue were like was enough to turn you into a Charlie Mansonite. Marcie Laster felt that if you gave the NYPD half a chance, they'd hop the midnight flight to Hollywood and bunk in *en masse* at the Chateau Marmont. Just get one of them on the budget as a "consultant" and it would be no parking tickets for the rest of your life.

Murray Sandler swore that he was different. Tenacious! If nothing else, Det. Sandler had staying power. For six months he had been shuffled down the political ranks at Metropolitan Pictures. He was bounced from the Chairman to the President to the Head of Production, to *his* secretary, and all the way back to the East Coast. Then Sandler was sent from the East Coast Creative Head to the Metropolitan Story Department, bouncing down lower and lower till finally he hit absolute rock bottom.

Marcie Laster would see him Friday at four.

Neither Marcie Laster nor Murray Sandler was aware of these corporate nuances. Murray Sandler, in fact, was just happy for an appointment. He was smiling when a pleasant-faced secretary finally waved him in, signaling that Miss Laster was done with her call. But she hadn't been. The girl with the mahogany hair shaped like a helmet and the nose tipped like a dart was screaming into a mouthpiece. She looked up, nodded, then motioned for Det. Sandler to sit down. Her voice rose like the wind. He wondered if she was talking to somebody thousands of miles away, if maybe they couldn't hear.

"I CAN'T GUARANTEE 250 PLUS TEN PERCENT. . . . I CAN'T

PROMISE YOU BUPKES, BUBBE," she yelled, then abruptly hung up. "Agents!" she said, then waited for more than a noncommittal stare. "I'd offer you some coffee, but I don't think it's very good. It was made this morning. You don't want any, do you?" she went on, not noticing his nod. She still couldn't make her new Yiddish vocabulary roll like velvet off her tongue. ". . . So if you could just tell me what I can do for you then-let-me-reschedule. . . . I'm awful-lee late." Her head shot out the door. "*Tina!* TEEN-A! TEEEEN-AHHHH!" She waited, lips pursed in a kiss. "TEEEEEEN-AHHH!!"

"WHAT FOR FUCKIN' CHRIST'S SAKES?" A voice boomed from half a mile down the hall.

"Coffee! Get me some coffee!" She turned to Murray Sandler, uncomfortable in his off-duty double-knit suit. "You don't want any, do you?"

"No thanks."

"Just one . . . Tina-love. . . ."

"GET IT YOURSELF. I'm Xeroxing." Her heels clacked like castanets on the other side of the wall.

Marcie Laster's face flushed, her index finger picked at the polish on her thumb. "I don't know what's gotten into her. Anyway, you were saying something about a 'property,' some crime case you're working on?"

"I wasn't saying anything. I was going to let this case speak for itself." Sandler pulled out a folder, laid it on the desk. "I can't leave this in your office. . . . Police property, you know."

Marcie Laster started on her other thumb. "*Listen.* Just forget it, then. I never read 'properties' the minute they come in to me." She leaned back in her chair, pointed toward a tower of scripts blocking her window. "I've got forty-seven projects that can't wait. They've been backed up for a month. Every day the coast is calling me and I'm putting them off."

"Look, miss. It's a city law."

Marcie Laster frowned, then forced herself to smile. You never could tell with these detectives, he might have a friend on the executive floor. Maybe Murray Sandler fixed the tickets for Metropolitan's president. She would be nice. "Okay. Now. I'm going to close my eyes and I want you to tell me the story.

146

Very slowly. And if I can see it play in my head—in panavision —then, Detective Sandler, you might have yourself a deal."

He began to talk, at first in spurts. Then gaining confidence, his voice expanded like yeast. At first his case played like a Police Story summer rerun, but as he expounded, the drama positively came alive. All the more so because of Murray Sandler's repeated insistence that everything in it—the rapes, assaults, homicidal intent—were certified and well-documented truth. "Right from this file in my hand," he said at the end of his three-minute synopsis.

Marcie Laster's eyes opened. "But why a movie? Why don't you just arrest the creep, throw him in jail?"

Sandler's face, already florid, deepened yet another full hue. "Because he gets off each and every time. He looks normal, talks normal. So he's released—I know, it's been three times straight—on his own 'recognizance,' for 'psychological examination.' You think he ever shows up?" He was agitated, his hands played with the file, flipping it over and over on top of his lap. "Listen. You think I like wasting six months of my life going from office to office, seeing TV people, movie people, magazine people? I don't know what the hell I'm doing here except that I saw David Durk on the news and he said any cop with a legitimate complaint should take it somewhere out in public . . . air it out." Sandler paused, pounded his hand on the manila casing of #654987. "*God damn it,* I'm sorry, miss. But for two years I've tracked this guy and I'm going to get him if it's the last thing I do; even if it means having to sit through a hundred meetings like this. I don't mean that *personally,* of course, but this is like a . . . I don't know, a thing with me, you know what I mean?"

"So I see." Half listening, she lit a cigarette.

"*I don't think that you do.* Don't you think there are some good cops here that actually might want to see the laws enforced, the streets cleaned up? Listen, I'm no pollyanna, but I got kids. And I don't want all these perverts, lunatics, the sickos keeping them from having a normal life. Have you ever thought that there are some of us who might not be on the take, despite what the newspapers say?"

147

Marcie Laster watched Sandler loosen his tie, then *silent,* she flicked an ash into her wastebasket. "To tell you the truth, I never really thought about it."

But from somewhere deep inside her psyche, a voice was speaking to Marcie Laster. She was beginning to respond to the policeman's heat. Murray Sandler's sincerity, his kamikaze zeal, his genuine emotional display touched her. She had never seen such true commitment.

At midnight the two of them were still closeted in Marcie Laster's tiny office. Into the morning they remained, reviewing Sandler's file, with Marcie taking notes and grilling him about the most minute elements of Case #654987. *Will this one talk; will she give me a release; how did you find out about that one; who told you to contact her; what kind of condition was she in when she called?* On and on into the dawn it went. For the first time, Marcie Laster, girl friday, knew she was on to something big, a possible turning point in her own life and maybe a springboard out of Metropolitan Pictures, if she did her homework right.

What was she going to do with this potential headline-making material? How could Sandler think she was going to squander it on a dumb movie treatment! She had other plans, but she would keep them to herself. No way she was going to discuss any of this with other journalists, friends of hers with so-called "media connections."

It was her turn to act. She would spend every weekend at police headquarters, she would seize the time, carve out her own opportunity. Lucky it was summer, the whole world would think she was out of town. And maybe, in effect, she was on her way *somewhere,* to an obviously better place.

The first sign how his day would turn out had been in the morning's *Wall Street Journal.* The lead story in the left-hand column had jolted him right out of bed: "McDonald's Encounters Problems in Suburbia, Oil Shortage, Shifting Neighborhood Patterns Held Cause." *Christ, if the VW of fast food was feeling the crunch—and in summer—then how, he wondered, was La Taquita going to survive?*

Who would have thought he'd ever have to wrestle with that question? He was depressed, but not just because business had slumped. Mike Markman had awakened alone. A vague sadness came over him thinking of the previous night. He was baffled, and a little annoyed. He thought he'd done everything right. At a dinner party two nights before he'd met a woman—a terrific New York type which meant blond, bright, and borderline frantic. She worked at the Kleiner Galleries, her specialty was African art. Perfect! He had called her promptly after taking her home in a cab. After dinner last night they had held hands and walked up through the park. He hadn't wanted to press, but would she like to come in for a drink? She had seemed to be having fun. She had admired his photographs. "An original Weston!" she had exclaimed, then lifted her face eagerly when he made the shyest attempt to kiss her. So they had collapsed, falling deep into his creamy butter-soft leather Chesterfield, a guaranteed turn-on just by itself alone.

He knew it had been one of the smartest buys he'd ever made—$2000 for a sofa! He thought he'd have apoplexy when he flipped the price tag in the D & D building showroom, but he let his better judgment get away from him and was he glad. The way the mocha kid felt to an arm, touching a leg, enveloping him, Mike Markman could lie on his Chesterfield for hours. It helped him relax. Women, he was sure, found it just as erotic.

Still, this one had left in the middle of the night. Now what the hell was he supposed to think about that? The way she zipped on her jeans, the swagger in her voice when she pecked him on the cheek, the utter disregard for *his* feelings when she said, "Thanks, I never like to stay over the first time, it's *policy,* you know what I mean."

No, damn it, he didn't know. His feelings had been trampled on. The way she said it was more like a war cry than a question. What was happening to women anyway, what were they trying to prove? This was the second time in a month this had happened to him, He was tired of being made to feel responsible for the *lumpen* sins of every unmarried male heterosexual. He had needs too, plenty of them. Somewhere

149

there had to be a woman who wasn't fighting the post-thirty blues.

He doubted he would call the Kleiner Gallery again, the more he thought about it. Who needed the aggravation? Not him, not now, not when Mike Markman had real problems to weigh him down.

This early heat wave wasn't making life any easier. Now he was walking through Central Park, cursing the humidity. Nothing stirred the air, children's voices coming up from the field seemed muffled. The temperature was a premature ninety degrees.

Why had he stayed in town? Mike Markman couldn't believe he had done this to himself, he was all alone on the last weekend in June. Everyone he knew—and their families—had gone to the beach; at least in Southampton there might be a chance for a breeze. He was lost in his discomfort, strolling miserably over the hill. A girl on a bike whizzed by him pedaling fast. Without warning, he'd felt her ten-speed come up behind him, then he'd heard her give a soft beep to her horn. Bicyclists! Seeing him jump out of his skin, she had smiled, then yelled, "Scuse me"; without slowing down, she flew past. Her curly hair and tennis racket became a dot disappearing over the crest of the hill. *Christ!* Was that the girl he'd been seeing in his neighborhood? Was she following him everywhere he went? For an instant Mike Markman wondered whether or not she had been making fun of him. Then he admired her abandon and let himself think that some free spirits might have manners as well.

Then the heat engulfed him again. God damn this weather, when would it rain? Not that he was concerned about this city, New York could be steamed off the face of the map for all he cared. Just let the heat wave subside in his territories; Virginia, Kentucky, Maryland, the Carolinas. Nobody ate *picante* in a heat wave, his tacos and burritos didn't have a Chinaman's chance. No way you could break even on grape drinks alone, and more: his Coca-Cola supplier had just doubled his costs.

What a fool he'd been in 1967. The blond man approaching Mike Markman on the Stanford campus had a plan. He'd been pitching 31 Flavors, Baskin-Robbins was the name of the firm. The guy had shown him figures, Mike Markman could have had his own franchise for a mere $4000 down. "Bubblegum ice cream? Licorice? Pumpkin Pie?" He had laughed, then made other plans.

Mike Markman sucked in a breath, thinking about who had the last laugh now. He knew the B-R recruiter was cackling all the way to the bank. Mike Markman was headed for the bank too, only he wasn't smiling, not today. Not when his New York location was held up in the courts, not when he could predict every word he'd hear from the mole at the Chase. The schmuck was a broken record. "Cut costs, cut costs; *standardize!* Get your overhead down," was the way he'd start out, then he'd move on. "Automation! Can't a machine replace two counter help; what about drive-through? Get rid of the free parking! Think about the property taxes you'll save." For a finale, he knew the mole would shove Pup 'n' Taco and Jack 'n the Box's latest figures right into his face.

Extending his credit line hadn't always been this tough. Once upon a time when he was starting out—could it now be eight years ago?—the bankers had clamored for his approach. Once upon a time, the mole had loved him. "Humanizing fast food," was how the Chase Manhattan had described what he was up to during their honeymoon days. Then they'd hailed him as some kind of hero, congratulated him on his strict avoidance of the plastic approach. Mike Markman had imposed his purist's vision on La Taquita. He was proud of all he had done; glad he'd rebuffed the men from Baskin-Robbins "31," especially after he'd read the list of ingredients that went into their ten-gallon drums.

All in all, if he should lose every dime tomorrow, he still wouldn't change one decision he'd made. Well, maybe *one.* His only mistake had been the expansion, he could kick himself for not staying small: he hated himself for not doing more to keep La Taquita under control. Twelve had been just the right size, but now there were twenty-four. Impossible! He couldn't find management, couldn't hire people who cared about little

151

things, who had an eye for detail: the hanging plants, the spotless ceramic counters, the authentic Oaxaca tile floors.

Mike Markman cared about every chair, every flower, he could recite from memory a list of every tile and pipe size his restaurant used. He was dogged, but not out of some perverse sense of aesthetics, not because he was anal or uptight. La Taquita was his childhood, thus a labor of love; his happiest memories were linked to its smells. Always a certain combination: mimosa spiked with garlic; bougainvillaea mixed with an ever-present *picante;* a corn tortilla being steamed over an oven of fiery stones. Mike Markman's mother's house in Cuernavaca—her "haciendita," as she called it—had always been filled with these smells. Her kitchen was the center of the world; Toby Markman had studied at Cordon Bleu but now taught *la comida típica four* times a week instead. "Grand cuisine no longer is relevant," she'd explain to each of her summer students when they'd plunk down their $100 fee.

Curling out of the Mexican kitchen windows would be other smells: La Haciendita was smothered with flowers, festooned with marching armies of red roses and pink camellias; purple azaleas and geraniums so brilliant they could aptly be called "jungle red." Carnations! Toby Markman had an entire trellis of peppermint-striped ones, she swore they were the only example of the species around. Come spring, she used to brag that she was "the one American who could convince an entire wall of English posies to bloom on command."

The flowers would still be there come the summer, when Mike Markman hopped off his plane. He was a child of Southern California, shuttled between parents like yesterday's dreams. Winters with his father meant twelve rooms, ocean view, in the Pacific Palisades. Which meant he went to Harvard, but not the right one. No, Harvard School for Boys, specifically Los Angeles' finest; he hated to think about what their worst might portend. Mike Markman's best friend—the son of a Paramount producer—was so sheltered, he was sent to tree-climbing school, only in Roddy's case that meant the tree-climbing tutor was brought to the house. On Halloween, the

Harvard class was dispatched to Beverly Hills to trick or treat in limousines.

Remembering Roddy Friedman, he broke into a smile, then continued walking down the hill. He had escaped Emmanuel Markman and Sons, fled from his father's pride in his craft. For Manny Markman, this meant throwing up nine-room Mediterranean-style ranches, docked on .75 acres of the Malibu hillside. The asking price, a steal, at 150 grand. And, paradoxically, Manny Markman's suburb was considered a bargain in Los Angeles realtors' eyes.

Mike Markman would rather die than be exiled back to the Pacific coast. He hated it, hated the endless vistas of shrapnel-colored water and man-made beaches; hated the foothills, the palm trees. He hated the way the Los Angeles freeways stretched on and on forever.

But now even Mexico was just as bad. Was no place out of the developers' grasp? Even the small towns were feeling the rub. Last time he'd gone, he'd gotten the honky-tonk blues from what had happened to the place. Kentucky Fried Chicken and McDonald's were more than just pockmarks, they'd given Cuernavaca a terminal case.

They'd driven out to his favorite bodega, the tiny grocería with the eat-in counter and the homemade molés, two blocks from Ivan Illich's institute.

A family had run it, had Casavera been their last name? *No matter*. His bodega was gone and his mother too, but he knew both of them would feel he'd done them proud. La Taquita had been modeled after his sense-memory of the roadside stand and his mother . . . well, she should have been named the first Jewish saint.

He kicked at a rock asleep on the road, then blinked very hard. Memories! Who needed to dredge up all that history, not today, not when he had to prepare to meet with the bank. Why were they after him? He deserved all the help he could get! He'd done all his homework before opening each stand; memorized demographics, what people read, where they shopped, ate, and played. He'd taken those damn suburban weeklies, congratulated himself on how well his amateur marketing tests had paid off. Still, even in this crisis he maintained subscriptions to one or two small-town bugles, a paper in Maryland, perhaps one in downstate Maine.

He loved newspapers. Like a machine, he would always chew up his daily twenty-two. Mike Markman had always wanted to be a reporter; his fantasy life was rich and all-encompassing, he wanted to be on the sidelines of every fire, he wanted to be in the next room when whole governments fell. But he'd also wanted money, to make it in carloads, all on his own. Even in school, he'd been aware that chasing after pipe dreams was no way to own the factory. One only became tired, never rich. But Mike Markman had never been an ideal-ist, he liked to think he was a "rational man." And now he was rich (on paper), but exhausted as well. What the hell was a rational man supposed to make of that?

A line of traffic slowed his progress as he stepped out of the park onto the street. Waiting for the light to turn green, he stopped, then wiped his forehead with a bare arm. *Damn this noise.* Weren't there laws against horns in the city? Why weren't they enforced? He was getting *really* annoyed. He waited, then made up his mind to buck the traffic clogging the street. He stepped off the curb resolute, but feeling somehow a whisper of change. Mike Markman seemed a sigh shorter, as if he had wilted imperceptibly. He hoped it was from nothing more than the force of the heat.

Transcript: Telemedia, "Tinseltown Wrap-up"
Date: 30 June
Time: 10:19 PM
Announcer: Rivers, C.

Hello, everybody. Tonight "Tinseltown Wrap-up" con-tinues its special series: UPDATE! And this evening's UPDATE! viewer question is: "Whatever happened to once-promising newcomer Jason Jaffe, nominated for his performance in *Day-Glo!!* as *Silver Screen*'s Actor of the Year?"

(Pause) A very good question from "Z.B.," of Yonkers, New York. And the answer, sad to say, is more than one of the theatrical world's few closely guarded secrets. It's also a sad commentary on the abuse of creative talent by producers whose only concern is for their profits.

We all remember Jason Jaffe from his stunning Broadway debut in the 1971 revival of *Streetcar Named Desire.* Some of us still recall his freshness, his candor—his very un-starlike willingness to meet the press. We didn't want to believe the stories that Jay Jaffe had changed after the success of *Jacaranda,* his second Broadway smash. And recently, we have been routinely denying that Jaffe's ego has swollen out of all proportion to reality, requiring his plant-doctor girlfriend to nurture him back to mental health at their Long Island beach house.

Now the cause of Jaffe's troubles can be named. It was Broadway mogul Sherwin Sunneson, the producer of Jaffe's third hit, *Day-Glo!!,* who apparently doubled Jaffe's asking price to get a run-of-the-play contract from the fast-rising actor. Then, when Jaffe tired of the role after a year and asked to be released, Sunneson branded him "an incredible prima donna." While he *did* give Jaffe his freedom, it's interesting to note that Jaffe hasn't worked since—for Sunneson or anyone else.

Jason Jaffe seems to feel that Sunneson had a hand in his current ill fortune. Six months ago, when the actor ran into Sunneson at New York's Russian Tea Room, just the sight of his former producer made him challenge Sunneson to a fist fight. Constant companion Pamela Rosen prevented that, but before he left, Jay Jaffe got in one last (wink) lick: he upended Sunneson's table, bathing the millionaire producer in a stew of Russian delicacies.

Now Jason Jaffe is in a pot of trouble himself. Who *will* he work for, now that Sunneson has sworn—at Jaffe's back, as he fled the Russian Tea Room—"You'll never work again!" (shuffles paper) Whoever won't have you, Jason Jaffe, you can count on one thing—you're welcome on this show *any* time.

(wink #2) This is Cherie Rivers and another "Tinseltown Wrap-Up." Sports and weather after this. . . .

An entire month had passed by and I was still headquartered at home trying to come up with a plan. I had so little time, so much to do. My career might be on the verge of going straight to hell, but I still couldn't be stopped from trying to execute the working girl's sure-fire cure. In a nutshell: If you can't get even, get married.

Florida Burns was back on the prowl, even in July, even with the whole world camped out on Fire Island. Believe it or not, none other than Ezra Matthews had been my inspiration. Some days before a postcard with the Golden Gate Bridge in four-color artwork had been slid under my door. "Dear F.B.," it began, "Pretty that you're not out here in this fabulous city for the most romantic time anybody could ever have in their life! Are you still working on the article? Lotsa Love, E.M." How's that for chutzpah? Love-Ezra-Love-Ezra-Love-Ezra! So there might be hope after all. I hadn't seen him in months, but if the bastard was thinking about me enough to paste stamps over my address, maybe our nonaffair hadn't yet breathed its last.

It was all the evidence I needed; I would refurbish one of my old time-tested tricks. I would interview one more "bachelor," take just one more husband candidate to a Tower Syndicate lunch. Obsessive! I combed every magazine, stayed glued to every talk show on my TV. I could have written a thesis on talk shows, could have lectured for hours on Not-for-Women-Only-Mid-Day-Live-Pat - Collins - Women - Alone!-The-Early-Evening-Report - The - Late - Evening - Report-The-Harry-Reasoner-Report. Sixty Minutes! I was like a hound dog, studying populning-Report-The-Late-Evening-Report-The-Harry-Reasoner-Report. Sixty Minutes! I was like a hound dog, studying popular culture's sludge pot. As a side benefit on Dave Altchek's "Business Alive" show, I thought I spotted a prime candidate for the role of Florida Burns' leading man.

But damn these unlisted phone numbers, these bachelors trying to play coy. Altchek had lined up five beauties, all members of the Young Presidents' League. In my book, that reeked money as well, but I tuned in in time only to get three of their names. *Fine and dandy!* I caught the name of the only masculine body that had an aura of I-am-smarter-than-Florida-Burns. *Michael "Barnum"* (I was sure that was the name I'd heard) was the trophy to be hunted down. He seemed high-energy, but calm; independent, but settled down. Something told me this Barnum-bachelor might be married, his darkish hair was riddled with gray. Why did he look so familiar? Like someone I might have passed several times (then processed out) during the course of a city day. New York! Live here a few years and *everyone*, no matter how exotic, begins to look familiar.

Barnum-Barnum-Barnum? The name was preying on my mind; something told me he would be getting a call from the Tower Syndicate before I lost both my column and my absolute last dime.

If only I could find him through the jungle of information operators and unlisted names. Why couldn't I, Florida Burns, convince "411" that I was the long-lost cousin and missing heir to the hallowed Barnum name?

So I forgot about *him,* and began tracking down Bachelor Number Two. Hobart Bordon Schaeffer was his name, tack a III onto all that and you'll understand that I was so desperate I could even imagine winding up in watercress-sandwich land.

And, I asked myself, would that be so bad? I was fed up with Jewish Princes, fed up with all those mothers who'd told their sons that someday some lucky lady would get down on her hands and knees and beg to play a Jewish Prince's queen. Well, not me! There was not going to be any forced labor; no hand-squeezing the orange juice or making the waffles from scratch for Miss Florida B. You know how a JAP behaves? A JAP says to his queen in the middle of dinner, "Where's the butter? There's none on the table." At least, with Hobart Bordon whatever, there might be a chance he'd jump up and get it himself.

Pundits say that the White Anglo-Saxon Protestant breed can always be identified by its aversion to publicity. The species, it is said, only appears in the newspapers upon its birth and upon its death. *So . . . nu?* Just that Hobie Schaeffer was living proof that the Wasp publicity cliché was no longer true. He came right onto the phone, what's more was delighted to see me, would four o'clock tomorrow be too soon? I look forward to it, I said, in my most modulated and gentile of tones. Within twenty-four hours, I had buttoned myself into my super-prep navy blazer and was on his Park Avenue doorstep, knocking hard.

Don't get me wrong, I knew plenty of gentiles, growing up

in Texas you have them coming out of your ears. But you don't have WASPS! You don't have Hobart Bordon Schaeffers appearing at their doors, which is to say tall blond asparagus spears lacking only a silver helmet for one to start yodeling Siegfried. Which is to say when Hobart Bordon Schaeffer opened his door, I nearly died. Not because of the slicked-back Gatsby hair, that I could deal with. Not because of the lanky body, the aquiline nose which, turned sideways, could slice bacon. Not because of his apartment with its *de rigueur* moss-green overstuffed love seats; its lush expanses of ancient Persian rugs. What did me in was what Hobart Bordon Schaeffer was wearing, framed in the door; an emerald silk smoking jacket cut like early Clifton Webb. Only, with Hobie Schaeffer this wasn't Hollywood camp because tucked into this sartorial gesture was an ascot of snowiest silk. But more: bedded down on that were three initials, HBS III, monogrammed in silver contrast threads.

Then he spoke. "Welcome. Do sit down."

I sank like the *Nautilus* into a mountain of oyster satin. By prestidigitation a drink appeared in my hand. Within seconds I knew the crystal—thin as onion skin—could be smashed by my least involuntary reflex. I set it down quickly. I already doubted that the two of us were going to make it onto the New York Times wedding page, *together,* I mean. I knew class when I saw it and this was the major leagues. I snapped on my machine. "Could we start off talking about . . . *politics?*"

"Politics?" Hobie Schaeffer was halfway out the library door. "Could you just bear with me one second? Won't be a moment." He strolled back in, then paused by one particular shelf. What a library! You didn't see rooms like this in Texas either, at least not in my crowd. But it wasn't just the thousands of old leather volumes that caught my eye, or the bibelots from the time of the Louies, which left not a surface exposed. *No.* There were silver trophies, gleaming bright as klieg lights, lining an entire wall of shelves. I asked what they were for. "*Oh.* Those old things? Just your run-of-the-mill regatta souvenirs from three generations of Schaeffer men sailing at Yale." He took one down for show-and-tell, then rubbed his fingertip along the edge of the bowl. "Awfully good for serving shrimp, but I'm afraid that's all." He replaced it, then stretched way up to the top and brought down an enormous three-foot-high Cantonese ginger jar. What a back! As he reached, his shoulder blades seemed to touch; they were like wings, only far more symmetrical. His back was so straight you could tee off from it. In defense, I slouched even deeper into my eiderdown burrow and just watched, mesmerized by what this exotic creature might possibly produce next.

From out of the ancient navy and cream ginger jar, a chocolate bar big as a brick was being extracted. With a silver knife, oh-so-gently, my host began to carve. "Do you indulge?" The shavings piled into a cone.

"No thanks. I'm on a diet."

For less than an instant his brow furrowed, then he shrugged. From out of a drawer came a Turkish water pipe, coils like freeways wove in and out, a moment later all the chocolate curls had been tamped into its bowl. "Sure you wouldn't like some? It's first-rate hash."

"*Oh.* I thought so. Sure, I'll try anything once." *Hmmm,* how perfect. A corner of the Woodstock Nation staked out at Seventy-fourth and Park. Hobie Schaeffer a druggie? A man who'd made his fortune starting an ecologically pure real estate trust? I closed my eyes and inhaled, then got stoned on the paradox of life. Florida Burns, who had managed to live through the electric kool-aid years, watching everyone else getting zonked, keeping rhythm with *Rolling Stone*'s prose, now finds herself on upper Park burning her lungs out with a lot more than some silly weed. I closed my eyes, drawing in, drawing in, imagining what it would be like to fuck my blond Siegfried. *Lousy* is what I decided it would be. *Turn off the lights,* he might say, taking a look at my chest. Something told me that men like Hobart Bordon Schaeffer III would not be into big breasts.

But he might be into geopolitics. I tried to focus on a clue to his loyalties. Books tell all! On the nearest table, a line-up: Adam Smith, Lionel Trilling, a tome by Henry the K. I cleared my throat and tried to go back to the business at hand. How would Barbara Walters begin if her throat was in flames? Would Barbara hit the air waves in a drug-induced daze? I took a breath, then waited for him to sit down. "May I call you Hobie?"

"Of course." He sucked in on the pipe.

I smiled. "Hobie. You seem to be a man of enormous sophistication. Are you . . . political?"

He waited, then fingered a malachite lion crouched on the end table nearest his chair. "All men are political in varying degrees. . . ." He looked up at me, indicating it was my turn to respond.

"*Right.* Well, now. Could you tell me a little bit about the nature of your political involvement?" I wondered if I sounded inane.

"*My* particular political involvement?" One well-manicured finger picked at an invisible piece of lint on his sleeve. "Frankly, I've never thought about it, a political involvement, I mean."

"But . . ."

"*But* one supposes that if one were to ascribe a label to my politics, then I . . . then one . . . would have to say one considered oneself a *radical.*"

"A radical?" This was a shock.

"Absolutely." For emphasis, Hobie Schaeffer gave a jerk to his head.

"How so? If you don't mind my asking. . . ."

"Not at all. In the sense that insofar as anyone is a radical, I am. One feels it's the only sensible position to take in the face of impending chaos, don't you agree?"

"Indeed."

But I didn't agree, not at all, not a bit. Radical my ass. Next thing I knew, Hobart Schaeffer would be summoning an Irish serving maid with a tray of roquefort balls. Anyway, I wasn't in any shape to stick around for his leftist homilies. Not when I was breathing rainbows, not when a beaver had come to roost upon my tongue. I was stoned. By an act of God, I managed to hie me home in the first passing cab. In the morning my tape sounded like a Gregorian chant, it was so formal and polite.

160

But one thing shone out loud and clear: I hadn't given Hobie Bordon Schaeffer III nearly an even chance. I would reschedule, let him have one more brief go-round.

I dialed the Schaeffer Real Estate Trust, launched into my spiel. Then waited for Hobart Bordon Schaeffer's secretary to say her boss had gone out of town.

"No problem. I'm sure Mr. Schaeffer would be delighted. Let me check." I was put on hold for an infinity. Her voice seemed to deflate when she returned to the line. "Oh. Miss Burns, Mr. Schaeffer wanted me to double-check . . . which *specific* periodical is this article for?"

I would have to lie. *"Town and Country."* All I needed was for Milman to get hip to my little scheme.

"Fine. Mr. Schaeffer would like you to be at his apartment—you have the address, don't you?—no later than six p.m. He'll need to leave promptly at seven."

Hobart Bordon Schaeffer must have left at 5:01. At the door a white-gloved butler handed me a note. I ripped it open, the pearl-grey writing paper weighed close to a ton. And read twice as heavy:

Dear Miss Burns:

I tried to reach you at *Town and Country* to cancel our appointment. My secretary said that they didn't seem to know anything about the article. They suggested I try to find you through Rona Barrett's publications.

Sorry if I have inconvenienced you.

Sincerely,

HBS III

So much for Bachelor Number Two. I'd been Ezra Matthewed again! Mollified, I stared at the note. His words dripped with contempt. Rona Barrett publications, indeed. How could he? Rona Barrett wrote fan magazines, had a militia under her that manufactured nothing but trash. Is this what Hobart Bordon Schaeffer III thought about Florida Burns? That I was some deadbeat from Flatbush wearing mink eyelashes and a patch-quilted rabbit-fur coat? I had never worn fake lashes or owned a pair of multi-level platforms in my life! Rona Barrett, the very thought of her made me want to . . . *Wow!!* Suddenly in my brain, a light bulb rang like the Liberty Bell! Rona Barrett! That was it; I'd read in *Celebrity Register* that the real Queen of Dish was coming to town.

Like a gyroscope my mind started to whirl. Rona-Barrett-Rona-Barrett-Rona-Barrett-Rona Barrett! All of the pieces were falling into place. Rona Barrett, the ticky-tackiest and the most declassé, had pulled herself up by the leg brace and stood like a rock as America's crowned Queen of Gossip. If she could do it, think what, under her tutelage, could happen to the daughter of Burns' Food Kings! Rona Barrett? Impossible, but who was I to doubt the voice of my muse? I had no idea where to find her or what I would say; but somewhere out in the fourth dimension a chorus of sirens was calling, *find her, listen to her.* At that moment I heard the clear chimes of The Call. For me alone, Rona Barrett held some kind of key to the future.

It had been getting worse and worse for Kenny Baer, Jason Jaffe's secretary-assistant-reader, ever since Pamela Rosen had become a fact of his boss's life. Oh, not at first; not in obvious ways, except for the big one. But in the beginning, even though it hurt him, Kenny Baer thought he could handle the loss of the sex. After all, sex wasn't everything, and Kenny Baer had plenty of other friends as well as lovers; he knew Jay would soon get over this phase and come back to him.

Now, that was out of the question. Jason Jaffe had told him that he never again wanted to fuck another man, not even for a change of pace. It was killing him! Seeing that little blond bitch every day falling all over him, knowing that she now had Jay's ear and he didn't. Everything was changing. Pamela Rosen had moved a jungle into the bedroom, forced Jay to change his pecan-colored walls to a feminine china gray.

Once, Kenny had tried to confront him, find out what he

was doing wrong. "Why are you so uptight about what we have?" he asked his boss.

"We have *nothing* and never did," Jason Jaffe replied. "Get this straight. I never *came* once, all the times that we fucked."

"Well . . . straights have bad sex too, it's not just limited to faggots, not just something fags . . ."

"I told you not to use that word around me. *Don't use that word.*"

"Faggot-faggot-faggot-faggot. Don't take it out on me, boss, just because you're in a bad mood. I didn't tell Cherie Rivers to dish you. It wasn't me that told Telemedia to find out why you haven't worked in a year."

Jason Jaffe stood up, then caught himself. He jammed his hands in his pockets, paced up and down the length of the room. He was silent-aggressive, he couldn't deal with any more shouting matches in his house. He'd already had his fight of the day with Peaches, she'd stormed out hours before. Now every few moments he checked out the window, he could feel Kenny's mocking eyes boring holes in his back. He thought if he had a pistol he might blow Kenny's head off, send it orbiting around the room. His anger was looking for a target, any target. Kenny Baer was as choice a target as they come. He wondered why he hadn't fired him months earlier, why he kept him around, a reminder of a past he was trying to forget. Jason Jaffe turned, his mouth was tight. "Hey, man. You got your scripts, think you could shove off for today?"

"You don't need to try to pretend that nothing is wrong— to ignore me—when you know something is. That's what straights do, they try to avoid. Pretend nothing's wrong, hottest-actor-in-America! Just do an improv of Mr. Cool. TRY TO KEEP UP A FRONT . . ." As his hysteria grew, Kenny Baer's normally boyish face puffed up, turned from raspberry, then swelled even more. He continued to scream. "The fact that you want to pretend that your life—that girl, what they said on TV—isn't eating you alive and instead of sharing it with someone who understands you and has feelings, someone who sits here day after day watching you ruin yourself with—"

163

"That's enough, Kenny. Quite enough." Jason Jaffe's voice was tempered steel; he'd used this tone in a San Francisco production of *The Merchant of Venice*, but now only whipped it out in the direst of circumstances. He felt himself ease into his most profound level of anger but, still, he was in control of his rage. He hated to think what would happen if he ever really let go.

"YOU THINK YOU CAN TURN ME ON AND OFF LIKE A FAUCET, THAT YOU CAN CONTROL ME LIKE YOU CONTROL EVERYONE ELSE IN YOUR LIFE. WELL, YOU'RE WRONG! IF ANYONE CALLS THE SHOTS AROUND HERE IT'S GOING TO BE ME . . . ME!" Kenny Baer's face suffused with blood, his hands clenched the top of a chair. He wanted to scream. But he managed to lower his voice. "Don't forget, we go back a long, long time."

Jason Jaffe laughed. "Are you threatening me? *Get out.* And I mean now. At least . . . if you're going to pull this soaper of a scene, don't do 'Tahlulah' on me, okay? Have a little more *taste.*" He spat out his words, letting the "t" hang in the air, a full beat after the living room grew still.

Outside in the hall, her leotards balled up in a baggie tucked under her arm, Pamela Rosen was pressed flat against the front door trying to hear. Usually the foyer door was open, to get the good cross-ventilation on these warm August days, but this afternoon it had been locked. Peaches fumbled in her bag for the key. She almost rang the bell, then stopped when she heard the screaming. She couldn't make out exactly what they were yelling about, not at first, not till she heard the word "faggot" fly back and forth. Thank God, Jay and Kenny were finally working it out! All this closet business, this veiled bisexuality, this secret life of Jason Jaffe's . . . boring! Peaches Rosen might be a JAP from Atlanta, but she knew two when she saw two. Kenny Baer and Jason Jaffe had been (or maybe still were) lovers; there was no doubt about it.

And what was the big deal? Not that Peaches Rosen liked gays, far from it! She despised them and had detested Kenny Baer in particular the moment they'd met. It was one thing to prefer men, but it was another to make your sexuality a crusade. Gays like that made Peaches Rosen nervous, feel less

164

womanly. She always felt a little responsible, as if something she, Pamela Rosen, had done had made them flee to leather bars. New York had become flooded with gays, which, many people insisted, gave it its liveliness, its kaleidoscopic pace. She wasn't so sure. She felt that for every fag let loose in New York, her life became tougher, there was one less man to be able to date.

She wouldn't have wanted Kenny Baer anyway, straight or gay. The way he looked—Missouri farm boy with a wide-open face and lumberjack shirts. The space between his teeth was his only blemish. She preferred gays with dancers' bodies wearing T-shirts with "La Salsa" stenciled across the front. At least they were out in the open, at least if they were playing midnight cowboy, they made no bones about it. "Why do you keep Kenny Baer around?" Peaches once asked Jay, trying to pry. Jay had mumbled something about "loyalty," but Peaches knew that explanation was pure sham. Loyalty? Some loyalty! Peaches was sure that blind devotion wasn't at the root of the screaming and the banging and the yelling coming from not so far inside the door.

Jason Jaffe's trump card had been ordering Kenny Baer to get out. If only it had worked. Now he had really dug himself in. He knew it was a mistake the first time he'd made it with Kenny. All his life he'd lived by the motto: never shit where you eat. He'd even told Kenny that in the middle of their first fight. Kenny Baer had turned and answered, "Is that what you think about sex?" How was he going to get him out of his apartment now? Or out of his life? He was standing there staring like an animal. Jason Jaffe tried to radiate back his Biff Loman gaze. If he couldn't get him out, what then? Maybe he would murder him, strangle him till he'd pulverized his neck. Or use a fireplace poker, like in vintage Raymond Chandler. He could bash his skull in, chop his body to bits, putting him out with the trash bags to be taken away in the morning collection.

"I'm asking you once more, Kenneth. Very calmly, *leave.* And we'll both forget that this happened."

"And go on like before? As if nothing had gone on? Seeing you resume this fake life, pretending that an entire section of your life doesn't exist, is a scene out of some play you were trying out on the road? What do you think we're doing? Playing *Sunday Bloody Sunday?*" He stopped, then ran his fingers through the top of his hair. "You make me sick. You disgust me. *I hate you.*"

For the first time all afternoon, Jason Jaffe broke into a smile. "I *disgust* you? Lovely! Then why are we even having this ridiculous discussion? We're in perfect agreement. *Now . . . get out.*" Jason Jaffe's voice bubbled up in the same timbre he'd used to play Thomas à Becket on a bus-and-truck tour of *A Man for All Seasons,* one of his first roles. What practice he was getting during this little melodrama! His smile became a laugh, overpowering Kenny Baer like a sudden thunderclap. Suddenly, Jason Jaffe froze; he'd heard the brownstone's front door slam . . . at least he thought it was the downstairs front. Any second, Peaches would be coming up. He smoothed out his hair, then nervously glanced out his window to check the street again. A blond figure, plastic bag bobbing up and down by her side, was turning west, running quickly, disappearing toward Fifth Avenue.

Just by looking at the newsstand, you could tell what had happened to the Ansonia Hotel over the years. The Spanish-language weekly *Novedades* fought for counter space with open boxes of halvah, grease-pocked from age. A fetid smell like rotten socks wafted up from the gym downstairs. And the lobby, once the caramel-cream center to the Ansonia's wedding-cake exterior, had been allowed to run down so far, even its orlon rug could inflict no further disgrace. Ringing for the elevator, Marcie Laster came up with a literary allusion. This stained and shiny carpet she was standing on reminded her of a once-beautiful woman who'd degenerated to a bum. Good line! She reached for her notebook to scribble it down, all the while watching the numbers above the elevator.

9-8-7-6-5-4-3-2- . . . A chill came over her, even on this stifling August day. Marcie Laster tried not to think about what was going to happen next. She was on her way to see Case

166

#654987, a rapist yet, in his room alone. She was going to "interview" him, at least she would try. What if he tried to kill her? Or worse? She tried not to think about the possibilities, surely Case #654987 would not try to harm a (self-styled) member of the press. Unless he was setting her up. Marcie had been stunned when he'd agreed to the interview, he almost seemed eager, as if he welcomed the publicity. She hoped that was all that it was, she'd hate to be Victim Number 74.

Seventy-three victims and still Murray Sandler hadn't been able to make one good arrest. He'd tried, God knows, he'd tried! Each time a judge had turned his man over to a shrink, let him out on bail, then been astonished when Case #654987 upped and jumped town. He was considered a psychopath, a nut case, a low-priority on a backed-up court roster.

He always worked the same way: hitting on prominent women, working women, names he pulled from newspapers, well-dressed career types he'd pick up on the street. What was worse, he got away with it, but Murray Sandler had figured out why. Case #654987 had typical, indistinguishable New York City looks: afro hair, small, darting eyes, Brooks Brothers clothes. Depending on who was talking, Case #654987 had been described as being everything from "sensitive" to "demoniacally intense."

No matter, he always scored. He worked on the vulnerability and guilt every woman feels about sex, then he took that guilt and exploited it, making each and every one of his victims feel responsible for her own rape. He played with their responses, made his crime a game, a sexual minuet. Let a woman encourage or come on to him in the slightest way—even if it was just something simple like inviting Case #654987 upstairs for a drink—and he had her in his control. His was a crime that in legal terms was only considered a borderline rape.

In point of fact, only lately was the law becoming sensitized to women's complaints. Classically, in legal terms, rape was a nine-foot nigger with a record the length of the Mississippi, cutting up some white woman bad, then sticking it in. But Case #654987 was no nigger, or even a "rapist" as the law viewed the term. Just your all-American satyr, your average red-blooded Don Juan, who had to penetrate anything in skirts. Marcie Laster wanted to research his seduction techniques. Specifically, to find out what happened at the magic moment where "seduction" became force and the victim was done in by her own blade.

Pity she'd have to make her debut on this feminist note. The entire subject of rape was smothered by rhetoric, obfuscated by pseudo-scientific legal definitions. She had read everything, attended speak-outs, gone to meetings, heard rape victims swap tales. Heresy! She did not think that a sexual crime was the worst form of assault in the world. Bad, yes. Traumatic, yes. But worse than having someone come at your throat with a three-foot-long knife?

All she'd wanted, her first time out as a reporter, was a good, clean-dirty crime story, a bank heist or a tax scam, something neat, nonpolitical, not an issue that bottomed out in consciousness-raising issues. Marcie Laster felt no allegiance to the women's movement, did not hold the view that any discrimination aimed her way had to be sociological in dimension. She was too young to have realized that she had experienced the benefit of a decade's worth of change.

Besides, she was an "executive." That's how she'd happened to glom onto this case. Murray Sandler had hyped it for a movie, Marcie had latched onto it to start her new career. Too bad. She could have made a mint by cannibalizing Case #654987 for its drama alone. A screenplay unspooled in her head. All the basics were there: an Ivy League psychopath let loose on the town, seducing, then terrorizing dozens of stars, each with stories so flimsy no lawyer could press charges. What cameos! All she needed was a script and a writer to supply both a climax and a denouement.

Marcie Laster never dreamed that she might be the vehicle to provide both. She strolled down a deserted hallway, more jittery than truly afraid. She wondered whether she would find Case #654987 attractive, even in a menacing way. She wondered whether a second Charles Manson was getting up to answer his door.

Waiting for Hollywood to come calling, Case #654987 had gotten an acute case of nerves. He wondered why Metropolitan Pictures was after him or what they'd found out, but on one thing he was clear. Finally he would be recognized, finally he would reach an appreciative ear. Screen tests! It was all coming together, all the friends he had made, all these women, these young professionals he had met. It was only logical that one of them would have a friend who had a friend at Metropolitan Pictures. His friendliness had obviously paid off. With this girl from Metropolitan, he might for sure hit on pay dirt.

For the occasion, he'd even taken a broom to his floor, tried to make his tiny room seem like a real home. He'd covered his walls with his artwork; the type of posterboard sold downstairs in the drugstore was perfect for his decorating needs. Zip-ee-draw, it was called, just the right size to fill in the names, draw little cartoons of all the new women friends he had made. Each poster could fit twenty-five along with the exact date and time he had scored. So far, he had nine manifestoes up on his wall. He wouldn't be truly content till there was a list three times the size.

Now he was looking at his Mickey Mouse clock, wondering when *she* would arrive. He checked himself out in the bureau mirror, made a last-minute spot inspection for fuzz. He had worn his best shirt: a pinstriped button-down, set off by his white corduroy jeans. Tennis shoes rounded off the look. Christ, he'd almost forgotten! He scurried into his bathroom, laid on some Canoë. He hoped that scent would offset Metropolitan Pictures' reaction to his cheap little room.

If only she would notice the books; he had hundreds of them, all stolen from the public library. What's more, some were even rare. He had psychology, best-sellers (fiction and non), how to guides, self-improvement, philosophy, and art. He wondered why more people didn't walk out with stacks and stacks. It was so easy! He liked to think he was someone who was always improving his mind. He was a sponge; he had imbibed a million facts through his books. If only he could find someone intelligent to cross-pollinate with, if only one time in his life he could meet a woman with whom he could share ideas.

He hoped Miss Metropolitan Pictures would have something besides trivia to say. Banalities! They made him fly into a chemical rage, made his head swell to the size of a globe. He had read book after book about anger and what brought it on, but he liked to think his problem was hormonal rather than neurotic in root. He'd been throwing these violent tantrums since he was a child, only then his mother used to beat him until he calmed down. It seemed strange for a pacifist mother to hit out at her child, but then Howie Leon's mother was never considered run-of-the-mill. He'd never read a treatise on immigrants and violence, so he wondered how many women out there in the Bronx were battering their kids. He would bet his last nickel that it was more than were reported, certainly more than anyone thought. Almost out of habit, he reached for a volume of Kraft-Ebbing and started flipping through it, until he heard Metropolitan knock. Howie Leon smoothed his hair once, and twisted his mouth into a smile.

For days I had waited for the Queen of Dish to answer my calls. For days I had prepared, worked over my spiel, memorized *appropriata* from her self-written bible, *Miss Rona.* Celebrityhood! What did it mean, the high-recognition factor Miss Rona had in spades? Did it mean the Rona Barrett one saw on TV, in photos, was actually The Real Rona? I wanted to get to her, the Real Rona, drill deep into her soul! I wanted her to open up, have a heart-to-heart, tell me what made this dynamo tick. I wanted her to help me. If only I could figure out how. Again, I would have to pretend, whip out the time-tested "interview" trick. Rona might not be a bachelor, but as time had gone by, I'd adjusted my motto. Now, the sign over my desk had been given an update: If you can't get married, get even.

And "even" was just what I, Florida Burns, intended to get. I decided the next time Harvey Kaplan called, I would indulge in a fireworks display of first-rate name-dropping. I would look to him for deep background, some off-the-record info in Rona that had never appeared in black and white. And maybe, just maybe, he'd take some word of my up-and-coming fame back to his client, Jason Jaffe, who, by extension, might repeat it to Miss Pamela R.

What I wasn't counting on was Harvey's response. "Why are you wasting, wasting your time on somebody so unimportant? Why don't you do something real, something important, something that might, might be useful in getting you on the media map instead of . . . Well, never mind. The point is, certain other people are right now working on projects that are so, so exciting and of such potential magnitude. . . ." Harvey paused for effect, then went on. "Don't ask me to tell you what 'they' are doing or who it is because I've been sworn to absolute, absolute secrecy. But, now I don't mean this in a negative sense, I mean, if you want to do an interview with her, Rona, I mean, the fact that she talks to anybody that calls up shouldn't necessarily be of any importance to you, but what should be important is not that your sick, sick article should be the duplicate of everything else that's been written about her, but that it should be at least better than all the other sick dreck which gets cranked out. . . . Not that anybody cares. Or even reads it. . . ." Harvey paused. "The most, most important thing is that you should just get on with 'it.' Get on with 'it.' "

"That's why I'm calling you, Harvey. I'm getting on with 'it.' Tell me about Rona, spare no details."

"I DON'T MEAN YOUR INTERVIEW, YOU SICK, DRECK KIKE. I MEAN YOUR LIFE! GET ON WITH YOUR LIFE! You're absolutely, absolutely, going to ruin your career, writing this sick, sick dreck."

I was desperate. "Okay. I promise after this one, I'll go and do something meaningful."

"No you won't. I know you. *And* you won't."

"But until that time comes, Harvey, just in two minutes give me a sketch of her, so I'll know how to behave."

"Can you hold on a moment? Someone is on the other line. . . ."

I was steaming. Just because Harvey Kaplan signed some

hot backwater blues singer, he expected me to give his client a hype. Well, I have some standards, though admittedly very few. Now I was getting punished for having put my foot down in last week's TIME. More: he was trying to best me at the Over-Achiever's Game—pin the tail on the mysterious donkey who's hard at work on the Big Story. Make me feel like vermin-on-wheels because I choose the jugular of the commonplace rather than some more relevant vein. He was always comparing me to some phantom-like, high-powered friend.

"Did-did I just hear you tell me that you're meeting with Rona Barrett?"

"Yes." Why did Harvey Kaplan dialogues always wind up sounding like a cheap imitation of a Harold Pinter play? I decided to press him. "*Harvey.* Come on, tell me about her. Or don't you know her?"

Harvey paused. "Well . . . I mean, let me phrase this right. I don't actually know Rona, I mean, we have met on several, several occasions which is probably what most people would think constitutes knowing somebody, but that's just *their* sick, drecky values. I mean, we're not friends, but we share many, many friends in common." He sounded distracted. I mean, we don't 'work' together, if that's what you mean . . . . *Listen.* If I could trust you, not that any of this is even important, but if when you 'meet' with her, you could do me the most enormous favor of maybe bringing my name up. . . . NO! WHY AM I EVEN ASKING YOU THAT? She would be lucky to be able to say she worked with me, Mr. Harvey Spencer Kaplan! Forget I just said that sick, drecky thing, will you forget it? Just do me that one tiniest, tiniest little favor and forget that we've even had this conversation, okay?"

Okay, okay, I'd forget it already. But I did remember that Harvey was needling me during his "meaningful story" riff. Especially when Rona Barrett in the flesh returned my call, especially when she seemed downright flattered that I, F'orida Burns, with a dozen papers like links in a chain, would well nigh relish the chance to spread Miss Rona over six pages with 7000 words and a guaranteed four-color layout. Yes, of course she'd have the right to approve the photography choice. She had manners, that to me was "meaningful." Later Miss Rona explained she always tried to help out "a fellow member of the press."

Wasn't it meaningful enough that Miss Rona was a walking advertisement for the triumph of the will? That she had risen above her stereotype of a mother, fought lawsuit after lawsuit, battering against the evil new networks who despised her till by some miracle of blind guts and determination, Rona Barrett had gone national and had hooked in with ABC? She was big business. And in the process she'd picked up a gold Rolls-Royce and a house in Beverly Hills and a husband, so that now she had become the sublime personification of the American Way. I hoped I wouldn't quake in her presence.

I didn't have to worry. The second Miss Rona sat down at the table and confided *her* body-beautiful secret, I knew that this would be a woman I could trust. Anyone who had gotten "pounded in the valley"—which Rona had translated as meaning that she'd gone to visit a Rolfer who lives in the San Fernando Valley in order to hack off the fat—just couldn't be anything other than A Real Person.

I got right to the point. "Rona . . . I can call you 'Rona,' can't I?" She nodded, so I went on. "Why do we do what we do, make all these enemies, have people hate us? Why are we columnists?"

Rona looked at me. I stared right back. I wondered how she kept every curl in place, like patent leather potato chips her hair folded into a hundred commas around her brow. Then she opened her mouth, her teeth were perfect too. "I don't know if *I* ever thought about being a gossip columnist, really. But I thought that . . . well, come to think of it, I don't know why! I guess it had a lot to do with my real desire of wanting to Do Something with myself and somehow I had this cockeyed impression just like a lot of teen-agers . . . Well, *columnists* have EVERYTHING. They have POWER! They have POSITION! And they're always invited to parties and openings and . . ." She stopped a moment, then continued. I was hanging on her every word. "I mean what did I know? I was a kid running Frankie Avalon's fan club! It wasn't till I went to Hollywood

173

and really had to function that I discovered that All That Glitters Is Not Gold and it was tough work and that if I ever really wanted to *make something of myself* then, the-parties-the-openings, all that was nonsense! It was work! Nothing but work! But it was the kind of work I enjoy, I guess because I always have had and I always will have an innate sense of curiosity about people. Maybe because of my *handicap.*" For a long moment, Rona looked down at her leg, then her voice dropped. "I know it looks all right, but to this day I can't walk up stairs withoug clinging to the banister. . . ." She let her words sink in. "But I got there! Because on every level and every front when I wanted a story there was no one who dogged a story more than I did. Yet, when it came to my own worth, I kind of dove into a little box."

Now I was getting somewhere. Florida Burns, so it seemed, wasn't the only one with problems. Maybe the Queen of Dish was more introspective than I thought. "How did you get out of 'the little box'?"

Rona's voice faded to a near-benediction. "*Analysis.* Of course, I didn't stay in long. The moment I hit 'analysis,' it was just a matter of a couple of weeks before I was able to figure out that what I was really upset about was *myself!* That I had allowed my business ability to far supercede my personal level and that the scale was *so* out-of-sync and *so* unbalanced that I knew I could no longer live this way. *It was a matter of either dying or saving myself!*"

A man in a white coat had been hovering by her, pretending not to listen. He cleared his throat, then Rona spun to face him. "I'll have the chicken salad, the special one; it's not on the menu . . . the one with the chunk of Port Salut." Rona frowned, for the first time since she'd sat down at the table the tiniest bit of the Grand Concourse was shining through. "*The chef knows.* Just tell him that 'Rona Barrett is ordering the special chicken salad' and he'll know which one it is. . . ." More to me than to the waiter, she continued, "I'm the only one he makes it for."

The waiter bowed. "Very good, madam." Then he took my order and disappeared.

174

I began to panic. The food was on the way and I still hadn't learned anything, still hadn't screwed up the courage to ask Rona if she had any Peaches Rosens in her life, still hadn't gotten the nerve to ask Rona how I could get to be *her*. Maybe I could get her to help me with the Rosen-Jaffe affair. "Do you have any enemies?"

Her eyes narrowed, then she exposed her teeth. I noticed she was smiling. "Enemies? *Weeellll* . . . I would say that the only one who really comes to mind is Frank 'Sinister.' . . ."

"Frank 'Sinister'?" I wondered whether I was supposed to have heard of this Sinister fellow or whether it was a joke.

"*Sinister!* Sinatra! Frank *Sinatra!*" Rona began to laugh, so I did too. "That's what I call him. And I'm not too sure who my other enemies are because Hollywood is a very fickle community and when you realize that . . . it won't bother you any more."

"I don't believe it."

"Listen, *Florence.* I've discovered one thing about celebrities and not just celebrities, but even the hierarchy of our industry. Which is . . . you write something horrendous? They hate you. You turn around and say something brilliant, *they love you!* And the love-hate relationship goes from morning to night and night till morning! And you would go crazy if you were to allow it to affect you!"

"I'm going crazy."

"I know, I know. I got very deep pangs at first too. Then, I realized something. When push comes to shove there are very few humans who can stand up and be counted, so it makes no difference." Rona spied the waiter coming our way, then she glanced at her watch. "I have to hurry, Florence. But, if I can leave you with just one thought, let it be this. PEOPLE ARE PEOPLE. Whether you're in the advertising business, the butcher business, the engineering business, or show business, everybody's the same! And when I realized that, then this all just became a One Big Job to me, nothing else. For me, Gossip is nothing more than . . . a business. *A very big business.*"

I took a breath. "But Rona, if 'a person,' say like it was one of my friends, wanted to get into this 'business' . . . I mean, wanted to really score on the tube, I mean the way you have with your magazines and everything . . . I mean, what would you advise 'this person' to do?

Rona smiled, then went on automatic pilot, as if she'd answered the same query a thousand times before. "Well, I would advise 'this person,' your friend, whoever it is, that if she wanted to make-a-name for herself, then once a month, she was going to have to take off after somebody and express An Opinion. I had to develop *opinions* and express them, otherwise, I'd never be where I am today!" The memory seemed to please her. "I was writing for a magazine with an enormous circulation, *Motion Picture,* it was called. And when I started expressing my feelings, people's attitudes changed. I was no longer everybody's buddy-buddy, now *everybody* began to say, 'This girl is serious,' 'This girl is going to make a name for herself'! And more: they would say, 'This girl is really *A Reporter!'* BUT THAT'S NOT ALL. On top of everything else there's another secret you have to know."

"A secret?" I watched Rona switch from platinum-blond yenta back to TV star. I wondered if she'd been acting. I hoped not.

"Yes, a secret!" She pronged a chunk of her Port Salut, jabbed it into the air. Her nails caught the light like mercury sparklers. "And that secret is as plain as the nose on your face. *'Make yourself special!'* Give them something they don't have! I gave them blind items, I gave them *Gossip.* I brought gossip for the first time in history onto the *Television medium!* That's what they didn't have and I gave that to my public. *Make yourself indispensable!* Give your audience, your editors, *your public* something that they can't get from your competition. Florence Burns, if you do that, *if you offer what the competition can't,* then nothing-but-nobody, Not One Thing will ever get in your way."

WOW! It was so obvious. I kicked myself all the way uptown for not having thought of it. *Offer What the Competition Can't!* Rona's words were like a mantra, but two things remained for me to figure out. What was so special or unique about me that

176

anyone in the American public, much less anyone that counted, would care about this "elusive Burnsism"? And, most important, who exactly *was* my competition? Suddenly, The Answer jolted me like St. Paul on the road to Damascus. Of course! My competition was Rona Barrett, none other than the Queen of Dish herself. Ridiculous? No way a stringer from the Tower Syndicate would be able to bump off the palace guard? All right, then I would wait. I knew my day would come. And I wouldn't be idle. I knew somewhere a cut-rate version of Rona was living in mortal fear that I would somehow ace her out, way, way in the backfield of the media's minor league.

Sherwin Sunneson, The Broadway Producer, was more than angry, he was borderline coronary. This time he had it; this was the time he finally was going to do something about that blond sleaze on Telemedia whose name he could never remember. Cherie Rivers! That was it. The name formed in his mind and his lips like a running sore. He swore to himself that after he got through with her, nobody would remember Cherie Rivers' name; much less her show. He was bringing out his heaviest artillery; Cherie Rivers had taken her last pot shot at him.

Sherwin Sunneson was a perfectionist, thus he was mounting a perfectionist's attack. All morning long he'd been sequestered like a demented general planning his revenge. He had locked himself into his office behind double oak doors, cut off from the rest of his nine-room Dakota apartment by a long corridor banked with posters from his forty-three theatrical productions. These were mounted on flame-stitched crimson silk which his decorator had assured him was a bargain at $25 a yard. The excess had stopped inside Sunneson's office. "Use props and backdrops from the warehouse," Sunneson had told the designer before he'd left on his annual English summer pilgrimage. For years, he had spent the warm months scouting what was new and importable on the British theater scene. His fastidious eye was, for his investors, more valuable than mint shares of Xerox, more precious than bargain warrants of

I.T.T. A "Sherwin Sunneson Presentation" meant quality, but more than that it meant profit. In his thirty-one years in the theater, he had failed to turn a profit only half a dozen times. Six bombs out of forty-three tries, which meant, to his backers and to Broadway, that Sunneson's batting average hovered around 80 percent.

He was a rug salesman in a Saville Row tailored suit. He would wait for his legendary ritual brunch held, as if by papal decree, the first Sunday after Labor Day. Then he would bring out his wares, his jewels, his treasure chest of scripts and ideas garnered from three months abroad. Like a Houdini of dramatic timing, he would keep his top ten "angels" in a state of ecstatic suspense while he regaled them over their gravlax and Norwegian flatbread, their truffled omelettes and vintage champagne, with a panoply of gossip and names, culled from his season in the theatrical bazaar. And just when his audience was beginning to fidget, he would dazzle them with descriptions of two, maybe three finished plays; two straights, one musical, an odd lot of works-in-progress or young playwrights to watch, finished budgets and production estimates and the day (calculated down almost to the hours) when his financial armada could count on receiving their first payback. Then, right on cue, his housekeeper would enter the dining room and announce a call for him—an "urgent" call, his calls were always "urgent"—from Paris or Rome. She would whisper the caller's name into Sherwin Sunneson's ear and then, like a dauphin he would rise, making sure every eye was upon him. Only then would he excuse himself into the velvet recesses of his office, where he would stay for no more than his preplanned twenty-seven minutes, giving him just time enough to peruse the book-review section of that morning's *Times* and stare out his seventh-floor windows at Central Park and the boathouse spread before him like a backdrop from a Sunneson presentation. Drama! He would re-enter his salon with abject humility, cursing his "emergencies" in a most audible *sotto voce,* then be delighted and profusely flattered to discover unanimous approval for his fall season (as well as the promise of over a million dollars to be raised long before the eleventh hour).

He was the old school. Different from a Hal Prince in that he preferred to spread his focus over a handful of ideas, rather than to concentrate on one at a time; different from a Joe Papp in that what interested him was raw commercialism and the promise of theater parties of ladies from Dubuque, not the arcane pursuit of the avant-garde.

But he wasn't perfect. There were only four days to go before his annual brunch, so Sherwin Sunneson was nailing down every last aspect, every minute detail of his trio of choices. Musical! His would be "To Tell a Song . . . To Sing a Joke!," the London blockbuster was a schmaltzy paean to vaudeville. Six stars had already agreed to share equal billing. He had only to hear back from Danny Kaye. Farce! There would be "Doctor! Doctor!," a take-off on the British National Health Service, scheduled for a Christmas Eve opening at the Longacre Theatre. It couldn't miss! The English cast had finally agreed to come over and give it a whirl. Any other producer would have been jubilant, but not Sherwin Sunneson. As he sat behind his massive English barrister's desk, he straightened pencils, piled up papers, and sucked on sugarless mints, all the while carrying on a nonstop barrage of threats and insults to the lawyers, advisers, agents, and accountants who were making his six rotating telephone lines blink like electronic Christmas trees. He played the buttons on his machine like a Rachmaninoff concerto, above the din his face—which years ago the *Journal-American* had described as "not dissimilar to those Mr. Potato Head games children often are caught disfiguring"—expanded and contracted like an accordian. He was fed up. Snipes and personal attacks Sherwin Sunneson could endure, but when a TV personality threatened his relationship with the *talent,* his bread and butter, then his entire career as an impresario was on the line. Much more than simple vanity was at stake during his morning's phone calls, "Sherwin Sunneson Presents" Number 46 was on the line. He planned to make his third play, the serious one, the season's hit. And the only way he could be sure of that with this downbeat epigrammatic statement about urban violence, was by landing Jason Jaffe.

179

And Jason Jaffe wasn't returning Sunneson's calls. He had tried three times a day for the last week, always he got the girlfriend, always the same response. "Can he call you back?" Actors! He hated their games; by Sunday at three he had to have a star. He had already eliminated several. DeNiro was in a film, Pacino was "unavailable"; Dustin Hoffman (or his agent) was demanding a half a million guarantee before he'd read the script. His best hope was Jason Jaffe and he had only seventy-two hours left to mend the fence, bury the hatchet, and get Jason Jaffe's name emblazoned in indelible ink on "S.S.P." Number 46's dotted line.

He had a simple but lethal plan. He hated to give the son of a bitch credit, but his dear, dear friend and arch-rival, Dwight Lambert, had come up with a King Lear of an idea. And it had been tested out of town with such success that it had become a part of his emergency repertory. Lambert's "hit" had forever eradicated one odious late-night screamer from an L.A. radio show, but Sunneson was convinced the scenario would play anywhere, anytime, with any cast. His rule of thumb—always stick to classics—would remain inviolate.

He watched couples rowing across Central Park pond, then smiled with aesthetic favor upon the trompe l'oeil book-cases his decorator had conceived from scrapped scenery flats. He made notes, approved codicils and expenditures. The title of his morning efforts would be longer than standard marquee length: "Sherwin Sunneson, Esq., and the 'Storm Warning' Production Corp. versus Telemedia Corp. Intl., and Cherie Rivers." Even so, he didn't envision a minor titular problem like length being able to alter the potential impact of a project with such obvious substance.

Pamela Rosen had never realized how much a little thing like junking the half-full Coppertone could mean. Packing the inflatable rafts, throwing out the leftover hot dogs, and jetti-soning the unfinished paperbacks had all been good signs. But for Peaches Rosen, the summer hadn't been truly over until she'd laid eyes on the Fifty-ninth Street Bridge. Jason Jaffe's

Fiat might have been packed to bursting for the trip home, but considering the mood he was in these days, Peaches could never be sure of anything. Jason Jaffe could have changed his mind any second, swung his sports car around in the middle of the expressway, and zoomed right back out to the beach, where all summer long he'd been threatening to "retire."

To put it mildly, Jason Jaffe was depressed. Actors! Let some little thing upset their emotional balance and you'd think their mother had died. Let some jerk on TV say they weren't the greatest since John Barrymore and you'd think they'd been hit by stomach cancer. Ever since Cherie Rivers' midsummer broadcast, Jason Jaffe's spirits had sunk from morose to bleak. He was impossible when he was down, which meant he was petulant, homicidal, and, in that much-overused term, *paranoid.* He was lashing out at everything and everybody. Everybody, that is, except Peaches Rosen. He didn't dare. Peaches had to smile when she thought about it, the twinge of power she felt at not letting Jason Jaffe off the hook. Bitch! Never once had she mentioned the Kenny Baer incident; never once had she made the slightest attempt to alleviate his fear that the dirty little secret might be out. The afternoon she'd listened outside in the hall, she pretended that she'd been away all day. Southern! She despised confrontation, shied away from heart-to-hearts, but more than that, her knowledge of Jay's peccadillos was Peaches Rosen's only ace-in-hand. All summer long she had used it, her conversation had become peppered with references to "fags." She pretended that she was on an anti-gay crusade, indeed asking probing questions, when the analyst next door had launched into a soliloquy about her technique for converting homosexuals. And all the while she watched Jay squirm, growing more and more insecure under her subtle but thoroughly insidious campaign. Betrayal! She believed none of it, couldn't care less about who did what to whom. But it was her trump card, her only weapon. And it had worked. The psychological tables in the Jaffe-Rosen merger had turned with a vengeance. Peaches was sure if she didn't let up soon, Jason's overwhelming sense of guilt might drive him squarely out of his mind. That she didn't want.

181

Peaches Rosen might be a little sadistic, but a kosher butcher she wasn't. She planned to collect on her emotional debt long before Jason Jaffe became totally incapacitated.

Besides, she was on her own little guilt trip. It wasn't easy being the female appendage to a male tarantula who also happened to be a star. Well, an almost-star. The trouble was Peaches Rosen couldn't be grateful, wasn't thrilled by the idea of occupying the rumble seat. She might be a man's woman, but she had been brought up to be more than a princess; little Pamela Rosen had been groomed to become a reigning queen. She knew she had rights, and plenty of them. In this relationship, she and her rights were clearly being oppressed. *That* was coming to a screaming end.

Now was the time to make her move. Peaches Rosen was a distinguished alumna of the school of not-biting-noses-to-spite-faces, which meant she would have to come up with the most delicate of plans. It had come to her after they'd driven past LaGuardia, she had been inspired when she knew they were almost home free. Passing the Queens-Midtown Tunnel, seeing Jay's jaw clench tighter as he held the wheel, she knew she had him in the perfect pathological space. Now was the time to get her payback, now before he'd had the ego salve of a session with his shrink. Now before he'd been "analyzed" into thinking his nagging worries were illusory; now before he regained his normal cutting edge.

She had started working on him as they cruised over the bridge, let him see a few pearl-drop baby tears forming in the corners of her eyes. She was crying about her friend, Florida Burns. And that was just for starters. Florida had become the pivotal issue, the symbol in Peaches' mind for everything that had begun to curdle between them as a result of the summer heat. Peaches' tears localized around the problem of her best friend; the fact that Jason Jaffe had forbidden her to come around; the fact that he had shut out parts of her life, her friends, as if they were vermin.

"It isn't fair," she began, "it just isn't fair. . . ." He'd never given Florida or anybody else half a chance.

She was taking a carefully calculated risk. Jason Jaffe had

always hated The Press, had never given an interview except under threat. Now, after the Cherie Rivers fiasco, the very mention of the term "gossip columnist" could send him spiraling on a downward curve. He was wound up tight as a top. As the Fiat made its way up First Avenue, Peaches never took her eyes off Jason Jaffe's face. She knew how to soft-pedal just when it looked as if he might be ready to blow. But she wasn't letting up either, not this time. "Just meet her," she said. "Just meet her. Is that asking so much? To do that one thing for me?" Then she made sure Jay was aware that she was crying just a tiny bit harder.

Almost to herself, she'd said, "That is . . . if Florida Burns will ever return my calls. . . ."

In the car there was absolute silence. Jay's stillness was oppressive, which was not an encouraging sign. The whole way uptown he'd been adamant, then something Peaches said seemed to turn the tide. "The thing is . . . we seem to be surrounded by *fags.* Nothing else. . . . Just *you,* me, and *fags.* I hate it! I hate our life. . . . I miss my girlfriends, I miss my life. . . ." Then she broke down. Now she could allow herself the luxury of a semi-hysterical, uncontrollable sobbing fit.

By the time their navy Fiat had turned into the Seventy-first Street All-Nite Garage, Jason Jaffe's hostility had been defused. By the time he and a now calmed-down Peaches had unloaded the Sony and the records, the TAD Imperials and the snorkles, Jason Jaffe had given in. Yes, he would agree to meet Florida Burns. Yes, he had probably been unfair. "Yes! Yes! Yes! *All right already,* but the minute she opens her mouth and asks for a favor . . . just one . . ." Jason Jaffe's words hung in the air like poison gas, once again his mood grew grim. Somehow, somewhere he smelled a trick; he had no evidence, could point to nothing that showed that the blond lynx had done him in. But he was an actor! Which meant his intuition was honed to the finest pitch. Watching Peaches loaded down with luggage, he brooded; seeing her struggle with the keys, he stood back, not offering to help. Then something deep within Jason Jaffe began to click. He was beginning to feel like the victim of some kind of ruse.

By the time he'd brought up their suitcases and settled in, their conversation driving home had faded to the back of his mind. Now he had other things to worry him. Waiting for Jason Jaffe on his answering service had been the startling news that Sherwin Sunneson had tried to call him not once, not twice, but eleven different times. Sherwin Sunneson! He'd sooner hear from Albert Speer. Suddenly, Jason Jaffe felt as if a tractor was digging tread marks into his stomach. Eleven messages! This was more than due cause for a terminal anxiety attack. Jason Jaffe prowled through his living room; he was panicked. Bad enough Sunneson should try to get him in the country, bad enough Jason Jaffe should have made Peaches lie for him.

But now he was being hounded, now there would obviously be threats and lawyers, now Sunneson was serious. Surely, after all these months he couldn't still be angry with him? Surely, after an entire season he couldn't still be simmering over some stupid artistic feud? Paranoid! Maybe he was going crazy, but maybe not. *Peaches!* He cried out, but she had gone down to bring up another load. In the dark, he sat and cursed the day he'd gone to see *On the Waterfront,* cursed the day he'd wanted to become an actor. There was no doubt he would have been happier doing anything else, even driving a truck. He was sinking like a stone, but before he touched bottom he had a flash of anger.

SCUMBAG-TOAD-S.O.B.-COCKSUCKER-MOTHERFUCKER!! Jason Jaffe was sure he knew that slimy pervert better than he knew . . . well, just about anything or anybody, including himself. After all, it wasn't like Sherwin Sunneson was a human Double-Crostic, he was a cinch to figure out. Simple! A thoroughly evil bastard was what he was, the lowest of the low. Wasn't it clear the way he'd plotted all summer to do Jay in? The way he'd waited like an executioner for Jason Jaffe's mood to slip from low to desperate? Then he'd struck. Emotional sabotage! He was being harassed by a thousand messages, hounded by a million calls. All year long Sunneson had waited in the wings for him to stumble, now he was kicking him when he was already down.

The perfect symmetry of Jason Jaffe's relentless vision pushed him back. He gasped, then collapsed upon a chair. For a moment he was silent, half dead, listening to his breathing echoing off the walls. Suddenly, he erupted. A thousand spasms sent him flying! "COCKSUCKER!!" he yelled, a half-beat before his fist smashed full force into solid brick. He crumpled like a rag onto the floor. By the time Peaches got back from the garage, put the teflon pans into the kitchen, and called his name, he had disappeared into the bathroom, was whimpering over the toilet bowl. She rushed to help him, but it was too late. His left hand had turned from chartreuse to eggplant, three of his fingers had started to swell.

The Ponce DeLeon was the only element of Marcie Laster's rigid daily routine that wasn't on the verge of changing. She had typed out her letter of resignation to Metropolitan, then run out and blown $500 on new clothes. She was moving quickly now, so appearances counted. She was in flight; up, up, and away to the land of lady journalists.

Marcie Laster knew that all the glamour associated with the media types was surely on its way. All her life she'd seen from afar those lady journalists, the sleek way they behaved; all her working life she'd wanted to take her place among them, to have those svelte conversations about subsidiary rights and what one's agent had said that day. Marcie Laster wanted to be in, but more: she wanted to be on the scene. Once a few years back she'd seen Sally Quinn all blond and in spaghetti straps. In her hand she clutched a notebook, by her side Bob Evans whispered in her ear. Marcie had hovered nearby, she didn't want to get too close, didn't want to disturb the magic of a *Washington Post*-Bob Evans interview. They looked so serious, all dressed up in formal clothes. Marcie Laster wanted to be part of that highly motivated, super-intense, overachieving world.

Power! She knew that getting Tell Me Everything was just a step. She smiled, then hung her clothes on the locker hook, pronged the suedes and silks with extra care. She was a rising media star, with a special grace. Without anyone telling her, she knew she had an aura. You never could tell, even in the Ponce DeLeon Health Club, which future fan might be watching her strip from head to waist. Marcie Laster smiled at the girl dressing next to her, with just a touch of *noblesse oblige.* Without any warning, the girl turned her back and walked away. Must not have seen me, Marcie thought; she frowned, then decided to forget about it. She was pulling on her new red leotards so as not to miss one second of Ronnie's Advanced Body Jazz championship-deluxe calisthenics class.

She couldn't live without the discipline, couldn't survive without the adherence to her strict routine. Tension! She had plenty of it. And the only way to get rid of it seemed to be by barreling around doing high-speed hip rolls, back pressed flat against the floor. She looked around the gym, checked out the other bodies crowded near her on the green shag rug. There was nobody she knew, not one of her friends. *Uh-oh.* There was Simone Ravitch. What? She had a tape recorder and a miniature cassette in her hand. She was talking for the benefit of the entire group. "So . . . I said to myself, 'Simone, you're going to Jamaica for two weeks, and what's the only way you're going to avoid getting so fat you want to die? Tape Ronnie's class! That's what I said to myself, 'Don't get away from your routine!' "

All summer long, Marcie Laster had been marooned at the gym. Florida Burns and Peaches Rosen never came around any more. Well, she understood about Peaches, what with the big love and all, but Florida? It wasn't like anyone was going to mob *her* for autographs, it wasn't like any of *les femmes* were going to crowd around begging her for gory details about Jason Jaffe. Not that she minded, Marcie Laster was glad for the solitude. She had too much to think about alone.

Mostly, she was thinking about her "interview" with Howie Leon. Mostly, she was thinking about the way he confessed everything (or was he bragging?) about his past, with the ease of one whose grasp on reality was not what she would describe as fine. He had confused her and he had scared her, his eyes seemed to take on an other-worldly shine. Frankly,

Marcie was afraid to write about Dr. Howie Leon. She was worried he might come after her, turn on her, perhaps even smear a little blood around. She couldn't be sure that he wouldn't try to do her in. Since her first half hour at the Ansonia a month had gone by; she had yet to commit a word to paper. Not that she hadn't tried. Murray Sandler had been on the phone every day ("Just get a story, *any* story done!"), threatening her, pleading with her, but she was completely blocked. Anxious now, Marcie looked at the clock. "God damn!" Why couldn't Ronnie start this class on time? Already, she was ten minutes behind schedule and she had a hurricane of a day ahead.

She was trying to keep her mind off Howie Leon. She would have to put the writing off. Torture! It was one thing to see a rapist's credentials (on paper), but it was quite another to hear him explain his *modus operandi* in the flesh. She had sat with him in the Ansonia, her Sony TC-55 by her side, endured his description of the kind of woman he hit on, "a woman who looked like she needed it. The tougher they are, the better. Challenge interests me, I like to break them down." He claimed to have "seduced" over three hundred women in the past year and a half. He said the posters on his walls would prove it.

Her skin had crawled, but she had stuck it out. She listened to his descriptions, heard him talk about his wife who'd died. She'd blanched when he'd brought out the Polaroid quickies, sat without flinching through the series that had dozens of almost-identical brunette heads going down on him. "Why do women respond to you?" she had asked him when he'd finished with his display.

Howie Leon had just looked at her. He could instill more fear without saying anything than anyone she had ever seen. She wondered if her terror was imaginary. Then he took her hand. "Women respond to me because . . . I know how to treat them," Howie Leon tried to look soulfully into her eyes. "I do the one thing that no other man on earth can do. . . ." He paused, then moved his face a fraction closer. Marcie Laster was sure he could sense her tension, sure that any moment she would begin to scream. He was letting the suspense build to a near-unbearable point. Spontaneous combustion! "I UNDERSTAND WOMEN!" he had bellowed before he tried to pull her down. She was sure if he hadn't remembered she was a reporter, she would have never gotten away.

An overpowering nausea crept over Marcie Laster, as if a sudden chill had found its way inside the gym. Getting dizzier, she began to fidget, then she looked around. Waves of women had taken refuge behind machines. "Yeeeccchh! I don't care what it smells like, ladies. *something* has to be done!" In Ronnie's hands was the murder weapon, an aerosol bomb. The heavy mist hung in the air, strawberry-flavored nitrous oxide. The sicky-sweet vapors attacked her stomach, then her lungs. One more second in that studio and she would . . . She ran, grabbed her abdomen, stumbled into a bathroom stall. She heaved and heaved, but nothing came up. For a moment, Marcie Laster forgot she hadn't eaten for two entire days.

She was dying, so she crawled into the steam room, made her way along the floor. She tried not to breathe, then she gulped for air. The noxious aerosol smell had been left outside the door. She was positively relieved to drink in large doses of steam and women's sweat. If only she could see. Billowing steam clouds attacked her eyes, her nose. Carefully she made her way to the center of the room, but she wasn't deft enough. She stumbled over a clammy body and fell flat on her face.

The body sat up. *"Are you all right?"* She was small and blond, her voice somehow familiar, breathy, well modulated with just a hint of a whine.

It took Marcie Laster a full three seconds to click. "Peaches Rosen! *I don't believe it!*"

"Marcie? This is . . . *to die!*"

They fell upon each other like ex-sorority sisters at a tenth reunion, with a mixture of curiosity, envy, annoyance, and affection. During the entire four months since they'd seen each other, neither one had tried to contact the other. Both had thought about it—Peaches because she wanted to find out about Florida; Marcie because she wanted Peaches to help her get a job. They had resisted their mutual temptation. Still, they were glad to see each other. The Laster-Rosen friendship depended on the coincidences of time and place. The Ponce DeLeon steam room was the epitome of fortuitous time and neutral place.

Peaches Rosen had resumed attendance at the run-down gym for only one reason. She couldn't care less about the Body Jazz, didn't need wet heat to help her obtain a more sanguine frame of mind. What she needed was to find Florida Burns, but she was afraid to pick up the phone and call her. What if she answered? Coward! She didn't know how to say "I'm sorry," she didn't know how to explain her seven-month silence without a total loss of face. She thought it would be better just to run into her than to brave the telephone or to send a fatuous note.

So maybe being stumbled over by Marcie Laster was a godsend. Maybe Marcie could help her gauge Florida Burns' state of mind. So much to catch up on! Peaches Rosen forced herself to smile, then stretched out in mock delight. She would gird herself for a ten-minute Marcie Laster monologue, she would emit the proper incredulous responses to a barrage of Laster *schtick.* She would wait, and then she would pounce, and ask the question that was uppermost in her mind.

But first she would have to submit to the bullshit. It was endless. How all summer long Marcie Laster thought she would go out of her mind at Metropolitan, how everyone had been telling her for months that she was much too bright to be there in the first place, my God, what did she need it for? How she had said to herself, why the hell didn't she do something about changing jobs and who would have ever thought it but without her having to lift a finger out of the fuckin' woodwork crawled this crazy cop who had sucked her into this most unbelievable case that come to think of it . . . would make a great property for Jason Jaffe. That is, if you still see him.

"I do," Peaches said through a rising screen of vapors the color of bullets.

"Well, then let me tell you about this guy. He's a . . ."

"Are you working on a script?" Peaches made herself ask.

"Not yet. I'm doing an . . . exposé." The words fairly

189

rolled off her tongue. "The case is unbelievable! He's a rapist, but it's more than *that*. He's a . . . Don Juan type. He's a psychopath who's likable, if you can picture that, kind of like a Bobby DeNiro or a . . ."

"Jason Jaffe?"

"Exactly!"

Something was beginning to register in Peaches Rosen. "What do you mean you're doing an exposé? You mean, like in a film? Something Metropolitan is doing?"

Marcie Laster hesitated only long enough to take a breath. Should she tell her? Could she count on Peaches not to go running to Florida Burns? *Of course.* They hadn't seen each other since spring, and everybody knew that Peaches and little Miss Tell Me Everything were no longer friends. Of course she would tell her. Maybe she could get Jason Jaffe interested in the film rights. Naked greed and ambition overtook her better instinct for discretion. For a moment she forgot about Murray Sandler, forgot about his imploring her not to tip her hand. What she was working on was just too hot not to share. "No, I'm not doing a script—that is, unless 'somebody' would want to buy it. I'm writing an article. I've become an 'investigative reporter.' This is a *crime story.* And when it hits, *wow!* Move over, Carl Bernstein and whatever that other guy's name is. . . . Hello, Barbara Walters!"

Now Peaches was really listening. "Who are you writing the story for?"

"*We-e-e-lll* . . . you swear you won't tell anyone?"

"Of course."

"Do I have your absolute word of honor, I mean it, this is like life and death to me."

"Marcie. I swear upon the lives of my unborn children."

"Okay, then. I'm doing it for *Close-Up,* you know, the magazine section of the Tower Syndicate?"

"Hey, wow! That's really great. Did Florida arrange that?"

"Are you kidding? She doesn't even know about it. Ohmygod, you're not still friends with her, are you?"

Peaches Rosen sat up, pulled her sheet around her.

190

"No . . . of course not. Isn't that common knowledge? We haven't talked since . . . I don't know when."

Lost in the clouds, Marcie smiled. "Thank God. Well, nobody has. Talk about someone who is 'over.' After this coup, I wouldn't be surprised if Florida . . ."

Peaches waited, then lowered her voice. "*Hey.* Have you spoken with her? What's she doing?"

"No idea. And I think after The Tower spreads this story around . . . I doubt if she'll ever speak to me again. Not that that would be any loss. The way I hear it from my friends at the Tower, Milman is so disgusted with Tell Me Everything, he's just waiting for me to get my act together before he gets rid of her." Marcie Laster tried to modulate the jubilation in her voice. "What can I say? If she's a writer, she should at least act like a professional. You know what I mean?"

"Sure, sure . . . I do." A towel draped Peaches' head, muffling her words. She had always viewed Marcie Laster as a conniving opportunist.

Paradox! Once she had warned Florida not to confide in her, not to think of her as a friendly camp. Now, the guilt Peaches had been feeling bloated into the world's largest anxiety attack.

Somewhere she smelled a rat. She had to do something, but what? She couldn't let Marcie Laster get out of this steam room without exposing her designs. She stammered, trying to collect her thoughts. She would have to stall. "Listen . . . this story sounds unbelievable! Who is the guy? I'd love to tell Jay about it, he's always looking for properties, projects, you know how actors are. . . ."

She took another breath, then pretended to stifle a yawn. Mustn't let Marcie Laster think that she's too interested, mustn't let Marcie Laster know that she had indeed turned Peaches on. "I mean, it's so *bo-o-o-ring* just to sit here in the heat. If you feel that you could, I'd love to hear about this rapist guy. How you found him and everything. Then . . . well, I shouldn't say this, but then maybe . . . if *I* think the idea is something that Jason might have the remotest interest in

. . . well, no. Forget that I said that. I mean, he's so busy, he doesn't even have time to think. *But,* maybe-just-maybe, if the story about this rapist is *faabulous,* then maybe I could arrange a little supper party and you could come over. . . ." Peaches waited. "I mean, I'd love you all to get to know each other, anyway. You have so much in common."

In the stillness, Marcie fairly glowed. At last. This would be her year, this was turning out to be her season to really shine. Her perspiration had formed an ocean on the floor. She was lightheaded, but not from the steam, she felt she could stay like this and talk for an eternity. Still, the Ponce DeLeon steam room was not exactly the setting she'd envisioned for her first story conference as a star. She grasped for a solution, found herself choking on the hot air. She had to do something, she couldn't let her golden moment, her chance for the consummate film/book/exposé subsidiary rights package deal, evaporate into nothing more than a promise not to tell. She would have to change the setting, then she'd figure how to operate from there.

She'd made a decision. *"Daarrlinggg* . . . I'd love to tell you all about it. I'd love for you to be the *only* one I'd tell. I'd love to get your advice on how to write it. But first, do you feel like having a little bite . . . of lunch? We have so much to talk about."

He wondered what the water bill must be like during the warm months, how the building could afford to keep those cast-iron lilies sprouting all summer and well into the fall. Mike Markman had been sitting by his window for hours, ever since he'd gotten the final call. Misery! He'd set the receiver onto its hook, then dragged his bentwood rocker to his favorite spot. There he sat, stiff as frozen rope, feeling the last rays of the sun as he slipped into shock.

He was in despair. He was unable to think, eat, or sleep. He was glued to his rocker, rooted to his post, for weeks all he'd had for exercise was a gentle back and forth. *Back and forth.*

192

But there was no going back. La Taquita was already in Chapter Eleven. Within six months (or maybe weeks) La Taquita would be in receivership, which meant that Mike Markman's paper worth, at one time an astounding $325,000, would have dribbled down to $14,500. Not counting his five rooms at the Dakota, thank God he'd paid for them in cash. Irony! By his thirtieth birthday he would have made and lost a paper corporate million. He wouldn't believe superior management and insistent quality had conspired to do him in. He would kill for twenty-six suburban Baskin-Robbins, fuck the goddamn *picante* and beans. He was a fool and his ambition had run away with him. One lousy write-up in the *New York Post* and seventeen consumer groups had come down upon his head. Two crummy talk shows and his competitors, Jack 'n the Box and Pup 'n' Taco, had begun to close in fast. How could he have known someone in their offices would both times have accidentally tuned him in? They were blanketing his areas, stealing his management, his ideas. Mike Markman didn't have a chance, not in Manhattan, where the ecologically pure didn't know from quality, didn't understand real class. And certainly not in his territories, not when he was thrown up against the big-time franchisers, against them he wouldn't have a prayer. Cut costs? Hah! They could fairly rape his price. Dollar for dollar, ounce for ounce, their imitations could be cranked out. They had beaten him by a price ratio of over two to one. Complicated! Mike Markman hadn't been able to whip the hamburger fetishists. Mike Markman had hoped—in his areas, at least—that those dedicated burgerphiles would switch. Then perhaps a miracle would occur: they would think of the taco and the burger as one patriotic lump.

He had been wrong. The taco was still considered something foreign, perhaps even a "luxury." Anyway, how could he have beaten Jack in the Box's so-very-unforeign marketing of three for eighty-nine? He had been slaughtered. *Christ.* They didn't even use real meat in their tacos, just beans laced with chile powder! Fate! He'd been killed by his home state; slain by an L.A. bowdlerization. Were these tacos? Not by his stan-

193

dards, not by the F.D.A.'s. He wondered if the F.D.A. even had standards. . . . What a question. Of course not, he read the daily *Times.*

He was being childish, needlessly bitter about the process of free trade. He wasn't cut out to run a business, to endure the *mishagas.* He couldn't take the constant traveling, the research, the hassling with the unions, the heat waves, the cold snaps, gauging his truckers' and suppliers' states of mind. *He was sick of it!* And completely out of touch. Mike Markman had been letting circumstances control him, he'd lost sight of what he'd always wanted to do in life.

His mind was floating miles away, but his eyes focused on a dining-room window across the courtyard. He didn't understand it, but there was Sherwin Sunneson at it again. How long could he have been back, around a week? And every night a different woman, the last three nights they had all been blondes. Mike Markman frowned. It was so anti-female, all of that, so old hat. How could he do it? Sherwin Sunneson was first and foremost A Producer, which meant he must be a bloodsucking, hard-nosed, grisly S.O.B. Three plays on Broadway! Who would think he'd have the strength to get it up at all, much less never miss a night. The blonde was laughing now, obviously at some *mal mot* Sherwin Sunneson had just tossed her way.

Mike Markman let his eyes close and tried to conjure up an imaginary conversation with Sunneson's blonde. *How's the steak?* he might start it out, then, if encouraged, cruise into, *May I teach you how to give perfect head?* In the dark, all alone, Mike Markman laughed out loud. Thinking about "giving head" reminded him of La Taquita Number 7's short-order manager Lou-Ann. Bananas! He'd hired her on a three-week trial basis, she had insisted that he put her special fried banana chips on the menu as an alternative to tostadas. One day, he'd overheard her talking to the counter girl. "Want me to show you how to give the world's most mind-blowing head?" Suddenly Lou-Ann flourished a banana, then she began gently sucking it into her mouth. He watched her tongue, circling it like a streamer on a Maypole. From the kitchen Mike Markman watched . . . transfixed . . . till he couldn't stand it any more. He'd barely made it to the john in time.

Maybe he should write about Lou-Ann, or one of his other serving aides. He had a million stories! He would hardly know where to begin. A book! Mike Markman could turn out his own version of *The Funny Money Game.* For a moment he felt cheered, then he sagged. How could he write anything, much less A Book, if he couldn't even muster the energy to leave his rocking chair?

All week long, he had avoided phone calls, hadn't bothered to open his mail. He had burrowed in, and he wasn't sure he ever felt like coming back. He rather liked his shell.

At least in his shell he could duck his obligations, pretend that he had totally withdrawn from community life. And certainly from the Dakota's "social committee," from its twice-weekly meetings planning the annual fête. A charming custom, that. Each fall the Dakota gave itself a courtyard supper, every resident pitched in to help. Which meant that Rex Reed would whip up his famous key lime pies and Yoko Lennon would send tubs of sashimi and vats of rice, garnished with the name of her baby artfully spelled out in peas. Ninety-five mini-feifdoms this grand old building contained and each principality sought to out-*gemütlich* the next; each resident hoped his contribution to the fête would earn him some sort of in-house fame.

Five of them were on the steering committee, whipping the soiree into shape. Mike Markman was in charge of the tables and chairs, tablecloths, and silver, just because he was "in restaurants." Now the Dakota's version of a "block party" was only a day away. The tables and the chairs were stacked like stage flats down in the basement, the cloths were, he hoped, on their way. He had done his bidding and he was tired. He couldn't take one more meeting. He couldn't take another pre-business social drink, couldn't take wrangling with the banker's wife about life-and-death matters like the number of serving trays.

195

So for days he had been dodging their attempts to press him into service. For over a week he'd ignored their phone calls and the avalanche of notes slipped under his door. He was taking a leave of absence, which meant Mike Markman was letting his ladies down.

He was feeling sorry for himself. He probably wouldn't even show up in the courtyard for the great event itself. Instead, he would sit in his rocker like a Sun City relic and he would just . . . watch. The entire world—starting with the group that would be gathering at tomorrow's Dakota party—would pass him by, and Mike Markman would be condemned to a voyeur's fate. Because that's what he felt like, a palsied geriatric. Any moment he'd be ready for a regime of shuffleboard and high colonics.

He was twenty-nine, and he was a has-been. He was powerless, unable to save himself. Even his handwriting had disintegrated. Illegible! Trying to scrawl out his last remaining financial statements, he had thought, so this is what a nervous breakdown must be like. He had to do something, but what? He closed his eyes and rocked, then it came to him. He grabbed for a pad, clutched a pen like he was on death row. He had just remembered something. An elevator converstaion, nothing more. A banker's wife had been speaking to a friend. "Whenever I feel 'out of control,' I just force myself to sit down. Then I write my name over and over till I get my handwriting to look . . . normal. Then *I* feel normal too." Common sense! He wrote Mike-Markman-Mike-David-Markman-Michael-David-Markman - M.-D. - Markman-Mike-Mike-Mike-Markman-Markman-Markman over and over again, covering three sheets. Useless! He might be able to get his handwriting back to Palmer Method standards, but perfect penmanship could do nothing to alter the reality of La Taquita's balance sheets.

Guilty! He was worried about how Manny Markman would react. He closed his eyes, imagining Manny Markman's probable reaction. "You can always lose your money, but you can never lose your name." Is that what Manny Markman would say? Of course not. Manny Markman would come up with an absolute pearl like, "So? This is why we dropped out of law school? This is why we turned up our nose at a 'professional career'?" The thought of it sent Mike Markman plunging even lower into his self-appointed emotional abyss.

What was the matter with him? Thirty years old any minute and he was still dying for his old man's approval. Humiliation! For the last few moments, he was stricken by the image of his mother weeping softly in her grave.

Remorse overcame him, then his tear ducts stung at the memory of the pain. There he sat, a solitary figure etched in electric light, and just . . . rocked. His mind was unoccupied, a ravaged and abandoned demilitarized zone. Now he was left to turn the other cheek.

But he couldn't. He didn't know how to recoup, how to fight back. Real estate! He didn't hold title to one inch. Not the kind he could unload on Jack in the Box, anyway. All he'd managed to obtain were dozens of extended leases. La Taquita (and its creator) would be slaughtered ignominiously, a vicious contrast to the noble dream out of which they had been born.

Or would they? From somewhere on the periphery of catatonia, Mike Markman was coming back. He had never been a quitter. He still had his dreams, somewhere. He still had that long-repressed desire to roll up his sleeves and write; he still felt printer's ink circulating in his veins. His days on the Pacific Palisades *Bear Paw* might have happened a decade and a half ago, but they were vividly enshrined in his memory. And his subscriptions to his twenty-two morning papers had over a year left to go.

He felt it was a small sign, but perhaps a promise that his life also had an extended run. Quick! Out came a legal pad, his pencil danced out a mathematical minuet. Let's see. He was down to $14,500 plus assorted nickels and pennies which put him far above—at least in cash—the minimal subsistence line. But he had not the promise of a future dime! So! With $900 a month taken by the Dakota, then if he figured another $100 or so for food or tossed in a few thousand "miscellaneous"

197

expenses just to cover cabs . . . Mike Markman's head was bowed, his lower lip was tucked under his front teeth. Taxes! Fun money! Clothes! He'd have to cut way, way back. No more tennis. No more special quail pâtés. Time for subway tokens and tuna fish, time to live lean. He had a year—one year!—to get an entirely new career organized and off the ground.

SHERWIN SUNNESON	X	
	X	IN THE JUDICIAL
Plaintiff	X	
	X	DISTRICT COURT OF
VS	X	
TELEMEDIA, INCORPORATED	X	THE BOROUGH OF
and Cherie Rivers	X	MANHATTAN, NEW YORK
	X	

PLAINTIFF'S ORIGINAL PETITION

TO THE HONORABLE JUDGE OF SAID COURT:

NOW COMES Sherwin Sunneson, hereinafter referred to as Plaintiff, and complaining of Telemedia, Incorporated, hereinafter referred to as Defendant, and Cherie Rivers, hereinafter referred to as Defendant Rivers, files this his Original Petition and as grounds therefor would show the court the following:

I.

Plaintiff has been the Chief Operating Officer and Chairman of Sherwin Sunneson Presentations for twenty-two years and at the time of the filing of this Petition continues in said position. The Defendant Telemedia, Incorporated broadcasts a weekly ten minute news show known as "Tinseltown Wrap-up." Such defendant's broadcast generally carries a series of news items relating to matters of show business interest involving various people, businesses, and organizations with some relationship to the entertainment industry. Plaintiff is informed and believes, and on such information and belief alleges, that the above referred to broadcast has a wide rating and a substantial audience in

198

Manhattan and outlying boroughs, New York; that it is widely publicized and receives a great deal of attention among the theatrical and entertainment communities of the City of New York.

II

Plaintiff alleges that the "Tinseltown Wrap-Up" broadcast of June 30th at 10:19 p.m. of the current year is the basis for this litigation. A copy of such broadcast is attached hereto, labeled Exhibit "A," and made a part hereof for all purposes. Plaintiff alleges that such broadcast is demeaning and belittling; that it was written with malice; that it contains statements which are absolutely untrue and false; that the whole tenor of the broadcast is to cheapen the Plaintiff's image, damage his reputation and make him look petty, small and otherwise ridiculous; that the broadcast holds Plaintiff up to public ridicule and is humiliating; that the broadcast was written at a time when the Defendants knew the Plaintiff was seeking both the talents and the services of one Jason Jaffe and that the broadcast would thus do the Plaintiff the greatest possible harm because of its timing; that the purpose of the broadcast was to humiliate and embarrass the Plaintiff and make him look bad in the eyes of the public, hence hurting the Plaintiff's image and clearly reducing his chances of being successful in the continuation of his theatrical career and in any business career the Plaintiff might undertake.

III

Plaintiff alleges that he has been seriously damaged by the actions of the Defendants; that he is entitled to be compensated in damages for the malicious and deliberate libel and slander which the Defendants have committed. Plaintiff sues for actual damages of $1,000,000 and for exemplary damages of $2,500,000. Plaintiff further sues for all costs and for reasonable attorneys' fees.

Wherefore, PREMISES CONSIDERED, Plaintiff prays that Defendants be cited to appear and answer herein and that on hearing hereof Plaintiff have judgment against the Defendants, jointly and severally, in the amounts set forth above, both actual and exemplary, such damages being for the libel and slander which have been committed against Plaintiff

199

with malice and willfullness. Plaintiff further prays for recovery of costs and reasonable attorneys' fees and for all other relief to which he might be in any way entitled.

KLEIN & KLEIN

BY

_____

T.E.D. Klein
One Park Avenue
New York, New York 10016

Attorney for Plaintiff

For the first time in days, Sherwin Sunneson had something to smile about. Beautiful! For him, nothing was as lyrical as a perfectly drawn legal document. He was convinced that this one had the touch of a poet. Sherwin Sunneson had always adored the intricacies of the judicial process. He had moved mountains (and walked on water) by applying his knowledge of torts to everyday problems. Titan! He was armed with a weapon more powerful than a .357 Magnum, he knew for sure he had both Telemedia and Cherie Rivers on the run. He was even more certain that within forty-eight hours he would have both a star and a fresh shipment of gravlax to serve at his annual fund-raising brunch.

He grabbed for his phone, then pressed the intercom buzzer. "Daisy? If you would be so kind as to take a tiny bit of dictation, dear lady. . . . Oh! And we'll need a messenger to run a small packet over to Sixty-ninth and . . . on the rolodex, if you could look up an address for—surely we have it—Jason Jaffe. . . ." He waited, then for the briefest instant he frowned. "Aha! We do have it! Good! Shall we begin, then?" He shuffled his notes, then cleared his throat. "Ready? . . . 'Dearest Jason' . . . Let me think, I know. . . . 'If I can forget my four-dollar cleaning bill and my equally stained pride, then what more do I need to convince you that you have done the American theatrical community a great disservice by your self-imposed hibernation. That Jaffe should be idle' . . . *parenthesis* . . . 'and at his own behest' . . . *parenthesis* . . . 'is shocking. But more. That

200

Jason Jaffe, one of America's gifted young actors, should be in hiding is positively criminal.' *Paragraph.* 'But rather than berate you any more, I propose that you peruse the enclosed documents. You will be gratified, I trust, to see that I have initiated a legal complaint which, one hopes, will eradicate the presence of Cherie Rivers from late-night television. The other item is much more important, however. It is the play that, God willing, will bring Jason Jaffe back to Broadway and to an audience, where he so truly belongs.' . . . Sign it, 'All best.' . . . One more thing. Another messenger, this one to go to Telemedia . . . to the President, whatever his name is. 'Dear So and So: I should be most pleased to discuss possible dissolution of the Telemedia-Sunneson suit at your earliest convenience. I only ask for a single pre-condition for negotiating a reasonable settlement. And that is this: replacement of your current columnist or eradication of the entire "Tinseltown Wrap-up" show.' Sign it, 'Sincerely.' Now . . . let's sit back and wait for the phones to ring."

"Florida?"

"Hi . . ."

"Did I wake you up?"

"No . . ."

"You sound like you were still . . ."

"MOTHER! It's ten o'clock on a Sunday morning, already. I've been up . . . for hours. *I've already jogged ten miles.*"

"Please take that tone out of your voice, dear."

"What tone?"

"I hate talking to you when you're like this."

"I'm not 'like this' . . . whatever 'this' is."

"All right, dear. Let's try to have a pleasant conversation. How are you?"

"Just couldn't be better!"

"Oh?"

"Never been happier in my entire life!"

"What's going on?"

"Let's see . . . just the usual. Parties every night, men

coming out of my ears, the phone doesn't stop ringing, and, well, this is minor . . . but, in the last week alone both Bill Paley and Punch Sulzberger have been fighting each other about who was going to be the one to get to offer Miss Florida Burns . . ."

"Darling, why are you being so sarcastic?"

"Me, sarcastic?"

"Darling, listen. If it's getting too rough for you up there . . . come home! Your father and I . . ."

"I really don't want to discuss this, Mother. If you don't mind."

"I know, dear. But not everyone has the constitution for that frustrating, nerve-racking, super-competitive, over-wrought existence. I don't know how you can take it. I never could."

"Well . . . *I* thrive on it."

"That's . . . great, dear. Just great. . . . I admire you for it, I really do. I don't know how you can take all that pressure. . . . Well, now. Let me see. There was something I wanted to ask you about . . . what was it? Oh! I know what it was. Your friend, what's-her-name . . . Pammy? The one who goes with that actor . . . who is it she goes with . . . Dustin Hoffman?"

"Jason Jaffe."

"Oh. Who's that?"

"He's like Dustin Hoffman."

"I've never heard of him. Well, anyway. That's not important. What I was starting to tell you is that I just read about . . . Pammy, where was it? In *Women's Wear Daily?* Did you see the article?"

"Mother. Her name is 'Peaches' or 'Pamela' . . . not 'Pam-mee.' She'd die if anyone ever called her that."

"Well, What difference does it make? All those names sound alike. Peaches! Pam-mee! Stop picking on me! I can't stand it! I don't think I deserve this treatment this morning, Florida. I'm just trying to have a nice, friendly, harmless . . ."

"Well, Mother, I'm just trying to help you. If you're going to drop names, at least you could get them *right.*" What was wrong with me this morning? The bile in my tone was even poisoning me.

"All right, Florida. You made the point. Well . . ." I could hear my mother breathing, trying to say something nice. "Have you seen 'Peaches' since she started living with . . . that actor? Have they been inviting you over a lot?"

"Are you kidding? I practically live there."

"Oh. That's nice. You haven't mentioned it much."

"Well, do I have to tell you about every single thing I'm doing? Can't I have a little privacy? Can't I lead my own life without feeling that you're breathing down my neck every second?"

"*Will you stop yelling? I wish I could figure you out this morning.* I just wish I could figure what's getting you down. All I did was ask a simple little question! Is it such a crime to think that if you and 'Pamela' and whatever that actor's name is are seeing each other all the time, that maybe you might want to share a few things with me? That's all I meant! I just was curious as to why you're not writing about them in your column! Is that so bad?"

For the first time all morning, I noticed the edges of my Wandering Jew were beginning to blacken from the sun. "I really have to go, Mother. I have to water my plants."

"What?"

"I mean, I have to get ready to go to a party."

"A party? Whose party?"

"You don't know them."

"You are so snippy!"

"Well, what difference does it make?"

"I'm just trying to figure out what your life is like, why you're always in such black moods."

"I can assure you it has nothing to do with the day's festivities. *Not one thing.*"

"Why? Who's going to be at the 'day's festivities?'"

"Just the usual schleppers. Lauren Bacall. Rex Reed. Roberta Flack. Maybe John and Yoko Lennon . . . you remember them, he was the English singer? Then . . . Paul

203

Simon, another music type, will probably put in an appearance. Lenny and Felicia Bernstein. A few socialites. The Shah's brother-in-law. The people who own Maxwell's Plum, that's a restaurant. What can I tell you? Just your run-of-the-mill New York social climbers out for some free food. Does that answer your question, Mother?"

"Yes, dear. Only one more thing. . . ."

I could feel my mother's pain, so I tried to soften. Margie Burns! What an advertisement for the sheltered life! At that moment, I could have torn my larynx out of my throat for the agony I was putting her through. Margie Burns, with your unfettered view of the romantic nature of Man; Margie Burns, with your undying optimism that all of life revolves around finding a dream husband . . . Margie Burns, I am your daughter, still joined by an unseverable umbilical cord. I hoped she sensed that my torment was as great as hers. "I'm sorry, Mamma. What's the other thing? . . . *These haven't been the best of days.*"

I could feel my mother's silent, but earth-shattering debate. Does she press me to tell her what the matter is and risk another emotional outburst? Or does she press on to the other "thing" that is weighing on her mind? I felt her hesitation. "Well. I just wanted to say, that if you're having problems with your work, have you ever thought about doing what Barbara Walters does? You know, on television? Is it hard to get those jobs? Because . . . darling, with your good looks and sparkling wit, there's nothing that *should* hold you back." My mother didn't wait for me to cut her off with my snide remarks. "*Honey.* I don't see what Barbara Walters has that my daughter doesn't have in spades!"

Ecstasy! She could see the difference now. All summer long, Pamela Rosen had watched parenthesis lines starting to frame her mouth. Each day, her mouth had been tightened into an increasingly tense line. Some days, she had screamed when she passed her hall mirror, floodlit by the sun. She had pored over her baby pictures, stared at her face at ages six, eight, and ten. Narcissus! She would moan, "What *happened* to that little girl?"

Now she knew. That little girl was all grown up and looking better than ever. All in the last forty-eight hours, ever since the messenger had found his way from the Dakota to East Sixty-ninth Street bearing his precious burden. A play! Jason Jaffe had been signed, sealed, and delivered three hours after the packet had arrived. He would open in Sherwin Sunneson's forty-sixth production, exactly four months from tonight. And he would start rehearsing in just sixty days. Happy! Peaches Rosen thought she would die. She flipped through her closet looking for just the right combination of peasant ruffles, turbans, and shawls to wear to the Sunneson brunch. The Dakota! She knew, she just knew, that not only would she be attached to a Broadway star, but she would also have her best friend back by the end of the day.

Sherwin—now they were on first-name terms—had tipped her off about the Dakota stuff-in. Not *his* party, not his "oh-so-boring, but *malheureusement* necessary" brunch, but the *other* one: the community smorgasbord. "Fabulous!" Peaches had said. "Because then you can meet my absolute best friend in the entire world, Florida Burns! Do you know her? She lives on the ninth floor."

"The ninth floor?"

"Right."

"Where they converted the maids' rooms?"

"That's it."

"How . . . *raffiné*."

"She is that, all right."

Pamela Rosen had it all planned. She would send Jason upstairs, then she would cruise the courtyard alone. Never for a moment did she doubt her abilities to sniff out her human prey. She would pounce! *"Darling! Oh . . . Darleeeng!"* she would squeal, but first she would make sure she had an iron grip on Miss Florida Burns. After all, Florida had feelings too, and Peaches Rosen was sure they were mostly hostile ones. So! There would be histrionics, maybe even *a real scene.* She wasn't a bit concerned. The crying and the screaming and the wailing

205

and the sniveling would all be worth it. She would tip Florida off about Marcie Laster only after she carried off the first prong of her ingenious attack. Fun! She hadn't enjoyed scheming this much since she'd left the South. She would escort a tranquilized Florida Burns upstairs, wheel her into the Sunneson *grand salon.* She would keep her there just long enough to introduce her, and from there on out it would be a snap. "Sherwin!" she would call, "could we excuse ourselves?" Peaches Rosen knew that within minutes she would be able to hondle, wheedle, and cajole him. Manipulation! They didn't call her "Little Miss Gets-Her-Way" for nothing. "Wouldn't Florida be faaabulous as Cherie Rivers' replacement on Tele-media?" she would whisper the moment they had locked them-selves safely behind the divine Mr. S.'s library door. How could he say no? Of course! He would agree. And only when she had his promise would she move in on Jason Jaffe holding court in the living room. She would whisper "Sherwin's idea" into his ear; she would mention that "Sherwin felt" thirty minutes with a new TV star could only boost his career.

She could hardly keep from spilling her plans in the cab. She barely could restrain herself from letting Jason in on the perfectly conceived machinations that were on the verge of coming about. But no. Let him think her effervescence was tied to his turn of luck; let him believe that everything that came to pass would be by merest coincidence of time and place. She plucked at her Yves St. Laurent raven silk skirt; rear-ranged its calf-length folds more delicately over the tops of her sable and tan boots. Chic! Over the summer she had turned from a thrift-shop sharpie into a boutique queen. She still knew from rags. From the waist up she had on one of her best. Your basic Hawaiian gothic abbreviated chemise, so gaily floral its exuberance left Jason Jaffe mildly depressed. Only today, no possible calamity could get the Tony Award winner down. She smiled, then squeezed Jason's hand as they drove through Central Park. Sunshine! The dazzling light broke into a million splinters all over Indian summer ground. For the first time in weeks, they both started to hum. Corny! "What a Day for a Daydream . . ." tumbled off their lips, they had barely finished the first chorus by the time the taxi had pulled up and stopped close to the front gate.

From inside the car, Peaches could see that the Dakota's party had already begun. By the time she and Jay were inside the gate, she had convinced him that he would be better off tackling Sunneson's brunch, at least at first, on his own. "I'll just be in your way," she had sighed. Then, seeing him hesitate, she added, "I'll be up in a second, just let me stay down here a few moments, greet some people, then check my face." Before he could argue she had whipped out her tortoise-shell compact and bared her teeth at the glass. She couldn't believe it, but those parenthesis lines that forty-eight hours before had been deep as ditches seemed hardly noticeable, more like two light pencil scratches. Radiant! She looked as good as she felt. She was soaring, so while the mood lasted she pushed Jason into the lift and disappeared into the crowd.

It had taken me an hour to figure out which pair of jeans I should wear. There were faded blue Levis (real) and faded green Wranglers-for-Women. There were tan cords and black Levis-for-gals with persimmon contrast stitching. What about the French brushed cottons that hugged my behind? Or the nailhead studded velvets with the belt set in just below the waistline? My anxiety grew along with the pile of discarded trousers on the bed. Twenty-six years old and I still couldn't get it together about a minor matter like clothes. Twenty-six years old and independent and I still had a wardrobe of disparate and uncoordinated parts. Psychology! I would have to try to look rich, as if I belonged.

And maybe I did. The fact that Brian Milman had put me "on notice" didn't prevent a note announcing the annual party from being slipped under my door. Ninety-five principalities representing the worlds of the arts and finance would be represented at this afternoon's convocation. The fact that I was a known sublet couldn't prevent me from getting *something* on. I would hustle my buns off, if only I could figure out what, for starters, to cover them in. Classic! I would rely on the formula which said "familiarity is best." From the bottom of the heap came my special Sigma Delta Tau model 28/31 stovepipe button-fronts. These were the real thing, like they don't make any more. A velvet jacket and well-worn Frye boots should finish off the look. *Not bad.* Half-dressed, I craned my neck out of the bathroom window to catch the courtyard view. Activity! Dozens of women were setting up tables hundreds of feet below. The autumn breeze was whipping checkered cloths around like flags while an army of khaki-uniformed handymen tried to hold them in place. Long banquet tables formed a battle line along the Seventy-third Street gate. I squinted, then leaned out a little more. Could those be silver platters which, from the altitude, glowed like fresh-minted dimes?

I didn't want to miss out on one more second of the action. Get it together! Within seconds I had blackened my lashes and fluffed up my afro, within minutes I had *schvitzed* on the Madame Rochas and was long out the door.

I was moving fast, but not fast enough. On the fifth floor I was stopped in mid-flight. "Scuse me, scuse me," someone drawled. "Are you going to the party? Because I could use some help." I turned just in time to catch an angular, tall, dark, post-graduate preppie in distress, yelling from the nearest staircase landing. In his arms were two enormous lime pies, only partially obscuring his camel herringbone jacket with the trademark suede elbow patches.

Rex Reed! I had grabbed one tin pie plate from him before he had time to ask me again. I smiled, then mumbled something banal. Suddenly I felt I had sixty-five tongues, a phenomenon I'd observed in myself upon coming in contact with celebrities in the flesh. I mean, what does one say to Rex Reed at such a cozy moment?

Thank God he spoke first. "*Thaaaank-ewe.* I tell you, I almost dropped the damn—" His words floated away in the air because just then he wheeled around and saw that the elevator was locked shut, the double bronze doors sealed absolutely tight. "*Gawd. Don't tell me* . . . Are they broken again? This building! With what the maintenance has gone up to, you think they could at least—"

"I think it's working. I just hate waiting."

"I know what you mean." He used the crook of his elbow to smash the button marked "down." "*Gawd.* Waiting for these damn things is worse than sitting through sixteen reels of a Cassavetes movie. . . . It's just *awe-full.*"

"The worst. . ." I paused, then stopped myself from saying something incredibly gauche.

"Well, should we break down and . . . walk?"

I was only too happy to agree.

We set off down the marble stairs as comfortable as two Dakota neighbors can be when only one is sure of the other one's name. And I tried, God knows I tried to make small talk, but I was distracted by cracks in the topping of the pie. What would Rex Reed say if I destroyed his meringues? I'd sooner die, so I clung to the oak banister for support. He'd have to be blind not to sense that I was uptight.

"*Listen.* You don't have to be *that* careful. I put in a teaspoon of cornstarch, they'll stay as hard as Plymouth Rock all afternoon."

Brilliant! Was it any wonder Rex Reed was a star? And popular as well. We shoved open the first-floor double doors; by the time we'd taken thirty steps it seemed as if half the building had stopped Rex to chat. Like an au pair girl I tried to pull a vanishing act.

It was no use. Suddenly we found ourselves next to a lady in blue, who took our pies. She was propped behind a table clutching a clipboard and pen. Contributions! It seems as if everyone (but me) had more than pulled their own weight. I hoped the general populace would view me as maybe a . . . Rex Reedian date. I was ignored, passed over, and looked around. Which couldn't have made me happier. Anonymity! I was free to soak up the color, what they call in the magazines "the general ambiance."

The Dakota courtyard was reeking with it. Food! Everywhere you looked a dish chafed or a tray steamed. On each one were banners made from tooth picks and felt hearts. "Ersatz Chasen's Chile by Betty Bacall" sat plate-by-jowl with a vat labeled "Moussaka from Maxwell's Plum, Apartment 54."

A barrel's worth of chopped iceberg lettuce had been tagged "The Bernsteins." Then there was a football field of butter-scotch brownies baked, so the sign said, "By Robbie and Clara Bingham." "Salmon Mousse compliments of David Marlow." A pot of meatballs, without a flag, perfumed the air with an essence of garlic and wine. There were sides of beef and foothills of cheese, kegs of beer and blueberry pies. Lakes of potato salad! Rivers of cole slaw! And three tubs of sushi, sashimi, and seaweed from, yes!, John and Yoko Lennon.

Excess! A bar mitzvah for three chunky triplets wouldn't have been equal to this orgy. And certainly not the residents of this special West Side address. Nobody was eating. Not one thing. Well, it was early. The food was still arriving; I watched transfixed as the checker stuck flags in more and more plat-ters. Around me my neighbors were oblivious. A blond kid had climbed way high on a ladder, tying pink balloons onto red and white Japanese lamps. Near him, one of the khaki handymen was fighting to get up a sign, "WELCOME! DAKOTA AUTUMN FOL-LIES!" Underneath was neatly stenciled, "Residents Only" Exclusive! Clusters of people swirled around me, breaking up and coalescing like balls of mercury. I noticed that Rex Reed had disappeared, been swallowed up by the crowd. I let my eyes fly past the tables downstage center, where cliques of residents were already staking out their own folding chairs. Aha! There was Rex Reed, leaning against the carriageway, and he was talking with . . . I strained to see. Oh! *That* guy. Who was that man? Tall and dark like you used to see in the movies, but he was decked out in cinnamon suede and faded denims. I noticed when he smiled his teeth caught the sun. Something told me he was foreign, maybe Italian.

Platzangst! I didn't know . . . anybody. Just faces: faces-of-the-famous, faces-from-the-elevators, faces-from-hurried-hellos-in-hallways. Still, I lived in the Dakota, didn't I? That meant that I belonged. I just wished I had someone to talk to.

Then I was rescued. The woman flagging the pies spotted me looking around. "Hey, are you doing anything?"

"Me?"

"Would you mind taking my place for a while?"

"No. . . . I mean, not at all. . . ." She showed me how to check off the names, where to prong the goods. With a wave, she too evaporated into the crowd.

I was overjoyed to have a job, to feel part of the action. I was only too grateful to be able to label watercress sandwiches and baby strudel; pickled artichokes and guacamole, trays of black breads and caviars. I was snowed under by the enormity of the task, I was trying to keep smiling under this avalanche of homemade *exotica*. And I was doing my darnedest to apply that age-old diet trick (keep a stiff upper lip), or, as my mother would say, "Use your mouth for words, dear." My fingers relaxed only after the tray of butterscotch brownies had been whisked away. Another crisis averted! *If only Marcie Laster was here,* I was thinking. *She could have a field day.*

But thank God she wasn't. Bitch! I remembered that she and I were no longer friends. I mean, how could you be, friendly, that is, with a patient who takes your career-counseling advice and uses it to try to get the doctor (ergo, me) out of her way? I knew a machete when I saw one, and I'd been tipped off by Andy Marks that the sharpest blade on the manufacturer's list was being readied. You didn't have to be in MENSA to know that it would have Florida Burns' name engraved on it. This was a sister? A fellow feminist? A comrade-in-arms? I'd sooner lie down with a rattler in heat, at least a real snake would make a noise before it bit me. Women like Marcie Laster set "the movement" back fifty years. At least, if she wanted a cat fight, let her come out in the open and scrap like . . . a man. Wasn't that the modern way, the post-liberated way, the enlightened way? Dare I call her and say, "Put up your dukes!"? No! She'd just pull a Pamela Rosen on me, which is to say never-but-ever return a single phone call. Deception! Had femaledom regressed to the era of Claire Booth Luce's vicious *Women* and then sadly left that era's wit and artfulness behind? Had we let our ambitions rape us of our sense of humor and, even more tragically, of our men?

I mean, Christ. If both Peaches Rosen and Marcie Laster wanted to fuck me over, the least they could do was tell me about it. It's not like I couldn't take it. Had honesty and

211

humanity gone out with the sixties? The enormity of this opaque concept swept over me amidst a torrential downpour of bagels and lox. *Ellman, check. Shiva, check. Wager, check. Segal!* I had more than philosophical musings on the decade to occupy my poor excuse for a mind. I had work to do.

A wooden washtub dropped like a bomb in front of me. A blanket of foil covered the top. "Fried chicken for . . . thirty. Markman. Apartment 87." Only then did I look up. Apartment 87 was young, middling height, head crowned by prematurely slate and white hair. I fixed on him from the waist down. Markman (87) was my twin! We had on matching peg-leg button-fronts, undoubtedly from the same year. I wondered if he was the ZBT fraternity boy I had been searching for all my life. I smiled and said, "Thank you." Then I looked to Number 87's left. Wouldn't you know he'd be attached to a streaked Madison Avenue blonde? Just my usual dumb luck. I knew my sagging features would give my inordinate disappointment away, so I averted my glance. I didn't want Mrs. Apartment 87 to know how I felt. I turned back to my clipboard, pretending more than casual dedication toward the task at hand. I didn't look up till I was sure the Markmans were safely gone.

But I could look down. Markman's 1968 "Levis Classic" model retreating over the Dakota cobblestones had been replaced by a black silk skirt and a pair of tan and ink size five custom-made boots. I heard my name spoken. "Florida?" a tiny little voice had by now repeated several times.

I forced myself to look up, then I wanted to die. What could she want? Surrounded by meatballs and fried chicken, I felt she had come to lead me to slaughterhouse five.

Was it just my vanity which made her seem as if she might be . . . *contrite?*

No. Clearly Peaches Rosen had come to make up. And just as clearly I would have no part of it. I pushed my chair back, almost knocking it over; then I ran! Down serpentine hallways, past byzantine doors, I vaulted up rosestone staircases, taking three steps at a time. Nine flights! Was it any wonder I was as overcome by asthma as by anger by the time I'd bolted behind my own sacred door?

212

That's right, *anger,* but more: what I was feeling was mortal rage. How dare she think she could intrude upon my space? How dare that bitch presume that because she was now a household word she could assert herself without the slightest regard for my feelings? She wasn't even *Madame* Jason Jaffe! And if she was, so-the-fuck what! I doubted that Jackie Onassis would display this much cheek. Pushy yenta! It just goes to show that you could take the Jewish princess out of Atlanta, but . . . *Oh, Christ. There she was, banging on my front door.*

Now what? Was I going to pretend I wasn't in? Yes. Which meant she wouldn't be fooled for a second; knowing Peaches, she'd stand out there whimpering till I broke down and let her come in. Too bad. Six months of agony she'd put me through. Every speech, every slap, every gesture I had rehearsed came rushing back to me. Revenge kept me as silent as a broken clock. I had waited too long for this moment to let charitable feelings undermine my resolve.

But I was beginning to crack. She had been out there ten minutes, and the attack showed no sign of receding. Instead, her hysteria was growing, her threnody resounded down every hall. Thank God the entire building was downstairs making merry. How did she know I was here? What made her so sure that her pleas weren't addressed to an empty room?

Because they weren't. She was crying, "It had nothing to do with you, it was all *Jason.* . . . *He was the one who was having a breakdown!* He was the one who said I couldn't even call you . . . that if I did, he would consider that I was being psychically unfaithful!" Then Peaches erupted into a spasm of petite but murderous cries. "Oh, Florida . . . would I have ever done anything so hideous, so god-awful, so mean?" Peaches paused. "That is, unless it was a matter of . . . Oh, I don't know what. OH PLEASE LET ME IN!"

I would not yet utter a word.

"GOD DAMN IT!" Peaches' voice had taken on a new edge. "IF YOU THINK I LIKE STANDING OUT HERE IN THIS FUCKING HALLWAY WHILE YOU SIT IN THERE LIKE SOME PRIMA DONNA WHEN FOR WEEKS I HAVE DONE NOTHING BUT TRY TO FIGURE OUT HOW I COULD FIND YOU . . . SHORT OF CALLING YOU, THAT IS . . . AND

213

FINALLY WHEN BECAUSE OF SHERWIN SUNNESON SUING CHERIE RIVERS WE HAVE A CHANCE TO GET YOU, THAT'S RIGHT . . . YOU! YOU BIG DUMMY, ONTO A NETWORK GIG, WHICH IF YOU'D STOP ACTING LIKE SUCH AN ASSHOLE WE MIGHT BE ABLE TO PULL THE WHOLE SCAM OFF THIS VERY AFTERNOON. . . . AND, DON'T GO ANY-WHERE BECAUSE I'M NOT DONE YET! IT MIGHT JUST INTEREST YOU TO KNOW THAT WHILE YOU'VE BEEN DROPPING OUT OF LIFE—THAT'S RIGHT! I HEARD!—MISS MARCIE LASTER HAS BEEN ONE BUSY-LITTLE-BODY AND I HAPPEN TO KNOW THE INSIDE GOODS—THE REAL STORY—OF THE EXACT NATURE OF THIS BIG EXPOSE SHE'S PROBABLY RIGHT NOW HOME AT THIS VERY SECOND TRYING TO TYPE . . . AND I HAVE A PLAN FOR HER TOO. SO FLORIDA, I'M WARN-ING YOU! FORGET FRIENDSHIP! IF YOU HAVE A SHRED OF SELF-INTEREST LEFT . . . YOU'D BETTER OPEN UP." Exhausted, Peaches Rosen crumpled against the wooden door. She wiped a drop of sweat from her upper lip, then, piqued, mumbled a silent curse. What if Florida wasn't there? What if she'd let her mascara and her blush-on melt for naught?

Misery! I couldn't take it any more, so I did the only thing a Florida Burns can do when she'd faced with this much pure feeling and overwhelming pain. I broke down and cried. But first, I made sure I'd flung open my front door. Going into self-imposed hibernation, saying one doesn't give a damn about career and fame may be noble, but you don't throw away a five-year friendship like the day-before-yesterday's trades. In the end, your friends will always pull you through. And, make no mistake, Pamela Rosen and Florida Burns went back a long, long time.

Marcie Laster was disspirited, despondent, dejected, and down in the dumps. She was back to square one; she was back in her pocket of melancholia at Metropolitan Pictures, Inc. Back to polite sneers from Arnold and Troy, and a desk piled high with the refuse of seventeen minor imprints. Weary! She was sick of the struggle, she was ready to crack. Maybe, in her heart of hearts, she was also relieved. She had discovered that trying to concoct journalism was no easy task; trying to cook up hard news was far from the *glaaamorous* (but hard-bitten) life touted by the mythmaking journalism reviews.

A heckuva lot worse than reading fifty pages a shot, anyway. That was a fuckin' picnic compared to the agony she'd just been through in her attempt to play hard ball. She supposed the problem was that she was just too *nice.* That she didn't have the cunty constitution necessary to make it in the world of the killers and ball-breakers that seemed to flourish on intermedia strife.

But she had also been humiliated. It wasn't every day one picked up the *Daily News* to discover the headline "PSYCHOLO-GIST ADMITS RAPED OVER 300" and worse: a four-thousand-word Dina Bellamy "You Are There" piece detailing almost every aspect of what Marcie Laster had already discovered about Dr. Howie Leon's crime. That was bad, but the worst was to come. Quoted in the body of the text was Telemedia's eleven p.m. anchorperson for their brand-new magazine-on-the-air, "Tell Me Everything." And she was named. Florida Burns! Right there in ten-point high-speed carbon type. "I felt Leon had the capacity for violence, certainly the capacity to carry off a persuasive sexual attack. And I see his crime, in particular, as being doubly insidious, which is to say that, at least from my limited experience, Howie Leon would probably be able to sabotage his victim into thinking she was the responsible party. And even in New York, with its heightened consciousness about rape, a twisted psychopath can have just about open season for lining up easy marks. It's tragic, simply tragic, but fortunately, my relationship with him was merely cursory. . . ." Marcie Laster had thrown down the *News* in a rage. But not before she discovered that Florida Burn's quote ate up another five lines, not before she discovered that her former friend was identified as "television personality," not before she had imbibed enough of Miss Two-Face's self-serving epistle to realize that through those lips had passed, *comme toujours,* nothing but bald-faced lies.

Deceit! Deceit! Even Brian Milman had turned against her and, in the end, helped to do her in. All she'd asked for was a job, any job, even doing something as menial as ghosting the

215

former Tower Syndicate version of "Tell Me Everything." *Nothing doing.* "Kid, I gave you your shot. Sitting on the biggest story of the season and what? To have it for a month and then be surprised when somebody tipped off the *Daily News*?" She couldn't help but notice that Andy Marks had skulked off into a corner to laugh.

Smarmy! Her mind spun back to a certain morning-after at the Ponce DeLeon. She had known something was up in the sauna, when Florida, ordinarily so talkative, would speak not a word. But nothing and nobody could fool Marcie Laster, which is why she had pressed Florida into revealing her blind date's name. *Howie Leon!* How could she have forgotten that Florida had had a date with him?

They could all have each other, they deserved whatever they got. Marcie knew all about that life. It's "lonely at the top," isn't that what they say? Let them have it! She was much too good to fight for tables at Elaine's. She knew all about those parties, was tired of feeling rejected when she'd read about an event that, with any luck, the old Marcie Laster might have muscled her way into.

The truth was she was sick and tired of being the least famous person in an endless series of rooms. She was tired of the ruthless, the ambitious, the more aggressively gifted than her. She had made a decision. Once, two years before, Werner Erhard and est, his self-help crusade, had worked miracles in her disturbed life. It was time now for a ten-thousand-mile tune-up. If she needed a crutch, so be it. At least with two hundred forty-nine other misfits, she might feel as if she had half a chance. Besides, every little bit helped. She might even go back to the Ponce DeLeon.

Yes, she would get it together, using every tool in her psychological kit. For the first time since she had been immolated, her old feisty feelings began to reappear. Maybe to celebrate, she'd fluff the reading and stick to magazines instead. Yes! A morning with Metropolitan's copy of *Women's Wear* and the *Post.* She even felt strong enough to flip to Earl Wilson.

Instead she wanted to cry. How could she have done such

216

a self-destructive thing? Third paragraph! Second item! There, bigger-than-wide-screen, was a squib about Harvey Kaplan, Florida Burns, Jason Jaffe, and "Penny" Rosen cracking crab claws at Joe's Pier 52. Treachery! With all the people he botched up, why did it have to be Florida's name that Earl Wilson would choose to spell right?

This was it! He'd had enough! What the hell was going on up there? All day long, workmen had been sawing and banging and hammering, all day long, he'd had to endure the noise of shattering glass. Mike Markman was at home working, crouched over a Smith-Corona portable, struggling with his— could it be possible?—*forty-seventh* nine-sentence lead. He had been an AP reporter for close to a year now, but grinding out these shitty financial fillers wasn't getting any easier. HEAVIEST DOW-JONES TRADING SINCE MARCH, '76! MARCOM-SITGO ANNOUNCE MERGER PLANS! OCTOBER CONSUMER INDEX DOWN .05%! Is this what the paper millionaire had rhapsodized about when he'd been lost in his journalism fantasies?

Hardly. But Mike Markman had been lucky to get a job, any job. Especially in these post-Watergate reporter-as-superstar days. Christ. The newspapers were besieged by willing bodies, the J. Schools were turning down magna cum laudes by the score. And where did that leave him? He was a thirty-year-old ex-millionaire who subscribed to twenty-two newspapers, but, in reality, he had never written a single published word. He was down to his last $14,000, desperate to stave off an ugly scene in bankruptcy court. Mike Markman had taken a long look at himself, his chances, his future career. He had *something:* if he had learned anything from bringing tacos to the Cumberland Gap, it was this: Offer Something that Makes You Special! Offer What the Competition Hasn't Got!

In Mike Markman's case, that meant a cannibalization of his own life. He would turn the La Taquita debacle around from corporate write-off to capital gain. So! He'd started writing La Taquita's story for fun and profit; in the process he'd sort of . . . invented himself. He'd started small: fifty pages of how he'd got going, another forty was his souped-up and fleshed-out financial report. Thirty pages of a rewritten *Business Week* cover story about fast food and franchising were lightened considerably by dishy stories and not-too-cynical asides about paper-wealth-gone-up-in-smoke. Only then had he been ready to blow $75 having this literary fragment gorgeously typed. Which helped him achieve his immediate aim: an introduction to DeWitt Browning, a literary agent who just happened to live next door in Snedan's Landing to the weekend home of a member of the Dakota's social committee.

Connections! That's what this city was all about. Take this building. Living in the Dakota for the last two years had taken care of practically all of Mike Markman's needs. His career needs, anyway. The Dakota was like some luxurious Welcome Wagon. He was invited to dinners, to lunches, to teas. In all these months as in-house Extra Man, Mike Markman still hadn't found his girlfriend-to-be. But, more important, he'd glommed onto his job. A downstairs neighbor had told him that the wire services were *always* looking for business reporters, why didn't he try the AP?

And his neighbor had been right! So with his $3500 Avon Paperback contract for a partial first draft of *Next Time, Belgian Waffles! (How I Made and Lost a Million with Mexican Food!)* and a bulging file of clippings he'd forged from the Stanford campus' *Palo Alto News,* Mike Markman had marched into the AP building, expecting . . . *nothing.* Instead, miraculously, he'd been hired, starting salary: $350 a week. He'd gritted his teeth, swallowed his principles, and joined the union, then sat down with seven hundred and fifty others to start hammering out his first assignment, "Business Briefs."

Boring! He was rewriting press releases, and at night, he would return bone-tired to his five rooms, then sit down for four more hours till he'd finished his regimented daily ten pages of *Next Time, Belgian Waffles* . . . his manifesto, his apologia, his work therapy for financial grief.

Everything was changing, nothing was changing; he still was staying up all night, writing through till the early hours of dawn. The difference was, *now* he was tired. Four hours of alpha waves a night, Mike Markman was convinced that nobody on this kind of schedule could thrive.

But god damn these carpenters, just god damn! Because of their air hammers, after sunset was the only time he could work. Someone on the ninth floor was ripping out a series of maids' rooms, demolishing cells, then *expanding* (!) onto the roof. Someone was turning a former rathole into two thousand square feet of sculpted space.

Ever-curious, he'd gone upstairs one afternoon to poke around. He'd asked a carpenter, "Who is renovating this space?"

He'd blanched when he'd heard the bad news.

Florida Burns! He had been hearing that name everywhere he went. "Oh! You live in the Dakota? Surely, you must know . . . she's so *funny,* can you introduce me to your neighbor . . . Florida Burns?"

Or: "Oh! You live in the Dakota? Isn't that where that talk-show hostess lives? What's her name, Florida Burns?"

Between *that* and her builder's noise, he was being driven up a smooth concrete wall. Florida Burns! Mike Markman had always despised gossip or anything else that was superficial in intent. He had resisted ever tuning in to the new super-hot "Tell Me Everything" show. Not for him was the naked exposé, the hatchet-job-of-the-air. Not for him was watching some bitch-on-wheels on the attack, hoping to reveal some kernel of viciousness which others might call "dish."

Anyway, he didn't need to watch her, he already had a visual on this gossip witch. Forty-five years old, divorced, and razor thin. So, it was visceral . . . Mike Markman had a mental barrier about Friday nights, Channel 8, nine o'clock. But it was more than a subjective problem; watching Florida Burns, for Mike Markman, was a physical impossibility.

Since his wire-service days had started, his daily regime at Yorkville Tennis City had been telescoped into one Nagasaki of an hour each week with Bobby Stein. Wouldn't you know it would be the exact match-up of the "Tell Me Everything" show; *that's right,* Friday nights at nine.

They had never missed one session, not once in their

playing days of the last five years. Unbelievable! This wasn't his day. Besides the banging and the drilling and the impossible first-paragraph lead; Mike Markman had just gotten the call.

Bobby Stein's secretary: "I'm sorry, Mr. Markman, but Mr. Stein has just gone home early. He's got 103 temperature; we think it's the flu."

An entire Friday afternoon and evening stretched before him, he had nothing to do. Desperate! He had even called the long-lost Kleiner Gallery for dinner, then getting a rebuff, he'd wondered, what about Brook Nicholson? Now that she wasn't his architect . . . but *no.* That low, he couldn't stoop. Better Mike Markman should sit home alone. He could get twenty pages done and, one never knew, maybe if he was lucky, some great old movies might be on the tube.

Andy Marks was in Xerox heaven and Watts-line paradise. Telemedia! Whoever knew that working for a multinational could bring him such a torrent of fringe benefits? Toilet paper! Telemedia had the real stuff (on rolls) in every stall, so each night Andy Marks had been pirating a few—"stockpiling," he called it—*just in case,* because after all, one never could tell. Andy Marks knew too well that it was one thing to have a plum gig like Head Writer/Production Assistant on Florida Burns' "Tell Me Everything" show, but it was quite another to stumble around blinded to the precariousness of life.

At least, if he and Florida got the network bounce-ola, a few things in his life would be secure. He had two years' worth of Charmin bulging out of his coat closet. One hundred twenty rolls! It had taken him ten months to collect it. He didn't want to grouse, but he knew he could have saved another fifty rolls if Florida had hired him six months earlier, maybe the moment the famous Jason Jaffe interview had catapulted her to minimedia fame.

What a show that had been! Jason Jaffe, who had belched on the *New York Times,* farted on the *Daily News,* shat upon *New York Magazine* and *Esquire,* and refused to answer anybody else's calls, had been landed by Florida! And all because of "connections." Well, he did have to hand it to her. The fact was she was a damn good interviewer; within minutes she had had Jason Jaffe talking about his secret desires and sexual quirks. Jason Jaffe discussing bisexuality on late-night TV! And in his first interview in five years! Telemedia, Inc. had locked Florida Burns into a three-year deal by five the next afternoon.

Only in the movies! But it had happened on TV. And now . . . well, what could he say? Just that they had come a long way since their days behind the desks at the Tower armpit. Now, Harvey Kaplan had been put on retainer and Andy Marks had to fight to keep the press away. But how were they going to get any work done if Florida insisted upon giving interviews to everyone from the *Denver Post* to the *Fayetteville Eagle?* "Never turn down somebody 'in the business,' " she had told him by way of trying to explain. "If it hadn't been for Rona Barrett, I wouldn't be where I am today."

So now Andy Marks was left to cool his heels (and answer the phones) till Florida got done with this guy from the *Elizabeth* (New Jersey) *Sun.* Elizabeth, New Jersey! Two hours she'd spent with this reporter, two hours frittering away moments of her best creative zeal. Andy Marks scowled at his desk, then picked up a phone to talk to an old friend from Brown now living in Rome.

Damn that Andy Marks. The reporter hadn't been in my office for ten minutes when Andy's stupidity almost caused me to blow my psychological edge. Nervous! It was bad enough to have to lie to any reporter (one's own kind), telling them everything about the glorious state of being a television queen. The truth is, it is pretty wonderful; but even wonderful is mined with back-breaking work, political treachery, and demanding potential pratfalls. But if you say *that* in an interview, you're just asking for it! I had nightmares that someday I might be quoted saying something as idiotic as, "It's lonely at the top." Instead, I tried to relax. Sure, I might work fifteen hours a day, which means there might be no time to have any fun much less ever any casual (nonbusiness) dates . . . *but.* Nobody can take away that magic moment when you're walking down Fifth Avenue and heads turn! Crowds would jostle you on the street, or you'd overhear someone on the bus say, "Isn't that Florida Burns?"

That's power! And it seemed to be worth every *centavo* of its price. Like now. I was leaning back in my Eames chair, watching the city lights playing tricks all the way out to the East River. I was getting stoned on this view from the thirty-ninth floor, lost in an inner haze that was muddling tricks with both my vision and my sense of total recall. In short, something was telling me I had seen this AP reporter before. All through our first hour, I kept trying to Get It. I was desperate to ask this Mike Markman where I had seen his face, how I knew his name. But I stopped myself. I remembered how annoyed I would get in the old TME days when some patsy I was interviewing would use that false-intimacy ploy.

Then I did something far worse, committed an egregious faux pas. "So . . ." I tried to sound calm. "How do you like working for the *Elizabeth* (New Jersey) *Sun?"*

Mike Markman looked at me one tortured beat too long. "I'd like it fine . . . if I wasn't on the financial desk of the AP."

But still he stayed thirty minutes, then an hour more. Was I crazy to be getting paranoid, to think this wire-service desk man was asking me questions that had a hostile edge? Well, at least at first, he let me blab on and on. I was only too glad to recount the slipshod nature of my meteoric, tumbleweed career. I perpetrated the charming (but studied) crime of the insouciant put-down. How I had been the absolute drone of a nowhere syndicate fighting for some respectability. How once I stopped fighting and just "let it happen," why little-old-luck came and set me free.

He didn't believe me. "Come on. Nobody hands anyone a network job. . . . I mean, you were writing some *schlocky* column that . . ."

"Schlocky?" I sprang to my own defense. "My dear Mr.

Markman, Tell Me Everything might not have had an over-whelming readership, but we were always read by those who knew . . ." I paused, then got nervous seeing the AP reporter smiling some strange little I've-got-a-secret smile. Who was he? I tried to focus on that name—Mike Markman—and that face, striking, yet somehow older than his years—Mike-Markman-Mike-Markman—the name spun like wire wheels in the corners of my minds. "I mean, we may have been small, my dear Mr. Markman, but the one thing TME never was . . . was *little.*"

Inscrutable! I couldn't make out the message behind his wire rims and pepper-and-salt hair. I shifted my gaze away from his face, trained my eyes on his waist. *Nice clothes.* Classic Brooks Brothers type, with navy crew-neck and faded jeans.

The real kind of jeans, of course, stovepipe button-fronts (exactly my favorite kind). I looked again. His were even my model's year: vintage '68, perhaps there was an outside chance they were a classic '69. *Then I died!*

STOVEPIPE BUTTON-FRONTS? VINTAGE '68, MAYBE '69? A wave of recognition upped and buffeted me. Was this the same Mike Markman of two-years-ago New Neighbor fame? Was this the same anal uptight creep who screamed to the concierge the very moment he heard the tinest bit of noise?

That Mike Markman was on the AP? I had felt for sure (from all reports) that the downstairs Mike Markman was either permanently married or positively gay.

Was I wrong! I wondered if this chunk of masculinity could hear my heart begin to pound. *Damn!* Wouldn't you know he'd be this attractive, they were the ones that always did you in. Then I got a little scared. What if Mike Markman were an in-house Howie Leon? No! Florida! That crazy and self-indulgent I couldn't allow myself to be. But . . . what did he want from me? I opened my mouth to ask exactly that, when he interrupted. I forced my lips to shut. *Interviewer-interviewee;* pupil taking notes from a willing star . . . forget all that, we were still woman and man, I obeyed Mike Markman, whoever he was; something told me I would only be too glad to give him the upper hand. I would not let on that I knew who he was. I wondered if he knew that I was the occupant of Apartment 99. I stared at his face but could not get a sign.

His smile (was it to throw me off?) bounced me back to the present. "Nobody accused you of being . . . *little.* I used to read you, all the time."

My God. So he was the Dakota's mystery-subscriber to the *Arnold* (Maryland) *Bugle,* his copy used to get tossed in with mine. What was going on here?

Was Mike Markman hinting that he wanted *me* to take the ball and run? Was he pulling an "Ezra Matthews" on Florida Burns? I dropped the ball like leaded steel, but smiled encouragingly.

"Yep. As a matter of fact, because of Tell Me Everything I used to save a lot of money in the market . . . you helped me, through your tips, unload some entertainment stocks."

Again, I smiled and nodded thanks.

"But you know and I know you were still . . . nobody. That that was a nowhere job. So how?" He was fiddling with his notebook, revealing an acre of white space on a virgin pad.

What the hell, he seemed nice. I would lay it on the line. "Connections. It's as simple as that. Work had nothing to do with it, not one thing." I warmed to my topic, felt my blood level begin to rise. "Well! It's not that I didn't work . . . I worked like a dog! For five years in this town, I bashed my head against the wall, spent ten hours a day chasing stories for the Tower—I don't have to tell you about that!—and I was . . . chasing men, making an ass of myself. . . ."

The reporter smiled as if he had won. "That's more like it. . . ."

But I was annoyed, my voice threw sparks. "Nonsense! Work had nothing to do with it! I had retired!" (For some reason, that made him smile.) "I was sick of having to prove myself, sick of competing in this vicious world of . . . I was sick of 'overachieving'. . . . I wasn't getting anywhere and I was ready to give it up."

Mike Markman asked me what happend after that.

"*Rona Barrett!* At a lunch, she said, 'Offer what the competition can't!' . . ." I paused, surprised to see a wide grin spread over Mike Markman's face. "But that was ridiculous because I had nothing going for me! Not a single stinking thing."

"I wouldn't say that."

I ignored him (was he flirting?), but, secretly pleased, I sailed right on. "So! Since I had absolutely nothing, I went into retirement, I was on the verge of a complete breakdown. Then what the cheap novels call 'fate' conspired in my favor and . . . *voilà!* Here I am! Rona was right. The one thing I had was . . . *friends.* But it took way too long to realize that, in the end, it's both your friends and even sometimes your enemies who help you to triumph over everyone . . . who help you, I guess, *to win.*" I could have shot myself for mouthing such utter tripe. Who was I trying to sound like, the Dr. Joyce Brothers of the graduate set?

It was Mike Markman's turn to switch this innocuous interview around. He forced a smile, but I could tell it was faked, *that* was a discouraging sign. "*Say.* I heard this crazy rumor that Sherwin Sunneson was suing Telemedia—really Cherie Rivers!—over an item she'd done about Jason Jaffe and . . ."

I tried to keep my features smooth as glass.

". . . that *you* were part of the deal, since you . . . what? Knew each other through Jason Jaffe—was it something like that?"

I thought, what should I do: deny it and refuse to tell an ounce of truth? I felt as if I were on trial, as if Brian Milman had reappeared in a different guise and had me manacled for my crime of forging clips. I told myself to get it together, this job on Channel 8 was mine, all mine. I had proved myself with show after show. Interviewed rapists, attacked stars, wrestled politicians to the floor. Was the unshakable Florida Burns about to crack over something as silly as a machete *somebody else* wielded at Cherie Rivers' back? *Yes!* Even so, I decided to tell the truth. What the heck? Everybody who was anybody knew about it anyway. Better Mike Markman should have it first, rather than some schlepp from *Daily Variety.* It wasn't like this little pearl had never surfaced in cocktail-party talk. Who cared about this stuff anyway? Why shouldn't we talk about something real like career ethics, woman to man? I sighed. "*Yes.* It was exactly like that. You're the first person who's been clever enough to figure it all out." I leaned back as he took a second out to glow. "And Mike . . . in your heart of hearts aren't you glad that crashing bore is off the air? God! She gave gossip a bad name. At least, with Tell Me Everything, I don't know, at least we try to fit in more relevant programs, I mean, *sometimes . . .*"

He nodded, then started to speak; what was that show? Ah, yes! he remembered now (at least the publicity): *that* was the breakthrough moment for the Florida Burns TV career. "Relevant programming—you mean like when you had that rapist on?"

I nodded, then announced the news that, believe it or not, Howie Leon was still out roaming the city, completely and totally scot-free.

"*Come on.* That guy?"

This was better, we had moved off of me and onto issues. Maybe I could begin to relax. "*Right.* They can't pin a thing on him, even with—what was it? six or seven seduction-rape victims of his on the air!"

Mike Markman mumbled something about how it had been an unbelievable, just unbelievable show.

"Thanks, *really!* Here I go again . . . forgive this bragging, but, the ratings! The drag of doing what I do is being locked to your Nielsen share. But that night! I think in the city alone, we got a 61, which was phenomenal. God, *what a share.* Too bad you have to admit you too are a rape victim to even come close to grabbing a percentage point like that." A noticeable edge crept into my voice, I swiveled in my chair. "This country. Air out your kinks and hang-ups in public and you're guaranteed to be made a saint." Again I paused. "Well, at least *something* came out of that rape group therapy, speak-out, whatever it was."

"You mean all those women who came forward, who said they too were victims of a sexual . . ."

I laughed. "Nothing that noble. Once we made the News-makers section of *Newsweek,* Telemedia said, 'Sign your name on this-here dotted line.' "

Now Mike Markman was laughing too. Did he like me? I couldn't tell, what if he thought my tongue was a poison dart? The old Florida-Burns-is-a-creep syndrome was sneaking over me. I forced myself to relax. Who cared! He could take me or leave me, just the way I was; these days, I was feeling more than a little fine.

If only we could get off the Howie Leon show. But no, Mike Markman was leaning back in *his* Eames chair as if he were settling down to stay. "Can I ask you something? Was it hard to come out 'on camera' and admit that you were raped?"

I waited; could he be so dumb to not yet realize that I, Florida Burns, was on top? That he was a floor below? "Of course, it was hard to admit . . . the worst! But *the absolute worst* was the fact that I was so stupid I didn't even realize that I'd been raped—a victim of a crime—till twelve months later . . . after the fact, till I picked up a copy of all things, the *Daily News.*" I started to laugh thinking about the Dina Bellamy-Peaches Rosen-Marcie Laster con, but then I caught myself. This reporter might think at this critical moment, a touch of mirth was rather strange. Anyway, the memory of the Howie Leon affair was beginning to fade and I wanted to sweep it under the rug for once and all. I had already used it, milked it for what it was worth, turned a negative charge into a positive electric force. So why couldn't we just drop it? "The point is, with Howie Leon, I guess with any rapist, the humiliation hurts just as much, if not more, than the entire three-minute sexual crime. I was the dupe. And I hated that."

"That sounds . . . logical." Sympathy appeared in Mike Markman's amber eyes.

"Hey, could we talk about something else? This is real-ly . . . past history, do-you-know-what-I-mean?" I squirmed in my seat, threw my legs over the side of the chair. Then I let them dangle loose and easy as if I didn't have a single care. I hoped this expansive gesture would fool Mike Markman, reporter from the AP.

He looked at me. "*No.* We don't *have* to talk about it, but I thought, well maybe, I could help you work through it . . . the pain, I mean."

"Work through it? Work through what?" I would mouth Florida Burns straight party line. "I did that a long time ago! Now it's just one more bit of experience that belongs only to me; for my memoirs someday! *I was lucky.* What went on with me and Howie Leon was no worse than one night of bad sex." Why was I telling all these things to Mike Markman? What if suddenly I saw them in cold type in the press? "This is all off the record, you know."

His nod made me forget my fears. Then he spoke. "Do you mind if I take my sweater off? It's really hot in here." I waved him on, then watched him peel off his navy shetland, to reveal a faded denim work shirt. A few dark hairs peered over the top button. He wrenched his sweater over his head, tossed it down on the sofa, and looked back up at me. We were quiet. It was the most nothing of moments, yet somehow intimate. I felt shy, nervous. I wondered if a stray hair clung to my shoulders. Quickly, I looked down and picked a speck of cream-colored fuzz.

Suddenly, I was talking way too fast. "Anyway, anyway. I really *adore* talking about myself, but I guess . . . could we, I mean, do you think this is going to go on much longer? It's been . . . what? Two hours or something? Not that I'm not having a great time, I am, I am. But I don't know anything about *you* yet, who you are . . . not one thing! And I guess, well maybe I'm just nervous being on the other side of the writing tablet."

"Well, *don't be.* You're a great interview. I only wish I could write more than a three-paragraph story about you for AP." Good God, he did like me, unless this was the place he'd screw in the classic zinger. I had an overwhelming feeling that Mike Markman was someone that I wanted to reach out and just . . . hug tight. Corny! Was this the-old-Florida-Burns-*avec*-fantasies? Hadn't I learned anything from Hobie Schaeffer, Howie Leon, or Ezra Matthews? Hadn't I learned that success carried its own sexual charge?

228

I had, I had, but Mike Markman was no ordinary pipe dream. And what the heck, you can take the girl out of her Texas dream world, but you can't expect that she'll completely give up all hopes of finding her Ideal Man. He was asking me questions and I was answering, I don't remember to this day (nor does Mike) what I even said. My thoughts were elsewhere: when do I ask him if he knows just who I am? When do I confess that we're neighbors, that, *yes,* the reason I chose to wreak havoc above him in the Dakota in my five infinitesimal rooms (rather than move into a downstairs *grand salon)* was that, I, Florida Burns, never wanted to forget that I'd started out in the servants' quarters.

Only later would I find out about La Taquita and the Mexican food, all the propinquities of our lives, our careers. But even on the long Telemedia Building elevator ride, *my* thoughts had landed on one phantasmagorical place. You'll never guess! *The New York Times,* second section? Sundays, which meant the wedding page? Already I was planning the photographer who would surely be there to catch us in mid-flight at the Carlyle Hotel's front entrance. Maybe we could have our own "Tell Us Everything" show! Maybe we could break through Apartment 87's ceiling and build a duplex combining Mike Markman's apartment with The Dakota's Number 99! Already I was thinking, Peaches Rosen bridesmaid, Harvey Kaplan, best man. For once in his life, I wanted Harvey to have shared billing.

But first I would have to get us home. We spilled out of the elevator into the marble lobby and still I nattered on. "You want to know if I felt guilty about my complicity in the Cherie Rivers thing? My God, Mike. I almost went to an analyst; I almost went to seek *professional* help. I almost quit the business entirely and went back to Austin, where I grew up. *Literally.* It was the most traumatic experience of my life, I couldn't sleep for days."

His eyes filled with concern, inadvertently, he took my hand.

I saw I had him, how easy! All I had to do was take the blame. In that case, I would lay it on with a trowel. "*Mike.* I hate to keep going on and on, but the Cherie Rivers firing was about the only thing I've ever been involved with that's been . . . I don't know, *unclean*. . . ." We walked easily toward the street, I sensed that he might get away. "But, *Mike* . . ."

He turned. "Yes?"

I waited a half beat, then smiled my emblematic Florida Burns smile. "There's only one thing. . . ."

"What's that?"

"I got over it." Before his laughter could shift to a look of horror, I took the offensive and grabbed *him* by the hand. "*Come on.* I insist. Let me give *you* a ride uptown."

He didn't argue.